D1526741

The Panama Affair

Jeffrey Miller

The Panama Affair

ISBN: 1507659164
ISBN-13: 978-1507659168

Cover Design by Anna Takahashi
annatakahashi.com

C-130 photo © tenboh siyaraku - Fotolia.com

Scenes from this novel first appeared in "Love Song from the Zone" from the author's Master of Arts thesis, *Response Time;* Western Illinois University, 1989.

DEDICATION

*For Howard, Chris, Larry, Dave, John M., Harry, Spud, Rusty,
Radar, Chester, Lee, Roly, John G., Hector, Roy, Animal, and
Moose—I miss you guys*

To all those who served in Panama or called Panama home

Operation Just Cause Veterans

ACKNOWLEDGMENTS

Special thanks to Anna Takahashi for her book cover design and for her never-ending support; Bud Tristano, who was there all the way for me with his insights, suggestions, and support; Lenny Johnson, who provided me a wealth of information regarding a Zonian's perspective of life in the Canal Zone; and thanks to my editor, Joyce M. Gilmour.

And finally, my heartfelt thanks to my wife Aon and our children, Bia, Jeremy Aaron, Joseph, and Angelina for all their love, support, and understanding. Without them, none of this would be possible.

Part I

PROLOGUE

MASTER SERGEANT KEVIN Rooney had never, in all his years of service, fired or even drawn his weapon in the line of duty. Now, his career and reputation were on the line: he was a prime suspect in the deaths of three men, including the reputed underworld figure that had tried to assassinate him.

While parts of the city smoldered, and bodies continued to be pulled from the rubble, the doves and hawks circled above ready to swoop down on the uneasy peace. Hundreds were reported dead or missing, thousands wounded and even more displaced by the fires that had ravaged some of the poorer sections of the city. The military continued its mop-up operations rounding up members of the defense forces that had terrorized the country for years. Meanwhile, the man responsible for those paramilitary units and who had brought the death and destruction upon his people had been led away in chains amid cheers and jeers after holing up in the Vatican Embassy. On a street corner, in front of a building peppered with holes from a .50 caliber machine gun on top of an M113 APC, a Cerveza Atlas sign hung lopsided over the entrance.

Jeffrey Miller

Next to the entrance, a middle-aged woman in a tattered, blood-stained dress with a naked sleeping child in her lap hacked away at a pineapple with a rusty machete. Neither the woman nor the pineapple seemed out of place; instead, both were symbolic and appropriate.

Rooney's small part in this drama—which unfolded over the span of two weeks—was also symbolic and appropriate and manifested in his injuries. He still walked with a limp as he was led into a small room that contained a steel table and four chairs. His left arm was in a cast, broken when he was slammed to the ground by a marine; his nose had also been broken when his head hit the steering wheel, the result of an accident the night the three men were killed. The rest of his injuries were a medley of cuts, lacerations, and bruises. The military clinic had patched him up as best they could after the more serious wounded had been treated.

He crinkled his nose as he smelled the presence of body odor, urine, stale smoke, and disinfectant. Having been on the opposite end of an interrogation, he knew the fine art of extracting information. Whoever had been in this room previously hadn't fared so well. One of the chairs had a bent leg as though it had been slammed against one of the puke colored walls. Rooney looked down and noticed a urine stain on the floor. A metal exhaust fan in one corner of the windowless room clattered and rattled from its uselessness. In the back of the room, an Air Force technical sergeant, there to videotape Rooney's testimony, placed a microphone on a stand in the middle of the table and then stood next to the video camera mounted on a tripod. Already seated at the table was a female airman first class with a memo pad in front of her. Rooney sat down on one side of the table facing the video camera. Following him into the room were two Air Force officers: Major Anthony Collins and Colonel Greg Johnson, who sat down at the table across from him.

The two officers, who looked like they had just stepped off an Air Force recruitment poster, opened their briefcases and took out yellow legal pads. It was obvious they had not spent much time in Panama, judging from how crisp and clean their Class A uniforms were—as though they just pulled them off the racks at the base clothing store. Kevin sat straight in the chair, with one arm on the table. His forehead was beaded with sweat, and his dress uniform was damp and wrinkled from having spent three hours in an adjoining room waiting for this procedure to begin. He hadn't slept in two days; his stomach growled from all the bitter coffee he had consumed and his arm in the cast began to itch something awful. He looked up and into the video camera, which had already started videotaping the proceedings, and then at the airman and the two officers.

"Sergeant Rooney, would you please state your name and rank for the record?" Major Collins asked.

Kevin nodded and looked straight into the camera. "Master Sergeant Kevin Franklin Rooney."

"Thank you, Sergeant Rooney. I would like it to be known for the record that you were in no way obligated to take part in this interview. You agreed to participate in our investigation surrounding the deaths of three Panamanian civilians while you were off duty," Collins continued. "This is an informal hearing and you have not yet been charged with any crime. The purpose of today's interview is to determine if there are grounds, based on the facts and your testimony for a more formal hearing. As such, anything you say in your testimony could be used against you if it is later determined that you were responsible for these deaths."

Kevin leaned forward toward the microphone and spoke in a weak voice. "Yes, that is correct."

"Could you please speak up?" Colonel Johnson asked.

"Yes, that is correct."

"You also waived your right to have military and civilian counsel present here today, is that also correct?" Johnson asked.

Kevin cleared his throat and nodded. "Yes, that is also correct."

"You do understand that this is an ongoing investigation. We're merely trying to ascertain whether or not certain military personnel violated rules of engagement during the first twenty-four hours of Operation Just Cause," Collins added.

Kevin looked at Collins and nodded again.

"Okay, good. Then let's get started," Collins said, glancing at some notes scribbled on his yellow legal pad before he looked over his glasses at Kevin. "For the sake of this investigation and a matter of record, can you take us back to the day before the operation when you stole a van from the motor pool?"

Kevin laughed to himself. He hadn't counted on them bringing that up right out of the gate. If these pencil pushers wanted to get at the truth, they were sure going at it the wrong way. And if he knew any better, these two probably had never interrogated anyone before. The funny thing was, he hadn't stolen anything, but if that's how they were going to start the proceedings, he couldn't wait to see what they had in store for him.

"Excuse me, Major," Johnson said, interrupting the proceedings and pulling rank on Collins. "There are certain extenuating circumstances involving Rooney, which we need to address."

Collins quickly frowned with an attitude of annoyance as he placed his hand over the microphone and motioned for the sergeant behind the camera to stop videotaping the process. "What do you mean *certain* extenuating circumstances? I thought we were only going to talk about the three Panamanians that were killed."

Kevin glanced at the airman first class and smiled. If these guys were going to pull a good cop/bad cop routine, his money was on Collins.

"New information has come to light," Johnson said, speaking in a low voice. "We have reason to believe that Rooney might have also been responsible for the death of an American civilian."

Kevin looked up from the table at the two officers and then looked toward the two-way mirror. He figured they would pin that death on him, too. Typical military bullshit. Someone at the top needed to cover their ass and they needed a fall guy. He felt they should be putting a fucking medal around his neck instead of jerking him off about some lowlifes that had been capped. Kevin continued to stare at his reflection in the mirror wondering who was on the other side. He figured there were at least two, maybe three men behind it watching and listening to him. That was fine with him. He didn't have anything to hide. If it were the CIA, DIA, and/or NSA, as he thought—he wanted them to hear everything. He wasn't about to go down—if things went south—without a fight.

"Excuse me," Kevin said glancing over at the sergeant next to the video camera. He didn't like the way Johnson was slowing down the proceedings with this Mickey Mouse crap. He wanted to get the hell out of here. "Would it be possible to have a copy of the video? My mom's always complaining that she doesn't have enough home movies of me."

The airman first class looked up from the pad in her hands and grinned. She was just as tired as the others.

"Make sure you get my right side, too," Kevin added.

"Just a second, Rooney," Collins said frowning.

Kevin turned around, stared into the mirror, and hoped that those watching him were not cut from the same cloth as these two pencil pushers. The one person who could put a stop to all this bullshit was one of the reasons why he was in this room. Unfortunately for Kevin, that person was in the base morgue.

On the other side, four men were watching the proceedings and taking note of Kevin's disdain for having been brought in for questioning. One of the men, with his arm in a sling and right foot in a cast, watched Johnson and Collins exchange verbal barbs. He was particularly interested in what the two officers were going to ask him, but so far these officers were questioning the wrong way. He knew they were merely toying with him to see what he would or wouldn't say. His money was on Rooney; there was no way these two officers were going to break him.

"Do you think he's going to say anything?" a man in the back asked. His right arm was in a cast and his shoulder was bandaged. He also had multiple lacerations across his face and part of his ear had been blown away.

The first man shook his head, which made him wince. Although the bullet only grazed his scalp, he sustained a more serious injury to his head, not to mention his broken foot, when he fell down the lobby staircase of the Mercado Hotel in downtown Panama City. They're just trying to bust his balls, that's all."

"Are *you* worried about him?" A tall man with white hair walked out of a dark corner and approached the two-way mirror. He was smoking a cigarette and in the darkened room, the smoke from it appeared to encircle his head like a halo. "He already knows too much."

The man standing in front of the two-way mirror stared at Rooney. "No, he's not going to give us any problems. We can trust him. In fact, when this is all over, we might even ask him to come and work with us."

The tall man smiled.

"I doubt that," the man with the broken arm said. "He's too stubborn and proud."

"How did you two end up despising each other so much in the first place?" the tall man asked the man with the broken arm.

"We loved the same woman," the man said.

The tall man nodded and smiled. It was always about a woman.

"You knew his father in Nam, didn't you?" A fourth man in the back of the room asked. He was a gray-haired man with a handlebar mustache; he wore an open-collar silk shirt and a gold chain around his sunburned neck. He moved out from the shadows and moved toward the mirror.

"That's right," the man with the broken foot said. "Like father, like son."

Back in the interrogation room, Johnson, after having conferred with Collins about the number of murders, was ready to continue with the proceedings. He had studied Rooney's file and didn't particularly like having to come across as a badass to get Rooney to open up about what transpired in the early morning of December twentieth, but there was no other way. Rooney had violated the rules of engagement, there was no question about it, but it was more than his innocence or guilt. Johnson wasn't so sure about what Rooney was going to tell them—if he even told them anything in the first place— which was going to make this a very interesting interview.

"Let's stick to our original questioning," Collins said, glaring at Johnson. "Sorry about that, Rooney."

Kevin liked Collins. He didn't seem as much of a prick as Johnson. "That's okay. I've got all the time in the world."

Collins grinned. "All right then. When did you first arrive in Panama?"

"September twelfth, nineteen seventy-six."

CHAPTER ONE

HECTOR RODRIQUEZ SAT in the backseat of the banged-up red and white 1970 Toyota Corona taxi and watched the entrance to the headquarters of the Guardia Nacional. For the past hour, he had been sitting here, hoping to catch sight of the man he was supposed to meet inside. His plan was simple: walk in and hand over a manila envelope with information pertaining to U.S. military and NSA surveillance in Panama and South America. If asked why he wanted to hand over this information to Panamanian authorities, he would tell the Guardia Nacional G2 that the Russians and the Cubans were not interested. Then, to prove he was doing this of his own free will and gain the trust of the recipient of this information, Hector would tell the colonel that he wasn't doing this out of any patriotic ideal or because he was offended by American involvement in Latin America. And just to make it sound even more legitimate, he would play the Latino card and tell the G2 that he was sympathetic to Panama's cause—for a price, of course.

Nothing had been left to chance; he switched taxis three times just in case he had been followed from the Army base where he was stationed. He wore a Hawaiian shirt, a pair of tan slacks, as well as a pair of cheap Foster Grant sunglasses and a straw-colored fedora hat which he had bought at the BX in Corozal so as not to draw too much attention. He wouldn't be caught dead wearing this ensemble on the streets of San Juan where he was born or Brooklyn where he grew up, but he would be able to blend in well with the locale.

On the seat next to him was the manila envelope containing the first set of transcripts, which he had removed from one of the listening posts at the military base where he was stationed. He didn't care what was on the transcripts; most of what he had read was about discussions regarding the ongoing canal treaty discussions and a few private conversations between some general and his mistress. What would be most important to whoever bought these transcripts from him was not so much the information as it was how the United States obtained it. For that, the Russians and the Cubans would pay dearly for it once they knew it was on the market—at least that was what Hector hoped.

Obtaining the transcripts had been easier than he thought. He told one of the guards at the facility on Fort Clayton that he had to work late, and then, by falsifying the log entries for that day and flashing his security pass, he gained access to a secure room. His primary job was logging all the tapes and transcripts the intelligence officers recorded, so none of the security detail had any reason to suspect him coming back after duty hours to work late. The only thing he had to do was make copies of the transcripts. It didn't matter what he copied: all he needed was just a sample to whet the appetite of the man he now waited to see.

Getting inside the Guardia Nacional headquarters had also turned out easier than he thought. He had done surveillance on the headquarters for the past month and knew exactly when the person he needed to see came and went. The real trick was getting past the guards. After weighing his options, Hector decided to walk right up to the main gate and flash his military ID card and tell whoever was in charge that he had classified military information that he would like to share. The worst thing that could happen to him at that point was someone might tell him to get the hell out of there, but he didn't think that was going to happen.

"Do I really want to do this?" he asked himself as he stared at the envelope next to him. It had been such a good idea in the beginning. He was sure that shit like this happened all the time—a disgruntled soldier wanted to get back at the military or something like that. There was always someone who believed in a cause and wanted to make a statement. Hector wasn't any of that, though. He saw an opportunity and took advantage of it. He just wanted to do it for the cash. Of course, if he did get caught—and there was no way that was going to happen unless the Panamanians turned him in—he could say that he had done it in the name of Puerto Rican sovereignty. The press would have a field day with that, and he would probably end up being a national hero back home.

Hector looked straight ahead and noticed that the taxi driver had been staring at him. He would ditch the clothes and cheap sunglasses later as soon as he pulled this off. He turned around and gazed out the window again. A black car pulled up in front of the entrance, and his man got out. There were two other officers with the colonel; however, there was no mistaking the man on the street: Manuel Noriega.

Hector was led down a dark, narrow hallway to a room at the end. In the outer room, three officers were standing at a desk looking at what appeared to be reconnaissance photos of some of the military bases in the Canal Zone. One of the officers, an older man with a dour expression, looked up at Hector and crinkled his nose as if he smelled a dead animal. The officer moved around the table and walked over to Hector.

"*Su tarjeta de identificación, por favor,*" the officer said, looking Hector in the eyes.

Hector didn't blink at all. However, he gagged from the officer's bad breath, which smelled of fish and beer. He reached into his shirt pocket, pulled out his ID card and handed it to the officer. It was the umpteenth time since he gained admittance that someone wanted to see his ID card. The officer, whose last name was Hernandez, looked at the card and then looked at Hector.

"*¿Por qué quiere ver al coronel?*" Hernandez asked crinkling his pockmarked nose as he stared at Hector. He couldn't understand why this soldier wanted to see his boss.

"*Tengo un paquete para darle,*" Hector said, pointing to the envelope he held in his right hand.

Hernandez motioned with his right index finger for Hector to turn over the envelope to him, but Hector shook his head.

"I'm sorry," Hector continued in Spanish. "Either I give this to the colonel or I walk out of here. What's it going to be?"

Hernandez grunted and snarled before he turned and walked to a door that Hector took for the entrance to his commander's office and walked inside. Hector took a deep breath and looked down at his hands, which were trembling. He could still turn around and walk out of here before anyone got hurt, but it was too late. Hernandez, who was gone for a few minutes, returned and led Hector into the office.

The man sitting at the desk stared at Hector as though he were looking at photographs in a mug book. He looked much older than he did in the photographs Hector had seen of Noriega, but there was no mistaking the man's bad complexion. It was as though someone had pricked his skin with an ice pick, which had garnered him the most unfortunate nickname, *Cara de Piña—Pineapple Face.*

Noriega stared at Hector, looked at the ID and then looked at Hector again. His eyes narrowed as he studied Hector's face. Noriega figured the kid was either Puerto Rican or Cuban which possibly explained his angle: it was all politically motivated. Still, when an opportunity presented itself to you, it was best to take it at face value. He motioned for Hector to hand over the envelope.

Hector swallowed hard and slowly handed it to Noriega as if he had just sold his soul to the devil. There was no turning back now.

Noriega took out one of the transcripts and began to read. Maybe this kid was setting him up. If he had the chance, he would take this punk outside and nobody would be the wiser. Suddenly, Noriega's demeanor changed as he came across something that piqued his interest. He licked his lips and twisted his mouth into a smile. His boss, General Omar Torrijos, had been talking about what would happen if there weren't a new canal treaty and what could be done to scare the Americans. He could only imagine what the Americans had on other leaders. And, of course, if the Americans were listening to Torrijos, they were most assuredly listening to him—even though he was on their payroll.

"What do you want?" Noriega asked.

"How much do you have?" Hector said, smiling.

13

Noriega smiled and with his right hand, opened the bottom drawer of his desk. This boy had balls coming in here ready to sell out his country. Noriega liked that. Hector swallowed hard as he stared at Noriega and expected the worst. Instead, Noriega set a bottle of Johnny Walker on the desk.

"Let's have a drink."

Hector walked quickly down the street. He was almost certain that Noriega had put a tail on him, but he wasn't about to turn around to find out. When he reached the end of the block, he turned right and hastened his pace. He cut down a narrow side street and ducked into a small restaurant. Sure enough, a minute later, two heavyset men in matching white *guayabera* shirts and tan slacks passed the restaurant. Hector peered out the window and watched the two men continue down the street. He waited until he was certain they were far enough away before he walked out of the restaurant and flagged a taxi going in the opposite direction.

Once safely in the taxi, he tried to catch his breath. His heart pounded in his chest. He couldn't believe what had just transpired.

"*¿A donde?*" the taxi driver asked.

"Fort Clayton," Hector said, settling back into the seat. He looked down at his hands. They were trembling. He looked out the window and smiled. No money had exchanged hands, but once Noriega saw what was on those transcripts, money wasn't going to be that much of an issue. However, that wasn't why Hector started laughing as he stared out the window.

"*Señor ¿está usted bien?*" The taxi driver looked at Hector in the rearview mirror and asked if he was okay.

"*¿Disculpa?*" Hector replied, not hearing the taxi driver the first time.

"*¿Está usted bien?*"

"Things couldn't be better," Hector said grinning. "*Las cosas no podrían estar mejor.*"

Once he felt the coast was clear, he took off the silly hat, tossed the sunglasses out the window, and pulled out a crumpled pack of Marlboros from his shirt pocket. He stuck a cigarette between his lips. He didn't feel so bad for having just sold out his country.

CHAPTER TWO

AS SOON AS the Pan-Am DC-8 dropped through the heavy canopy of clouds dominated by towering, puffy plumes of white and gray, Howard Air Force Base could be seen in the distance. The plane buffeted a strong headwind as it continued its descent through the last remaining cloud coverage before making its final approach to the air base's single runway. Farther in the distance, the Thatcher Ferry Bridge could be seen rising from the canal it traversed. Beyond it, Balboa and Panama City appeared through the diminishing cloud layer.

Located on the Pacific side of the canal, Howard was the point of entry for all military personnel stationed in the Panama Canal Zone. Gary Lee Taylor, one of the passengers on the MAC flight from Charleston AFB, had his face pressed against the cool window as he got his first glimpse of the base that would be home for the next two years. Awake since the day before, when he flew from Chicago to Charleston, Gary was both excited and apprehensive about arriving at his first duty station. He could see that the center of the base was dominated by huge four-story white buildings with reddish-brown tile roofs on either side of a parade field about the size of five football fields. Four massive hangars stood at a ninety-degree angle along the tarmac, flanked by rows of various aircraft—Vietnam War-era Bell UH-1N Hueys, Cessna O-2A Skymasters, Ling-Temco-Vought A-7 Corsairs, and Lockheed C-130 Hercules and C-141 Starlifters—which stood sentry, waiting for their next mission.

The DC-8 tilted slightly to the left and began a slow and steady turn over the Pacific Ocean. A sudden bump and hydraulic groan from underneath the plane told Gary the landing gear was lowered. Feeling his ears pop, Gary opened his mouth as wide as he could in an attempt to release the pressure. He looked down and saw gentle undulating blue waves and whitish-brown foam breaking on a strip of beach cluttered with garbage and driftwood. As the plane continued its descent and made landfall, palm trees and other tropical vegetation whizzed by. The aircraft slowly dropped onto the waiting runway, ending the flight with a mild screech and rumbling as the tires kissed the hot tarmac. Although he had flown a few times before, Gary gripped the armrests as the plane shook and vibrated as it rolled down the runway at an Indy 500 speed before the captain applied the brakes. There was the sudden rush of air and distinct blowing noise as the air brakes were deployed with increased engine sound as the engine's thrust was reversed. The captain needed every foot of that 8500-foot runway to bring the aircraft to a stop. A one hundred and eighty degree turn at the end of the runway followed by the slow taxi onto the tarmac edged the plane toward the MAC terminal.

Gary still had his face pressed against the cool window, but he could already feel the intense heat outside. The plane shimmied to a stop. The captain switched off the no smoking and fasten seatbelt lights.

Panama.

Howard AFB PC Zone, which was what his orders said when he received them two months earlier at Lowry AFB, was not one of his base preferences when he filled out the so-called dream sheet during basic training. In fact, when orders had been distributed to airmen that cool Denver morning, he had no idea where he was going. Neither did his buddies standing in formation with him nor his squadron sergeant. PC Zone? What the hell was that? It wasn't until he asked his instructor, a retired colonel, later that afternoon when he learned that he was going to Panama.

"You're going to love it, Taylor," the colonel said. "I was stationed down there in the 1960s. There's this beautiful golf course right in the middle of the isthmus."

"I don't play golf."

"Learn."

Panama. It sounded both exotic and frightening. It reminded him of the TV series, *Mission Impossible* when the IMF team was sent to some Third World Latin American country to depose a dictator or rescue a scientist. While most of his buddies were heading to Europe or Asia, Taylor was heading south. He knew a little about the Panama Canal: in sixth-grade geography class, he was in a group of students that had made a clay relief model of the Americas; Gary was responsible for making the canal.

"Jesus, Taylor, what the hell did you do to get that kind of assignment?" his buddy Palfi, who was going to England, had asked when he found out where Gary was going. "Shit, Canal Zone? I didn't even know we had bases down there."

"Did you request that base?" another buddy, Fultz, who had known Gary since basic training, had asked. "You're dumber than I thought."

That night, after he finished studying, Gary went to the base library and read as much as he could about Panama. He knew that Panama was in the news a lot because of the canal and talk of a new treaty with the country; what he didn't know was America's colonial underpinnings in the Canal Zone. As soon as people started talking about returning the canal back to Panama, everyone suddenly started screaming that the U.S. had built the canal, therefore it belonged to the U.S.—including Ronald Reagan, who was running for president.

The canal ran north to south, not east to west as most people believed.

A person could see the sun rise in the Pacific and set on the Atlantic.

The U.S. dollar was the official currency.

The rainy season lasted from May to January.

The Canal Zone was only ten miles wide and fifty miles long.

A ship normally took eight to ten hours to transit the canal.

Gary's head spun with all these facts. That same night, after he came back to his barracks, he heard "Panama Red" by New Riders of the Purple Sage on a local Denver radio station for the first time. Whether that was a weird omen or just a coincidence, Gary couldn't sleep at all that night, lying in bed wondering what Panama was going to be like.

Gary's first feeling upon arriving at Howard Air Force Base was not excitement, but panic: there was no one to meet him at the airport. His sponsor hadn't shown up, and Gary had no idea where he was supposed to go.

"I'm sure it's just a paperwork thing," the attractive airman first class behind the information desk at the MAC terminal said. She already had her hands full with two irate officers and their families trying to locate their sponsors who also hadn't shown up at the terminal. A chief master sergeant who had just learned he had been bumped from the Freedom Bird back to Charleston was not very happy, either. She looked at a copy of Gary's orders. "Didn't you contact your sponsor while you were on leave?"

"S-s-sponsor?" Gary's panic skyrocketed. No one at Lowry had told him anything about a sponsor. The only thing he had been told to do when he was out-processing after finishing his training was to be sure to make his September nineteenth port call at Charleston.

Still skinny from all the weight he lost during basic training, Gary's uniform hung on his body like a scarecrow. He had opted to wear his dress blues and in the heat and humidity, he was paying for it dearly—even more so from the stress and anxiety—for not contacting his sponsor. He had been in the Air Force long enough to know what it meant to screw up, something he learned the hard way when he reported to basic training at Lackland Air Force Base four months earlier wearing a bright orange Three Stooges t-shirt.

After having been yelled and screamed at—from the time he and the other new recruits had landed at San Antonio Airport until they reached the Welcome Center on the base where all the recruits did some preliminary in-processing and were yelled and screamed at again—they had been bused to a chow hall for a late dinner and then taken to their barracks. However, the best was yet to come for Gary when the bus pulled up in front of the 3708 Basic Military Training Squadron. It was dark and quiet on the bus as the recruits waited for their basic training nightmare to begin. Gary's name was the first one called and ordered to get off the bus and stand in formation in what would soon become Flight 242. As soon as his training instructors (TIs) in their Smokey the Bear hats saw him, they berated and yelled at him non-stop for what seemed like thirty minutes but in reality was only ten. And in that time, they used up most of the clichés from their training instructor playbook.

"What's your name, Airman?" the taller of the two TIs asked.

"Gary Lee Taylor."

"Where are you from, Taylor?"

"Illinois, Sir."

"Do you mean to tell me that you came all the way down here from Illinois just to piss me off?" the TI asked. He got as close as he could to Gary's face as he could, with the brim of his hat lightly touching Gary's sweaty forehead. Gary's pale complexion, long red hair, and boyish looks made him fair game for the training instructors to have a little fun at his expense.

"Yes, S-s-sir," Gary stammered.

"Don't call me sir. I work for a living."

"Are you a stooge, Taylor?" It was time for the shorter training instructor to have a go at Gary. He pointed at Gary's shirt.

"No, Sergeant."

"You're a stooge, Taylor! Take that shirt off, turn it inside out, and put it back on!"

Gary did as the shorter sergeant instructed as quickly as possible, but the sergeant was not finished with him yet.

"Now stick out that chest, suck in that gut, put your shoulders back, and stand at attention!"

Gary didn't know whether to laugh or cry.

Later, during basic training, the taller training instructor, Sergeant Mike Abshire, laughed about that night with Taylor.

"Got to hand it to you, Taylor, you showed some balls wearing that shirt to basic," Abshire said, grinning. "We thought you were trying to pull one over on us."

"Sergeant, I didn't even think about it that morning when I got up and put it on."

"Then you were dumber than I thought."

He had showed them, though. There were a lot of people back home who didn't think he was cut out for the military. He went in with six friends from high school and now only he and his friend Greg were still in.

Fortunately for Gary, his sponsor worries were soon over—all it took was a phone call to the 24th Supply Squadron to clear everything up.

"They'll be sending someone soon to take you to the squadron," the airman first class said.

Not far from where Gary was standing and waiting for his sponsor, Kevin Rooney turned around and noticed that most of the passengers who had been on the plane with him had already left the terminal. Kevin smiled and waved at Gary; they had met at Charleston Air Force Base last night and spent a few hours talking in the departure lounge.

Kevin's dark hazel green eyes, which seemed more soulful than his youthful looks warranted, moved from one side of the terminal to the other, searching for the three security police officers who had been on the plane with him. While the passengers on that flight were collecting luggage and waiting for sponsors, another group of passengers in the departure area was waiting to board the same plane back to the States. He loved the protocol and the uniformity that the military provided him. It made him feel safe and secure. Part of that was growing up as a military dependent and being accustomed to the military rank and file. It never bothered him having to move every two or three years like it did some of his friends. He looked forward to each new military assignment the way his father did. Most of those assignments had been Stateside though his father had spent two years in Vietnam and another year in Korea.

Just a shade under five-and-a-half feet, to look at him, most people would think that he was the runt of the litter, but that's where they were wrong. Despite his size, he had proven himself at school on more than one occasion with his fists and on the baseball field with his arm. His grades were good enough to get into most colleges, and his athleticism and baseball prowess as a shortstop at his last high school were good enough for a baseball scholarship to North Carolina State. There was never any question as to what Kevin would do after high school, however. Kevin followed in his father's footsteps and enlisted in the Air Force.

Kevin had spent most of his life trying to please his father. Unlike his older brother Chet, who could do no wrong in their father's eyes, even when he protested against the war in Vietnam and ran off to San Francisco for a year, or his younger sister, Karen, who was the brains of the family, Kevin always felt he had something to prove to their father. Getting good grades wasn't enough. He had to be at the top of his class. Being a good baseball player wasn't enough. He had to win a scholarship. Simply enlisting in the Air Force wasn't good enough, either. He had to be a cop, just like his old man. "Why do you bust your ass to get Dad to like you?" Chet had often asked him. But life never came as easy and sweet for Kevin as it did for Chet, who was happy drifting from one job to the next.

And then their father had to drop dead from a heart attack while cutting the grass—the day after he retired from the Air Force. If only his father were still alive, Kevin knew that he would be so proud of him.

He adjusted his blue security police beret on his head and finally located the three other security police officers. They had recently completed their training, too. One of them, John Bradshaw, was from Georgia. His father was a peanut farmer who was friends with the family of the Democratic presidential candidate, Jimmy Carter. Kevin had met Bradshaw in basic training and had gone through security police training together. As soon as Bradshaw and the other security police officers collected their baggage, Kevin slung his duffel bag over his shoulder, picked up his suitcase and followed them out of the terminal to a waiting van.

When Frank Costello walked out of the plane, he felt as though he had just walked into a wall of heat and humidity. He gagged as soon as he got a whiff of the heavy smell of rotting vegetation and JP-4 jet fuel. He had gotten used to the heat at his last duty assignment—George Air Force Base outside of Victorville, California—but this shit was going to take a while. Both uncomfortable feelings soon passed as Frank walked into the cool terminal. He removed his aviator sunglasses and waited until his dark blue eyes adjusted to the dim light before he continued to the baggage claim area and grabbed his duffel bag. A security police officer with a drug-sniffing dog at his side gave Frank the once-over as he passed—Frank's jet-black hair and mustache (which far exceeded the Air Force's grooming regulations) reminded more than one person of a young Elvis Presley. Frank tipped his head to the security police officer and slung his duffel bag over his shoulder.

Frank's tall frame swayed with feline grace as he moved through the terminal. His sponsor, Chris Shea, had called him the night before last and said that he would be waiting just outside the arrival area. As Frank walked toward the crowd of sponsors waiting to meet the new arrivals, he couldn't spot Shea's name on any of the uniform name tags.

It sucked that MAC didn't allow any alcohol to be served on the plane coming down. However, what Frank could go for right now, though, was a big fat joint with some of the local herb. It made his eyes water just thinking about it.

He had peddled pot in high school, which supplemented the income he made busing tables at the local Holiday Inn. Selling drugs wasn't what got him into trouble, though. Frank's life had changed forever when he had *borrowed* his neighbor's car and had gone joyriding one autumn afternoon with his best friend, Eddie Cahill.

"Well, at least we filled up the tank," Frank had muttered, casting a sideways glance at his father, who had come to the police station to bail out his son.

His father, a sanitation worker for the city of Cicero who didn't want his son to end up in some dead-end blue-collar job, had answered with a slap against the side of the head. "You think it's funny, don't you? I should have let the police throw your ass in jail."

"And miss this quality father/son time?"

"Don't get wise with me, boy," his father replied, slapping his son again.

The following day, they were back at the county courthouse. Before Frank and Eddie went into the judge's chambers, their fathers, as well as Tom Witek, the owner of the car, and the chief of police had already conferred with the judge and agreed to a deal. The judge, who knew Frank's father from high school, went easy on the two boys.

Frank and Eddie didn't think so.

"You boys have two choices: the military or juvenile detention," the judge said, looking up from his desk at Frank and Eddie. "I've already discussed this with your fathers, law enforcement, and Mr. Witek. Upon completion of your military service, your record will be expunged."

They had no idea what branch of the military to join though they wanted nothing to do with the U.S. Army or the U.S. Marine Corps. They just wanted to do their time and get out. Eddie thought the Navy would be cool, but Frank couldn't swim. Then Frank saw a recruitment poster for the Air Force that mentioned the Air Force's buddy system. If the two of them selected the same field, they could go to basic training and technical school together and possibly be stationed together. That's all they needed to know to make up their minds. Both of them loved to tinker with cars and had taken auto mechanics when they were in high school, so it was only natural for them to choose the aircraft mechanic field when they enlisted. They went off to basic training together and were in the same flight as guaranteed by the "buddy plan." Halfway through basic training, however, Eddie had broken his ankle while running the obstacle course. Frank finished basic training and was sent to helicopter mechanic school at Sheppard Air Force Base.

The Air Force wasn't that bad of a gig—it sure beat doing three to five at the Sheridan Correctional Center. He liked working on helicopters, Vietnam-era UH-1Ns, and didn't mind all the military rank and file bullshit—especially all the exercises and drills. He was just biding his time and counting the days until his discharge. And it certainly didn't crimp his style. At George Air Force Base, Frank was soon peddling pot and speed to his buddies, thanks to his supplier, an old biker friend who had been living in Baker at the time.

While he waited for the crowd to clear out, he checked out the blonde airman first class helping this kid he met on the plane down from Charleston. That's when he saw a heavyset man with a mustache in wrinkled, faded fatigues walking toward him.

"Costello?" Shea asked, holding out his hand.

"Yeah," Frank said. "Chris Shea?"

Shea nodded, shaking Frank's hand. "Sorry to be late. Welcome to Howard."

"Thanks."

"Well, let's get you over to the squadron and squared away," Shea said, grabbing Frank's duffel bag.

They were just about to walk outside when the sky, which had turned dark and gray while Frank was waiting for Shea, opened up with a heavy rain. Slick sheets of rain came pouring down hard making it impossible to see most of the base in front of the terminal.

"Does it rain a lot here?" Frank asked.

"So much you won't even notice," Chris replied, grinning.

CHAPTER THREE

HOWARD AIR FORCE Base, which was built in 1939, was one of thirteen military installations in the Canal Zone that included Quarry Heights, Fort Clayton, Fort Amador, Fort Kobbe, Rodman Naval Station and Howard on the Pacific side and Forts Sherman, Gulick, and Davis on the Atlantic side, which were all part of SOUTHCOM (Southern Command). Originally called Bruja Point Air Base, the installation was renamed Howard Field later that year and Howard Air Force Base in 1962 after it had been separated from the adjoining Fort Kobbe. Once part of the United States Air Forces Southern Command (USAFSO), in 1976 the Tactical Air Command (TAC) assumed command of the base and its mission in Central and South America.

Like most of the buildings on these military installations, one of the base's more noticeable and prominent features were the large four-story white buildings, six of which straddled the parade field in the middle of the base. Gary's sponsor, Staff Sergeant Johnny Rodriquez, who had finally showed up after thirty minutes, took Gary to one of the barracks on the south side of the parade field next to the chow hall. They went to the orderly room on the second floor where he was introduced to Airman First Class Mike Clark and the first sergeant's secretary. In a corner window, an air conditioner rattled and groaned as it worked as hard as it could fighting the tropical heat and humidity to keep the room moderately cool.

After Gary had shown the secretary a copy of his orders, he was led into the first sergeant's office on the right. Behind a desk at the far end of the room sat Chief Master Sergeant Daniel Bartlett. Despite the heat and humidity, the creases on his sleeves and pants were so heavily starched and sharp that they probably could cut paper, Gary thought, as he stared at Bartlett behind his desk. Gary had been warned about these lifers, sergeants who had been in the service since the brown shoe days and didn't take crap from anyone, not even the wing commander. Bartlett looked at a copy of Gary's orders and then looked up at Gary over his Air Force standard issue black horn-rimmed glasses.

"You're early," Bartlett said, pushing his glasses up his nose. He wasn't too pleased that Gary hadn't contacted his sponsor. They had to scramble to find him a room. "We didn't expect you until November."

"I finished school early," Gary beamed, hoping that Bartlett would notice his enthusiasm and overlook the fact that he'd forgotten to contact his sponsor.

"I see," Bartlett grunted and stared at Gary with the kind of look reserved for those who fail to see the humor in anything. "I'm going to give it to you short and sweet, Taylor. You do your job, stay in line, keep your nose clean, and stay out of trouble, and you'll have a good tour of duty.

"Don't do drugs and don't bring women back to the barracks. There are some folks here who think they can get away with anything they want, but I've already got their number. People think they can have the life of Riley here, but I will not tolerate it. There are guys walking around here thinking that just because they served in Vietnam gives them the right to do as they please. Well, it doesn't. These clowns were still sucking on their mother's teat when I was fighting the commies in Korea. Just keep that in mind here, Tyler."

Gary knew better than to correct the first sergeant and let him continue with his tirade.

"You screw up one time and I'll be all over you so fast you'll wish that you were never born. You got that, Airman?"

Gary nodded; so much for the short and sweet. "Yes, Sergeant."

"One more thing, do you go to church?"

It had been years since Gary last went to church regularly. However, in basic training, he volunteered to be a chapel guide when he found out that they got out of extra duty on Sunday by escorting new recruits to Sunday services. The guides were supposed to attend one of the denominational services, but they usually hung around outside in the parking lot in front of the Army Air Force Exchange Services mobile food truck—or roach wagon, as it was affectionately called by airmen—filling up on soda, sandwiches, and chips. Gary's little surefire excuse to get out of those extra duties backfired when he left a group of recruits standing out in the rain. He got a good ass chewing from a master sergeant TI and was replaced as a chapel guide.

"Frequently," Gary said, hoping to get on the first sergeant's good side.

"My wife and I run a Bible study group on Wednesday and Saturday nights if you are interested," Bartlett said, looking over his glasses at Gary. "We're Baptists, but our house is open to all denominations."

"I'll keep that in mind," Gary said.

Bartlett grunted knowing what that kind of answer meant. "Airman Clark will see you to your room. Remember what I said, Tyler. Don't screw up."

Gary gritted his teeth when Bartlett got his name wrong again. He didn't know whether he should continue to stand in front of the first sergeant's desk or to leave because he hadn't been properly dismissed. Gary cleared his throat to get Bartlett's attention, who already had his head buried in the latest issue of *Southern Command News*.

"You still here? What is it now?" Bartlett looked up and realized that he hadn't dismissed Gary. He grunted and motioned for Gary to leave with a wave of his right hand as if he were shooing away a fly. "Dismissed."

Before Gary left the orderly room, Clark issued standard Air Force bedding, including the *fart sack*, a cloth cover for the mattress all of which carried the distinct chemical odor of Air Force requisitioned mothballs.

"You can leave your luggage here and collect it later," Clark said, removing a key from a wooden cabinet and handing it to Gary. He was tall and thin and had a bad case of acne. He smelled of Aqua Velva. "It's not going to get up and go anywhere."

Gary didn't know whether to laugh or not, so he played it safe and grinned. Of the few airmen that Gary had already seen at Howard, Clark was by far the most disciplined. His 1505s— the number assigned to the tan shirts and pants that were slowly being phased out of the Air Force clothing inventory— like Bartlett's uniform, were starched just as heavily and his dress shoes were spit-shined to a high gloss.

"Just your dumb luck to arrive this week," Clark said as they walked out of the orderly room.

Gary frowned. "Why?"

"We're restricted to base."

"Restricted to base?" Gary didn't like the sound of that.

"University students are up in arms about something, probably the canal again."

No one bothered to tell Gary that Panama could be dangerous. He remembered reading something about these riots in 1964 when some American soldiers had been killed, but he thought that was all in the past.

"Can you swim?" Clark asked.

Gary furled his eyebrows. "What do you mean?"

"In case someone sabotages the canal. We'll be under water," Clark said nonchalantly as though he had rehearsed this part of his orientation. "But I wouldn't worry about it any. If it did happen, the Pacific Ocean would rush in so quick, we'd be dead before we even knew what hit us."

"You're not serious, are you?" Gary asked with a quizzical look on his face. "There's no way that could happen."

"Good thing you live on the fourth floor," Clark grinned as they started up the large staircase.

Gary heard the familiar strains of "Rock and Roll All Nite" blaring from a room on the second floor and smiled. One of the first things he was going to buy was a stereo when he got paid. His cousin Bernie had been a loadmaster in the Air Force during the Vietnam War and came back home with all kinds of stereo equipment.

Originally constructed as tropical open-bay barracks, the Air Force in its attempt to improve the quality of life for its airmen, renovated the World War II-era barracks by making individual two-men rooms. On both sides of the latrine— located in the middle of the floor—six rooms were constructed. Four more rooms were built at both ends of the floor. The only problem was the rooms in the middle had no windows. Large sliding glass windows ran the length of each floor of the barracks, but it was much easier and convenient to have the hallway, which was wide enough for a Volkswagen to drive on. Some people said the reason the rooms were built that way was because it was more practical given the heavy monsoon rains; others said it was just easier to construct rooms that way. Those who were lucky enough to live in one of the rooms at the end of the floor had their own windows— they could care less about the poor saps stuck in the middle rooms.

The Air Force, in its infinite wisdom and cost-saving efficiency, had devised a central cooling system to cool the barracks. Airmen who were unfortunate enough to end up in one of the middle rooms were at the mercy of the base's ingenious cooling system, which occasionally broke down.

"Did the old man ask you to join his Bible study group?" Clark asked as they climbed the stairs to the fourth floor.

Gary nodded.

"Let me guess, you told him you would think about it?"

"Yeah," Gary replied, smiling.

"I did it for a few months. If you want to get on Bartlett's good side, I advise you to attend. He runs a tight squadron and doesn't take shit from anyone. He's one of the few people who thinks this place is the *real* Air Force. His room inspections can be a real pain in the ass if you know what I mean, white gloves and all."

"Thanks for the advice."

"Did he talk about fighting the commies in Korea?"

Gary nodded.

"He's a trip, that's for sure," Clark said laughing. "Do you get high?"

Gary raised his eyebrows. "Get high?"

"I've got a friend, Gus Santiago. He can get pretty much anything he wants in town," Clark said, pretending to take a hit off an imaginary marijuana joint.

Gary tried marijuana a few times his senior year in high school, usually when it was offered to him at a party but never bought any.

"I'll keep that in mind," Gary said, trying to be diplomatic and making a good impression on Clark at the same time.

"Well, here we are," Clark said, stopping in front of a room on the third floor and unlocking the blue door. "Wait until you see who your roomie is."

Gary gasped as soon as the door was opened and he looked inside. His new roommate had taken over most of the room by dividing the room with two ten-feet high steel metal wardrobes on the left side and a refrigerator on the right, leaving Gary with about a third. He had also commandeered most of the furniture leaving Gary only a bed, chair, and chest of drawers. His roommate had taken great pains to decorate his side of the room into some swinging bachelor pad with black light posters of buxom, scantily clad women, a poster of K.C. and the Sunshine Band and another one for Colt .45 Malt Liquor. A lava lamp, a candle stuck in the neck of a Chianti wine bottle with multicolored wax drippings stood on a table in the far left corner; along the rear wall, wooden and metal ammo boxes had been converted into bookshelves filled with various knickknacks, empty wine bottles, and a stereo system. Finally, a parachute suspended from the ceiling made that side of the room seem like the inside of a tent.

"Yeah, old J.J. is a real trip," Clark said, handing Gary the key to his room. "You two ought to get along well."

J.J. must have been one of the people Bartlett warned him about.

CHAPTER FOUR

BUCK SMITH WAS fit to be tied. Six months after being assigned to the CIA station in Panama, he was still dealing with his first crisis: an Army sergeant from Fort Clayton, who had been caught selling information to the Panamanians.

Hector Rodriquez was quite the piece of work. He was just a librarian, but over a five-month period, he had turned over hundreds of documents to Manuel Noriega, Panama's Guardia Nacional's G2. In what would soon be known as the Singing Sergeants Affair, this sergeant had been supplying Noriega with transcripts of wiretaps of high-level officials in Panama including Torrijos, which included sordid conversations about his love life, as well as ongoing discussions pertaining to a new canal treaty. Buck laughed and ran a hand through his short-cropped sandy colored hair as he glanced at the report he had been writing about the incident. He wished he could have heard some of the juicy exchanges between Torrijos and one of his lovers. What he found most amusing was how everyone—the Panamanians, Americans, the Russians, and even the Cubans—thought it was all a CIA operation that had gone afoul. Truth be known, Buck wished he had come up with the idea.

He had to admire Rodriquez's handiwork and sense of humor. Imagine, turning over transcripts of Torrijos talking to his mistress. It wouldn't do Noriega any good though, other than to give him a hard-on, knowing Noriega's penchant for graphic pornography. Sexual proclivities aside, as a competent intelligence officer under Torrijos, he knew how valuable these transcripts were, and it wasn't long before Noriega had his hooks into Rodriquez. At the same time, Noriega recruited a few more sergeants. By the time these sergeants were caught, they had turned over transcripts, which included not only surveillance of Panamanian targets, but also other targets throughout Latin America. The pièce de résistance, and the most damaging information that was passed to Noriega had nothing to do with anything scandalous about Torrijos or discussions about a new canal treaty. Instead, the information passed along to Noriega included what amounted to the NSA playbook for its listening posts and surveillance targets throughout Latin America.

What Buck and others also understood was that Central America was ripe for round two of the Cold War and this so-called Singing Sergeants Affair was a wake-up call. If there was going to be another showdown, why not Panama? All the major players were here already: the Soviets, Chinese, Japanese, Cubans, and, of course, the Americans. All eyes were upon Panama. Maybe Rodriquez didn't just show up at the Guardia Nacional one day and demand to see Noriega. If he wanted to get people's attention, he did just that. All Buck could figure was someone put him up to it. The real question that remained: Who was it?

In the meantime, everyone was screaming for someone's head on a platter until Noriega's name started being batted around. Although the NSA wanted to come down hard on the sergeants, the CIA director told the NSA to back off—and for very good reason. Noriega was on the Agency's payroll. Noriega, who had been in bed with the CIA since 1967, right around the time Buck had gone through jungle training school before he was sent to Vietnam, was off-limits. He was providing valuable intel on the Cubans which for now, made him indispensable. He was untouchable as far as the Agency was concerned—just as long as he minded himself and did what he was told.

While Buck was musing over the mess, Rodriquez and Noriega had created, Tom Kelly, the Panama station chief, stuck his head into Buck's office.

"Any breaks in the investigation?" Kelly asked.

Buck looked up at Kelly and shook his head. "Rodriquez and his buddies are still not talking which has really pissed off the NSA. They want to hang those soldiers up by their balls."

The NSA, which stood the most to lose if the story ever was leaked didn't like being shackled by interagency politics and dysfunction. Buck's job was to make sure that the Agency came out of it unscathed for having been caught with their pants down and avoid a scandal that could hurt Gerald Ford's chances in the upcoming presidential elections.

"Can you blame them?" Kelly asked.

Buck still remembered the day when Kelly briefed him on the security breach. "Nothing like jumping right into the frying pan, Smith," Kelly had said when he explained to Buck the role he would have in the investigation. Buck was eager to lead the investigation and make a good impression on his boss. Little did Buck know what was in store for him.

Buck picked up a photograph of Noriega and Torrijos taken in the early seventies and showed it to Kelly. "They make a great couple, don't they?"

"You're the Panama expert, you tell me."

Buck rolled his eyes. That's what he got for having been a military brat at Quarry Heights in the sixties and later, attending the Army's Jungle Survival School at Fort Gulick. After he had returned from two tours of duty in Nam, they made him an instructor at Gulick before the CIA recruited him. He spoke Spanish fluently, and he knew Panama better than most people in the Agency, even the station chief. Although he had only been with the Agency for a little over five years as an analyst, he had quickly proven to his superiors that he was a person who could get things done.

The Singing Sergeants Affair wasn't the only thing that was taking up all of Buck's energy and time. Ever since he had been assigned to Panama, he had been closely watching Torrijos as the likelihood of a new canal treaty between the United States and Panama moved closer to becoming a reality. Ever since his rise to power in 1968, Torrijos had been a headache for the Agency. He was a shrewd player when it came to getting what he wanted, but his volatile temperament and lack of confidence made it difficult in the beginning to figure out what kind of political course he was going to chart and who he was in bed with. Everyone suspected the Cubans—which meant the Russians, which equaled another Cold War hiccup in Central America. Moreover, he was the kind of person who acted first and asked questions later, which when combined with his impetuous, impatient behavior, when it came to dealing with complex political issues such as securing a new canal treaty, made him all the more unpredictable and dangerous.

It was Buck's job to compile all the information on Panama that came in from the various agencies as well as outside sources, specifically about Torrijos, his number two man, Manuel Noriega, and their known associates. While most people were watching the latest developments on a new canal treaty, Buck had his hands full with other issues. The file he had already started on Panama, Torrijos, and Noriega was already bulging with memos and reports, teletypes from other stations in Latin America, and articles from a variety of news sources. The more he learned, the more he believed the Agency and the country were headed down a road they did not want to travel. Buck offered assessments and recommendations. And what he had learned so far scared him. Torrijos, they could handle; all he wanted was a new treaty and barring any unforeseeable roadblocks with whoever ended up in the White House in November, he was going to get what he wanted. Noriega, on the other hand, was an entirely different problem that as far as Buck could see in the little time he had been in Panama, was only going to get worse.

Torrijos might be the Agency's and Washington's biggest concern and headache right now, but it was Noriega who was the wild card in all of this. The Singing Sergeants Affair had brought that reality home: Noriega's position and reputation were too important for the Agency to overlook. Thanks to Buck's Panama background, he had been chosen to shadow Noriega. If the Agency had Noriega on its payroll, the Agency damned well wanted to make sure that it was getting its money's worth. Although Buck's priority was Torrijos, his boss at Langley made it quite clear what Buck was supposed to do once he got to Panama: "Watch our boy and make sure he doesn't embarrass us."

Buck soon learned that was easier said than done.

CHAPTER FIVE

FRANK STUDIED THE ice cubes in his Jack and Coke and listened to Chris Shea and Rusty Phillips give him the lowdown on the squadron—who to watch out for and who to stay clear of—if he wanted to have a good tour of duty. He nodded every few seconds, paying more attention to the Panamanian waitress, who was leaning over a table to clean it causing her tight beige dress to creep up her thighs showing a glimpse of her pink panties, than all the gossip and bullshit Chris and Rusty were feeding him. He'd heard the same thing from nearly a dozen people so far, and everyone agreed that the commander was a buffoon but that the first sergeant was the one who really ran the squadron.

Most of the week was spent in-processing and going through an orientation with the other newly-assigned airmen—filling out a shitload of paperwork, as well as listening to lectures about drug and alcohol abuse. Frank thought it was all a joke and a waste of his time—he hadn't been at Howard for more than a couple hours before he had been getting high with his roommate. He filled out more forms, sat through a boring lecture from the OSI about practicing good OPSEC (it focused on what to do if approached by a Russian spy, and featured a poorly-made training film about two Russian spies with an uncanny resemblance to Boris and Natasha from the *Rocky and Bullwinkle Show*) and attended a safety briefing. He met some of the guys he came down on the plane with—Kevin Rooney, Gary Taylor, and John Bradshaw—and they all decided to meet on Friday at the NCO Club.

After Frank had met the first sergeant and commander, Chris took him to the hangar where he would be working. There he met David Harrison, who had arrived just a few weeks earlier, Jack McFarland, a crew chief and door gunner as well as Greg Sobkowiak, who worked in munitions.

Most of the people he had met in the squadron and the barracks were cool, with a few exceptions, true of any military outfit. Tonight, many of them were now all seated along the heavily varnished mahogany bar just down from where Frank, Chris, and Rusty were sitting. Chris and Rusty also worked in munitions, loading rockets on the observation planes and helicopters as well as 7.62mm NATO rounds in the two miniguns on the helicopters. Here, most of the higher-ranking NCOs gathered, away from the meat market in the other room; those who wanted to sit down and have a drink before or after dinner in the restaurant at the opposite end of the club.

"So, what's with this nightlife that I've been hearing everyone talk about around here?" Frank asked, sipping his drink while keeping an eye on the waitress. From the jukebox, Freddy Fender sang about wasted days and wasted nights. After being restricted to base all week, he had seen enough of the NCO club, and couldn't wait to check out the bar scene downtown that he had heard so much about. "Is it as wild and decadent as I've heard it is?"

"It's not Bangkok or Manila, but it's the next best thing,"

41

Jack said, swirling the swizzle stick in his Jack and Coke. The sleeves of his denim shirt were rolled up over his thick, sunburned arms. His weatherworn face, chiseled jaw, and dark blue eyes set low in their sockets reminded more than one person of the Marlboro Man. "Stick with us, we're heading down there later this evening."

Jack was one of the oldest, not to mention the highest-ranking resident of Barracks 714 and the ringleader of The Barracks Rats. The group was composed mainly of personnel assigned to CAMS (Consolidated Aircraft Maintenance Squadron) who lived on the second floor and a few guys from the 24th Supply Squadron on the third floor. The term "barracks rat" was a misnomer; in the Army it meant a soldier who never left his room or barracks. It was quite the opposite for the 714 Barracks Rats who worked hard but partied even harder. Jack, who had done two tours as a crew chief/gunner on a Huey gunship during the war and later had trained other gunners, had recently returned to Howard for another tour of duty.

Everyone in the barracks looked up to him. In his early thirties, he already had fifteen years in the Air Force. He had an aura about him that made men want to be his best friend and women want to fuck him. He might have survived two tours in Nam, but his dick was constantly getting him in trouble. He already had two ex-wives and had been banging the wife of a colonel at his last base in Florida. The base commander, whose ass Jack had saved in Nam, pulled some strings and had Jack reassigned to Howard, just before the shit hit the fan.

"I'll never forget my first morning here," David said, turning to Frank. He was wearing a *Keep on Truckin'* t-shirt and jeans. "I went into one of the shower stalls and this woman walked out with only a towel around her that just barely covered the biggest boobs I have ever seen."

Harrison held out his hands in front of his chest to illustrate how large the woman's breasts were. Frank looked at Harrison and grinned.

"You sure that wasn't one of your wet dreams, Harrison?" Rusty laughed. "I hear you haven't had your cherry popped yet."

David blushed and took a drink of his Tom Collins. His fair skin and freckled complexion reminded most people of Opie from the *Andy Griffith Show*, and that's what most people had started calling him.

"Don't let old Rusty bother you, kid," Jack said smiling. "Stick with me tonight and I'll make sure you get that cherry of yours popped."

These guys are tight. Frank eyed the waitress one more time as she wiped off the table next to where he was sitting. It was nothing like he encountered at his last base. At the same time, rules were looser here, which was fine by him. Today, for example, everyone had stopped working around three o'clock; someone had gone to the base package store and filled a metal garbage can with ice and two cases of Old Milwaukee. When the beer was gone, they staggered over to the NCO Club just in time for happy hour.

"So, Frank, what do you think of our little slice of paradise?" Jack asked.

"Seems like you guys got everything pretty much under control down here," Frank said, smiling. "From what I've seen so far, you guys hardly do any work."

Chris and Rusty looked at each other and grinned. Chris already told him that the guys in munitions worked about half the time. When the observation planes or helicopters didn't have gun missions, they sat around the office and played cards, read, or caught up on some sleep after having spent another night downtown. It had never been like that at George where there had been one exercise after another.

"It's what you make of it," Jack said. "Do you know what they used to call command down here?"

Frank shook his head.

"Well, the command used to be United States Air Forces Southern Command, but you know how everything in the military has to have a unique acronym, so it became USAFSO. People here at Howard—and elsewhere—started calling it 'You Laugh So' because discipline was so lax, and the people stationed here could get away with almost anything," Jack explained grinning. "There were guys who came here right from Nam and you know they weren't about to bust their balls for anyone. Well, some people think that's changed now since the Tactical Air Command took over but we still like the way things were before if you catch my drift."

Frank didn't particularly like Jack's condescending tone, but he would play along with him.

"No prob there, man, I'm cool," Frank said, looking at Jack.

Jack nodded and held up his beer bottle in a gesture of approval.

"There's not much that I don't know about," Jack said, staring at Frank with his piercing blue eyes. "We all look out for each other here. As long as you do your job no one's going to give a rat's ass what you do off duty. Screw up on duty and people will be on you faster than buzzards on a shit wagon."

Frank looked at Jack with a startled look on his face. There was something about Jack's tone that frightened Frank and made him feel a little uncomfortable, as though Jack was letting him know who was in charge.

"Ah, I'm just fucking with you, Costello," Jack said, slapping Frank on the back. "If you want to enjoy your tour of duty here, you can't take everything so serious."

Frank twisted the corners of his mouth into a smile. Although he didn't appreciate Jack's sense of humor, as long as he didn't try to bust his balls, Frank didn't think they would have any problems getting along.

On his way to the bathroom, Frank wanted to see what was happening in the main room. As he passed the main entrance, he could see the line of Panamanian women, who were outside waiting for someone to sign them in, extending down the steps and along the sidewalk to the corner of the building. In the main room, he noticed Gary, Kevin, and John who were sitting at a table with another of Kevin's buddies listening to him go on and on about the women who came to the club.

"You have two types of women," the tall lanky man said, pointing to a trio of women sashaying past their table. "You've got your ladies looking for a ticket to the Land of the Big BX and those wanting to polish your knob for ten bucks. More often than not, they are one and the same."

Gary's eyes widened as he ogled the three women. One of them was wearing a skintight purple t-shirt that accentuated her large breasts. Written across the front in bright yellow letters was "Hot Stuff." Gary wondered if she knew what it meant. "Ten bucks, huh?"

"That's the going rate," the man said grinning.

"Damn," Gary replied. Ever since he arrived in Panama, all he heard from the guys in the barracks were stories about pussy, drugs, and booze.

"But you might want to make sure she's on the clock first," the man added laughing, "before you ask her to fuck. Otherwise, you might find yourself on the wrong side of a backhand to the face."

Gary looked at the man with a quizzical look and then realized what he was talking about. Kevin looked at John and rolled his eyes. Everyone in the squadron warned them about Mike Brodsky whose propensity for pontificating about his views of women and dating was second only to the number of times he had been to the Howard Clinic for VD.

"And one more thing, don't ever let anyone kid you about free pussy," the man said, taking advantage of the receptive audience he had to share his thoughts on women and dating. "There's no such thing as free pussy. Men always end up paying for it one way or another."

"Hey, look, it's Frank," Kevin said, relieved when he noticed Frank approaching their table.

"*¿Qué pasa?*" Frank asked, leaning over Gary and Kevin from behind and putting his arms around their shoulders. "Fancy finding you gents here this evening."

"Looks like this *is* the place to be on a Friday night," Gary said, keeping an eye on the three women. "I've never seen so many hot chicks in one place at the same time."

Frank smiled at Gary's naivety and wide-eyed innocence. Frank got along with most of the guys he met during orientation, especially Gary, who reminded him of a friend back home. He wasn't so sure about Kevin, though. He was a cop—even if only a sky cop—which meant that Frank already had a skewed opinion of him.

"You ought to join us," Frank said turning to Gary. "There are a bunch of us from the barracks going downtown."

Gary looked around, hoping to see someone from his floor, but couldn't see anyone. "Sure, why not."

"I'll catch up with you guys later," Kevin said. "John and I are waiting for some other guys from our barracks to show up."

"Fair enough," Frank said, as he and Gary walked back to

the smaller bar.

After Frank had introduced Gary to Jack and the others and another round of drinks had been ordered, it was time for the evening's revelry to change locations.

"Gentlemen," Jack said, tossing down his drink and turning to the new guys, "now, your real orientation begins."

CHAPTER SIX

THE COOL NIGHT air was both sweet and pungent with the slight fragrance of pink plumeria, yellow frangipani, and pink hibiscus flowers dripping with moisture and the undefined scents of rotting vegetation. With Jack in the lead, Chris, Frank, Gary, and the others staggered across the street and waited for a bus in front of the base theater. The first one that came along was a brightly colored *chiva* bus with salsa music blaring from the inside. *Chiva* in Spanish meant baby goat and that pretty much described the way the bus would jump forward in small movements—like a baby goat trying to walk—each time the driver double-clutched as the bus slowly moved along.

Chiva buses in Panama were an art form, and some owners went to great lengths to customize and decorate them. The buses were painted in bright colors and adorned with a variety of traditional Panamanian scenes including ones of Old Panama, village life and women wearing *polleras*—a big one-piece traditional skirt embroidered with flowers. Some owners even gave the buses a nickname: this one had Juliet written on the front, either the driver's mother, wife or girlfriend. The inside was another story: colored Christmas lights were strung along the ceiling, which was decorated with various black light paintings depicting similar scenes of traditional Panamanian life. In the front, above the driver was a mural of Jesus seated on a cloud above the Panama Canal. The glass had been removed from the windows and replaced with iron bars. The bench seats were hard and uncomfortable. From the front of the bus, the music they heard blared from a cassette deck jerry-rigged to a multicolored dashboard.

Jack and the others found empty seats near the back of the bus and plopped down as the bus lurched forward.

"How do we know when to get off the bus?" Frank asked as he bounced up and down on the seat. An elderly Panamanian lady sitting across the aisle laughed at him.

"You yell *parada* and hope the bus driver hears you," Jack said above the din of the salsa music and the rumbling of the Ford motor.

"What does *parada* mean?" Gary asked, pronouncing the word more like "parade."

"Bus stop," Jack replied, "but don't worry, all the buses stop where we are going."

"Where's that?" Frank asked.

"Right in front of the Ancon Inn," Jack replied with a wide grin that reminded Gary of Cesar Romero as The Joker.

"*El paraiso de los hombres solteros,*" Rusty said smiling as he recited from memory the phrase, which in English meant, "the paradise of single men" from the Spanish translation of the Ancon Inn's double-sided business card.

"Roger that," Jack said.

Gary and Frank looked at each other and grinned.

The bus chugged and rumbled along a winding road through the base before it turned onto the Pan-American

Highway and then began its long, slow climb up the Thatcher Ferry Bridge. The 5,425-foot long bridge, built from 1959 to 1962, had been named after Maurice Thatcher who first proposed the idea of a ferry that had operated across the canal for many years in the same spot where the bridge now stood. Though it was called the Thatcher Ferry Bridge, many Panamanians preferred to call it The Bridge of the Americas—*Puente de las Américas*. The bus slowed to a crawl to the dismay of the line of traffic behind it as it reached the crest of the bridge, 384 feet above sea level, where one got a good view of Miraflores Locks in the distance to the left and Panama City straight ahead. A cool breeze blew in from Panama Bay and filled the bus.

"Pretty exciting, huh?" Frank asked above the din of the salsa music, and the driver grinding the gears as the bus started down the other side of the bridge.

Gary smiled as he looked out the window and saw the Panama Canal for the first time. Even at night, with the lights of the Miraflores Locks in the distance, it was breathtaking. It finally hit him that he was in Panama and a part of something bigger than he could have ever imagined.

Although the bar scene and the nightlife paled in comparison to Bangkok or Manila, as Jack pointed out, the handful of bars and clubs—starting with the Ancon Inn and ending with the Ovalo (affectionately known as The Office) the Golden Key or The Foxhole—could be just as raunchy, decadent, and wild as their Asian counterparts. Nights that started out at the Howard NCO Club or other enlisted clubs, usually ended up downtown and the first Canal Zone bus back to base in the morning for the more serious, well-seasoned and pickled veterans. Almost everyone who was newly assigned to the bases on the Pacific side of the canal and ventured downtown for the first time started off with the Ancon which was located right in front of the bus stop on Fourth of July or Kennedy Avenue (which bordered the Canal Zone), as it was still called by most foreigners (though Panamanians officially referred to it as *Avenida de los Mártires* following the 1964 riots), across the street from the Gran Morrison Department Store. A man could step or stagger off the bus, take ten steps and be inside the Ancon; five minutes later, a drink in one hand and one of the beautiful hostesses—the bar advertised on its business cards—in the other.

Like the Pied Piper of Hamlin, Jack led the entourage from the Ancon Inn down J Street to the Paris Bar. Gary and another airman from the barracks brought up the rear of the column, already feeling the effects of having too many rum and Cokes.

"Come on, no stragglers," Jack said laughing.

After that first or second trip downtown, people gravitated to their favorite watering hole when they had their fill of bar-hopping, which didn't require much effort; the bars and clubs were located in a three-block radius. Only The Foxhole, located down one of the narrow winding streets away from the critical mass of bars and casinos, presented any real challenges for those flying by the seat of their pants. The allure and temptation that awaited customers in dark, red-lighted rooms might have been too much for the eighteen-year-old grunt or airman away from home for the first time. The nights ran their course as smooth as a Cuba Libre and as wild as shots of Panama's national alcoholic beverage, Seco Herrerano, a clear beverage distilled from sugarcane.

If the night happened to get too wild and too much testosterone turned even the scrappiest kid into a fighter instead of a lover, the presence of the U.S. military town patrol was there to make sure things didn't get too far out of hand.

Their presence was more symbolic than a deterrent against any rowdy or unlawful behavior, though. On the other hand, no one wanted to cross the dark, grim-faced Guardia Nacional in their tight fitting green uniforms and campaign hats pulled down on their heads. They were both Panama's police and military and looked every part the mean SOBs they wanted everyone to think they were, but it was not for show. They made sure that the service members behaved themselves and stories of them harassing service members were not uncommon.

"Gentlemen, we're standing in the heart of all that is holy and debauch," Jack said, stopping in the middle of the intersection with his arms stretched outward. A few Panamanians walked by and stared at Jack and the others with puzzled looks on their faces. Then, as if he were a tour guide, Jack began to point out some of the more popular establishments. "Just down the street on the left side of the street is the Paradise Bar. Across the street is the Paris Bar and right next-door to it is the Ovalo."

"What about that bar on the corner?" Frank asked, pointing to a bar not far from where they were standing.

"That's the Buffalo Bar," Jack said. "It's off-limits."

"Why is it off-limits?" Gary asked.

"Some grunts got into a fight there with some locals a few months ago so the military placed it off-limits, though that hasn't stopped a couple guys in our squadron from going there, including myself," Jack said smiling, with a twinkle in his eye. "They love us in there."

Gary had already heard about most of the bars from Steve Wilson, who worked in the Base Service Store. Wilson had been a trove of information describing the bars and the women who worked in them.

"Now you're going to hear rumors about something

called the black clap that the ladies have in the Paris," Jack continued. "Don't believe a word of it."

"Black clap?" Gary asked, remembering the VD training film (which had been produced by *Walt Disney*) that was shown to recruits during basic training; there was no mention of the black clap.

"It's worse than your everyday gonorrhea," Rusty said. "Supposedly if you get it you'll die in two weeks, that's after you get all kinds of boils on your body and your dick falls off."

"Damn," Gary said. His eyes were wide with apprehension. Just thinking about that shit gumming up the works made him wince from the imaginary pain.

"Just make sure you wear your rubbers, kid," Jack said, casting a sideways glance at Chris and Rusty and winking. "And you'll be okay."

As they continued down the street, the spicy aroma of cooked meat soon filled their nostrils.

"What's that smell?" Frank asked, twitching his nose as he tried to determine the source of the aroma which got stronger the closer they got to the Ovalo. "Someone grilling meat around here?"

"Monkey meat!" Chris said as they stopped outside the Ovalo in front of a man grilling meat on a small grill. "Ain't nothing else in the world like it!"

"Best monkey meat in all of Panama, right, Hernando?" Jack said, grinning, as he bent over and breathed in the smoke rising from a small charcoal grill on a stand with wheels that could be easily moved from one location to another.

Hernando, a skinny middle-aged man with shaggy black hair, flashed a toothless grin and turned over the strips of marinated meat which were on wooden skewers. Called *carne en palita* in Spanish that translated as "meat on a stick," the meat supposedly was a low grade of beef, but there was a lot of speculation as to the origins of this mystery meat. Some said it was iguana; others said it was cat or coatimundi, a member of the raccoon family. Wherever it came from, it was the perfect complement to a bottle of Panama's national beer: Cerveza Panama.

Hernando took a barbecue brush, which looked more like a paintbrush with worn, stained bristles and brushed a dark sauce onto the meat. Flames shot up through the darkened charred metal grate as the sauce and juices from the meat dripped down on the hot coals.

"It's not really monkey meat, is it?" Gary asked bending down and sniffing the meat.

Chris grinned. "No one knows for sure."

"Come on, boys, get them while they're hot," Jack said, passing out the sticks of meat to everyone crowded around the grill.

"I'm going to bring some of the sauce home when I rotate back to the States," Rusty said, gnawing at a piece of the meat, the sauce dripping off the wooden skewer and onto his fingers. He licked the sauce off his fingers and smacked his lips. "Damn, that's good monkey!"

"We're here, boys," Jack said as he turned and opened a heavy glass door that had been painted red.

"Where?" asked Frank.

"Your home away from home," Jack replied.

As soon as Jack and the others entered the Ovalo, they were immediately hit by a blast of cold air seasoned with an olfactory overkill of sweet, sugary perfumes, cheap cologne, and stale cigarette smoke. The room was bathed in red and yellow which embodied the sexual allure and carnal pleasures waiting inside. On their right was a long, red upholstered bar which ran the length of the cavernous room. Standing and sitting along the bar was a bevy of Colombian women, who rotated in and out of Panama every sixty days. Although prostitution was legal, Panamanian women were prohibited from working in the bars that catered to service members. Some of the women were scantily clad in bikini tops and shorts; others were in halter tops and jeans. On the left was a maze of tables and chairs occupied by service members and some of the women. In the corner, a jukebox played David Bowie's "Fame."

Gary turned to Frank, his eyes wide as saucers. "I think I've died and gone to heaven."

Frank smiled. "That makes two of us."

Jack led the gang through the larger room on the left to the back where there was the entrance to the other room. In the back of the room was a small stage where on some nights, depending on the crowd, some of the girls would dance. They moved along the bar, eyeing some of the women without a customer. Two of the women threw their arms around Chris and Rusty and planted kisses on their cheeks.

They finally stopped near the center of the room as Jack pushed a couple of tables together for everyone to sit down. It didn't take long for a couple scantily clad women lingering at the bar to swoop in for their kill. One of them found an empty seat next to Gary and had her arm around Gary before he knew what happened.

"Hey, Gary, I think she likes you," Frank said grinning.

The girl, wearing a bikini top and pair of shorts which rode high on her large, rounded buttocks already had her hand between Gary's legs. She had thick lips painted red and wore too much blue eye shadow that camouflaged her age in the dim red and yellow illuminated interior.

"Buy me drinkee," the woman said as she continued to rub Gary's crotch. Her breath was hot and sweet from all the Cokes she drank.

Gary gritted his teeth. He felt an erection stirring in his jeans. "She wants me to buy her a drink. What should I do?"

"Buy her a drink, kid," Jack said.

Gary blushed and ordered a drink for him and the girl. From another jukebox—this one in the corner next to what had to be the dirtiest and raunchiest bathroom up and down J and K Streets—Gary Wright sang about being a dream weaver. The town patrol trio—an MP from Fort Clayton, an SP from Howard, and a stern-looking Guardia Nacional with his cap pushed down so far on his head that his rat-like eyes were just visible beneath the shiny black brim—slowly moved through a crowd that gave them a wide unobstructed path. Only the Guardia Nacional carried a sidearm; the Americans carried nightsticks. The MP and SP recognized a few service members from their respective bases and smiled as they continued their way through the room, but the Guardia Nacional with his beady eyes stared at everyone with disdain, especially Jack and the others.

"I bet that's the prick that shook down Steve Wilson," Chris muttered after the Guardia passed their table.

Jack and Rusty nodded.

"What happened?" Frank asked.

"One night, a Guardia, caught a kid, who lives on the fourth floor of our barracks trying to take home a girl from one of the bars," Jack explained. "The Guardia told the kid if he didn't give him some money, he would arrest him."

"That sucks," Frank said.

Steve had mentioned that he had gotten into trouble one night downtown when he told Gary about the Ancon and other bars, but he didn't go into much detail.

"Can they do that?" Frank asked.

"They can do anything they want," Jack said. "They can throw your ass in prison like they did to this Navy guy who tried to buy some pot from a local when his ship made a port call at Rodman, and not tell the military authorities because there's no Status of Forces Agreement. The fucking Guardia let that poor swabbie sweat it out in one of Panama City's prisons until his shipmates finally figured out what happened to him and bailed his ass out of jail before the ship sailed."

"They're all a bunch of pricks," Rusty said. "Right, Chris?"

"Fucken-A, Bubba," Chris said.

Chris often joked about his fifty-dollar finger—that's how much a Guardia shook him down for after he flipped off the driver of a slow-moving vehicle on the road to Colón not knowing that it was an off-duty Guardia officer behind the wheel. Rusty raised his bottle of Cerveza Panama in a salute and clinked it with Chris's bottle; he had been with Chris the day he was pulled over and harassed by the Guardia.

The girl sitting next to Gary was getting restless. She continued to rub his crotch and flick her tongue around his ear. Gary squirmed in his seat. He didn't know how much more he would be able to restrain himself from creaming in his jeans right there and then.

"You, me, fuckee, fuckee, suckee, suckee," the girl finally said.

Gary looked at Frank and Jack for help; everyone else at the table laughed. His face turned red and then he turned back to the woman and nodded.

"Ten dollars for me, three dollars for the bar, two dollars for the hotel," the girl said giggling.

"Welcome to Panama, Gary," Jack said, slapping Gary on the back.

"Do I give her the money now?" Gary asked, looking around the table for some assistance from his buddies.

"Not unless you want to do it right here," Chris said

laughing.

The girl looked at Gary with a puzzled expression. "¿*Problema?*"

"Come on, give the kid a break," Rusty chimed in. "Can't you see he's ready to shoot his wad in his jeans."

"Just pay for the bar now, Gary," Jack said. "She'll show you what to do afterward."

A chorus of catcalls, jeers, and hoots erupted around Gary, who smiled sheepishly as he pulled out three damp dollar bills and handed them to the girl.

"Congratulations, Gary," Chris said. "You've probably set the record for the fastest time to take one of these girls out of the bar."

"Wait," Jack said, motioning to a short Panamanian man with a Polaroid camera around his neck, one of a half-dozen men who made their living taking photos of service members and their dates, as he moved his way through the crowd. "You're going to need a photo to preserve this moment forever."

Jack, Chris, Frank, and the others all laughed as Jack motioned for the photographer to take a photo of Gary and the girl. The photographer positioned himself in front of the two of them and took their picture.

"Now you have something to write home about," Rusty said grinning.

"Go get her, tiger!" Jack said, clapping Gary on the back.

The rest of his buddies served up another round of catcalls, whistles, and cheers. On the way out, after the girl had collected her purse, they stopped at the door where a balding, overweight man sat on a stool. The girl handed the man the three dollars who gave the woman a laminated chip with Ovalo written on it in return before they walked outside.

Frank walked up to the bar and motioned for another

rum and Coke. He already had that Spanish down. "*Cuba Libre, por favor.*" He turned around with his drink in his hand and sipped the sweet but potent concoction.

Jack slid up next to him and ordered the same. "Well, what did I tell you, Costello? You like it?"

Frank turned around and looked at three women standing a few stools down from him. "Feels like I am in paradise."

"You got it, buddy."

Jack got quiet. At the far end of the bar, he saw Gustavo Santiago, an airman who worked in the transportation squadron, talking to Chris.

"Look at that son-of-a-bitch," Jack said, shaking his head.

"Who?"

"The guy at the end of the bar talking to Chris," Jack said, motioning with his glass to a tall man standing at the end of the bar. Santiago—who had large brown eyes and a bushy, droopy mustache that exceeded grooming regulations and reminded more than one person of the popular TV actor, Freddie Prinze—arched his head back and laughed at something Chris had said. "Watch out for him."

"Why?"

"He peddles pot on base," Jack said. "Not that I mind anyone who likes their weed, but rumor has it, he's mixed up with some local hood with ties to the Guardia. He's bad news if you know what I mean."

"Oh, really?" Frank said, trying to mask his interest, but he couldn't wait to meet Santiago.

CHAPTER SEVEN

GUSTAVO SANTIAGO HAD all the right moves. At six-foot-three, he was the star forward for the 24th Transportation's basketball team that had won the base basketball tournament two years in a row. He was also one of the key players for the squadron's volleyball team and quite good in the ring; he came in third in a boxing tournament at Fort Clayton last year. Off the court and out of the ring, Santiago still had all the right moves peddling marijuana to his buddies.

For over a year, Gus had been selling drugs on base courtesy of Diego Guerra, who his Panamanian girlfriend, Cecilia, had introduced him to at a party in the city. Guerra had an electronics store on Vía España, a main thoroughfare through the heart of the oldest part of Panama City, which was a front for his little drug operation. Most of the stereos he sold were stolen from ships transiting the canal, which meant that Diego could sell them cheaper than his competitors and still make a hefty profit. Not long after Gus met Diego, he walked into Diego's store one day to buy a Yamaha stereo receiver. He walked out with it and a couple ounces of Panama's finest, a week later, he walked out with half a pound.

Originally from a Puerto Rican neighborhood in the Lower East Side of Manhattan, Santiago had supplemented his meager stock boy salary at a bodega in his neighborhood by peddling pot to his high school buddies. It would be nothing like the kind of action that he would soon have in Panama.

Though there were some guys on base who had been weaned on Thai Stick laced with opium, Panama Red was an entirely different kind of smoke. One or two hits and a person soared higher than a kite. However, what made it legendary was the natural, psychedelic high many got smoking it. And at a couple dollars a lid, he couldn't keep up with the demand. Once folks tasted Red, they were hooked, and Gus was the man who kept them hooked payday after payday. It wasn't only the enlisted men and women or a handful of officers either; he had just as many bored housewives as customers who preferred getting stoned instead of drinking their troubles away.

Getting the drugs onto the base was never a problem. He made sure to have a few friends in the 24th Security Police Squadron who informed him when there was going to be a raid or when vehicles were going to be searched. All they asked in return was their few ounces of Red. Although things had been tightening up ever since TAC had assumed operational command of Howard, Gus wasn't worried about how it would affect his little operation. In fact, business had never been better thanks to the sudden wave of personnel fresh out of technical training schools.

Right now, what he was worried about most as he walked into the dimly lit bar just down the street from Napoli's Pizzeria, was what Diego would do when Gus told him that he was two hundred dollars short this week. Diego had fronted him drugs in the past, even let him slide a few days when he couldn't make a payment on time. However, what worried Gus the most was Diego's boss, Alejandro Vega, a local businessman and renowned figure in Panama's underworld. Gus had never met Vega, but he had heard a lot about him and it wasn't good. Vega had grown up in El Chorrillo, one of Panama City's poorest neighborhoods that bordered Fourth of July Avenue. Rumor had it he had killed a Zonian during the 1964 riots, and that was what had led him down the road to a life of crime. He was also supposed to have ties to an officer in the Guardia Nacional, Manuel Noriega. He had heard stories about some of Vega's thugs and how if you double-crossed him, you ended up in a ditch with your throat slit.

"Gustavo, *mi amigo*," Diego said, getting up from the table and walking across the room to where Gus was standing. He was a dark, beefy man with a shaved head and a gold-capped front tooth. "*¿Cómo estás?*"

"*Bien.*"

"*Bueno, bueno,*" Diego said. "*¿Cómo está tu esposa, Cecilia?*"

Gus nodded. "*Bien.*"

"*Ah, me alegra,*" Diego said. "*Por favor, sientate y toma una copa conmigo.*"

Gus glanced at his watch and nodded. One drink wouldn't hurt. He didn't have to be back to the motor pool until the afternoon.

"*Bueno,*" Diego said.

Diego motioned for the bartender to bring them a bottle of Seco Herrerano, a bucket of ice, two glasses, and some milk. Known as *Seco con vaca*, whenever Diego drank this sweet drink, it was difficult for him to stop. Likewise, those he asked to drink with him had a difficult time saying no.

"I'm really sorry, but I couldn't come up with all the money this week," Gus said. "I had police augmentee training for two days."

The security police recruited airmen, most of them newly arrived at Howard, and taught them some basic riot control skills in the event that the base was ever attacked or threatened by civil disturbances. The runway at Howard was the lifeline for bringing in more personnel and supplies, as well as evacuating nonessential personnel if the base or the Canal Zone came under attack. Supposedly the idea was that the security police would defend the runway and that the augmentees would assist where needed. Besides having to spend most of one day marching back and forth across the parade field in full riot gear practicing various crowd control tactics, which was a real pain in the ass in the heat and humidity, the augmentees had to qualify on the M-16.

"And the police have been cracking down again," Gus added starting to feel a little nervous having to explain to Diego why he had come up short this week. "The night before last they raided CAMS and Supply. Two guys I sold some weed to last week got busted."

Diego didn't say anything. He picked up a pair of metal tongs and dropped a few ice cubes into each glass; each one clinked and rattled around before another one was dropped into the tall glass. He then filled the glass three-quarters full of milk and finally added Seco. When he was finished, he slid one of the glasses across the table and motioned to Gus to take a drink. Gus sipped the cool, sweet concoction and felt the alcohol rushing to his brain. Panamanians referred to drinking Seco and milk as *vuelve loco con vaca*—which meant, "makes crazy with cow." It took the edge off his nervousness.

"Is it good?" Diego asked.

Gus nodded.

"I'm happy that you like it, Gus because your happiness is important to me and I wouldn't want to see you unhappy,"

Diego said staring across the table at Gus. "So when you come here and tell me that you can't pay me this week because of this and that, I can tell that you are unhappy. And that, my friend, makes me unhappy."

"I can—"

Diego wagged a finger in front of Gus. "If you are unhappy with our arrangements, I am sure there is someone else I can depend on. And that would be most unfortunate for you. I know what happens on base. I know about your training, and I know about the barracks being raided. There are a lot of things that I know about. Sometimes these things are inevitable. However, you and I have an arrangement. We have to put our personal interests and matters aside. Business is business. *Negocios son negocios. ¿Lo entiendes?*"

Gus nodded his head. He understood perfectly where Diego was coming from and was relieved that he was off the hook—at least for now—with just a stern warning. "I promise next time not to be late and to have all the money."

"Of course you will, Gustavo," Diego said. "I have all the faith in the world in you. Now drink up and we shall talk of this no more."

It could have been worse Gus thought as he drove across the Thatcher Ferry Bridge. Diego was cool—it was Vega he had been worried about. Gus took out a hash pipe that he wore on a chain around his neck and put a small piece of hashish into it. He needed something to settle his nerves and take the edge off the Seco coursing through his brain. He knew the next time he might not be so lucky. And it wouldn't make any difference that Diego was Cecilia's uncle.

After he had returned to the motor pool, he signed out a pickup and drove over to the CAMS hangar. It was one of those days when there was nothing going on. A couple of guys were tossing a Frisbee around; a couple others were reading comic books.

Gus spotted Frank in the back with his shirt off, lounging on a makeshift chair made from empty wooden rocket boxes for the rocket pods on the UH-1Ns. Frank had a portable radio pressed against the side of his head listening to *SCN*, the *Southern Command Network*—the military broadcast network for the Canal Zone. Gus heard the end of popular radio series, "Chickenman," which spoofed comic book heroes, before the *Charlie Tuna Show* continued with the famous radio personality playing "Show Me the Way" by Peter Frampton. As soon as Frank saw Gus, he smiled and got up from the wooden crates.

"What's up, man?" Frank said, grabbing Gus's hand in a mutual handshake, followed by patting the backs of their hands, and ending with lightly pounding each other's closed fists.

Gus looked around. "Are you ready to do some business?"

"You read my mind."

CHAPTER EIGHT

THE FIRST TIME Kevin laid eyes on Inés Herrera he could tell that she was not like the other women who lined up outside the NCO Club on Friday and Saturday nights waiting for club members to sign them in. She seemed a bit out of place as though she had gotten lost and only stopped at the club to ask for directions.

Kevin hadn't planned on going to the NCO Club when he finished the day shift. There was a good movie playing at the base theater, but at the last minute, he changed his mind and headed to the club instead. Although still early, already a dozen or so women were lined up on the sidewalk and the steps to the club on the second floor. He ended up standing behind a tall man and two women who were waiting to get into the club.

"Hey, buddy, can you do me a favor?" the man asked, turning around to Kevin. "I'm not a member of the club yet. Can you sign in these two women for me?"

Kevin nodded.

"Thanks, man," the man said, clapping Kevin on the

shoulder. "If you like, you can join us."

Kevin followed them inside. The shorter of the two women that were with the man must have been a regular at the club, Kevin thought as they walked inside. Before they made it to the main room on the right, at least five men had said hello to her, including this one guy who lived in Kevin's barracks. Kevin glanced around the room and didn't see anyone he recognized, so he reluctantly joined the man and the two women. They found an empty table just inside the ballroom.

"Thanks a lot again, bro, for signing in the ladies," the man said, pulling out a crumpled pack of Kools from his shirt pocket. He shook one free and stuck it in the corner of his mouth. "My name's Mark Brown. I'm here TDY from Myrtle Beach."

"Don't mention it," Kevin said. "My name's Kevin."

"Nice to meet you, Kevin," Mark said, reaching across the table and shaking Kevin's hand. "This is Rosa and her friend, Inés."

Rosa, the shorter woman, had dark skin with numerous chickenpox scars on her face which she tried to cover up with too much makeup. Inés, on the other hand, was pretty in a very plain way which made her seem all the more attractive compared to her friend Rosa and the other women. She wore a sheer long-sleeved blouse and a pair of black slacks whereas Rosa had on a low-cut halter top which barely covered her breasts and a pair of shorts. Inés didn't say much at first. She hardly touched her soft drink and had to be coaxed by Rosa to dance with Kevin. Music was provided by a Filipino band, The Kiwis, which made the rounds at all the bases in the Canal Zone. Rosa was also making the rounds; every time she and Mark came off the dance floor she stopped at a table to say hello to one of her male friends.

Inés's English was not as good as Rosa's; between Kevin's

limited Spanish and Inés's limited English, the two of them stumbled through a number of topics about the weather, food, and family with Rosa providing the necessary translation along the way. Although she seemed to be enjoying herself, Kevin thought that the only reason she came along was to keep Rosa company. One thing was for certain, as the night passed by and they danced a few more times, Kevin was becoming more interested in her.

"Hey, buddy, long time no see," Frank said, stopping by the table. "How's it hanging?"

Frank startled Kevin, who had been staring at Inés. He knocked over his drink and started to clean it up as best he could.

"Hi, Frank," Kevin said sheepishly. "How's it going?"

"And who do we have here?" Frank asked gazing at Inés.

"Oh, this is—" Kevin began.

"*Hola, amiga,*" Frank said, sliding up in a chair next to Kevin and Inés. "*¿Cómo estás?*"

Inés looked at Frank and smiled. "*Muy bien, gracias.*"

Kevin had picked up a few Spanish words and expressions but not as many as Frank, who already had a good command of basic Spanish.

"*¿Cómo se llama usted?*" Frank asked looking at Inés.

"Inés."

"*Mucho gusto. Encantado. Mi nombre es Frank.*"

"Hey, you're not moving in on my girl, are you?" Kevin said grinning.

Frank laughed. "You better pick up some more Spanish, pardner, if you want to dazzle the ladies."

When Rosa and Mark returned to the table after having danced, that was Frank's cue to leave.

"*Nos veremos de nuevo,*" Frank said, smiling before he stood up. "See you around too, Kevin."

After one too many rum and Cokes and Rosa's male friends chatting her up, Kevin could sense that Mark was starting to feel a little desperate about what to do with Rosa. It was obvious that she wasn't that interested in him, but he had invested too much time and effort in the night already to cut his losses. Kevin, on the other hand, hadn't thought about what he and Inés would do when they left the club, but he was definitely aroused by her. He was equally buzzed from the steady flow of Cuba Libres.

While the two women were engaged in some conversation, Mark took Kevin aside. "Listen, I really want to get Rosa in the sack, but if her friend doesn't come along, she's going to want to go home."

"Sure, I'll tag along," Kevin said. It was against regulations to bring a woman back to the barracks after hours, but it was one of those regulations that no one knew how to enforce and that everyone broke.

"Her friend's pretty hot, too," Mark said, sweetening the offer and slapping Kevin on the back. "Maybe you'll get lucky, too."

Kevin glanced over at Inés and Rosa and wondered what they were talking about.

Rosa let Mark grope and feel her as much as he wanted and didn't seem to be bothered by other couples watching them. After several more drinks and dances, Mark finally made his move.

"What do you say we get a bottle of something at the package store and go back to my room?" Mark suggested. "My roomie is gone for the weekend."

Rosa and Inés chattered away in Spanish with Rosa gaining the upper hand in the conversation. Kevin could tell by Inés's body language that whatever they said must have been something about going back to the barracks room because Inés looked over at Kevin and smiled.

They walked out of the club into the cool night. Even though it was the tropics, the trade winds which blew in from the ocean always made the night seem cooler. Rosa chatted away, talking some nonsense about how she knew some pilot, which she probably felt was supposed to impress Mark as he staggered along trying to keep up with Rosa who was on autopilot as she glided along the sidewalk. Kevin cast a sideways glance at Inés and smiled.

As they walked across the parade field, after buying a bottle of TJ Swan's Mellow Nights, Kevin's arm accidently brushed against Inés's arm. She looked over at him with her big brown eyes and smiled. He was feeling just drunk enough to show a little bravado and gently take hold of her hand; it felt cool and clammy. In front of them, Mark carried Rosa piggyback across the field.

"Rosa is funny," Inés finally said. "She's very lonely, though. She had a boyfriend who went back to the States. It broke her heart, *se le rompió el corazón.*"

"That's sad," Kevin said.

"*Ella realmente quiere casarse,*" Inés said. "She wants a husband."

Frank was right. He needed to learn more Spanish.

"Don't mind the mess," Mark said, opening up the door and turning on the light. The transient barracks for TDY personnel was on the third floor above the 24th Supply Squadron office just down the street from Kevin's barracks. The room was like other barracks rooms at Howard, which came with the same standard furniture though these rooms had more of a hotel room feel to them. In order to have more privacy, Mark, and his roommate had placed the two steel wardrobe cabinets in an "L" shape in the middle of the room and hung a bedspread from one of the wardrobes to the wall. Judging from the way they had the rest of the room organized, they were going to be TDY at Howard for a while.

"Make yourself at home, man," Mark said, motioning to his roommate's side of the room. Mark turned off the overhead light, grabbed Rosa and plopped down on the bed with her. He reached over and turned on a portable radio which was already tuned to *SCN* and a country and western oldies show. The Sons of the Pioneers serenaded them with a scratchy version of "Cool, Cool Water." Kevin took the cue from Mark, who already had his other hand inside of Rosa's shorts and proceeded to the other side of the room with Inés.

Although the other side of the room was dimly lit, the violet glow from the radio made it easy to find the bed, which, fortunately, had been made. Kevin sat down on the edge of the bed next to Inés. On the other side of the wardrobe, they both heard Rosa giggling followed by the sound of kissing. Kevin moved closer to Inés, put his arm around her waist, and pulled her closer. He had been with lots of women, but this night he felt as though he was back in high school in the backseat of his father's Dodge with Suzy Wilson. There was just a brief moment of awkwardness with the mood nearly broken when Rosa started giggling again, but when he finally moved in for the kiss, Inés responded by kissing him first. Her breath was hot and sweet. The frequency of their kisses increased as they rolled back and forth on the bed, their two bodies intertwined. Both their hearts were pounding as the depth of their kisses increased, their tongues darting in and out of their mouths. Her perfume and the faint, flowery scent of the shampoo she used were intoxicating.

Kevin fumbled with her bra strap before she reached around and unhooked it for him. She slowly slid her arms out from the bra and held her hands in front of her small pert breasts. His hands slowly moved down her body; he removed her pants and panties and dipped a finger inside of her. Already wet, she softly moaned as he worked his finger deeper. She guided his head with both her hands until she felt his tongue inside of her, then she clasped her breasts. He felt her arch her body and groan as he continued to work his tongue inside of her.

He worked his way up her body with his tongue, pausing to kiss her large erect nipples. He could feel her body quivering as he tongued and nibbled each one. She slipped her hand down his pants and felt for his penis. She gasped when she felt how long and hard he was. After she had helped him off with his pants and underwear, she closed her hand around him and ran her thumb back and forth across the sensitive tip. She kissed and tongued his penis before she took him into her mouth. Kevin lay back and closed his eyes. He gritted his teeth as she licked him with long flicks of her tongue and sucked him harder.

Kevin suddenly remembered the condom in his wallet, in his pants on the floor, but it was too late as Inés rolled over and mounted him. Kevin was a little shocked that Inés was as aggressive in bed as she was when she had been so quiet and shy at the club. He felt her hand guide him deep inside of her. She moaned softly as she rolled her hips back and forth and arched her back. She grabbed his chest with both hands as her hip thrusts intensified. Kevin squeezed her breasts and gently pinched her nipples. Inés let out a small shriek, enjoying the brief moment of pain as she pressed her hips against his hips even harder. Her brown eyes were wide and frantic as she slowly lifted her hips off his body, drew her knees up, and finally squatted over him. Uncontrollable tremors coursed through her body as she moved up and down—slowly at first and then fast and hard—until she climaxed. He looked up at her and felt her insides quivering. That's when he could no longer wait as he felt himself explode inside of her.

She stayed on top of him before she lowered her body onto his. They lay together for several minutes trying to catch their breath. On the other side of the wardrobe, they heard Rosa and Mark talking. Kevin slowly caressed Inés's arm. She took his other arm and placed it around her shoulder. They heard movement on the other side of the wardrobe. Rosa started chattering away in Spanish. There was the sound of a glass or a bottle breaking.

"Shit!" Mark yelled.

"I want to go now," Rosa said. *"Inés, quiero ir a casa."*

"What's wrong?" Kevin asked, looking over at Inés as she sat up.

Inés sighed. "Rosa wants to go home. I'm sorry."

"That's okay," Kevin said dejectedly, wanting to spend more time with Inés, who began searching for her clothes on the bed. Rosa flipped on the overhead light startling Inés, who quickly covered her breasts and midriff with her blouse. Kevin quickly located his clothes and tried not to look at Inés as not to make her feel any more embarrassed. He had just pulled on his pants when Rosa stuck her head around the edge of the wardrobe to see why Inés was taking so long.

"Pa' lante, Inés!" Rosa said with an edge to her voice.

Inés slipped on her panties, pulled on her jeans, and grabbed her shoes. When she passed Kevin, she kissed him lightly on the cheek.

"Thanks for a really nice time this evening," she said smiling. "You're not like most men."

Her English was flawless.

Kevin looked at her with a quizzical look on his face but decided not to bother. "I'll walk you to the bus stop."

"That's okay," Inés said matter-of-factly. "I know the

way."

When Kevin walked to the other side of the room, Mark was sitting on the bed with a cigarette dangling from his lips. He looked worse for the wear. "Well, did you get any?"

Kevin nodded sheepishly.

"Lucky you. That Rosa was a little prick tease," Mark said, swigging some of the TJ Swan. "Would you believe she's got a boyfriend? She could have at least given me a blowjob."

"She did seem like she knew a lot of guys at the club."

"It's still early," Mark said, scooping up a handful of condom packets scattered on the floor. "Do you want to head downtown?"

Kevin shook his head. "I think I'm going to call it a night."

"Whatever. I still need to get laid, unlike some people I know."

On his way back to his barracks, Kevin could still smell Inés on his lips and fingers. He had never made love to a woman as he had made love to Inés this evening. He had slept with a half-dozen girls in his life and thought he knew a thing or two about making love and what a woman wanted, but Inés was unlike any of the women he had slept with. And what did she mean when she said, "You're not like most men?" Maybe his buddy Rick Grimes in the squadron was right; most of the girls who went to the club were looking for that ticket to the Land of the Big BX.

Back in his room, he stripped down to his shorts and sat at the desk writing a letter to his mother. He wanted to tell her all about this wonderful lady he met this evening.

Inés. He liked the way her name sounded as it rolled off his tongue.

CHAPTER NINE

THE FIRST EXPLOSION occurred at four o'clock in the afternoon the last week of October in front of the Balboa Retail and Commissary Store.

Harold Walker, an employee of the Panama Canal Zone Company, had just put his groceries in the trunk of his car when he noticed one of his friends walking into the commissary. Harold had just raised his hand and opened his mouth to yell to his friend; the next thing he knew he was knocked to the ground when an explosion ripped through the parking lot. About a hundred yards away, a Toyota Land Rover that had been parked in front of the commissary had suddenly exploded and caught on fire.

Fortunately, no one was injured though the parking lot was crowded with afternoon shoppers. Harold got up off the ground and brushed some broken glass off his shirt. He was lucky; the trunk of the car which had been opened at the time of the explosion had blocked the blast waves and saved him from being injured.

The Army sent their Explosive Ordinance Disposal Team

(EOD) to the scene to investigate, but neither they nor the Canal Zone Police (CZP) were initially able to determine the cause of the explosion. At the time, it was believed that lightning from a thunderstorm had struck the car causing the gas tank to explode. In fact, people who were near the commissary when the gas tank exploded didn't even realize they had heard an explosion, thinking that the sound they did hear was a combination of the heavy rain and thunder.

Nonetheless, the reaction of the American powers-that-be was swift to enact tighter security measures, led by the Canal Zone Governor, who was an Army general but opted to use the CZP. The police were put on twelve-hour shifts to provide additional patrols both on foot as well as vehicular. He set up checkpoints at all entrances, at both ends of the Thatcher Ferry Bridge, and in the middle, and gave the CZP authority to search vehicles at will entering the Canal Zone. Citizens were also warned to be careful and on the lookout for any suspicious individuals or activity. Hotlines were set up. The governor wanted people to go about their business but advised them to remain vigilant.

Five days later, there was another bombing. This time, the intended target was Canal Zone policeman William Drummond, who was an outspoken critic of a new canal treaty. He had become somewhat of a folk hero among Zonians who felt they were being ignored by Washington. The EOD Team was called in again and they discovered a timer mechanism which had been used to detonate the bomb that most likely used C-4 plastique. Again, there were no injuries because the bomb had been detonated at around two o'clock in the morning. Unlike the first bomb, the fact that one person had been singled out and targeted raised anxiety levels across the isthmus. Many Zonians thought the bomb had been planted by Panamanians to scare Drummond; on the other hand, many Panamanians thought someone in the Zone had done it to influence the upcoming presidential election.

That evening, in Coco Solo near the Atlantic side of the Canal Zone, there were three more bomb blasts which were the most destructive of the Canal Zone bombings. Three separate timed explosions destroyed three cars in the parking lot of the Coco Solo Hospital. Windows were blown out, a total of seven cars were destroyed and buildings were evacuated. The next day, another bomb went off, this time in a residential area on Amador Road near the east approach to the Thatcher Ferry Bridge. Two houses were damaged by the bomb blast; fortunately, there were no injuries again

These latest bombings sent shock waves of fear from one end of the Canal Zone to the other. Zonians and military personnel alike were fearful that there would be more bombings. Unlike the 1964 riots, it was the first act of terrorism committed in the Canal Zone and reminded everyone how vulnerable facilities and American personnel in the Zone were to acts of terrorism.

Whoever was behind these bombings had sent a very strong message.

In his office, Buck stared at a copy of the teletype he had sent to Washington. Although the CZP and EOD personnel were still in the early stages of their investigation, Buck felt that whoever was responsible for these bombings wanted to send a clear message to Zonians and Washington alike.

Buck and others, specifically the U.S. State Department, feared that the failure to produce a new canal treaty would complicate U.S. relations in Latin America. It was still the Torrijos show. Since he came to power and prominence, he had become less erratic and he learned how to handle people and situations better. To be sure, one of his masterstrokes was being able to bring various groups together who at one time had opposed each other such as the Guardia Nacional and university students. He was, in Buck's assessment, no longer uncertain of his ability to run the country, and in many ways believed that he was destined to right the wrongs his country had suffered since 1903.

Buck poured himself a glass of bourbon from a bottle he kept in his desk drawer and continued to stare at the teletype. He wondered what would have happened if Reagan had won the Republican nomination. During the campaign trail, Reagan declared that the canal was America's: "We built it. It's ours. We're going to keep it." Politicians could get away with that kind of rhetoric to gain support and win votes, but there was no place for it in Buck's world. Although Reagan failed to win the Republican nomination, there were many people who still thought the canal should not be turned back over to the Panamanians. Buck, who once felt the same way when he was a military brat, now couldn't care less one way or another; however, public support for keeping the canal smacked of the kind of nationalism that made his job interesting.

Of course, most everyone knew that the canal and the Canal Zone were more symbolic issues that tugged at one's nationalistic heartstrings than anything else. There were far more important issues at stake that were crucial to American interests in the region. One of those issues was Torrijos's active support for the Communist Sandinista guerillas in Nicaragua which convinced many Panama watchers, Buck included, that Torrijos was not to be trusted. Although Torrijos had already threatened to blow up the canal should the United States fail to deliver on its promise of a new treaty, he had his hands full with other pressing issues such as the civil unrest in Panama regarding the country's weakening economy which had been affected by drought and world-wide inflation.

Torrijos might get a new canal treaty, but his problems at home were giving him a new headache. Last month there were massive protests but unlike other protests, none of the students were shouting, "Yankee go home." The bigger issue at hand though, remained stability in the region; if something had to be done about Torrijos to keep him at bay during this critical period as well as beyond, those in the Agency and the State Department were going to need help.

Buck was well aware of the colonial underpinnings that the Canal Zone and the military presence had for Panamanians and how it strained relationships between the two countries. Having lived in the Canal Zone for two years when his father was stationed at Quarry Heights, he heard both sides of the story—why many Zonians didn't want to relinquish their little piece of paradise and why many Panamanians wanted what was rightfully theirs. Without question, it was an emotionally charged issue on both sides. He knew most Zonians didn't really understand things fully who felt that the Canal Zone was completely theirs forever from a technical point—which smacked of the kind of rhetoric Reagan used on the campaign trail. But mostly, as he knew from his years in the Canal Zone, the Zonians didn't want to give up their way of life; it didn't make any difference whether they were right or wrong. They claimed patriotic notions about how the canal belonged to the United States and that if the United States were to withdraw, communism would move in. However, it was almost entirely their hatred of getting kicked out and their society destroyed which motivated them the most.

The flip side of the issue, for those people who were for a new treaty, was that the canal had run its course. In ten or fifteen years, it wouldn't be able to handle the big container ships that were on the drawing boards. Maybe it was time to move out, perhaps even construct another canal. Nicaragua still looked inviting, though the unrest there had many people nervous.

It was easy to understand the Panamanian position: The Panamanians were never satisfied from the very first treaty in 1903 because they felt it was lopsided when Philippe-Jean Bunau-Varilla negotiated a treaty with the United States without consulting with any Panamanians who were pretty much blackmailed into accepting it. Throughout the decades, as they protested more and more, changes were made to give them more, but they wanted complete ownership eventually in the distant future, as was traditional with such projects. John Kennedy actually sympathized with them and opened talks on the subject. After he had been assassinated, it was thought that Lyndon Johnson would continue what Kennedy had started. However, Johnson was embroiled with his own problems in Southeast Asia as well as dealing with Congress on passing a civil rights bill.

The riots in 1964 were a wake-up call for both Panama and the United States, but it took another decade before any serious discussion of a new treaty began. Talk of a new treaty and righting the wrongs of the past dragged on through the sixties and early seventies with Panamanian tempers escalating, especially commoners, college students, Communist and Castro groups, as well as politicians promising a new treaty for them. Eventually, all this public clamoring gave them more steam to get behind Torrijos when he came onto the scene.

Put simply, Buck knew that what it all came down to was Panama wanted a future and that future was to have the Canal Zone and the canal turned over to them. They never wanted it overnight even though they realized they knew nothing about running the canal, but that didn't matter to them. They wanted something even if it was just symbolic of a new distant future.

Ironically, wealthier Panamanians didn't seem to care.

They were more content. That's what Buck couldn't figure out. In the words of one Panamanian, who sarcastically pointed out, "Will I get a new house or a new boat for free if we get the canal?" The biggest brain trust and pushers for a new treaty were the commoners, politicians, and college students, along with Communist groups prodding them on. As such, this created mixed signals to most Americans, especially Zonians, who believed that the Communists were behind all the demands.

Buck rubbed his temples and leaned back in his chair. Solving the Canal Zone issue with a new treaty wasn't going to be easy.

However, it wasn't Torrijos who worried Buck the most; nor was it the fallout should the ongoing treaty negotiations fail to produce a new treaty. His headaches were still with Noriega that started when Rodriquez walked into Noriega's headquarters and turned over classified information.

Panama had been ripe for espionage for years; it was the nature of the country's location connecting the rest of Central America with South America. While the Americans and Panamanians hammered out a new canal treaty, the Americans had upped their surveillance activities—from listening posts to satellites and spy aircraft in the skies above. And it wasn't only the Americans who were doing all the spying. The country was crawling with spies: the Russians, Cubans, Japanese, and Chinese, not to mention the Colombians. Everyone wanted to know what was going on between the Americans and the Panamanians.

One thing for certain, Buck was earning his pay.

At first, Buck thought whoever planted the bombs only wanted to make a statement because those who detonated the bombs were careful where the bombs were placed. With a presidential election in a few days, the timing of the bombings couldn't have come at a more opportune time. Or was it much more? Was someone trying to sabotage the treaty negotiations before they even got started should Carter win the election or were those involved just sending a deadly message? Buck also wondered how involved their man Noriega was in all of this. And if he was involved, what kind of message was Noriega trying to send?

These latest events were most disturbing. Both he and the station chief didn't think it was a Zonian; however, rumors making the rounds suggested otherwise. *A fucking hospital.* Buck stared at the teletype again. It was fortunate that no one was injured. As he read the teletype again, lost in his thoughts, he was startled by a knock on the doorframe as Kelly stuck his head inside the door.

"Well—," Kelly began.

"The police are interviewing witnesses and still searching through the rubble for clues," Buck said. "It's a fucking mess."

Kelly nodded. "I just got off the phone with the ambassador. He's furious about all of this. He's going to meet with Torrijos to make sure this doesn't get sensationalized by the press."

"Good luck with that, huh?"

"Just what we need, too," Kelly said, "another headache with the election just a few days away."

"If someone wanted to get our attention, they sure did a good job." Buck put his hands behind his head and leaned back in the chair.

"What's your gut feeling on this one, Buck?"

"I don't think it was a Zonian; however, it seems that this Drummond fellow might have sparked it all since he was the only one targeted. And I don't think it was Drummond either, as some people have suggested," Buck explained. "This suit he filed in the U.S. District Court in the Canal Zone last week against Ford, Kissinger, and Ellsworth Bunker to prevent a continuation of the treaties might have ruffled a few feathers but I don't think it has anything to do with that. What I really think is that someone is sending us a message."

Kelly grunted. "Okay, so if it's not a Zonian, then who?"

"You're not going to like it."

"Who?"

"Noriega."

"Are you sure?"

"If I were a betting man, I'd say when the smoke clears from this one it's all going to point back to our friend Noriega," Buck continued. "It might be Noriega's way of keeping things interesting down here. His way of letting us know who's really in charge and how vulnerable the Canal Zone, as well as the canal, is to random acts of terrorism. This could just be the beginning."

Kelly frowned. "It'll be just like Tel Aviv or Jerusalem."

"You've got that right. Ever since 1964 that has always been one of the biggest fears and concerns, which brings us right back to Noriega," Buck said. "Torrijos doesn't want to get his hands dirty, so he lets Noriega do it for him. Whether or not he orchestrated it or simply gave the order, the end result is the same."

"Washington's not going like it, Buck," Kelly said.

Buck bit down on his bottom lip and nodded. Although Buck wasn't one hundred percent sure if Noriega or the Guardia Nacional had anything to do with the bombings, it certainly added an element of suspense to an already volatile situation. "You do realize that we're going to have to deal with this Noriega fellow sooner or later. We're not paying him for nothing."

"That's not for us to decide, Buck," Kelly said, rolling his eyes again. "That, my friend, is above our pay grade."

Buck grinned. He knew that it was only a matter of time before Noriega really started to become a problem, not only for the Agency, but for the person sitting in the Oval Office.

CHAPTER TEN

IN THE AFTERMATH of the bombings of various locations around the Canal Zone, military authorities promptly issued an advisory restricting the movement of military personnel in Panama except those service members living off post. While most of the personnel on Howard were not affected by the restrictions, the security police and law enforcement officers went on twelve-hour shifts. Unfortunately for Kevin, this meant he ended up working the evening shift and couldn't meet Inés. And then the next weekend, Inés couldn't make it because she had to work.

Since they started seeing each other five weeks earlier, a few movies at the base theater, dancing at the NCO Club and one Saturday of swimming at Kobbe Beach had been highlights, but they hadn't gone on a real date off base yet. When they could finally see each other, Kevin couldn't make it again: some of his buddies who lived on his floor were throwing a bachelor party for a friend.

"We're going to start off at the Ancon, and after that it's anybody's guess," Steve Martinez, one of his buddies, had said two weeks earlier when he invited Kevin.

"Count me in," Kevin had replied at the time. But that had been before the week of bombings across the Canal Zone and the extra duty. He had forgotten all about the party until Martinez reminded him on the Saturday morning of it.

"You're still coming tonight, aren't you?" Martinez had asked, Kevin when they bumped into each other in the latrine.

"Oh shit, that's tonight."

Ever since Kevin began seeing Inés, he hadn't been spending enough time with some of the guys in his squadron and he didn't want them to think that he was aloof or anything.

Martinez had furrowed his brow as he spat out some water and toothpaste. "Just be there man. It's going to be a blast!"

The problem was Kevin didn't know how to get in touch with Inés to tell her that he had to cancel their date. The few times he had called her before, her father answered the phone and immediately hung up when Kevin started speaking. Kevin really didn't want to go out this evening either, but after he said he would, he had no choice; he would never hear the end of it if he didn't. He was afraid that she would think that he blew her off if he wasn't at the club.

He was still mulling over his dilemma that afternoon in the chow hall, pushing his tray along the service line, when he bumped into Frank, almost knocking his tray off the line.

"I hope you don't drive the same way on the flight line," Frank said, laughing when he saw who it was.

"Sorry," Kevin replied, embarrassed for not having paid attention.

"What's up?" Frank asked, noticing that Kevin seemed troubled about something.

"You remember that girl I was with the other week, don't you?" Kevin asked as he set two bowls of lime Jell-O on his tray. "We bumped into you outside the base theater."

"Inés, right?" Frank replied, motioning for the macaroni and cheese to one of the San Blas Indians behind the serving line. San Blas or Kuna Indians were from the San Blas Islands on the Atlantic side of the canal. Noted for their small stature, as well as the colorful *molas*—colorful panels of cloth comprised of geometric patterns—many San Blas men worked on military bases throughout the Canal Zone. Frank sniffed the contents on his plate before he set it on his tray and continued to move down the line with Kevin in tow. He remembered her exactly. She wasn't one of those painted-up hotties hanging outside the NCO Club on Friday and Saturday nights waiting for someone to sign them in. She was much prettier. He envied Kevin.

"Yeah, that's her name."

"What's wrong, she's not giving it up for you?"

Two airmen behind Kevin snickered.

"I've been trying to get in touch with her, to tell her that I can't meet her tonight because of this bachelor party," Kevin explained as he motioned for the same entrée that Frank chose. "Every time I call her house, her old man answers and I don't think he has a thing for Americans."

"At least Americans banging his daughter," Frank said grinning.

Two guys from CAMS in front of Frank laughed. Kevin felt embarrassed for bringing it up in the first place. It was true, however. He was having the best sex of his life, two and sometimes three times a week, every time Inés came to the base. Almost every Friday and Saturday night that started off with dinner and dancing at the NCO Club or a movie at the base theater ended up back in his room.

"Let me guess, you want me to tell her that you can't make it tonight?" Frank said, grabbing two empty glasses and filling them half full with ice cubes from an ice machine.

Kevin hadn't thought about it, but it sounded like a good idea. After all, Frank spoke Spanish well.

"Yeah, that's what I mean," Kevin said, hoping that Frank would be able to help him out. "And if you could tell her that I will see her tomorrow night at the same time that would be great."

"What do I look like to you, a fucking secretary?" Frank said trying to suppress a grin.

Kevin looked at Frank with a startled expression on his face.

"Come on, Frank, give the kid a break," Jack said, sliding his tray up to where Frank and Kevin were standing. "Can't you see the poor guy is in love or heat?"

Frank ignored Jack as he filled his glasses with Coca-Cola. "Don't worry. If I see her, I'll be sure to tell her that you can't make it this evening."

"Thanks a lot, Frank."

"In the meantime, I'd work on letting her father know you've been banging his daughter, just in case you two decide to get married one day," Frank added.

Jack and a few others in line laughed.

Kevin looked at Frank with a sheepish look on his face. "Is it that obvious?"

"Yup," Frank said nodding. "You are definitely pussy-whipped."

* * *

The party started off at the Ancon where fifteen of the groom's friends had taken over one corner of the room, pissing off a group of sailors on liberty hoping to get closer to the stage. One of the girls, remembering Kevin from a previous visit to the club came up to him and put her arms around him. She planted a kiss on his cheek, leaving a noticeable lipstick mark. Then she plopped down on his lap and asked him to buy her a drink.

"Go ahead, Rooney, your old lady isn't going to find out," Todd Jackson said. "Have some fun, for Chrissakes."

He bought the woman (he vaguely remembered her name as Lily or something like that) a drink, and then another. Someone pulled out a bottle of tequila and everyone at the table did shots until the bottle was finished. At some point, after some needling and coaxing from some of the older SPs, Kevin, John, and two other guys from his barracks floor got up on the stage and started dancing with some of the girls to a K.C. and the Sunshine Band song until the owner chased them off the stage. Then someone yelled they should move the party to the Golden Key Disco.

Lily didn't want Kevin to leave and started hanging all over him, grabbing his crotch, kissing him—which culminated with a large hickey on his neck.

"You're going to catch hell for that, Rooney," one of his buddies said when he saw the size and location of the hickey.

Kevin grinned as he turned his head and looked at the purplish-red mark in the reflection of a mirrored post behind his chair. One of his buddies went ahead and paid the bar fine as a joke, and the next thing Kevin knew, he was being pushed out of the door with Lily in tow.

He was already feeling the effects of the rum and Coke, tequila, and a potent cocktail called the Motherfucker—similar to a Zombie—that contained five different kinds of alcohol. Kevin, in his inebriated state, didn't think it would be a problem to go to the disco with Lily. After all, he was just having a little fun with the guys.

* * *

Frank had gone to meet Gus, who had to work late at the motor pool, for a late-night drug buy and was walking back to the barracks after he smoked a couple bowls with Gus. At the bus stop in front of the base theater, he saw a woman sitting by herself with her face in her hands as if she was crying. He did a double take when he walked past the bus stop and noticed that the woman was Inés, the woman he was supposed to meet in the club. He had lost track of time and forgotten all about meeting her and telling her that Kevin wouldn't be able to see her tonight. Well, that was Red for you.

"Inés, right?" Frank said. He could tell that she had been crying.

She looked up at Frank and tried to figure out where she had met him before. Then she remembered she met him the same night she met Kevin and another time in front of the base theater. He was the one who spoke Spanish well. She dried her eyes with a lace handkerchief.

"*Sí*," Inés replied. "You're Kevin's friend, right?"

Frank nodded.

"Kevin was supposed to meet me, but he never showed up," Inés said with a frantic edge to her voice. "Then my friend Rosa went off with some guy and left me at the club by myself. Then I went to Kevin's barracks and one of his buddies told me he was downtown."

"Oh, shit."

Inés arched her eyebrows. "Excuse me?"

Rooney was going to catch hell no matter what he said. The best thing for him to do was to smooth things over for Rooney.

"It's all my fault," Frank said. "Kevin asked me to tell you he couldn't make it, but I lost track of time."

"Humph," Inés muttered as she craned her neck to see if a bus was coming.

"No, really that's what happened. Kevin went to a bachelor party for one of his friends. That's why he wasn't at the club or his barracks."

She scrunched her nose as she thought about what Frank had said and bit her bottom lip.

"Listen, let me make it up to you," Frank said thinking fast. "I'm hungry. Do you want to get something to eat? I'll make sure you get back home even if I have to take you myself."

"*Eso estaría bien,*" Inés said smiling.

They still had time to get something to eat at the BX cafeteria, which didn't close until midnight. Frank ordered a burger and fries; Inés ordered a chicken salad sandwich. Frank wolfed down his food; Inés picked at hers.

While they ate, Inés couldn't take her eyes off Frank. She had only been out with a few men before she met Kevin. She liked Kevin at first; he wasn't like the soldier she'd dated from Clayton, who was rough and only wanted sex. She was not like Rosa, sleeping with anyone she could hoping one day to meet the right man to marry. Of course, she thought about that, too. Her daughter was already three. The father had been that same soldier from Clayton. He had rotated back to the States before she found out she was pregnant.

"How are things with you and what's-his-name?" Frank asked jokingly.

91

Inés frowned not catching the humor in Frank's question.

"*¿Cómo estás tú y Kevin?*"

"*Estamos bien.*"

Frank nodded and shoved a couple fries into his mouth. Inés was quiet for a few seconds, lost in thought before she spoke again.

"*Es una especie de joven, todavía un bebé,*" Inés said staring into Frank's dark blue eyes. She had never seen such blue eyes on the men she dated in the past. She also liked his jet-black mustache, which reminded her of a famous Panamanian actor. She loved his accent, the way he tried to pronounce certain words in Spanish.

"In English, we say 'still wet behind the ears'," Frank said.

Inés smiled and sipped her Coke. She swept her bright pink tongue over her lips and let the tip flick the end of the straw. Frank took a bite of his sandwich and continued to stare at Inés. He liked how she wasn't all painted up like many of the women who trolled the club. He liked the way her dark brown eyes smiled, teased, and glinted all at the same time when she spoke.

"He's already talking about marriage and wanting me to meet his mother," Inés said.

Frank grinned; he couldn't take his eyes off her small pert breasts. He could just make out her nipples pressing against the tight fabric of the halter top she was wearing. He was jealous, in a mild sort of way, when he thought about his friend sleeping with her. She was one of the fairer skinned Panamanians, which meant her ancestry was more European, which seemed odd when you considered who she hung out with when she came to the base. Most of the women were from the poorer sections of the city and looking for that ticket back to the Land of the Big BX. There must have been something more to Inés, something in her past. Frank had been with several women the past couple of weeks, including an airman first class who worked at the MAC terminal, another one at CBPO and a cute piece of tail at the Foxhole, but none turned him on as much as Inés.

"He probably means well," Frank said, feeling a little guilty for what he knew he was doing. He could have easily stopped flirting and made sure that Inés got back home okay. But that was not what was going to happen. "But what do you want, Inés? *Pero, ¿qué es lo que quieres?*"

Inés shrugged her shoulders. Although Kevin wasn't like the other men she had dated and slept with, she wasn't sure that he was the one.

"I don't know," Inés finally said, gazing at Frank.

"I see," Frank said, taking another bite of his sandwich. "I'm sure you'll make the right decision. *Estoy seguro que cuando llegue el momento, que va a hacer la decisión correcta.*"

"*Su español es muy bueno,*" Inés said smiling.

Two years of high school Spanish finally paid off for Frank. Although he only took the class to impress Glenda Mason, he must have learned more than he thought.

Frank smiled. "I studied in high school."

"*¿En serio?*"

"*Si.* I had a crush on this girl."

"Crush?"

"I liked this girl, but she didn't know I was alive."

Inés grinned. "Puppy love."

"Where did you learn that?" Frank asked.

Inés had learned that from the man she had met before Kevin, but she didn't want Frank to know. "I learned it in school."

Frank smiled. "*Tengo una confesión que hacer.*"

Inés tilted her head and continued to gaze into Frank's eyes. Frank liked the way her eyes sparkled and got big whenever he said something that she enjoyed. He liked the way her long eyelashes fluttered. She loved how deep and profound his eyes were as though they were two pools that she could lose herself in.

"*Confesión?*"

"My Spanish. I wanted to impress you."

"*Por qué?*"

"*Te encuentro tan fascinante.*"

Inés blushed and looked down at the table, then looked up again as Frank's gaze met hers. Frank knew there was no turning back now. Once he wanted something he wouldn't stop until it was his.

* * *

Kevin wasn't having a good time; the more Lily tried to hang onto him, the more he refused her advances to the amusement of his friends.

"Come on, Rooney, join the party," John Bradshaw said grinning.

Kevin smiled and nodded. He had switched from a Motherfucker to Jungle Juice, a crazy concoction of Ron Cortez rum, Seco, and whiskey. He was working on his third when the room started spinning, and he felt as though he was going to pass out. On the jukebox, the lead singer from Nazareth lamented how much love hurt.

"I need to get some air," Kevin mumbled, as he tried to stand up. He lost his balance and fell onto the table, knocking over most of the drinks, including one that fell into Lily's lap, immediately staining her white shorts.

"Jesus, Rooney!" John exclaimed. "Watch out."

"I'm going back to the base," Kevin mumbled.

"What? It's only eleven," John said, stuffing a five dollar bill inside the bikini bottom of the girl he was with. "The night is young."

"I'm too fucked up."

"Man, don't be such a lightweight."

Kevin grinned and stumbled past Lily, who wasn't too thrilled about losing out on ten dollars.

"*¡Hijo de puta!*" Lily said as she stormed off.

From the Golden Key, it was just a few yards to Fourth of July Avenue. He staggered across the street, almost getting hit by a slow-moving *chiva* bus, and flagged down the first taxi that came along.

In the back of the taxi, he rolled down the window to get some fresh air and rested his head against the door. The cool night air felt good on his face, but it wasn't sobering him as much as he had hoped it would. He hoped that Frank had been able to deliver the message to Inés and that he would still be able to see her tomorrow. He was also going to have to work something out with her so they could get in touch with each other in the future. And Frank was right, he was going to have to start learning some Spanish if he ever wanted to impress her parents. The next thing he knew, the taxi came to a stop, and one of the law enforcement officers at the Howard gate was shining a flashlight on his face.

"Oh, it's you, Rooney," a familiar voice said. "How was the party?"

Kevin mumbled something as he opened his eyes and sat up in the backseat.

The airman at the gate waved the taxi through as Kevin stared out the window and breathed in the cool night air. Everyone joked that he was pussy-whipped; maybe he was, but he knew what it was: he was in love with Inés. Guys who said shit like that were jealous that they didn't have a girlfriend.

Kevin was about to tell the taxi driver to turn right when he looked out the window and saw Frank walking with Inés.

"What the—"

Kevin screamed for the driver to stop and threw a dollar bill into the front seat. By the time he caught up with Frank and Inés, they were at one of the bus stops, sitting on a bench underneath a concrete overhang. Frank had his arm resting on the back of the bench, but in Kevin's drunken stupor, it appeared that Frank had his arm around Inés.

"What's going on here?" Kevin asked, out of breath.

Frank and Inés were surprised to see Kevin standing in front of them. Frank could tell that Kevin was drunk and then realized, with his arm still on the back of the bench, Kevin probably thought that he was putting the moves on Inés. Frank immediately removed his arm from the back of the bench.

"Hey, Buddy, what's up?" Frank asked, taking out his cigarettes and removing one from the pack.

"Don't 'Hey Buddy' me, Costello," Kevin said. "What the fuck's going on?"

Frank knew where this was headed. "Listen, Kevin, I can explain everything. It's not what you think. I forgot to meet her at the club, and I was—"

"Some friend you turned out to be. You had your arm around her."

Frank could tell that Kevin was drunk and tried to reason with him as best he could. "It's not what it looks like, Kevin. As I said, I forgot to meet her, and we had something to eat at the BX. Really, dude, I just walked her to the bus stop when you saw us. Why don't you go to your room and sleep it off? I'll make sure Inés gets home okay."

"And then what? Fuck her?"

"Oh dear, you had to go and say that, didn't you?" Frank said, shaking his head. "I think you owe your girl an apology."

"That's what happened, Kevin." Inés stood up and grasped Kevin's arm. "Please darling—"

Kevin shook his arm free and continued to stare at Frank. "You promised you were going to tell her, but all along you just wanted to get into her pants."

"Kevin, you're drunk and you're not making things any better by arguing with me in front of your lady friend." Frank stood up and got between Kevin and Inés. He didn't want this to go any further than it had already. "You need to cool it, bro, if you know what I mean."

"I should have known better," Kevin said, casting a sideways glance at Inés. "You're no different than the rest of them."

"Kevin, stop it!" Inés screamed, having heard enough. Her ex-boyfriend from Clayton had also been the jealous type. "Listen to Frank."

"No, I want to settle this now." Kevin rocked and weaved back and forth; he nearly stumbled and fell, but he managed to maintain his balance.

Just then, the rattle and rumble of the last *chiva* bus from Veracruz could be heard coming toward them. Kevin came at Frank, but he tripped and fell. He tried to pick himself up off the ground, but he keeled over and started vomiting.

"I'll make sure he gets back to his room," Frank said, looking at Inés. Then he knelt beside Kevin. "That's right, buddy, get it all out of your system."

When she got on the bus, she turned and smiled. Frank helped Kevin to his feet, put an arm around him and started for his barracks.

Frank had already won Inés.

CHAPTER ELEVEN

FROM THE MOMENT he smoked his first bowl of Panama Red, Frank had been thinking of a way to smuggle the tasty herb back to the States.

"Imagine if you could send some of this stuff home," Frank said one afternoon as he got high with a couple of friends in Roy Mitchum's room on the third floor of Barracks 714. "I know friends back home who would pay top dollar for a chance to smoke this tasty bud."

"A few have tried, but they either got busted here or at the other end," Chris said. "It's not worth the risk."

Frank, who had already broken apart a thick bud of Panama Red on an opened copy of Pink Floyd's *Dark Side of the Moon*, took a Zig-Zag paper, courtesy of a "care package" Roy got from home, and proceeded to roll a fat joint. Then he lit up using his trusty Zippo. The paper on the end burned a bright yellow as he took his first puff. He held the smoke in his lungs as long as he could before he slowly exhaled; two intertwined lines of bluish gray smoke climbed toward the ceiling. He loved its zesty, crackly taste and speedy, intense high.

"A risk is always worth taking for a price. Weed this good could go for twenty or thirty dollars an ounce back home, and it only costs us a couple of bucks," Frank said, as the lyrics from Floyd's "Breathe" sounded through the room. "I can't believe you guys haven't even thought of the fucking gold mine you're sitting on."

"You could mail it in something," Rusty suggested. "Wrap it up tight and put it in a baggie and place it in a box of laundry detergent or something like that. I doubt the drug-sniffing dogs could smell it."

"Too messy," Frank said.

"How much are you talking about?" Rusty asked.

"A couple of pounds," Frank replied.

"You've been smoking too much of this shit," Chris laughed, exhaling a cloud of smoke that he hadn't been able to hold in.

Everyone in the room laughed.

"We're not talking about mailing a couple joints or even an ounce or two back home to a friend," Rusty said. "Sending that amount of weed back home is just asking for something to go wrong. And how are you going to sell it and get the money back here?"

"It can be done."

Roy, who had been sitting on a beanbag chair in the back of the room strumming his guitar, set his guitar down and sat up on the chair. He took the joint from Tom as it was passed around.

"What's that, Roy?" Chris asked.

"Mailing weed, shit like that back to the States," Roy said. He had spent his youth surfing up and down the California coast before Uncle Sam needed him for Vietnam. Roy had other plans. He joined the Air Force and liked it so much, he re-upped for another four years. He was constantly in trouble with the first sergeant, mostly for never keeping his blond hair and mustache in regulation as well as for keeping a parrot in his room. Supposedly, Roy trained the parrot to pick the seeds out of his weekly marijuana purchases from Gus—though no one had seen the parrot do this feat. "That's what you're talking about, right?"

Frank nodded.

"It can be done."

"How? You're not serious about mailing it through the military postal system, are you?" Frank said. "Shit, they'd catch you before it even left the post office."

Roy took a hit off the joint and passed it to Frank. "Nah, I'm talking about shipping it another way. I know this guy who works in this section called packing and crating. He's been sending all kinds of shit back to the States for the past year."

"And it's safe?" Frank inquired.

"That's what he says," Roy replied, picking up his guitar again and strumming a few chords of a Beatles' song. "He's sent some weed back, too. He says it's foolproof."

"Nothing is foolproof," Rusty quipped.

"This guy says it is," Roy said.

First things first, Frank had to get the marijuana from Gus without raising too many flags which meant Frank had to include Gus in his little scheme.

Gus rolled up in a Dodge pickup and walked into the cool hangar. There was nothing scheduled that day for the UH-1Ns or the O-2As—no maintenance or practice on the gunnery range; most of the guys were reading copies of *Playboy* and *Penthouse,* tossing around a football and a Frisbee, or sleeping off last night's downtown excursion. If the Air Force ever found out that he was using one of the squadron's trucks to make his deliveries, they would have his ass in a sling. Of course, that would be the least of his worries.

Gus removed his aviator sunglasses and strolled past one of the Hueys in the middle of the hangar. He spotted Frank at the far end of the hangar tossing a football with Chris Shea and Larry Tschida. Frank dropped back as though he was a quarterback and had Chris and Larry go long, in this case, the other side of the hangar. He set the football spiraling across the hangar into Larry's outstretched arms. When Frank saw Gus standing off to one side, he motioned to Chris and Larry that he was finished playing football.

"Nice arm," Gus said. "You ever play ball in school?"

"Nah, I never cared much for being part of a team," Frank said, motioning with his head to the smoking area just outside the hangar.

Gus smiled. "I talked to my man and he's interested."

"What do you mean?"

"He wants in, too."

"Of course he does," Frank said. That made five people already including Gary, Gus, and himself as well as Roy's friend. Frank still had to arrange for someone on the other end to pick up the "package" and find someone who could bring the money back.

Jack came around the corner of the hangar and walked toward Frank and Santiago. When he passed, he didn't say anything to either man; instead, he shot Frank a dirty look.

"Jesus, if looks could kill," Gus said after Jack was out of earshot. "What the fuck is his problem?"

"I don't know, man," Frank said. "I guess he thinks his little pond here is not big enough for the both of us."

"He's just a lifer biding his time until he gets out," Gus said. "Fuck him."

"Yeah, fuck him."

"And one more thing," Gus added. "My supplier wants the money up front."

"Of course," Frank said. "I wouldn't want it any other way."

Two days later, Roy took Frank to meet Mike Casey one afternoon. Casey was quiet and a little suspicious. He had a good thing going and didn't want too many people in on his secret. Casey had been stationed at Howard for two years and had recently extended for another year. Right now, his piece of action was taking military hops on C-130s down to Peru to buy up as many hand-woven llama rugs—round, brown and white rugs made from the pelts of alpacas and llamas—as he could to bring them back to Howard. Here, he sold them at a considerable markup and then sent what he couldn't sell to his brother in California. Frank and Roy felt as though they had stepped into a surreal bazaar as soon as they entered the room. In one corner of the room, llama rugs were piled on a table alongside stacks of Kuna *mola* panels that could be framed or used as pillow covers. Strands of white puka shell necklaces, animals carved from soft, brown stone, wall tapestries of traditional Panamanian scenes made from bamboo and brightly colored thread, and stereo equipment took up the rest of the room. It was difficult to move from one side of the room to the other without banging into all the stuff Mike had accumulated. Either Casey's First Sergeant was one of his customers or the First Sergeant didn't care. Either way, there was no way this room passed anyone's room inspection.

"Don't mind the mess, boys," Mike said, picking up the latest issue of *Playboy* and plopping down on a beanbag chair. "Find a place to sit and let's talk business."

Frank and Roy looked at each other with furrowed brows, which both translated as, *get a load of this fucking place.* The only place they could sit was on the floor across from Mike.

"I understand you want to send some stuff back to the States," Mike said, looking up from the copy of *Playboy.*

"That's right," Frank said, finding a spot on the floor and sitting cross-legged across from Mike.

"Something illegal, I take?"

Frank nodded.

"Hey man, can I play some music," Roy said, looking at Casey's record collection.

"Sure, just be careful, okay?" Mike said.

Roy nodded and pulled out Bad Company's 1974 debut album from a stack of albums next to Mike's stereo system. He carefully placed side two on a Technics turntable and played the first track, "Bad Company." He sat down across from Frank and pulled out a baggie of marijuana. "Mind if I roll a jay?"

"Just be sure to put a towel along the bottom of the door," Mike said, pointing to a towel hanging on a rack on the door. He continued to thumb through the magazine until he came to the centerfold. He unfolded Miss May and licked his lips at the airbrushed beauty staring at him. "How much product are we talking about?"

"Two pounds."

Mike grinned and took out a can of Pabst Blue Ribbon from a small refrigerator next to where he was sitting. He popped it open, quaffed half of it, and wiped the foam from his mouth with the back of his hand. "Two pounds? You've got to be joking, right?"

"I just want to know if it can be done," Frank said already despising this smug little worm, "and not get caught."

"Of course it can be done. I've been doing this for over a year," Mike said in a sharp and condescending tone. He said goodbye to Miss May and tossed the magazine aside. "And it's my ass, not yours."

"Fair enough," Frank said. He didn't care much for Casey's tone, but he had to respect a guy who had this nice little operation on the side. "How do you do it?"

Mike finished his beer and belched. "It's quite simple. One of my jobs is to send stuff back to stateside depots for repair or disposal. Most of the shit that can be repaired is high tech stuff, avionics, communications, stuff like that. Some of this equipment is repaired locally, but other times it needs to go back to the depot. Most of the time, the equipment still has the original box and packing material, but when it doesn't, that's where I come in. First, I make sure whatever it is that needs to be packed is wrapped in plastic or some other protective material. Next, I spray expanding foam on it."

Roy took out his Zippo lighter and got the joint going. After he had puffed on the joint a bit, he handed it to Frank.

"What's expanding foam?" Frank asked, taking a long hit off the joint.

"Liquid foam that is stored under high pressure," Mike continued. "When I spray this stuff, the pressurized contents spurt out and begin to expand and finally harden around the equipment in the box. I spray the bottom half of the box first and then the top half; that way there are two halves which make it easy to remove the equipment."

Frank liked what he was hearing. This guy Mike might have been a little repulsive and nerdy, but he knew his shit. Frank offered the joint to Mike, but Mike shook his head. Frank drew on the joint again before he handed it back to Roy.

"Now, all I have to do is take your two pounds—you did say *two pounds*, didn't you?"

Frank furled his eyebrows. "That's what I said."

"Okay, so I take your two pounds of weed and have it vacuum packed. Then I put it in the box with the equipment and then spray this expandable foam on it. I pack up the box nice and tight, slap a packing label on it, and take it to the terminal where it is put on a pallet for loading aboard a C-130 or C-141." Mike said, going over all the details. "From here it goes to Charleston or Dover and then down to Warner Robins Air Materiel Area in Atlanta."

"That simple?" Frank asked.

"That simple."

"It sounds too easy."

"Who said something had to be difficult for it to work?"

"Far out, Mike," Roy said taking another long puff off the joint.

Mike looked across the room at Roy and smiled.

"What happens when the box arrives at the other end?" Frank asked.

"Now comes the tricky part, but don't worry, I've already got it covered," Mike explained. "I've got a buddy, a civilian, who works at the depot. It's his job to process all the cargo that comes through. He'll remove our little two-pound package and deliver it wherever you want. You do have someone on the other end, don't you?"

Frank already had someone in mind. Eddie, who had been living with his sister ever since he washed out of basic training, hadn't had a steady job in three years. Not unless you counted fencing stolen goods and writing bad checks as steady. If this turned out to be the windfall Frank thought it could be, there would be no problem bringing Eddie on board.

"What about the sky cops and their dogs? Dogs will be able to detect the weed."

"That could pose a problem because they do bring their dogs around to sniff the pallets," Mike said. "The good news is that once the product is vacuum packed and sealed in the foam, it's really hard for a dog to be able to detect it. They usually don't mess around with the stuff I have to send back to the depot. Still, we don't want to take any chances. I know a couple SPs here who will look the other way if the price is right."

Frank nodded. It was all coming together better than he had expected.

"Now all you need is someone to bring your package to packing and crating," Mike said, "and leave the rest up to me."

Frank didn't know anyone off the top of his head.

"Don't worry, I know someone. It's this new kid, Gary Taylor. He used to work in the Base Service Store, but he was recently transferred to the Repair Cycle Support Unit. He drops off parts that can be repaired at depots in the States. All you have to do is get the marijuana to him to bring when he drops off the parts. No one will be suspicious."

Frank smiled. "I know Gary very well. We came down here on the same plane."

"He's brought some stuff in a couple of times already," Mike said. "He seems like a pretty good kid."

"I'll talk to him," Frank said. "We're pretty tight."

Everything was now complete, Frank thought. He still had to talk to Eddie back home, but it was all coming together nicely.

CHAPTER TWELVE

AFTER THE CANAL Zone bombings and the presidential election, things quieted down a little for Buck. As it turned out, his hunch about someone in the Guardia Nacional being responsible for the bombings wasn't too far off base. Although most of the bomb's components could have been purchased anywhere, it seemed more and more likely that the Guardia, given evidence found at some of the bomb sites, had played a role in them. It didn't make any difference, however. Carter won the election and talk of a new treaty kept everyone busy.

Keeping busy was a bit of an understatement. The file he kept on Torrijos and Noriega grew thicker and thicker; his superiors at Langley demanded more reports and updates. Each time he filed an update, he shook his head and reached for the bourbon.

There was something else that kept him busy: his goddaughter, Estefani.

Just off Vía Espaňa, near the Canal Zone Bus Company, was La Rosa de Vía Espaňa, a small family-owned Panamanian restaurant that Buck first visited in the 1960s. His father had been stationed at Quarry Heights then, and he'd kept on coming back ever since. They had been out exploring the city one day when they came across this quaint little hole-in-the-wall restaurant. The rich aroma of the food cooking inside was all it took.

It wasn't only the food and the gracious hospitality of the owner Estevan and his charming wife Ascension that brought Buck back time and time again. It was one of the few places in the city that he truly felt at home—in no small part to the personal ties he had with the family. Buck had once helped out the family. They had been so touched by his kindness that they asked him to be Estefani's godfather. It was a great honor to be asked to be her godfather—or *padrino*; just being asked implied the respect and the trust Estevan and his wife had for Buck, who gladly accepted. In Panamanian culture, refusing to be a child's godparent for whatever reason was disrespectful and even an insult.

It had been a little over a month since the last time he stopped at his favorite restaurant in the city for some of Estevan's delicious cooking as well as the family's warm and gracious hospitality. If it wasn't Estevan arguing with Buck over who was a better boxer—Sugar Ray Leonard or Roberto Duran—it was Ascension trying to fix Buck up with one of her friends. Although Estevan and Ascension were both happy to see him, Buck sensed that something was bothering his friend. After most of the evening crowd had filtered out, Buck and Estevan sat at a table in the rear of the small restaurant and enjoyed a late dinner.

"When are you going to find yourself a nice lady to settle down with one day?" Ascension asked, setting down a plate of *Carimañolas*—a meat pie stuffed with ground beef and vegetables—in front of Buck and her husband. "I have a friend who you might be interested in."

"Watch it, my friend," Estevan said grinning. He was a short, balding man with a thin mustache. "If you're not careful she'll have you married and on a honeymoon before you know what happened."

"Shush!" Ascension said laughing.

Buck smiled and glanced up at Ascension. She towered over her husband by at least a foot and wore her long jet-black hair in a center-parted ponytail. "Now, if you could find someone as lovely, charming, and intelligent like yourself, maybe I would take you up on your matchmaking advice."

Ascension smiled back and returned to the kitchen.

The two men caught up on the latest news and gossip regarding the ongoing canal treaties and one of Panama's most famous personalities next to Omar Torrijos, Roberto Duran. Unlike most Panamanians that Buck knew, when it came to a new treaty, his friend had mixed emotions. Although Estevan was like most people who wanted a new treaty, he didn't like the prodding of the Communists who were more concerned with pushing their agenda than helping the country in the long run. When he talked to his friend, Buck got a feel for what Panamanians wanted, which he was sure to include in his weekly reports to Langley.

"There are some people who say we should keep things the way they are," Estevan said. "Of course, those people have nothing to lose and everything to gain."

Buck nodded and smiled. He knew that most of Panama's wealthy and elite were fine with the way that things were now.

"Personally, I don't care much for Torrijos," Estevan said, lowering his voice, "but I appreciate what he's doing. I know people in your country don't trust him and think that he might even be in bed with the Communists, but for better or worse, he has the best interests of our country in mind. You of all people should appreciate that."

Buck nodded and ate some more of his meal. There was no doubt in his mind that the stakes were never any higher than they were now if Torrijos didn't get what he wanted. When Buck was here in the sixties, during the time of the riots, his father was hardly home. While Buck never knew what his father did exactly during that time, he knew that it had something to do with the defense of the Canal in case of sabotage. What would people think if Torrijos went ahead with his threats to blow up the Canal if Panama didn't get a new treaty? Having gotten to know the General, Buck believed that Torrijos would follow through with his threats.

"Yes, you do have to admire what he's tried to do for the country," Buck added, appreciating his friend's candor. "But you know what they say, politicians and generals make very bad bedfellows."

Estevan smiled.

"Is that all you two men can do is talk about politics?" Ascension asked, standing over the table.

Both men had been so engrossed in their conversation they didn't notice Ascension walking back into the room.

Estevan looked up at his wife and smiled again. "We're in trouble now, my friend."

Buck grinned and pushed his plate away. In a smaller room, just off the dining room, he heard a young girl's voice. "Now where's that lovely goddaughter of mine?" Buck asked loud enough for the girl to hear.

Estefani came running into the room, her long, black, braided pigtails flapping behind her. She had grown up so much since the last time Buck was here.

"*Padrino*!" Estefani said, bending over and kissing Buck on the cheek. "I missed you."

"I missed you, too," Buck said. "Let me see."

Estefani flashed her godfather a smile and then showed him her new braces that he had arranged for her to get through the Howard AFB dental clinic.

"Soon you will have the prettiest smile in all of Panama," Buck said.

"We want to thank you again so much for helping out with her braces," Estevan said. "We'll find a way to—"

"Don't worry about it, my friend," Buck said. "How's school?"

"I'm an A-student!"

"*Bueno*," Buck said. "You get your good looks and your brains from your mother."

Estevan looked over at Buck and smiled. "Watch it, my friend. You never want to have these two ladies ganging up on you."

"That, my friend, would be the least of my worries."

Estevan smiled, but the smile soon faded as he stared at the cup of coffee Ascension had set on the table. Estevan didn't even bother to look up at his wife as he continued to stare at the cup, lost in thought.

Buck looked at Estevan with a concerned look. "I was right. As soon as I walked in tonight, I felt as though something was bothering you."

"It's nothing," his friend said trying change the subject.

"Your poker face says differently."

"*¿Qué significa cara de póquer?*"

"You know, when you're playing cards, and you don't want the other people to know whether you have a good hand or not," Buck explained. "You try to show as little emotion as you can."

Estevan grinned and nodded. "Is it that obvious?"

"Just a little."

"Can you help me with my homework?" Estefani asked.

"Of course, when I finish talking with your father," Buck said.

Buck kissed Estefani on the forehead and watched her help her mother clear some of the dirty dishes from the table. Estevan spooned some sugar into his coffee and slowly stirred it. He took a sip and then looked across the table at his friend.

"Business hasn't been too good ever since some new restaurants opened down the street. It's been difficult having to compete with them," Estevan said. "The economy is not good, as you probably well know."

Buck's cover, (at least when it came to telling people what he did) was that he worked for the U.S. Agency for International Development (USAID). Ironically, there were some people who believed the USAID and the CIA were one in the same. It was a good cover because Buck did his homework. He knew that despite Torrijos's popularity, he was having problems with Panama's economy. A lot of people were going through some hard times, which made any new canal treaty all the more significant in terms of helping to turn the economy around for the country. He also knew that small business owners like his friend were feeling the pinch. The past couple of times he visited the restaurant there were only a few customers.

"Is there anything that I can do?" Buck asked.

Estevan shook his head. "You've done enough already for Estefani."

"You're just as much my family as I am of yours," Buck said. "It's the least that I can do. You and your wife have been so kind to me over the years and before that, my father and mother."

"That's very kind of you, my friend, but this is something that I have to do on my own," Estevan said. "There are some things that a man must do, even if it means swallowing a bit of his pride."

Buck looked at his friend and nodded. When it came time to pay his bill, he slipped a fifty dollar bill under his plate.

CHAPTER THIRTEEN

ALTHOUGH GARY'S PART was minor, just transporting the marijuana from Santiago's office to the hangar where Mike worked—the one with the least risk if this operation was ever discovered—he wondered if an extra couple hundred dollars a month was worth the risk. It was one thing getting stoned in the barracks or popping Captagon, a local diet pill that was the next best thing to speed and that could be bought legally over the counter at any drugstore in Panama City, but smuggling drugs back to the States was something else.

There were a couple guys who mailed some joints back home to their buddies now and then and never seemed worried about the risks they were taking. What Frank wanted to do was too much of a risk.

Frank assured him there was nothing to worry about and that it could never be traced back to him, but he still wasn't convinced. He was worried that someone might see him with the marijuana before it was put inside the box, but he finally gave in after Frank and Santiago told him that there were too many people counting on him.

*   *   *

Gus never cared much for Gary. There were some people that just rubbed other people the wrong way, and that was how he felt about Gary. There was just something about Gary that worried Gus. Even though Gary was pretty tight with Frank and a few other people in CAMS and Supply, he sometimes came across as aloof and a loner. Although Frank vouched for his friend, Gus still wasn't convinced.

Those fears became all too real when Mark Thompson arrived at Howard. Thompson, who was assigned to CAMS, worked in Transient Alert—the unit responsible for parking and servicing aircraft, which landed on the base. Thompson was a likable enough of a guy who had a trophy wife stateside that he bragged about constantly, but that didn't stop him from hitting on anything in a skirt, and was constantly entertaining everyone with his stories—from working on oil rigs in Oklahoma to his hair-raising exploits during the Vietnam War.

One story that got a lot of mileage and free drinks whenever he told it was his courage under fire story. During the height of America's involvement in Vietnam, Thompson was at some remote base trying to repair a C-130 that had broken down on the runway, all the while under machine gun and mortar fire from VC just outside the perimeter of the base. After twenty-four hours, he managed to get that C-130 fixed and back in the air.

The first time Gary met him was on one of those Friday afternoons when many of the duty sections stopped working at three o'clock, broke out the cases of Old Milwaukee and Pabst Blue Ribbon from the package store, and got an early start on the weekend. On this particular Friday, the beer was on ice in two metal garbage cans inside the welding shop in the same hangar where Gary worked. There were about ten CAMS personnel gathered around Mark listening to him tell the story for the umpteenth time.

"I bet the pilot a couple cases of Hamm's that I could get the bird fixed by morning," Mark said, stopping to take a drink of his beer. "The only problem was Charlie had other plans for me. So, there I was, with my toolbox in one hand and an M-16 in the other. I'd work a little bit, then fire off a couple rounds. This shit went on all night."

There was usually someone in the crowd who said, "Damn," or "That's fucking intense, man," when Mark told the story, which he used to set up the last part of the story.

"Fucken-A, Bubba, you've got that right. And somewhere in the Air Force inventory, there's a C-130 patched up with a case of flattened Hamm's beer cans that I used to repair all the bullet holes," Mark laughed. "Just as soon as I patched one of the holes, Charlie made another one. I sure did develop a strong fondness for Hamm's that day, though Charlie's accuracy left something to be desired."

Everyone standing around Mark and the two beer-filled trash cans laughed.

"What about the bet?" someone asked Mark.

"Oh, yeah, the pilot paid off his bet the following morning," Mark said laughing. "And we made sure to save the cans for the next time Charlie shot up one of our birds."

More laughter followed by a chorus of beer cans popping open.

Gary looked up to him, not the same way he did to Frank, but the same way he did to Jack and the other men who had served in Vietnam. There was an aura around these men—of people who had looked death clearly in the eye and hadn't flinched. They had once been kids too, no older than Gary, who had been asked by their country to put their asses on the line. Wars fought by kids sent into harm's way by adults.

Not everyone liked Thompson, however.

One afternoon, Fred Matthews, who was a friend of J.J.'s and a regular customer of Santiago, cornered Gary in the latrine. "Don't you know he's OSI?"

"I don't know what you're talking about," Gary said, looking up at the six-foot-three Matthews, who spent most of his free time, when he wasn't getting stoned in the barracks, working out in the base gym.

"Thompson."

"Thompson?" Gary asked. "He asked me if I knew anyone who could sell him some pot."

For over a month, there had been rumors of undercover OSI agents at Howard trying to crack down on the increasing problem with drugs after two airmen were busted trying to smuggle a few pounds in their duffel bags when they DEROS'd back to the States. Airmen grew suspicious of anyone new assigned to their squadrons and barracks until they got to know the person. Although Thompson got along well with most of the people in the barracks, there were some, such as Matthews, who didn't believe Thompson's courage under fire story.

"What did you tell him?" Matthews asked, looking down at his thick biceps, which bulged underneath a fishnet tank top. His eyes were red, and his nostrils flared as he spoke. "You didn't give him any names, did you?"

"I told him I knew where I could get some," Gary said, "and he asked if I could bring him a sample."

Matthews' eyes narrowed, and the veins in his neck tightened. "Are you that fucking stupid?"

"He just asked me, that's all," Gary said, pleading his case. "I didn't tell him any names."

"You better watch out, Taylor. I'm fucking watching you." Matthews stepped back and pointed two thick fingers at Gary before he turned and stormed off.

As it turned out, Thompson wasn't OSI but the damage had already been done. Santiago, who was already wrapped too tight for his own good and just as paranoid, decided that Gary couldn't be trusted.

Gary sat in the blue pickup truck and waited for Santiago. Through the intermittent sweep of the windshield wipers, Gary could see the motor pool office where Santiago had entered fifteen minutes earlier. It was coming down hard outside as Gary kept an eye on the door. Despite assurances from Frank and others that there was nothing to worry about, Gary still felt a little apprehensive. He just wanted to get this over with as soon as possible.

On the seat next to him was a box containing the radio transmitter he had already processed back in the hangar where the Repair Cycle Support Unit was located. All that was left to do was to put the *package* of marijuana inside the box and go to packing and crating.

On the radio, Gordon Lightfoot sang "The Wreck of the Edmund Fitzgerald."

"What's taking you so long, Santiago?" Gary muttered as he looked through the windshield.

Gary's heart skipped a beat when he happened to look up at the rearview mirror. In the reflection, he saw a security police truck pull up behind his truck. His heart started pounding in his chest. He didn't know whether or not he should sit there and wait for Santiago to come out or to get the hell out of there. In the meantime, he hoped that Santiago had also seen the truck and would know what to do.

As Gary was contemplating what he should or shouldn't

do, he didn't see the driver of the truck get out and walk up to the side of his truck. Gary jumped when the officer knocked on the window. There was nothing that they could prove, Gary thought, as he rolled down the window.

"Are you waiting to see Santiago, too?" the airman asked.

Gary looked up at the airman standing at the side of his truck and recognized him as one of Kevin's friends. "No, I mean, he went inside about fifteen minutes ago. I don't know where the hell he is."

Just then, the door to the office opened and Santiago walked outside. Gary didn't know if he should do something to warn Santiago about what was about to go down. He didn't have to. As soon as the security police officer saw Santiago, he turned around and walked back to his truck.

"Sorry about the wait," Santiago said, tossing two brown packages about the size of a brick into the truck. "You didn't think these cops were here to bust us, did you?"

Gary shook his head and tried to cover the packages with a rag that was on the seat.

"Bet you pissed your pants when you saw that truck pull up, huh?" Santiago said. "Well, I better go and see what they want. Just make sure you don't screw this one up, Taylor. There are a lot of people who have put their asses on the line."

CHAPTER FOURTEEN

FRANK'S LITTLE OPERATION worked like a charm. Just as Mike promised, once the *package* arrived at the depot at Warner Robins, the friend on the other end delivered it to Eddie. It had been no problem convincing him to hop on a Greyhound bus bound for Atlanta to collect the package. Within a week, the marijuana was on the streets in Frank and Eddie's old neighborhood. Two weeks later, a loadmaster on a C-130 out of Dover AFB delivered a package to Frank. Inside a gym bag was five thousand dollars.

* * *

That night, Frank, Gus, Roy, Gary, Mike, and Diego celebrated at Napoli's. The wives and girlfriends were also with them. Normally Diego wouldn't want to be seen in public with a bunch of gringos, and especially the ones that he kept in drugs, but tonight was special. Thanks to Frank's little operation, he was two thousand dollars richer this evening.

"What's next for you, Frank?" Gus asked, leaning toward

Frank. "Was this a one-time deal or are you in it for the long haul?"

"I think we should up the ante," Frank replied.

Gus nodded. "And I have just the thing."

"What?" Frank asked.

"Come on," Gus said, standing up and motioning to the bathroom in the back of the room. "I want to show you something."

Frank and Gus excused themselves from the table and walked to the bathroom at the back of the room. Once inside, Gus checked the stall to make sure no one was inside and then locked the door. He pulled out a tiny amber-colored glass vial from his shirt pocket. Gus held the vial up to the light; inside Frank could see a white powder.

"Have you ever tried cocaine?" Gus asked, slowly twirling the vial around for Frank to get a better look at the white powder.

Frank's eyes got big as he continued to look at the vial. "I've tried it a couple of times. I read something in *Penthouse* about guys who put it on their dicks to stay hard."

"Yeah, I heard that too." Gus laughed as he walked into the stall and wiped off the top of the toilet tank with his hand. He opened the vial and tapped out half the contents into a small mound. Then, taking out his military ID card, he spread the powder into four identical lines. Finally, he took out a twenty dollar bill, rolled it into a straw, and handed it to Frank. "Go ahead, man."

Frank pinched one nostril and snorted one of the lines; then he did the same thing for the other nostril. He felt a powerful tingling sensation that shot straight to the brain. It didn't burn like it did the other times he had snorted coke. It was pure, unadulterated, uncut high-octane ecstasy.

"*Chuleta*! This shit's unbelievable!" Frank exclaimed,

sniffling. His eyes widened more as he felt the effects of the cocaine rushing to his brain.

"I knew you'd like it," Gus said, sniffling and wiping his nose after he did his two lines. "So, are you ready to up the ante?"

Frank smiled. "You read my mind."

Gus laid out four more lines for them. The second time was just as exhilarating as the first. Gus cleaned up the residue with his finger and rubbed his lips with it. "Let's talk later."

Frank and Gus glided back to the table. He tossed down his drink and motioned to the waiter for another one. The coke he had done before was nothing like the shit he snorted tonight.

"Everything okay?" Inés asked.

Frank sniffled and wiped his nose. "Yeah, yeah, everything is fantastic! Everything couldn't be better."

Inés smiled and put her arm around Frank. "I'm so happy—"

"Well, look who we have here," a drunken voice said behind them. "If it ain't Frank and his buds."

Frank turned around in his chair and saw Kevin with two of his SP buddies moving through the crowd. He could tell that Kevin had been drinking.

"How's it going, Kevin?" Frank asked.

"Looks like the gang's all here," Kevin said, walking up behind Frank's chair. "Hey, Gary. Long time no see. What's the matter, you don't like hanging out with me anymore?"

Gary looked at Frank and then looked at Kevin. "I've been busy, you know."

"Who's this guy?" Kevin asked, pointing at Diego.

"A friend," Frank said.

"*Hola, amigo. ¿Cómo estás?*" Kevin asked in a loud voice that got the attention of a few customers at nearby tables. "See,

Frank. I can speak Spanish, too. Hey, *amigo. ¿Cómo te llamas?*"

Diego shifted uncomfortably in his chair. Some of the customers looked over in the direction of the table and Diego, who smiled and motioned that everything was okay.

"Kevin, we're kind of in the middle of something, if you don't mind," Frank said. He could sense the uneasiness that Diego and others around the table were feeling—not the least of which was the scene Kevin was making in front of Diego, as well as Kevin's two security police buddies. Besides, Kevin was bringing him down from his high fast. "It's our friend's birthday and—"

"Come on, Kevin," one of Kevin's friends said. "Let's go back to the Ovalo."

"Birthday, huh? Where's the fucking birthday cake?" Kevin, who had been deliberately ignoring Inés, finally looked over in her direction. "Hello, Inés."

She looked up at Kevin, with a sheepish look on her face and looked embarrassed. "Hello, Kevin."

After the scene he had made in front of Frank and Inés a few months earlier, he hoped to see her again and apologize for being so rude, but she stayed away from the base. He tried calling her, but he still couldn't get past her father. Then one night when he had gone to the club he happened to look at the sign-in book and noticed the Frank had signed her in. That's when Kevin knew that Frank had stolen Inés from him.

Kevin bent over, put his arm around Frank, and pointed across the table to Inés. "So tell me, Frank, is she as good in bed for you, as she was for me?"

Frank had had enough. He abruptly stood up, knocking over his chair and pushing Kevin away from the table. "I think you should go now."

"You don't frighten me, Frank," Kevin said, trying to maintain his balance. "I know all about you."

Diego frowned and stared at Frank and then at Kevin.

"Come on, Kevin," his friend said again. "Let's get out of here."

"No, I want to know if he enjoys fucking Inés the same way he enjoys fucking his friends over," Kevin said.

Frank only gave Kevin a slight nudge, to move him back, but Kevin responded with a punch to the side of the head. Kevin didn't put much behind the punch and Frank barely felt it. However, when Kevin attempted to come at him again, Frank caught his arm and prevented him from connecting. Kevin's friends, sensing that this was going to get out of hand quickly, pulled Kevin back. That's when it turned ugly. Kevin lunged again at Frank knocking him to the ground. Diego tried to intervene and got punched on the side of the head. He fell onto the table; plates and glasses crashed on the stone floor. By the time Kevin was pulled off Frank, two Guardia had arrived on the scene.

* * *

Kevin's head was pounding. He tried to open his eyes, but each time he did, his headache pounded more. He noticed that he was naked and that there was a naked woman in his bed. Slowly the previous night started to come back to him. He had been downtown drinking at the Ovalo when someone said they were hungry for pizza. The next thing he knew he was staggering past a table where Frank, Gary, and some of their friends were sitting along with Inés and some other Panamanian women. The rest of the night was still a little fuzzy—like how the woman ended up in his bed and his bruised knuckles.

His head wasn't the only thing pounding. Someone had been pounding on his door for the past couple of minutes. By the time Kevin hid the girl under a blanket, wrapped a towel around his body and opened the door, his first sergeant, Senior Master Sergeant Donald Brown was not looking at all pleased.

"You better get your ass dressed and get down to my office now, Rooney," Brown bellowed, looking at Kevin with a disgusted look on his face. "And when I mean dressed, I mean in your uniform."

Fighting off base, a run in with a Guardia Nacional, and a woman in his bed—they were going to throw the book at him.

When Kevin walked into the first sergeant's office ten minutes later, the ass-chewing that he thought he was going to get from his sergeant took a turn for the worse. Standing next to the first sergeant and squadron commander, Major Fletcher, were two plainclothes men, neither of whom he had seen before.

"Rooney, these two men would like to talk to you regarding Sergeant Frank Costello," Brown said. Although he had calmed down after having yelled at Rooney, his lowered tone conveyed concern. "I understand that you two are pretty close friends. What can you tell us about his relationship with Gustavo Santiago?"

Kevin looked at the two men, and then his first sergeant and commander. He cleared his throat. "I'm not sure I understand the question."

Brown leaned forward, resting his thick forearms in front of him on his desk. "Just answer the question, son."

"Maybe some introductions are in order, Sergeant," the shorter of the two plainclothes men said, taking over the proceedings. "We don't want to waste too much of this airman's valuable time."

Kevin didn't like the man's condescending tone. He wasn't going to like the rest of what the man had to say.

"Airman, my name's Jake Flagg. I'm with the OSI, and my colleague is Skip Gordon of the DEA," Flagg said as he stood up and walked to the front of the first sergeant's desk. Flagg, who looked as though he spent most of his free time at the base gym or on the tennis court, stared at Kevin with piercing blue eyes. "We have reason to believe that some airmen on Howard have been dealing drugs. We were hoping, because of your, let's say 'special relationship' with Costello, that you might have some information to help us in our investigation."

Kevin looked at his first sergeant and commander for some sign as to whether he should answer the question or not. The OSI was one thing, but the DEA was some serious shit.

"You've got to be kidding me." His head might have been pounding and his stomach doing somersaults, but Kevin was alert enough now to know that he didn't like where this was headed. "What do you mean *special* relationship?"

"You two dated the same woman, didn't you?" Flagg said. "Inés Herrera, right?"

Kevin furrowed his brow. "How did you—"

"Just answer the question, Rooney," Brown said, just as confused as Kevin was.

Kevin cleared his throat again. He didn't like Flagg reminding him about Inés, but that was beside the point. Although he had no idea what Frank and the others were mixed up with, he knew it wasn't good. They could have easily asked anyone in the 24th CAMS Squadron who worked with Costello or someone who lived in the barracks. He shuddered to think that the OSI and DEA thought he was somehow involved in this.

"I know him pretty well. We all came down together on the same plane."

"That much we know," Flagg said. "Go on."

"We hung out for a while after we arrived here, went to the NCO Club, hit the downtown bars a few times, those sorts of things," Kevin said.

"You're also pretty good friends with Gary Taylor, is that right?" Flagg asked.

"That's right," Kevin said. "We came down on the plane together, too."

Flagg looked over at Gordon and nodded.

"I still don't understand what this has to do with me," Kevin said. "Did something happen to them?"

"Well, that depends," Flagg said.

"I'm sorry?" Kevin said. "I still don't follow you."

"Your buddy, Taylor, he's pretty tight with Costello," Flagg said. "We would like for you to find out what he knows without raising too many flags."

Kevin stared at Flagg and Gordon with his mouth agape. He couldn't believe what he was hearing. "You want me to spy on my friend?"

"Not exactly," Gordon said.

"So, you guys put a lot of thought into this, huh?" Kevin said. His head continued to pound, but that didn't dull his senses. "You know, me being a security police officer and all."

Brown and Fletcher grinned. Although they often worked closely with the OSI, there was sometimes no lost love between the security police and the Office of Special Investigations.

"I know your commander, and maybe even your first shirt—if he's on the up and up—are going to call me a liar, but it's no big secret that quite a few of the junior enlisted personnel warn folks when a raid is going down, maybe one or two senior enlisted. Who knows, maybe you are just the kind of person who would do such a thing," Flagg said. "You guys might serve and protect, but you also look out for your buddies no matter what. So, I think getting to know your buddy Taylor a little better, for the greater good, isn't going to hurt you too much. And just to show you how much we appreciate you doing this for us, we'll make sure your commander writes you a letter of commendation."

"Flagg, that's quite enough," Fletcher said, shooting Flagg a dirty look.

"We're not asking you to lie to your friend or deceive him in any way," Flagg continued. "All we're asking is that you—"

"Follow him. I got it. You want me to spy on my friend. Isn't this something you guys in OSI should be doing? I thought that's what you got paid for?"

"Well, what do you know?" Flagg said, turning to Gordon. "Our boy here has got a pair on him after all."

"Flagg, I'm not going to tell you again," Brown said, shooting Flagg a dirty look. "Do you think we can get back on track here?"

Flagg smirked and motioned for Gordon to continue with the questioning.

"Your buddy Costello has been seen in the company of Diego Guerra, a Panamanian businessman who has ties to Panama's underworld. He's the one you slapped around a bit last night," Gordon said, moving forward. He was a tall man with cropped blond hair and piercing blue eyes. "He also is suspected of dealing to service members at Howard—that's where your friend must have met him. We have reason to believe that he might be using your friends for one of his smuggling operations."

"Wouldn't it be easier for you to bring Santiago or Costello in for questioning?" Kevin asked. "Why do you need to drag me into this?"

"We've been trying to get Guerra for over a year now, but every time we get close, he manages to avoid arrest," Gordon said, careful not to reveal too much of his investigation. "If we alert your friends or if they even suspect that something is going down, we might not have the chance to get him."

"First you want me to shadow one of my good friends here to find out what he knows," Kevin said, trying to wrap his mind around what Flagg and Gordon were telling him. "Now you're telling me that you want to use them to get this Guerra guy. You guys are too much."

"When you put it like that, I guess it does sound kind of bizarre, but Rooney, these are some dangerous men," Gordon said. "We don't know what he's up to here, but the company he's keeping is rather suspicious, wouldn't you agree?"

It was right there in front of him, but Kevin still refused to believe that Frank was mixed up with the wrong crowd. He knew a couple of cops who were dealing some grass on the side and Flagg was right; he knew of at least two men in his squadron who notified their buddies in the other barracks when there was going to be a raid. Smuggling drugs to the States was a sure ticket to a dishonorable discharge and a couple years at Leavenworth.

Then, of course, it was still too personal for Kevin having lost Inés to Costello. Still nursing a bruised ego, he would like nothing better to get back at Costello, but spying and ratting out his friends went against everything he believed in.

"At the same time, Rooney, I would be more concerned about your buddy Gary. He's caught up in all of this just as much as Costello is," Flagg added. "You wouldn't want him to throw away his career because you were too stubborn to lend a hand. As I understand, he wants to go to film school when he gets out. He'll have a difficult time doing that when he's in prison."

Both Kevin and Gary shared a fondness for movies, especially classic Hollywood films. The first couple of weeks they were at Howard they spent most evenings watching whatever movie was playing at the base theater. Kevin knew all about Gary's dream of going to film school in California; in fact, one of the reasons why Gary joined the Air Force was to take advantage of the GI Bill.

"Why are you pressuring me like this?" Kevin asked. "I told you I have no idea about the company Costello keeps. As for Gary, shouldn't you be talking to him and warning him?"

"You're his friend," Flagg replied.

"I won't be after I do this."

"I can understand if you're worried about their safety," Flagg said. "We are, too."

"I doubt it," Kevin said.

"You don't want us to have to threaten you with an Article Fifteen, do you? Here you are, in line for a promotion; your whole Air Force career dangling in front of you and you're ready to throw it all away because you're too stubborn to help us," Flagg added. Think about the consequences of your actions, Rooney."

"Sergeant Brown?" Kevin said, looking at his first sergeant.

"Son, you were fighting off post and according to three eyewitnesses at the restaurant, you instigated the fight with Costello," Brown said. "At the very least you're looking at an Article Fifteen."

Kevin swallowed hard. Flagg was right; his Air Force career meant everything to him, but he couldn't betray a friend.

"Gentlemen, is that all?" Fletcher asked. He had heard enough. "Unless you're going to charge Rooney with anything, I think it is best we conclude this little inquisition of yours."

"Yeah, we're through here for the time being," Flagg said. "I'm sure Rooney's going to come to his senses and do what's best for all the parties concerned."

Flagg and Gordon started for the door, but before they reached it, Gordon stopped and turned around facing Rooney.

"By the way, Rooney, Lori Stewart says hello," Gordon said.

Kevin's jaw dropped when he heard the name. Brown and Fletcher look at each other with dumbfounded expressions.

"You two are still talking to each other, aren't you?" Gordon added.

Kevin's father had been stationed at Dyess Air Force in Texas when Kevin was a senior in high school, a few months before his father passed away. One night Kevin snuck out some beer and schnapps from his father's liquor cabinet and met two of his friends and Lori at the base golf course. Lori, who was known for her sexual prowess, ended up giving Kevin and his buddies blowjobs when the base police showed up. Kevin and one of his buddies managed to get away, but their other friend couldn't get away in time because some of Laurie's long hair got caught in his zipper as he was zipping up his pants. Laurie's father, who was the base commander, was furious when he found out about what happened to his daughter. It created quite the scandal on base, and the commander personally requested that Kevin's father lead the investigation. It quickly got covered up in no small part to Kevin's father making sure that his son was untouched. No charges were filed though the fathers of his two buddies were transferred immediately. Kevin thought it had all been forgotten until now. What he couldn't understand was how Gordon or Flagg knew about it and why they were bringing it up now. And he certainly didn't like his father being dragged into this.

"Never mind," Gordon said, as he looked at Kevin. "I guess I must have been mistaken."

"Are we finished here?" Brown asked.

"Yes, we're finished for now," Flagg said, glancing across the room at Gordon, who motioned that he didn't have anything else to add. "We'll be in touch, Rooney."

"What should we do about Rooney?" Sergeant Brown said after Rooney, Flagg, and Gordon had left. "He's a good cop. I'd hate for all of this to put a blemish on his record."

Major Fletcher sat down across from his first sergeant with a cup of coffee in his hand. "Just to make it look good, in case anyone asks, write up a letter of reprimand and have him sign it. We can shitcan it later."

"What the hell was that about some girl who knows Rooney?"

"I have no idea," Fletcher said. "I don't like any of this, but it's out of our hands. OSI must have a real bug up their ass to want Rooney to spy on his friends."

"There's another thing, too. There was something about Gordon that I can't quite put my finger on," Sergeant Brown said, leaning back in his chair. "I don't think he was DEA at all."

Major Fletcher drank some of his coffee and nodded. "You know, I think you're right, Top."

"

CHAPTER FIFTEEN

EVENTUALLY, FRANK'S LITTLE smuggling operation was brought to the attention of Alejandro Vega and a meeting between the two was set up. The marijuana Frank was moving meant nothing to Vega, but when he started asking around about cocaine, that was entirely different. There had been other GIs who wanted to make a little cash on the side peddling drugs to their friends, but nothing like the kind of action this airman from Howard was after.

After his dealings with Diego, Vega wasn't anything like the criminal mind Frank envisioned. He looked more like a schoolteacher than the man responsible for running most of the drugs, prostitution, and gambling in Chorrillo and a black market operation on the side. He was wearing a light-blue silk shirt, revealing a gold chain around his neck. He had a pencil-thin mustache and wore his jet-black hair slicked back. On his right cheek was a scar he had received in a street brawl when he was fifteen. His eyes were narrow and dark which made most people feel uncomfortable when he stared at them. On the desk in front of him was a glass with a white beverage inside that Frank knew was *Seco con Vaca*.

"We've been using Tocumen with success, but your DEA has been cracking down hard in Miami," Vega said, sipping his drink. He leaned forward and stared across the table at Frank. "So when my friend Diego tells me that some gringo has been smuggling *my* drugs to the States, of course, I'm interested."

Frank looked around the room. The way Vega emphasized that the drugs were his worried Frank. He wondered if they were going to let him walk out of here alive. It was one thing to cross one of the Guardia when out on the town; eventually they would have to notify the military authorities. The men seated in front of him were a different story entirely. They could slit his throat in a heartbeat and dump his body in a ditch outside of town; it would be days before anyone knew what happened to him. Back in Chicago he knew some guys who got mixed up with some of the gangs in a very bad way but nothing like what could happen here.

"At the same time, I have to be a little cautious, *sí*? Diego is happy with Gustavo, though Gustavo can sometimes be a pain in the ass, but Diego and Gustavo are blood-related. If it's just a little money and no one is going to get hurt, what do I care?" Vega said, glancing at Diego and Gustavo, who both looked embarrassed. Vega still hadn't forgiven them for the incident at Napoli's. "Of course, I was a little concerned when Diego didn't come to me first, but seeing how he had *my* best interests in mind, I can forgive him."

Vega cast a sideways glance at Diego and Santiago which made them both shift uncomfortably in their seats.

"I don't care much about *la marihuana*. It grows everywhere. It's pocket change for me," Vega continued. "But, when someone starts inquiring about *la cocaína*, well, that's going to get my interest."

"Mr. Vega, before we go any further, I want to make one

thing clear," Frank said, carefully choosing his words. "I mean no disrespect to you. I don't want to intrude on your operation in any way."

"Relax, Mr. Costello," Vega said. "If I were worried about you, this conversation would not be taking place."

Frank smiled nervously.

"I'm curious, how do you do it?"

"I have an associate who packs the drugs in shipments going back to the States. They're vacuum-packed and sealed in a packing compound. On the other end, we have a friend who removes the drugs and hands them over to another friend." Frank explained, careful to reveal just enough detail to pique Vega's curiosity. "Finally, I have someone who flies down here once a month with the money."

"Hmm...." Vega sat back in his chair and rubbed his chin. He liked what he was hearing. "Seems like a lot just to move a couple pounds of marijuana."

"I'm not talking about marijuana," Frank said, looking across the table at Gus and Diego, who both nodded.

"Ah, you're talking about something more powerful," Vega said, twisting his large black onyx ring on his left ring finger.

Frank nodded.

"*Bueno, bueno,*" Vega said. "And that is how you and I have come together in this little drama. You want to make money, and I want to make money. I have the product; you need the product. Now, we get down to business."

Vega rubbed his chin. *No hay honor entre ladrones*—there's no honor among thieves. For months, he had been skimming a little here and a little there from the cocaine that found its way into Panama courtesy of Noriega and Pablo Escobar. He mainly relied on mules to smuggle the cocaine to his associates in Miami, but he wanted something bigger. He wanted a bigger piece of the action without raising too many flags. Now this gringo walked into his office with a plan that could net him some serious cash. When life presented you with an opportunity, you have to seize it. What Manuel and Pablo didn't know, wouldn't hurt them. With the amount of drugs flowing in and out of Panama, no one was going to miss a few kilos here and there. He loved the idea.

"Aren't you afraid that you might get caught using military transports?"

Frank shook his head. "No one checks cargo pallets containing avionics or radio transmitter parts. And just in case the dogs are brought in, we have a few security police officers working with us."

"See, Diego, what have I been telling you all along? There's no reason not to trust these gringos. After all, they have our best interest at heart," Vega said laughing.

Diego chuckled, which would have been more appropriate had he farted and wanted to cover up his embarrassment.

"How much product do you want to move?"

Frank figured half a kilo. He didn't want to be too greedy. "It all depends on how much you're going to charge."

Vega laughed again. "You're sitting on a gold mine and you're worried about how much it's going to cost you? *Pensé que iba en serio, Señor Costello.*"

"I am serious, Mr. Vega," Frank said, still trying to come up with a number. "It's just—"

"You don't have enough money," Vega said.

Frank nodded.

"Mr. Costello, you have a lot to learn about the drug business. Diego, I thought you said that Mr. Costello was a player?" Vega glared across the room at Guerra, who shifted uncomfortably in his seat again and tried to avoid eye contact with his boss. "You do understand that I have a *reputación*, or as you Americans would say, a reputation to live up to, but I also like to gamble, especially when I like the outcome."

"I like to gamble too, Mr. Vega, but I don't like to gamble with other people's money. It makes people nervous when someone else has their money. And when they feel nervous, they make me nervous. You spend too much time looking over your shoulder. I think you know what I mean."

Vega started laughing; the laugh started out as a low rumble in his stomach that increased in volume and timbre as it rolled upward, reminding Frank of Sydney Greenstreet as Kasper Gutman in the *Maltese Falcon*.

"Tell me, Mr. Costello," Vega began, "Why should I trust you? You have nothing to risk in this little venture whereas it could really inconvenience me. I think you know what I mean, *sí*?"

It was time for Frank to play his cool hand. "A man in your position does not get where he is at without taking some risks."

"I like you, Mr. Costello. You're obviously a man who knows what to say and what not to say," Vega said smiled. "I think you and I will be able to do business together."

Frank nodded. Vega wasn't so tough after all.

"Now, how much product could you move for me?"

"My friend tells me no more than two kilos."

Vega looked at Diego and nodded. That would be a hundred grand. After paying a couple thousand to the people they would have to pay off, and a little something extra for Costello, it would still be around seventy-five grand—and no one would be the wiser, not even Noriega or Escobar.

"When can you do this?"

"When do you want to?"

Vega glanced at Diego and laughed. "See what cocaine

does to a man's mind, Diego? Five minutes ago he was nearly pissing himself; now he's filled with bravado."

Diego and Santiago laughed.

"Come, let's have dinner to seal our little deal," Vega said.

As they walked out of the office, Vega put his arm around Frank's shoulder.

"On a more serious note, one of your associates, Gary Taylor, is he a person who we can trust? I understand he is friends with a military police officer who has already been questioned by your OSI," Vega said. "And as I understand, this security police officer, Rooney, was also once your friend."

Vega's comments caught Frank off guard. He wasn't aware of any OSI investigation, but if there was one, Rooney had nothing on him.

"Rooney and I were never friends," Frank said. He knew that Vega was checking him out, making sure that he wasn't going to be burned later. Diego had probably already told him about the fight at Napoli's. "We were on the same plane to Panama from Charleston, and sure we hung out together for a while, but that's all."

"I also understand you stole his girl."

Frank grinned. "She was never his to keep."

"And Taylor?"

"He's like a brother to me."

"And he won't be a problem, *sí?*"

"He won't be a problem," Frank said looking Vega straight into the eyes. "I'll bet my life on it."

Vega took them to the restaurant on the roof of the Mercado Hotel. The view from the top of the hotel and the restaurant wasn't exactly breathtaking as it looked out over the urban squalor of Chorrillo. Frank was able to make out the Gran Morrison Department Store sign in one direction and the

Thatcher Ferry Bridge in the opposite direction. The maître d' led them to a table in an open air section of the restaurant. At least a half-dozen people came up to the table and paid their respects to Vega, which reminded Frank of a scene from *The Godfather.*

"To business and success," Vega said, raising his glass. "*Por los negocios y el éxito.*"

At the same time, everyone at the table joined Vega in the toast. A roving photographer who was two tables away pretended to take a photograph of a group of tourists seated at a table; however, his real subject was Frank and Vega. When Vega proposed the toast, the photographer who had been watching Frank and the others since they entered the restaurant, slowly turned and quickly took a photograph. The photographer knew better than to use a flashcube and hoped that the natural light would suffice for the Polaroid print. He wasn't worried about the quality. His orders were to get a photograph of Vega and whomever he was sitting together any way possible.

CHAPTER SIXTEEN

BUCK WAS PERPLEXED, which was a bit of an understatement when it came to the daily reports he filed to Langley. Although the new canal treaty negotiations were going smoothly with Carter in the White House, the fallout from the Singing Sergeant's Affair still had everyone worried about how much of the Agency's activities in the region had been compromised. Rodriquez and his cohorts were still not talking which alarmed many people that it wasn't an isolated case of some disgruntled soldiers trying to make some quick cash by selling secrets to the highest bidder.

And then there was Manuel Noriega, who was no longer a nuisance, but a certified pain in the ass.

Despite Noriega's growing laundry list of illicit activities, he continued to be a valuable asset which always made it easy to look the other way. Buck knew that Noriega was a ticking time bomb. As far as he was concerned, the Singing Sergeants Affair, the Canal Zone bombings, and an assorted medley of illicit activities in Panama were just the tip of the iceberg. There was more to meet the eye when it came to Noriega. Buck could

140

see that; he hoped his superiors in Washington did as well.

However, that wasn't what had Buck worried this morning as he sat in his cramped office and studied the blurry black and white photograph in front of him. The photograph, taken at an outdoor restaurant on the rooftop of the Mercado Hotel in the older part of Panama City, immediately caught his attention when it ended up on his desk. He had been to the hotel several times; though it paled in comparison to other hotels in this part of the city, the Mercado was a landmark. Although it had fallen into disrepair since the first time Buck stepped inside, it still exuded a special charm all its own.

As Buck studied the photograph, he nearly spilled his coffee. Though there was no mistaking one of the four people in the photograph, Alejandro Vega, it was two other people in the photo which alarmed him.

Vega was small time, strictly black marketing, gambling, and prostitution, but he had been quickly moving up the food chain adding drug trafficking and money laundering to his résumé. More importantly, Vega's connections with Noriega made this photograph even more interesting, not to mention raising Buck's blood pressure.

Vega's part in this merry-go-round was a minor one, but an important one. Unknowingly, he had been providing Smith with important intelligence regarding Noriega's illicit activities—including his comings and goings, as well as his contacts with a number of shady characters, not the least of which were some known underworld figures. It was Vega who provided Buck with some dirt on Noriega's proclivity for hookers and hardcore porn. It was Vega who provided him and the Agency information about the Singing Sergeant's Affair last year. And it was Vega who provided Buck with the first real evidence that Noriega's drug and gun smuggling operations were much more extensive than the Agency thought.

Although Vega's résumé paled in comparison to Noriega's, his criminal activities were also overlooked given his important source of intelligence. Likewise, Vega knew that Buck was using him for intelligence in return for various favors, not the least of which was making sure his bars and clubs were never put off-limits. Two of those bars were co-owned by Noriega's wife; rumor had it that Noriega's wife and Vega had a little side action going in a hotel on Balboa Avenue making it that much easier for Buck to squeeze Vega for whatever intelligence he needed.

Buck was so engrossed in the photo he hadn't seen Kelly walk into his office and stand in front of his desk.

"I see you got the photograph," Kelly said grinning and looking down at the photograph. "Looks like Christmas came early this year."

"Just what I needed," Buck said, setting the photograph aside. He wasn't sure how he was supposed to interpret Kelly's expression. Did Kelly know something that he didn't? Vega was strictly hands off. He was Buck's problem or concern depending on how one looked at it and right now it was leaning to the latter. "As if I didn't have enough on my plate already with keeping up with the treaty negotiations and making sure our friend Manuel behaves himself."

"Never a dull moment around here, eh?"

Buck grinned.

"I know you've already thought about it, but just in case you haven't, here goes. What the hell is Vega up to? He's not going to give us any trouble, is he?"

Buck shook his head. He was confident that Vega wouldn't pose a problem. Vega was someone he could trust and someone he could use. "He's not going to give us any problems."

"I've got Langley breathing down my back on this one, Buck," Kelly said, still not convinced that the Agency's latest operative was going to be any better than Noriega. Both he and Buck had caught a lot of heat for the Noriega spying fiasco, which was far from being over. "They're still smarting over Rodriquez and his buddies. We can't screw the pooch on this one."

"I understand."

"Then I guess we'd better tighten the reigns a little," Kelly said with a hard edge to his voice. "I just have to know one thing, Buck. Do you trust Vega?"

Buck nodded. "As if he were my brother."

"How can we keep him in the loop without raising too many flags?" Kelly asked, staring at the photograph on Buck's desk. "We don't need Washington breathing down our necks if this ever comes back to us."

"Trust me on this one, Tom."

Although Kelly and Buck had done their best to deal with Noriega's illicit activities, the new director surprised them all by doing nothing to investigate Noriega or question the Agency's friendship with him. Either that was a blessing in disguise or a harbinger of things to come. The spying continued as though nothing had happened. It was, as Buck put it eloquently during a security briefing, "Noriega gives us the least amount of information for the largest amount of protection. He's got us by the balls and he knows it." If Noriega was ever going to be a valuable asset, Buck was going to have to find a way to extract the information indirectly.

Kelly gave Buck a "that's good enough for me" look and picked up the photograph of Vega. "Find out what you can about the people in this photograph. Find out what the hell these airmen are doing with our informant."

"I will."

Buck waited for Kelly to leave his office before he looked at the blurry blown-up photograph again. It was a copy of a Polaroid taken by these roving photographers who plied their trade wherever GIs hung out in the bars and clubs in Panama City and Colón. However, this wasn't just any photographer; it was one of their contractors, whose job it was to tail Vega. Buck had a file folder bulging with photos of Vega meeting with some of his associates, frequenting his favorite brothel, and entertaining high rollers at his hotel, including Noriega—nothing out of the ordinary for a man who managed to stay off most people's radar screens. What puzzled Buck the most about it were the three men seated at the table with Vega. Two of them were definitely military. He already knew that a Panamanian civilian, Diego Guerra was mixed up with some airmen on Howard and that the OSI had one of these men under investigation. Guerra, he could handle; it was these two airmen who also raised his blood pressure.

What Buck couldn't understand and what he couldn't tell Kelly was how two airmen at Howard Air Force Base had gotten involved with one of their operatives in Panama and his oldest friend.

CHAPTER SEVENTEEN

GARY FISHED FOR the keys in his pants, but he wasn't having too much success. His hard-on wasn't helping matters any, nor was the girl he had picked up at the Paris hanging all over him, tonguing his ear and neck. It was the first time he had brought home a girl from one of the bars, and he was convinced that the security policeman at the main gate, who had warned him about bringing a girl back to his room, had probably already radioed ahead and dispatched a patrol truck to his barracks. He should have told the officer a different barracks number. It was too late for that now, as he finally pulled out his keys along with a wad of bills and coins.

It turned out to be a good night, all things considered. At the Paris, he ran into a few of his friends from the barracks and joined them for a drink. Ever since he started running with Frank, he had been seeing less and less of his buddies from the squadron. He would have still been with them if the girl he brought back to the barracks hadn't plopped down on his lap and started pestering him for a drink.

That was all it took to take his mind off Patti.

Gary had met Patti his senior year in high school. Although she had been going out with a friend of Gary's, Patti and Gary started hanging out together at school and on evenings and weekends. They both had part-time jobs at a local mall and they took turns taking each other to work. One night, after Gary had given her a ride home from work, they split a six-pack of Pabst Blue Ribbon and had started to make out in his car behind her house. They would have probably gone all the way if Scott hadn't shown up, threatening to kill Gary for making out with Patti. That in itself was interesting because Gary and Scott—along with six other friends—had all signed up for the Air Force's Buddy System and were scheduled to report to basic training six days after they graduated. They even had their photograph—standing next to a static display of an F-104 that was on exhibit at a local mall—on the front page of their hometown newspaper. Although Patti ended up getting back together with Scott, she and Gary still remained friends.

Before Gary left for Panama, he stopped in to see Patti one afternoon. They sat on the patio outside her house and drank lemonade and ate an apple pie her mother had baked. Of the seven friends who left for the Air Force, Gary was the first one to come home on leave after finishing his training. Four of his friends never made it out of basic training. His other two friends, Greg and Scott, were still at tech school. According to Patti, Scott had deliberately washed out of aircraft maintenance school so he could come home and marry her.

"I don't know what the hell he's thinking," she said, brushing her bangs off her forehead. "I'm still in high school."

"Guys wash out all the time. I knew a guy at Lowry who did the same thing," Gary said, lying to Patti to make her feel better. "He just wasn't cut out for the military. Better to realize that sooner than later."

"Do you really think that's what Scott did?"

What Gary really wanted to tell Patti right there and then was that he still had feelings for her and that Scott was a jerk. Instead, he continued to lie, which was probably worse because when Patti eventually found out about Scott, it was going to hurt her more.

"Yeah, it must have been too much for him," Gary said. "Of all the services, the Air Force is the most competitive—and the most selective. We might not be the marines looking for a few good men, but we're looking for someone who can keep million-dollar aircraft from falling out of the sky."

Patti grinned, sipping her lemonade. Gary loved the long brown hair which curled over her shoulders and her cute, pudgy nose—especially the way it crinkled when she smiled.

"We had it all figured out. I was going to finish high school and go to college," she said. "And then we were going to get married."

"I'm sure everything is going to work out for the two of you," Gary said.

"Thanks for being such a good friend, Gary. You always know what to say," she said.

"Friends forever, right?" It was the noble thing to say, but it was another missed opportunity.

Patti nodded, wiping away a tear from her eye. "When do you leave for Panama?"

"The day after tomorrow."

"Excited?"

"I guess so."

"You'll write to me, right?"

"You know it."

The first couple of letters had been about her going to school and waiting for Scott to come home. Although he might have deliberately washed out of the technical school, the

Air Force was going to get their money's worth. They had kept finding things for him to do, and by the time he finally came home, it was the beginning of November. Gary wrote long letters about Howard, the Canal Zone, and Panama. He wrote about visiting to Miraflores Locks, taking a train across the isthmus from Panama City to Colón with one of his best friends, Howard Hakkila, who he had met at Lowry the day they both had to get yellow fever shots, and getting his first stripe. He had told her about his job and the people he'd met including his best friend, Frank.

And then she wrote him *the* letter.

She confided in him about how she had been wrong about Scott. How she should have stayed in the car with Gary that night, instead of going with Scott and been the one waiting for Gary to come home to her.

I wish you were here with me now, Gary. I need you so much. I love you, Gary. I have always loved you.

Gary's hands were trembling by the time he reached the end of the letter. Patti needed him. Patti *loved* him.

A letter back to Patti would not do—he wanted to call her and tell her that he felt the same way but the only way he could call the States was to patch a call through an overseas operator—which could take a couple of hours—or go to the MARS (Military Affiliated Radio Service) unit across the street, and place a call with them.

It had been almost two weeks since she wrote the letter. Was she waiting for his reply?

It took almost two hours to patch a call through to her, and despite other people listening in on their call and having to say "Over" when he was finished speaking, as he pressed the key button on the microphone and said, "Patti, this is Gary. Over," it didn't make any difference. In the three hours since he had first read the letter and decided to call her, he knew exactly what he would say to Patti. Unfortunately for Gary, though, much had changed in those two weeks.

"Wow, it's great to hear your voice, Gary," Patti said, surprised that Gary had called her. "What a surprise. There's someone here who wants to say hello. Over."

"Someone? Who? Over."

"Hey, Gary, how's it hanging?" Scott asked on the other end. "Guess what? Patti and I are finally going to get married. Over."

Gary's heart sank as soon as he heard Scott's voice.

"Getting married? Wow, that's some very happy news," Gary replied, trying to hide his sadness and fighting for the right words to say at the same time. "I'm happy for the two of you. Over."

The radio operator pretended not to listen to the conversation, but he had sat through similar radio calls and felt sorry for Gary.

"And I owe it all to you, Gary. I don't know what you told Patti, but whatever it was, it worked. Over."

He wasn't too sure what he said or what Patti said after that. He might have said congratulations or wished them all the best again. He thought he heard Patti say that she wished he could be there for the wedding. He couldn't even remember saying goodbye to Patti.

*   *   *

On his way back to the barracks, he bumped into Frank, who had just returned from dropping off another payment to Guerra.

"What's wrong, Gary?" Frank asked. "You look a little down."

"It's nothing, really," Gary said.

They started to walk toward the barracks. Suddenly they heard a ruckus from somewhere on the third floor, followed by someone yelling, "Get back here you little son-of-a-bitch!" There was more yelling, even some swearing in Spanish. Frank and Gary had looked up at the third floor at the same time—a dilapidated shoeshine box was flung out one of the large bay windows. It landed at their feet smashing into a half-dozen pieces. Frank and Gary stared at the broken shoeshine box, and then at the same time, looked back toward the third floor.

There were a lot of perks about being stationed at Howard that made for a very easy and laidback tour. No one had to pull KP or do other chickenshit details like having to clean the latrine. They had a Panamanian houseboy for that. And no one had to shine their boots. There were at least one or two shoeshine boys hanging out in the barracks on any given day hoping to make a couple bucks. But that was the problem: they hung out in the barracks too often, and sometimes they did more than hang out, slipping into unlocked rooms and stealing whatever they could.

Frank and Gary had heard more yelling and then saw a new guy from the third floor come running out of the barracks with a towel wrapped around his skinny body in pursuit of a shoeshine boy.

"Stop him!" the man yelled. "The little fucker grabbed my wallet while I was in the shower!"

Frank stuck out his foot, tripping the little thief as he ran by, sending him sprawling onto the ground. Frank retrieved the man's wallet and picked up the boy by the scruff of his shirt.

"Here you go, man," Frank said, handing the wallet to the man.

"Thanks, man, I owe you," the man replied, looking inside the wallet to see if all his money was still there.

"You ought to be more careful next time," Frank said,

staring at the boy trying to wiggle himself free of Frank's grip. "These kids will steal you blind."

"What should we do with him?" the man asked, adjusting the towel around his waist.

"Hmm…that's a good question," Frank said setting the boy down while still tightly holding onto his shirt. "*Yo digo que lo encerramos en la cárcel y tirar la llave.*"

The boy's eyes got as wide as saucers.

"What did you say, man?" the airman asked.

"I told him that we should lock him up and throw away the key," Frank said, smiling. He turned the boy around and kicked him gently in the buttocks. "*Chico ahora lárgate!*"

The boy picked up the pieces of the shoeshine box and ran off in the direction of another shoeshine boy who had watched what transpired.

"He'll be back again tomorrow," Frank grinned.

"Thanks again, man," the man said, holding up his wallet as he headed back into the barracks.

"Now do you mind telling me what's wrong with you?" Frank asked Gary as they walked into the barracks. "You look as though you just lost your best friend. You didn't lose your best friend, did you?"

"It's my girl."

"And let me guess, she sent you a 'Dear John' letter, right?"

"No, it was nothing like that. We were friends," Gary explained as they started up the stairs. "I mean I wanted to date her, but we were friends and there was this other guy, a friend of mine. They're getting married and—"

"The guy she's marrying is a real jerk?"

Gary nodded.

"Come on, Gary. This is Panama. You can be banging beaver any time you want."

"I know, but this girl was special. After she sent me this letter telling me how she felt about me and how she didn't love this other guy, I thought that there was a chance for us to be together."

"Life's a bitch, ain't it?"

Gary looked at Frank with a puzzled look on his face. It wasn't what he expected his friend to say.

"Come on, I have something that will make you feel better," Frank said, motioning Gary to follow him to his room.

After smoking a few bowls of Red, Gary was definitely feeling better and caught the first bus downtown.

* * *

He was surprised when he realized that the door wasn't locked—J.J. was already home. That's great, he thought, as he opened the door and ushered the girl inside. In his roommate's half of the room, he heard Manfred Mann's "Blinded by the Light" playing and smelled incense which barely masked the odor of marijuana. J.J.'s "fuck light"—what J.J. referred to a table lamp with a red light bulb—and a black light cast an eerie glow in the room.

"Is it okay?" the girl asked, looking up at him with large brown eyes.

He had already forgotten her name. It was Lily or Sara, or something like one of those. He had been pretty buzzed when she landed on his lap and asked for the first of four "drinkees" before he paid the bar fine and stumbled out, nearly crashing into a trio of soldiers standing on the sidewalk gnawing on sticks of monkey meat. At that point, he hadn't even thought about bringing her back to the barracks until she suggested something about all night and he nodded. The next thing he knew, she was pulling him across the street in the opposite direction of the hotel where most of the ladies from the Ovalo and Paris took their customers. First they had to get past the Guardia Nacional outside the bars and clubs—he didn't want to end up like Steve Wilson and the run-in he had with the Guardia—then, he had to worry about the police on base, but what he hadn't counted on was his roommate being home.

Gary shrugged his shoulders. He hadn't been on speaking terms with his roommate since the two of them got into a fight over some stuff one of J.J.'s lady friends had stolen, so it wasn't like Gary could ask him to step out for a while. He probably should have taken her to the hotel and gone back to the Paris where his friends were probably still partying.

"Yeah, yeah, it's okay." Gary turned on a lamp next to his bed and sat down on the edge of the bed with the girl.

They started kissing, groping, and caressing each other's bodies. Gary wasted no time liberating her large breasts from the halter top she was wearing and began to tongue and nibble on her nipples. She moaned softly and started rubbing his crotch, but all the Cerveza Panama's he had tossed down at the Paris had caught up with him when he suddenly had an aching urge to urinate.

"I have to go to the toilet," Gary said bummed that he had put a damper on their lovemaking. "Make yourself at home. I'll be right back."

The girl didn't look too happy as she covered her breasts with her top, but it wasn't like she was going to go anywhere. He leaned over and kissed her on the cheek before he walked out of the room and down the hallway and into the latrine. He had just started to piss—laughing to himself about telling the girl to make herself at home—when he heard a woman screaming. He zipped up hastily and ran out of the latrine to see what all the commotion was about. That's when he saw Lily, Lisa, or Sara or whatever-her-name-was, standing outside his room screaming.

"Jesus, Taylor, what the hell did you do to her?" Charles Marshall asked, walking out of his room in only his underwear to see what all the screaming was about. "She's going to wake up half the barracks."

Gary tried to calm the girl, who continued to scream and look toward Gary's room. "I was just taking a piss when she started screaming."

"Maybe she saw how tiny you are," Marshall said, laughing.

"Screw you, Marshall." Gary shot Marshall a dirty look and then turned to the girl. "What's wrong?"

"I-i-inside," the girl stammered, her heart pounding inside her chest.

Gary walked back inside his room and looked around. Everything looked okay, but when he happened to look into J.J.'s half of the room, that's when he saw the lower half of a man's body on the floor. *That's what must have frightened her.*

"Hey, J.J., you okay?" Gary asked grinning. "What the hell are you doing there on the floor? Did you pass out again?"

"What's wrong?" Marshall asked, looking into the room.

"It's J.J. He passed out on the floor," Gary said. "Hey, man, wake up."

When his roommate didn't answer, Gary parted the beads which hung down across the entrance and looked inside. That's when he saw J.J.'s partially clothed body on the floor, his glassy eyes staring at the ceiling. His head was in a pool of vomit. There was a syringe near his body. Gary dropped to the floor and immediately checked for a pulse but found none. Behind him, the girl saw J.J.'s lifeless body again and let out a blood-curdling scream.

By then, she had woken up most of the barracks.

CHAPTER EIGHTEEN

BUCK WAS ALMOST certain he was being tailed when he entered the bar in the Intercontinental Hotel. There were two men who had taken an interest in him the moment he slid up to the bar and ordered a Jack and Coke. He figured them for Guardia Nacional right off the bat as he watched them watching him in the mirror behind the bar. He couldn't go anywhere in the city without at least someone being interested in his comings and goings.

The men weren't the only two people in the bar interested in Buck. He turned on his barstool and eyed a leggy, fair-skinned Panamanian woman sitting by herself. She tongued a cherry on a swizzle stick and made it obvious that the titillating gesture had been intended for Buck's viewing pleasure. Buck nodded in approval; *Tas buena, mami*—Panamanian slang for *You're looking good, mama*. Buck put her in the three hundred dollar a night range, and wouldn't be surprised if Noriega hadn't sent her around just in case the two Guardia stooges couldn't do their jobs. Buck smiled at the woman and watched her slowly uncross and cross her long legs for his benefit. He gave her a *maybe some other time* look before he turned back to the bar and motioned to the bartender for another drink.

When the bartender brought him his drink, Buck noticed that the two men watching him earlier had moved to the back of the room where they pretended to feed quarters into a slot machine. It's not that he minded Noriega paying this much attention to him—as the Guardia's G2, he expected as much. The woman was a nice touch, however. It was Noriega's way of saying; "I know you're curious about one of my associates, so why not have some fun before we get down to business?"

The associate, according to the tip he received from Vega, was one of Buck's old Vietnam War buddies, Danny Patterson, who had been recruited by the Agency to fly special ops in and out of Laos, was in town and staying at the Intercontinental. In Vietnam and Laos, Danny had been a hotshot pilot for Air America, flying everything from reconnaissance and air support to cargo missions. Known for flying in and out of hot landing strips, he never lost a plane or a cargo. However, after the war he had disappeared; some people, Buck included, felt that if Danny were to turn up anywhere, it would be Central America.

What Patterson was doing in Panama was of special interest to Buck and the possible headache that it could cause for the Agency. There were rumors that he was flying again; this time guns and drugs. Noriega may have been on the CIA's payroll, but that didn't stop him from pursuing extracurricular activities.

Buck's thoughts circled back to the two men. His best bet was just to walk out of the hotel, get in a taxi and lose them in the labyrinthine traffic maze around Vía España. Then, out of the corner of his eye, another person, a tall man with short-cropped hair in an expensive suit, got his attention. He was standing near the entrance to the casino talking to another man. *Well, so much for rumors.* Patterson was definitely in town.

This was turning out to be quite the evening. Even the bartender seemed to part of the night's entertainment. He had made sure that Buck had a fresh Jack and Coke in his hand, and just to make sure that none of this was to be taken too lightly, he was offered a Cuban cigar. Buck smacked his lips and glanced at the woman again who made sure he could see that her long legs went all the way to her thighs and once they reached their final destination, they left nothing to the imagination. Buck sighed, nodded to the woman, and slid off the barstool. In the reflection of the mirror behind the bar, he could see the two beefy Guardia trying not to be too inconspicuous as they occasionally glanced in Buck's direction. Buck was going to have to lose the two Guardia. The woman and Patterson would have to wait.

Buck noticed two young women standing near the entrance to the bar looking bored and lonely as they waited for the right moment to swoop down on an unattached male walking into the bar.

"*Buenas noches, señoras,*" Buck said, walking up to the two ladies. "*¿Cómo les gustaría hacer cien dólares?*"

They pretended they didn't hear him. Buck had started too low. He offered them one hundred dollars each. That got their attention.

"Do you see those two guys standing over there?" Buck said, pointing to the two Guardia.

The two girls nodded.

"Just go up to them and put your arms around them," Buck said.

"*¿Eso es todo?*" one of the girls asked.

"*Sí*, that's all you have to do," Buck replied.

The two girls looked at each other and shrugged their shoulders. Buck peeled off ten twenties from a roll of bills and handed each girl one hundred dollars.

"Make it look good," Buck said.

"¿Estás loco?" they said in unison.

Buck grinned. "Yeah, I'm crazy all right."

He moved off to the side, still maintaining visual contact with the two Guardia and watched the two girls earn their hundred dollars. They each threw their arms around one of the two Guardia, momentarily blocking their view of the lobby. That was Buck's cue. He slipped out of the bar and through the lobby before the two Guardia realized they had been had.

Buck caught a taxi outside the hotel and in less than twenty minutes, he was back in his old stomping grounds. At the corner of J Street, where it finally ended its short meandering route onto Vía España, Buck got out and headed up the street toward the cluster of bars, casinos, and clubs. He blended into the throngs of soldiers, airmen, sailors, and marines out on the town. He knew this area like the back of his hand; he knew all the side streets that even most locals could get lost in during the day. He passed the bars that catered to service members every desire and carnal pleasure, even the one where at the tender age of sixteen he had lost his cherry to one of the golden-skinned beauties who took him to an upstairs room and made him a man.

He was almost tempted to stop in the Ovalo, but a quick glance at his watch told him to keep on going. Maybe he'd stop on his way back and see if one of his favorite girls was working tonight. Of course, there was always the woman back at the Intercontinental.

He followed the narrow side street for about a hundred yards and turned up another narrow street and then down another until he came to a wider avenue. If he had been tailed, it would be easy to lose whoever it was in the labyrinth of streets in this part of town. At the end of the street was a nondescript five-story building. Three men sitting outside paid no attention to the gringo in this part of town except one who nodded his head to one of the upper floors.

He had reached the bowels of Chorrillo; the stench and poverty of third world strata rose all around him. He climbed the stairs to the fifth floor and walked to a room at the end of a dimly lit corridor. There was another man at the end of the corridor in front of the door. The man knocked on the door twice then opened it for Buck.

As soon as Vega saw his friend standing in the doorway, he stood up and walked over to Buck, putting his arms around him.

"Buck, what took you so long?"

CHAPTER NINETEEN

IT HAD ALL started with a flag. When it was over, four U.S. soldiers had been killed and over eighty Americans wounded. On the Panamanian side, the numbers were staggering: twenty-four were killed and more than two hundred wounded. More than thirty thousand Panamanians had taken to the streets; at one point some of the protestors stormed into the Canal Zone, tearing down sections of the "Fence of Shame"—a fence which divided the Canal Zone and Panama City. American businesses in Panama City, including the Pan Am building, were set on fire. President Lyndon Johnson had his first foreign policy crisis. It was, for all practical and semantic purposes, the beginning of the end for the Canal Zone.

* * *

For years, Americans had flown the Stars and Stripes wherever they wanted to. Throughout the Canal Zone, from schools and government buildings, to courthouses and hospitals it flew— to the continual dismay of Panama, who demanded that their flag fly alongside the American flag. Finally, President John F. Kennedy had stepped forward to issue an ultimatum: either take down the American flag or put up another pole to fly the Panamanian flag. It made Kennedy a hero in Panama, but it didn't sit too well with the Zonians.

Then, on a sunny day in January 1964, everything changed. On the first of that year, Canal Zone officials said that *no* flags would fly in front of schools. The declaration hadn't sat well with a group of high school students who had taken matters into their hands and ran "Old Glory" up a flagpole outside Balboa High School.

Buck had been in Panama for about a year and had understood what this meant to his classmates, as well as other Zonians. Two of Buck's classmates had stayed up all night on two consecutive nights, guarding the flag in front of the school making sure that no one would try to lower it. Buck had wished he could join his friends, but his father, stationed at Quarry Heights hadn't allowed it. Buck had missed the demonstration later that week when two hundred Panamanian students had marched to Balboa High School and demanded that the students take down the American flag and raise the Panamanian flag. The Balboa High School students refused and a large group of Zonians surrounded the group of Panamanians and started singing the *Star Spangled Banner*. A light scuffle had broken out which had to be quelled by the Canal Zone Police who dispersed the Panamanian students, but as they left the Canal Zone, the students smashed car windows and knocked over trash cans—pretty mild, considering what was about to transpire.

Though he missed the school demonstration, Buck had gotten caught in the middle of the protest later that day, trying to cut across an intersection to get home. When the

Panamanian students marched back to Balboa High School and demanded that their flag be flown, the flag had somehow gotten ripped in the scuffle. Tensions and tempers flared as things quickly got out of hand. Buck and the others who had witnessed the first demonstration suddenly found themselves in the middle of a massive demonstration. Thousands of Panamanians rushed into the Canal Zone claiming that the Panamanian flag had been torn. It just wasn't any Panamanian flag, though; the flag had flown during a demonstration in the late 1940s when Panamanians protested against the United States attempts to maintain military bases outside the Canal Zone and had become symbolic for Panama's claims of sovereignty in the Canal Zone.

Buck and his friend Mark Jones sought cover when they saw the mob of Panamanians. They jumped over a fence and were about to start down a street when Buck saw a Panamanian youth sprawled on the street. From where Buck had been standing, he could see a small pool of blood around the boy's head. There was only one thing for Buck to do.

"Buck, what the hell are you doing?" Mark yelled as he watched Buck jump back over the fence and race across the street to save the boy.

* * *

"How's the spy business these days?" Vega asked after they had moved next door to the spacious and much cleaner surroundings of his office in the Mercado Hotel.

Buck grunted. "You tell me."

"You're looking rather peaked tonight, my friend," Vega said. "Would you like for me to have the kitchen grill you up a steak?"

Buck shook his head.

"I see, so there's something else which brought you here," Vega said, stroking his pencil-thin mustache. "Something tells me that it's not good."

"It depends."

"Depends on what?"

"On what you say in the next couple of minutes," Buck said. Vega was the master of the subterfuge. He didn't get to where he was at today without a little manipulation along the way. "Do you know anything about the two men that followed me here?"

"Which two men?"

"Two men followed me from the Intercontinental. Someone had better teach them how to do a better job of tailing. They were so fucking conspicuous it almost hurt how easy it was to lose them."

Vega feigned a look of surprise as he stirred his Cuba Libre. "Don't look at me. I didn't have any men follow you."

"Why don't you ask them yourself?" Buck said. "I figure by now, they're downstairs in the lobby, pissing themselves for not doing their job."

"Why are you in such a foul mood, my friend?" Vega asked. "Have I done something to upset you? Haven't I always been there for you when you needed me?"

Buck nodded. "Yes, you have, my friend. You've always been there for me."

"Then tell me, my friend, what's on your mind?" Vega inquired.

Buck wanted to be careful how he played his cards with this friend. What Vega had going with the servicemen was his own business, but it might come in useful later if Buck needed someone to keep an eye on his friend. Buck threw a photo down on Vega's desk.

"Since when did your little business involve a couple of

airmen from Howard?"

*   *   *

The boy's eyes widened in fear when Buck approached. At first the boy had wanted to get away from the approaching *gringo*, but his leg was too banged up.

"Are you okay?" Buck asked, helping the frightened and dazed boy to his feet. The boy couldn't have weighed more than seventy-five pounds dripping wet. "We had better get out of here before the police arrest you."

The boy looked up at Buck with wide eyes. His skin was pockmarked and dirty. The blood from the head wound had already started to clot. Most of the high school students and the Panamanian demonstrators had dispersed.

"Come on, let's get you out of here. *Vamos, vamos a llevarte de aquí*," Buck said, putting an arm around the boy help him walk. "Let's get you back across Fourth of July Avenue."

Buck had never tried to help someone along like this, and they nearly fell over a few times, but once they had synchronized their movements, it became a lot easier. A squad car sped by, but the officers inside paid no attention to Buck and the boy. Buck stepped up their pace. They passed some stragglers from the demonstration who were yelling and raising their fists into the air. It seemed as if they were regrouping and planned to return the way they came. Buck's heart pounded in his chest. Ahead he could see Fourth of July Avenue. Just a few more yards and they would be out of harm's way.

*   *   *

He hadn't intended to broadside his friend but also didn't like being tailed by two off-duty Guardia. "Do you want to explain this?"

"You mean to tell me that is why you came all the way down here? About a photograph?" Vega asked, looking at the photograph, but not trying to show too much interest in it. "I have a lot of photographs. I've got albums full of them. You want to see some of my trip to Contadora last month?"

"I'm serious, Alejandro," Buck said.

Alejandro picked up the photograph and crinkled his nose as if he just smelled something rotten. "Whoever took this photograph should seriously consider looking for another line of work. Look, you can't even make out who the people are in the photograph."

"You wouldn't be expanding your business in any way, would you?"

Alejandro tossed the photograph on his desk and shook his head. "I'm just exploring some new business opportunities."

"And the two airmen in the photograph?"

"They were guests in the hotel. When did taking a photograph with your guests suddenly become a crime?"

"When one of them is dealing drugs."

"Seems *you* should be talking to them about this."

Buck frowned. "And Manuel is okay with this?

"What Manuel doesn't know, won't hurt him."

* * *

Once Buck and the boy had gotten across Fourth of July Avenue, the boy had started pumping Buck's hand wildly.

"*Gracias, gracias,*" the boy said.

"*De nada,*" Buck replied.

In the distance, they heard people yelling that someone had ripped the Panamanian flag, and it appeared that some of the protestors were regrouping. Buck hadn't thought about the danger he was in by crossing into Panama, but hearing all the yelling and shouting had made the hair on the back of his neck stand up. He had gotten the boy to safety. Now, all he wanted was to run back across the avenue to the safety of the Canal Zone, but the boy, still dazed and frightened didn't want Buck to leave yet. The boy grabbed Buck's arm and started to lead him down a narrow street. Buck tried to free his arm, but the boy wouldn't let go. The boy started to cry, and, not wanting to make a scene with the protestors, Buck decided to follow the boy.

They continued down the narrow side street for about fifty yards before coming out on another narrow street. Buck recognized the area, having gone here with one of his friends one afternoon to explore the older parts of Panama City. The road they were on jogged to the left and then to the right until it came out in a small plaza. At the far end was the Mercado Hotel. A group of older Panamanian men, had been sitting on a bench in the middle of the plaza, and they stared at Buck as the young boy led him across the plaza and into the hotel.

The hotel felt cool and smelled of cigars and disinfectant. In its heyday, it must have been quite the place, Buck mused as he stared at the high ceilings. However, on this day it was eerily quiet because of the demonstrations not far away.

"Alejandro!" a man's voice echoed across the lobby.

"*Papá!*" Alejandro cried when he had noticed his father.

The elder Vega took one look at his son and frowned when he saw the boy's injuries. "What happened?"

After Alejandro had explained the situation to his father, his father nodded and thanked Buck for bringing his son home to safety.

"If you ever need anything, you are always welcome here," Alejandro's father said, clapping Buck on the shoulder.

Buck still had to get back to the Canal Zone and his new friend's father made sure of that.

* * *

Vega poured Buck another shot of whiskey. Buck never cared much for the rum in Panama, having had his share of Ron Cortez after he completed jungle training at Fort Gulick. That had been Buck's second trip to Panama. Before he shipped off to Vietnam, he looked up his old friend, Alejandro, who by then had taken over his father's hotel and import/export business. Later, when Buck started working at the Agency, he had called upon his friend from time to time for information. It wasn't long before Vega was on the CIA payroll.

"How's your buddy Rodriquez doing these days?" Vega asked grinning.

"He's not my buddy," Buck answered.

"Manuel still thinks you set him up."

"What *doesn't* Manuel tell you?"

Vega laughed. "Come on, Buck. Where's your sense of humor?"

"I left it at the office."

"He still believes that the CIA was behind it."

Buck grinned and sipped his drink. There were rumors that Rodriquez had been a plant by the Agency or the DIA— rumors that were not denied by the Agency or anyone connected with the ongoing investigation. As long as Noriega thought he wasn't free from the Agency's grip, they could still reel him in whenever they needed.

"He does, huh?" Buck tried not to be too surprised. "Manuel thinks what he wants to think. There's nothing I can do about that."

Vega smiled. "Of course not."

It was getting late, but Buck wasn't through with his friend.

"Oh, one more thing, this so-called exploring of new business opportunities wouldn't have to do with the rumor that you're using military transports for your business?" Buck said.

"Not at all."

CHAPTER TWENTY

THREE DAYS AFTER the death of his roommate, Gary had been summoned to the orderly room by the first sergeant as part of the ongoing investigation. Though it appeared that J.J. had died from an apparent overdose, the police and OSI hadn't ruled out the possibility of foul play. Gary, who was still in shock over what happened, thought for sure he was going to somehow be punished in all of this—either for knowing that J.J. used drugs and not reporting him or for using drugs himself when some marijuana seeds and resin were found in a wastebasket on his side of the room during the police investigation.

While he was waiting to see the first sergeant, Gus Santiago came into the orderly room. Santiago didn't say anything to Gary; in fact, he didn't even look over at Gary. Instead, he walked across the room to Clark's desk, leaned over the front of his desk, and started talking to Clark in a low tone. Clark looked up from his desk and glanced across the room toward Gary. It was only then that Santiago turned around and glanced at Gary before he left the orderly room.

When he walked into Bartlett's office, Gary thought that he would only be talking to the first sergeant; instead, there were two other men: Master Sergeant John Kerr and Jake Flagg. Flagg sat in the corner and let the security police ask all the questions. He didn't think that the kid was involved in this; maybe he was smoking some weed and popping some speed but nothing more than that. If the kid didn't cooperate, the seeds and the resin they found in the wastebasket were enough to bring him up on an Article Fifteen. Flagg didn't think it would come to that. He figured the kid was still in shock over finding his roommate dead, and whatever information he did have, it was going to be a while before he shared it.

"Did you know that Sergeant Washington used drugs?" Kerr asked him. Kerr, who was leading the investigation, had seen Gary around the base with one of the men in his squadron, Kevin Rooney. Kerr's long, thin face with a pointed nose and chin was a perfect match to his unpleasant personality. Ground down by fifteen years of service and still only a master sergeant, Kerr had a feeling that Taylor knew where his roommate had gotten the drugs. He was going to find out, no matter how long it took. "Do you have any idea who might have sold him drugs?"

"I wouldn't have any idea about that," Gary said. "My roommate and I didn't get along too well."

"You lived together, Taylor," Kerr continued. "You must have noticed something."

Gary shook his head. "Like I said, my roommate and I didn't get along. In all the time I knew him, we probably spoke no more than a couple of sentences."

Kerr looked over at Bartlett, who nodded.

"You're not trying to protect anyone, are you?" Kerr asked.

Gary shook his head.

Kerr, who talked to a few of Washington's workers in POL (Petroleum, Oils, and Lubricants), hadn't had much luck with them either, but one of the newer guys mentioned that Washington sometimes hung out with someone in the 24th Transportation Squadron. If Taylor was trying to protect someone by using this "I don't know anything" defense, Kerr decided to try a different tactic.

"I know this has been a nightmare for you, Taylor, and I'm sorry that you had to get dragged into all of this. But if it comes to light that you did know something and you failed to tell us, you're going to find yourself on the wrong end of an Article Fifteen—or worse." Kerr glanced over at Flagg for a nod or some other gesture—a sign of approval—that the OSI concurred. Flagg nodded.

Gary's eyes widened when Kerr mentioned Article Fifteen.

"We found seeds and resin on your side of the room, son," Flagg said, trying a softer approach. "That's an Article Fifteen offense."

Bartlett grunted. He had a feeling that Tyler would end up in the trouble.

"How well do you know Mike Casey?" Flagg asked.

"I've seen him around the base," Gary said.

"What's this about Casey, Flagg?" Bartlett asked. "What's he got to do with Washington's death?"

"Casey's a real piece of work," Flagg continued. "He's been smuggling shit home on C-130s and C-141s for about a year now. He thinks the Air Force is his private delivery service. Well, we suspect he's moved up to narcotics. You used to deliver stuff to him didn't you?"

Gary's heart skipped a few beats. They had him dead to rights. He could feel the beads of sweat forming on his forehead. He was certain Kerr or Flagg could see them. He swallowed hard. If he confessed now, maybe the OSI would go easy on him. Of course, he would have to give them a few names. "Yes, that's right. When I worked in the Repair Cycle Support Unit."

"I see," Flagg said. "So it was work-related."

Gary breathed a little easier, but he knew he wasn't out of the woods yet. "Yes, that is correct."

Bartlett grunted again and stared at Gary.

Flagg looked at Gary closely. The kid hadn't flinched. As much as he admired Taylor's resolve for not giving up his friends, Flagg still had a job to do.

We just want you to make it easy on yourself, Gary," Kerr said, moving to the front of the room and picking up where Flagg had left off. "I know when you're in the military far from home, you want everyone to accept you, to like you. I've been there, too, Gary. But you've got to ask yourself one question: Would someone you might be trying to protect do the same for you? Think about it."

Gary looked at Kerr and Flagg. Frank had told him that there was no way that he would be connected. It would be his word against theirs.

"The truth is, Airman, we don't want to see you throwing away your Air Force career should anything come to light that could connect you with this," Kerr added.

Kerr looked at Flagg, who nodded in approval. That was good enough for him.

"Yes, Sir," Gary said.

"There is one more thing," Flagg said, stepping forward with a manila folder in his hand. He opened it and handed Gary a photograph. "Have you ever seen any of these men?"

It was a black and white photograph of Vega and Guerra taken outside the Mercado Hotel. Kerr and Bartlett looked at each other with puzzled looks. Flagg had not told them about a photograph.

Gary shook his head. "No, I haven't."

"Are you sure about that, Airman?" Flagg asked.

Gary studied the photograph. He recognized one of the men from the night he went to Napoli's with Frank, the night Frank got into a fight with Kevin. That was the only time he met the man.

"Yes, I'm sure," Gary said. "Sorry."

"That's okay, Taylor," Flagg said, taking the photograph and putting it in the folder. He noticed that Gary had studied the photograph for a bit. "I'm good."

"That'll be all, Taylor," Kerr said.

Gary stood up and walked to the door.

"One more thing, Gary," Flagg said, "if you do hear of anything, you will let us know, won't you?"

Gary, who had already opened the door, turned and nodded before he walked out. He started walking toward the stairs when Clark caught up with him, pulling him aside.

"What did they want to talk to you about?" Clark asked in a low voice.

"They wanted to know if I knew anything about the people J.J. hung out with," Gary said.

"What did you tell them?"

"I didn't tell them anything," Gary said. "I'm not *that* stupid."

"You were in there for a long time," Clark said. "What else did they ask you?"

"They asked me if I knew any of his friends, stuff like that."

"And—"

"I told them that I hardly saw my roommate," Gary said. "We weren't exactly on speaking terms with each other, you know."

Clark grunted. "Anything else?"

"The guy from the OSI showed me a photograph."

"A photograph?"

"Yeah, it was a real blurry one of some Panamanian taken at a downtown hotel."

Clark raised his eyebrows. "A Panamanian?"

"Yeah, they wanted to know if I or anyone I knew might have seen this person when we were downtown," Gary said.

"And—"

"I told them that I never saw the man before."

Later that afternoon, Gus met Clark outside the orderly room after Clark got off duty.

"What did he say?" Santiago asked.

"I don't think he told them anything that they don't already know about J.J.," Clark said. "I think you're still safe. But they questioned him for a long time."

A door opening upstairs and then the sound of someone walking down the hallway toward the stairwell startled Santiago, who waited until whoever it was moved out of earshot. "I still don't trust the kid. If the police or OSI didn't think he knew anything more, they wouldn't have questioned him."

"I don't know, Gus," Clark said, sticking up for Gary. "I've known him for over a year now, and he's always been on the up and up. He just doesn't seem like the kind of person who would narc on someone."

"Narc or no narc, people get nervous when the OSI starts questioning them," Santiago said. "You remember that guy at Kobbe last year, don't you?"

Clark nodded. Most everyone at Howard had heard the story of the soldier at Kobbe, suspected of being a narc. Depending on which version of the story one heard—the one where he lived or the one where he died—the soldier had been stuffed into a steel locker and thrown out of a third-floor window.

"I feel sorry for the kid," Santiago said, now convinced that Gary couldn't be trusted. "But business is business."

CHAPTER TWENTY-ONE

BUCK SAW FRANK standing at the far end of the visitor center at Miraflores Locks. It wasn't Buck's first choice to meet him here, but it was much easier to blend in with the tourists—both local and abroad—who came to watch ships transit the locks. He had driven his car to Corozal; hopped on a Canal Zone bus to Coco Solo; and then returned by a *chiva*—just in case Noriega or Vega had him tailed. The timing of their meeting couldn't have been any better; a ship had already entered the locks and was the perfect diversion.

"You're a very hard person to meet," Buck said, standing a few feet from Frank as they both watched a cruise ship pass slowly through the locks in front of them.

Six "mules"—electric locomotives that guided ships through the locks, so the ship didn't smash into the sides of the canal—guided the ship. It would be lowered in two steps, dropping more than fifty feet, before proceeding to the Pacific Ocean. The entire journey across the isthmus and through the locks took approximately ten hours. It was both breathtaking and fascinating, an engineering feat unparalleled in the twentieth century. It was no wonder that the canal was one of the seven wonders of the modern world.

"Maybe it's because I don't want to be ratted out."

"You needn't worry about me, Frank. Right now, I might be the only friend you've got."

"I've got plenty of friends."

"Not this time. The police and OSI are going to be on to you soon enough with or without my blessings. Smuggling drugs to the States on a military transport? They're going to throw the book at you, my friend," Buck said, casting a sideways glance at Frank. "On the other hand, all it will take is just one phone call and I can make twenty to thirty at Leavenworth go away in a flash. Or you can take your chances. What's it going to be, Frank?"

It hadn't taken long for Buck to find out that it was Frank who was one of the men in the photo. Thanks to the little incident at Napoli's as well as Flagg's ongoing investigation of Santiago, Buck soon found out that Frank was one of the men in the photo. Getting Frank to meet him was a little trickier, until Buck threatened to expose his little operation, but not before he made him squirm a little; getting Frank to work for him, even trickier.

"How did you find out it was me?"

"We have our ways."

"It was Rooney, wasn't it?"

"Do you think your little operation wasn't going to go undetected?"

"You're OSI, aren't you?"

Buck laughed. "If I were OSI we'd be having this conversation on the base inside a cell."

Frank thought for a moment and then smiled as if he had just won on a game show. "DEA."

Buck grinned and shook his head.

"If you're not OSI, or DEA—" Frank's face turned pale. The greasy burger and fries he had for lunch that was now churning in his stomach wasn't the only thing making him nauseous. "Let me guess, DIA?"

"You're getting warmer."

Frank's jaw dropped as he looked at Buck with a dumbfounded expression on his face. "You're CIA."

"I see that I got your attention now," Buck said. "That's good."

Frank shaded his eyes with his hand as he watched the ship coming toward them. First of all, he couldn't figure out how the CIA found out about him and his operation and second, why the CIA was interested in helping him.

"Now here's my dilemma, Frank. I don't care if you're smuggling a pound or two of weed back to the States. What I do care about is how you and your buds got mixed up with Vega and Guerra," Buck explained. "Either you're very smart or very stupid. I don't think you know who you are dealing with. You're in some serious shit, pal, and way over your fucking head with Vega and his cohorts."

The ship reached the end of the locks and slowly began to descend to the next chamber. It took ships approximately one hour to transit the locks. Frank and Buck stared at the hull of the ship and looked up at the people lined along the deck. A buxom blonde in a flowing floral print dress caught their attention as she blew kisses to the crowd below.

"Spare me the lecture," Frank said, taking out a pack of cigarettes. "I know what I'm doing."

"I don't think so. Have you ever heard of Manuel Noriega?" Buck asked.

Frank shook his head.

"I didn't think so. Most people haven't heard of him but if you're in bed with Vega, you're also in bed with Noriega.

He's a Guardia Nacional and doesn't take too kindly to some gringo pissing in his backyard."

Frank took a long drag from his cigarette and looked up at the woman in the dress again. A gust of wind blew her dress up to the top of her thighs, which reminded him of the iconic Marilyn Monroe photo. "What do you want from me?"

"Information, Frank. That's all. You're on the inside now, and whether you like it or not, you're working for us."

"And what if I don't want to?"

"To be honest with you, Frank—" Buck stopped talking as two men around his age walked very close to where he was standing with Frank. One of the men did a double take when he passed Buck, who waited until the two men were out of earshot before he continued. "You don't have any choice."

Out of the corner of his eye, Frank noticed a photographer taking a photograph of two women, who looked like models, with the cruise ship in the locks as the backdrop. Ever since the Canal Zone treaty negotiations had taken place, tourists had been flocking to Panama. He thought about what Buck had said that he had no choice but to work with the CIA. When Frank looked away, the photographer turned and took a photo of Frank and Buck.

"I know you're probably wondering how you can get out of the predicament you're in. Right now you're in so far over your head, working with us is your *only* option." Buck turned back to watch the ship in the locks, shading the sun with the back of his hand. "You're a person of interest in an ongoing OSI and DEA investigation."

Frank furrowed his brow and stared at Smith. "You already told them, you bastard."

"What they know and what I know are two different things, Frank. And I'll keep it that way—if you cooperate." Buck said.

"What do they know?"

"That all depends."

"Screw you."

"Come on, Frank. Is that any way to talk to the one person who can save your ass if the shit hits the fan?"

Frank had been leery of meeting Smith, but he couldn't be sure if Vega were somehow behind it. It might have been Vega's twisted way of checking up on him to find out what he knew about this investigation. Frank had a hunch that Vega was well-connected to some Americans; maybe Smith was one of them. Now he didn't know what to think. Both men fell silent. A noisy group of tourists with cameras dangling from fleshy sunburned necks jockeyed for a position not far from where they were standing to take photographs of the ship as it slowly moved toward them.

"How's your friend Eddie Cahill these days?" Buck finally asked.

Frank winced when he heard the name, but didn't want to telegraph his surprise to Smith. "I don't know who you're talking about."

"It's okay if you want to pretend that you don't know him," Buck said. "He's looking at ten to fifteen for possession, but if he gives up some names, the DA is looking to make a deal with him. And guess whose name came up?"

Frank looked away from Smith and watched the cruise ship continued its drop to the next level. People on the decks above waved to the visitors and tourists below and dropped chocolate bars, flowers, and cigarettes.

"You don't scare me," Frank said.

"What do you think would happen if Vega found out you're under investigation? How do you think he would react?"

When backed into a corner, Frank usually came out swinging, but that seemed unlikely with the corner Smith had him backed into now. If Smith was for real, there was no telling how big the shit storm that was coming his way if he didn't go along with the plan.

"Go on, I'm listening."

Buck grinned. Frank wasn't as tough as his file said he was.

"You're going to be my eyes and ears, Frank, while you and Vega do your little song and dance. I just want to know what he's up to, that's all."

"Why? Did he *piss* in your pool or something?"

Buck laughed. "Something like that."

"So what you're saying is that you want me to shadow the man who is my partner? Boy, that's choice."

Buck nodded. "I'm not asking you to follow him into the bathroom when he takes a shit. Just be on the lookout for anything unusual or out of the ordinary."

"Like a person following him into the bathroom when he takes a shit."

Buck smiled. He enjoyed toying with Costello, but there was something about the guy that he liked. For one thing, he seemed more intelligent and sophisticated than what Flagg had led him to believe. The kid also had balls teaming up with Vega. Frank might have been an amateur in this comedy of errors, but he had a lot of potential. The bottom line was he liked Costello.

"You know what I mean. And when the time comes, if it comes, that'll be your cue to make good on our little arrangement."

"Nothing like being caught between the proverbial rock and a hard place."

"You're a fast learner, Frank."

"And that's all?"

"That's right. Just carry on as if nothing happened."

"How do I know you're not going to turn me in?"

"You're just going to have to trust me, Frank."

Out of the corner of his eye, Frank panicked when he thought he saw someone he recognized from the Mercado Hotel. However, when he turned to see if it was who he thought it was, it turned out to be someone else.

"There is one more thing, you, and this kid you hang out with, what's his name—"

"Taylor."

"Yes, Taylor. You two better watch your backs."

"What's that supposed to mean?"

"I'm just saying you and your pal are mixed up with some people who don't take too kindly to special investigations."

What Frank still hadn't figured out though, was how Smith knew about their little operation. Someone had tipped off someone somewhere. Smith was right about one thing, though, Frank had no choice in the matter; he was screwed either way. On one hand he would get busted for the drugs; on the other hand, if Vega ever found out, he was as good as dead.

"What kind of assurances can you give me that no one will find out that I talked to you?" Frank finally got around to asking.

"None, but I guess you've already figured that out."

CHAPTER TWENTY-TWO

KEVIN BUMPED INTO Gary at the BX cafeteria two weeks after J.J.'s death. He was working the night shift on the flight line and had stopped in to grab a bite to eat. It had been over two months since Kevin last saw Gary, to the dismay of Flagg who had hoped that Kevin would have had some information about Costello and Gary to share. Problem was, Kevin had been working nights and Gary had been transferred to a new section.

"Mind if I sit down?" Kevin asked.

Gary looked up from the grilled ham and cheese sandwich he was eating and nodded.

"I haven't seen you around for a while," Kevin said. "Everything okay?"

"I'm getting by, you know," Gary said, studying the triangular half of the sandwich in his hand before biting off a piece.

Of course, everyone on base knew what happened to J.J. and how Gary and some girl he brought home had discovered the body. As such, there were a lot of rumors regarding J.J.'s demise including one—which had gotten a lot of mileage—about how Gary had been screwing the girl he brought home right in front of old J.J. on the floor. If it hadn't been for the girl turning her head and looking into J.J.'s glassy dead eyes, they probably would have kept on screwing all through the night.

"That's cool," Kevin said, trying his best to keep the conversation going. "So I understand you started working in a new section."

"That's right. It's called the After Hours Support Unit," Gary said.

"What do you have to do?"

"I have to do everything in supply that is done during the day," Gary said, chewing on his sandwich. "I have to take orders on the phone, type up the paperwork, drive to the warehouse, pick up the item, and deliver it within a fixed period of time depending on its priority."

"Sounds like a lot of work."

"Yes and no. It depends on what's happening on base," Gary explained. "If it's a weekday, it's a sixteen-hour shift. If it's a weekend or holiday, it's a twenty-four-hour shift."

"A twenty-four shift, huh?"

"It's not as bad as it sounds," Gary said. "We have a cot in the office, so we can get a couple hours of sleep if we want. The neat thing is that the three of us who work in the section work one day and two days off."

"You supply weenies have it made," Kevin said laughing.

Gary smiled and drank some of his Coke. "What's really trippy is seeing all these women from downtown traipsing up and down the stairs all night turning a trick or two with all the TDY folks."

It was no secret on base that a group of Panamanian women made the rounds from barracks to barracks. The real goldmine for them was the two floors above the 24ᵗʰ Supply Headquarters, where most of the TDY personnel stayed. The LE's—Law Enforcement personnel—did their best to round them up and escort them off base to no avail.

"I bet it is," Kevin chuckled. At least once a week there was an incident where an airman got into it with one of the local women, either for refusing to pay or for having something stolen. Then he remembered the night he had gone to one of the rooms with Inés. He got quiet as he stared at graffiti someone had scribbled on the table.

"Always something, huh?" Gary said as he chewed on his sandwich.

"What's that?"

"Always something about the local girls making the rounds," Gary said. "There's this one gal, I call her "forty-fours" because of her big boobs. I swear she goes from one room to the next. Just the other night she accosted me outside the supply office and asked me when I got off. Well, just one look at those boobs of hers, I wanted to say, 'right now, darling.'"

Kevin chuckled again. He was happy to see Gary in better spirits. After Gary's roommate had been found dead, Flagg and Gordon let Kevin off of the hook while they did their investigation. Still, Kevin couldn't help but feel a little worried that Gary was still under investigation for his association with Frank and Santiago. He was also worried about how he was dealing with his roommate's death.

"Gary, if you ever—"

Some chatter on Kevin's Motorola radio interrupted his train of thought and informed him that he needed to get back to the flight line.

"What was that?"

"Nothing," Kevin said getting up from the table. "I just

hope to see you around more."

"Yeah, I think so. I'm much better now."

However, Gary wasn't much better. He never told the shrink his commander made him see that he couldn't sleep much, even after he pulled one of his sixteen or twenty-four shifts. He didn't talk about the nightmares he had been having, especially the one about having sex with a woman from one of the bars while J.J. stared at him, but J.J. didn't have any eyes—just two empty sockets. And the base chaplain wasn't much help either. The chaplain was pretty cool when he told Gary what he could talk about, but Gary just didn't feel comfortable talking to him. He did get along with his new roommate, Greg Martin, a staff sergeant who worked at POL but that was because the two hardly ever saw each other. Thanks to the shift Gary worked in his new job, he was getting off work when his roommate was going to work.

One night, during one of his two days off, he staggered into the Paris and nearly knocked over the girl he brought back to the barracks the night J.J. died. She took one look at him and started screaming.

He had to be escorted from the bar and told never to come back again.

* * *

A week before Christmas, Frank, Gary, and a few other guys went to the MAC terminal to say good-bye to Chris Shea, who was finally leaving after having been stationed three years at Howard.

"The place is just not going to be the same without you," Frank said, giving Chris a big bear hug.

"I think you guys will manage all right down here," Chris

said. "Just be sure not to catch the black clap or eat any bad monkey meat."

Frank and the others laughed and then took turns shaking Chris's hand.

"Hey, check out that staff sergeant over there," Chris said. "He worked in CBPO, didn't he?"

Frank, Ben and the others turned around and looked at a short, balding man in dress blues looking inside a black briefcase. Next to him was a Panamanian woman in a floral print dress which accentuated her curves in all the right places.

Frank nodded. "Is that Rosalie with him?"

"I'll be damned, she finally snagged herself a husband," Ben Kowalski, a tall, lean man with curly brown hair said. Ben, who worked in munitions, had only been at Howard for a month, but he had caught on fast. "Who would have thought?"

"I swear she's slept with half the men on base," Chris said grinning.

"You?" Frank asked.

Chris grinned. "Yeah, I took her to one of those push-button motels."

Push-button motels, similar to love hotels in Japan and South Korea, were a unique experience in Panama. They gave new meaning to the term, motor lodge. A push-button motel was a long narrow structure comprised of a series of garages and private rooms. A person drove into one of these garages and pushed a button to close the door. Then the couple got out of the car and entered a room with a bed. Everything was done discreetly; there was a slot for payments and a small compartment where drinks and food that had been ordered were placed. When it was all over, the *guests* picked up the phone and called the management who tallied up the bill, and paid through the slot. Then the couple got back into their car, pushed the button, and drove away.

"I borrowed the first shirt's car one day and told him I had some errands to run," Chris said laughing. "Boy was he pissed when I returned the car the next day."

"Why was he angry? Did you do it in the car?" Jimmy Baker asked. Baker, who had recently arrived at Howard, didn't waste any time getting on everyone's nerves with his endless supply of questions. "Is that why Sergeant Wild was angry? You didn't clean up after, right?"

Ben rolled his eyes. "You don't do it in the car, you moron. You get out and go into a room."

Baker's face turned red. "Why not just go to a regular hotel? Why go to all the trouble borrowing Sergeant Wild's car? Then he wouldn't have gotten angry. And why do they call it a push-button hotel if you have to get out of the car?"

Ben and the others laughed.

"Oh shit, she's seen us," Chris said, quickly looking the other way.

When Rosa saw Chris and the others, she waved to the dismay of her husband who struggled with their luggage.

"I wonder if the poor son-of-a-bitch knows," Ben said.

"Probably best that he doesn't," Frank said grinning.

"You're cruel, you know that?" Chris said.

"Jesus, will you look at that," Frank said, pointing to a couple guys from the civil engineering squadron. "Looks like a few other people heard she's leaving."

The three uniformed airmen who were seeing one of their friends off at the terminal had also spotted Rosa and were saying goodbye to her and her husband.

"If he didn't know before, he probably does now," Chris added.

"Aw, come on, you guys," Ben said smiling. "Leave her alone."

"What's the matter, Ben?" Chris asked. "You jealous that you never got any?"

Ben shot Chris a dirty look and then smiled at his friend. "More than you'll ever know."

Chris and Ben pretended to box with each other before Frank stopped them and pointed to Rosa, who continued to look in their direction. While the sergeant checked in their baggage, Rosa waved again to Chris and others before she walked over to where they were standing. Frank remembered her from the NCO Club; she still wore a lot of makeup—blue eye shadow and dark mascara—which might have been okay at night, but during the day it made her look a lot older and worse for the wear.

"Hello, Frank, Chris—" Rosa began, saying hello to the men she knew. "Are you leaving too, Chris?"

Chris nodded. "That's right, back to the Land of the Big BX."

Frank elbowed Chris in the ribs.

"How's Inés?" Rosa asked.

"She's fine," Frank said.

"Tell her I said hello and to take care of herself," Rosa said.

"I will," Frank replied.

An announcement was made that boarding would begin soon. Service members and dependents began to move to the exit.

"Well, boys, I guess this is it," Chris said, picking up his carry-on bag. "Take her easy, boys, and if she's easy, take her twice."

"That never gets old," Ben said laughing.

Rosa's husband, who had been watching with resignation as she said goodbye to more of her male friends, waved his arms to get his wife's attention. Frank noticed and hurried things along.

"Good luck to you, Rosa," Frank said.

Rosa smiled. "Goodbye, guys."

Frank, Chris, and the others watched Rosa walk back to her husband who looked as though he had just lost his best friend. Chris held a hand to his mouth and blew her a kiss which resulted in another elbow in the ribs from Frank.

"I'd hate to be in his boots," Chris said watching her sashay across the terminal to her red-faced waiting husband. "Then again—"

"You're disgusting, you know that?" Frank said smiling.

Chris grinned. "That's what she said."

Gary and Frank didn't say anything until everyone had left and they were outside.

"You were awful quiet in there," Frank said as they walked outside into the bright sunlight. "Are you okay?"

"I'm fine," Gary said. "Just a little tired."

Frank glanced at Gary with a concerned look. He hadn't seen or talked to Gary very much after J.J.'s death and hoped that his friend was holding up okay.

"Do you have any plans for New Year's Eve?" Frank asked, slipping on his aviator sunglasses.

Gary shook his head. "Nothing definite. I know a bunch of guys from the barracks are going downtown."

"Well, if you're not doing anything, Inés and I would love for you to stop by our apartment," Frank said. "We're having a few people over for dinner and drinks."

"Cool."

As they neared the road, that led back to the center of the base, Kevin and other security police drove by in one of the security vehicles. As soon as Gary noticed it was Kevin, he waved to his friend, but Kevin didn't wave back; instead he shot Frank a dirty look.

"Far out. I'll draw you a map," Frank said. "One more thing—"

"What's that?"

"Never mind. I'll tell you later."

CHAPTER TWENTY-THREE

THE APARTMENT WASN'T much, kind of high-end though for the squalor that made up this part of the neighborhood and its third world stratum. In one corner of the sparsely furnished room, a Christmas tree with colored miniature lights blinked on and off. Against one wall, a wooden table transformed into a makeshift bar was laden with various bottles of liquor. There was a poster of Sylvester Stallone as Rocky on one wall; on another wall was a black velvet painting of Roberto Duran. A few of the people at the party were associates of Guerra or Vega; the rest were friends of Frank and Santiago. Gary helped himself to a beer from the refrigerator and searched the room for Frank. Salsa music played from a stereo in the corner of the room; a few couples were dancing off to one side. Guerra was also there, but he didn't seem too happy to see Gary when he walked in. There was another man, Luis Soto, who sat off by himself. He was a friend of Guerra's and spent most of the night watching who was coming and going. One of the people that he kept an eye on, as he nursed a rum and Coke, was Gary. When he saw that

Gary was staring at him, Luis got up and walked into another room.

Gary walked outside and up a flight of stairs to the roof where most of the people had gathered. Strands of multi-colored Christmas lights strung above the roof swayed in a warm breeze that blew in off the ocean. The sweet aroma of Panama Red wafted across the roof courtesy of Santiago, who passed out joints to all his friends. Gary took a hit of one of those joints as it was passed and chased it with his beer. At the far end of the roof, he saw Frank talking to a few of his guests.

"My enlistment is up next year and I'm thinking of getting out," Frank said. "Inés and I have enough stashed away that we might open up ourselves a little bar."

"That's cool," one of Frank's friends said. "I can see you owning a bar."

"Just make sure you don't drink up all your profits," one of the guests said laughing.

As soon as Frank saw Gary standing off to the side, he excused himself from the people he was talking to and walked over to Gary. "Glad to see you could make it."

Gary took a drink of his beer and smiled. He looked at all the people gathered on the roof. "It's a great party."

They moved to the edge of the building away from the crowd. In the distance, they could see the twinkling lights of boats in Panama Bay and beyond a large container ship that had transited the canal.

"Remember last Christmas?" Frank asked, sticking a cigarette in his mouth. "And how we all piled into the back of Mark's dune buggy?"

Gary smiled. "And we were all singing 'Jingle Bells' at the top of our lungs as we crossed the Thatcher Ferry Bridge?"

"Jingle bells, shotgun shells, rabbits all the way. Oh, what fun it is to ride in a one-horse Chevrolet," Frank said, singing their version of the traditional holiday song. "How could I forget that? Good times, indeed."

"Some things are just not meant to last, I guess," Gary said sadly.

"Cheer up, buddy. Next year is going to be a great year for us."

Gary nodded and thought about what his friend had said. His life had changed a lot in the past year. He wasn't the same naïve kid he was a little over a year ago when he stepped off the Freedom Bird, but then there was still a part of him that was that same kid.

"I have some good news to share with you," Frank said.

"What's that?"

"Inés and I have decided to get married."

"That's great, Frank," Gary said, putting an arm around Frank and giving him a hug. "Have you set a date yet?"

Frank shook his head. "Not yet. But I would like you to be the best man."

"I'd be honored."

"Here's to good times, my friend," Frank said raising his glass. "May the new year bring us peace, prosperity, and happiness."

"I'll drink to that," Gary said, raising his bottle of beer. "Not exactly champagne, but it will have to do."

Clusters of firecrackers exploded somewhere on the street below punctuating the festivities. Downstairs, the familiar strains of "Hotel California" filtered up to the roof top. Soon a chorus of voices from the party downstairs was singing along with the Eagles.

Frank smiled. "We're all going to the Paradiso Hotel later to ring in the new year in style. You should join us."

Gary thought about it, but he didn't feel right about tagging along. He didn't like the way Guerra or one of Guerra's friends had been looking at him all night.

"Nah, I think I'll pass," Gary said. "I promised a few people from the barracks that I'd meet them at the Ovalo."

Frank nodded. The two of them were silent for a few minutes as they listened to the end of "Hotel California" before they went back downstairs to the party.

* * *

The Paradiso Hotel was one of the more modern buildings in El Chorrillo, but it was more famous for its tenth-floor discotheque than its rooms or restaurant.

"This is only going to take a couple of minutes," Vega said to one of his bodyguards in the elevator on the way up to the tenth floor.

Vega first stopped at a table where three men and their wives were sitting. Vega wished them all a Happy New Year before he continued to work his way through the labyrinth of tables, stopping at a few tables to extend more holiday greetings. His goal was a table at the far end of the room near the dance floor.

"Happy New Year!" Alejandro said as he reached the table where Frank and Inés were sitting along with Gustavo, Guerra, and their wives. "I see everyone is here this evening. *Bueno*. I hope everyone is having a good time."

"*Si, Alejandro*," Guerra said, taking it upon himself to be the spokesman for the table. "*Gracias por el champán.*"

"*De nada*," Vega said, smiling warmly. "And there's much more where that came from."

Guerra smiled. Thanks to Frank's recent "package" to the States, it was going to be a *very* happy new year. He poured more champagne for everyone at the table

Vega turned to Frank. "Frank, could I have a word with

you?"

Frank nodded and got up from the table and followed Vega to the rear of the room to a door that opened to an outdoor balcony. Vega's bodyguard pushed open the door and surprised a couple who were making out on the balcony. The man had his hand up under the woman's dress, and judging from her soft moans, had already found the perfect way to satisfy her. She opened her eyes briefly and as soon as she saw Vega, she let out a shriek and quickly removed her boyfriend's hand from under her dress. Vega, his bodyguard, and Frank laughed as the man—seeing who had stepped onto the balcony—apologized before he ushered his embarrassed girlfriend back inside the disco.

"Glad to see some people are enjoying themselves this evening," Vega said smiling. He took out a gold-plated cigarette case and removed a cigarette. He lit the cigarette and slowly exhaled before he turned to Frank with a concerned look on his face. "*¿Hay algo que te molesta?* You don't seem to be too happy this evening, Frank."

"I'm fine, Alejandro," Frank said.

"Inés treating you well?"

Frank nodded. "She loved the diamond bracelet. That was very thoughtful."

"A woman of her beauty deserves only the best," Vega said. "Am I treating you well?"

"Of course you are."

"*Bueno.* Then if I were to ask you whether or not people have been poking their noses where they shouldn't be, this wouldn't be something that would be of concern to you, *sí*?"

"No, of course not."

I'm glad to hear that, Frank because sometimes what might appear to be one thing to one person, can be something entirely different to another person."

"Yes, that's true."

"Take for instance this investigation into the death of that poor airman who died of a drug overdose. If someone is not too careful, with what they say or not say, a lot of people could find themselves in trouble. And we certainly wouldn't like that, would we?"

Frank pretended not to be alarmed, but he had a feeling that Vega was referring to Gary. "No, we wouldn't, Alejandro."

"He's not going to be a problem, is he?"

"No, he isn't."

Vega looked at Frank closely and nodded. "*Bueno.* Then we have nothing to worry about. Come, my friend, I've taken you away from that lovely woman of yours too long this evening. Have you set a date yet?"

"Not yet."

"By the way, you haven't been to the Miraflores Locks recently, have you?" Vega asked matter-of-factly.

"No, not recently." Frank flinched slightly but did a good job of hiding his surprise. "Why do you ask?"

"Someone said they thought they might have seen you there," Vega said gazing at Frank. "Must have been someone else."

"Yeah, must have been someone else," Frank said.

"Come, my friend, the celebration awaits us," Vega said, taking Frank by the arm and walking back inside.

If Vega had been trying to catch Frank in a lie, he couldn't have made it more obvious by asking Frank if he had been to Miraflores Locks recently. However, it had been almost a month since he had met Buck there. As soon as he saw Inés, he smiled and forgot about it for now.

When they reached the table, Vega motioned to his bodyguards that he wanted to go. Without being too obvious, the bodyguards began to move toward the elevator.

"*Feliz año nuevo otra vez, mis amigos,*" Vega said.

"Happy new year," everyone at the table said in unison.

Frank and Vega exchanged glances before Vega started for the elevator. It wasn't a casual parting glance; it was more like one that said, "You and I have some important matters to discuss." Inés put her arm around Frank and kissed him on the cheek.

"*Te amo con todo mi corazón,*" Inés whispered into Frank's ear.

Her hot wet breath made Frank's skin tingle. He forgot all about Vega, Buck, and Gary. Tonight it was all about Inés.

"*Vamos a casarnos pronto,*" Frank said.

Inés's eyes widened and lit up, the way they always did when they made love. She kissed and hugged him again. "Really?"

Frank nodded. He couldn't wait for the new year to begin.

After he had left Frank's apartment, Gary walked up one of the narrow winding streets, which characterized this section of El Chorrillo. The streets and sidewalks were crowded with revelers singing, laughing, and yelling. A cluster of fireworks exploded not far from where Gary was walking, which made him jump. When he realized what the sound was, he smiled sheepishly, hoping that no one had noticed him.

One person did notice him. When Gary left Frank's apartment, one of the guests, Luis Soto also left shortly after Gary did and had been following him. His orders were simple: he was to make sure Gary didn't get back to base.

Gary walked along the winding street and passed the pharmacy on his right where he and others often stopped to buy their night's supply of Captagon. Farther up the street, Gary passed the tattoo parlor where one of his buddies in the squadron, Jerry Miller, got a tattoo last New Year's Eve. They all celebrated later that night at the Foxhole Bar. Gary still had the Polaroid photo of that night in a picture frame on his desk. At the end of the street, around the corner from the Buffalo Bar, there was a lot of shouting and yelling. A crowd had gathered around two soldiers from Fort Clayton fighting over a woman from the Paris; an MP and SP on town patrol were in the process of breaking up the fight. Luis lost Gary momentarily in the crowd but soon saw him emerge across the street in front of the Ovalo.

Gary walked into the first entrance and pushed his way through the crowd. He didn't recognize anyone in the larger of the two rooms and continued to the smaller room. There, he recognized a few people from CAMS including Jack, Ben, John "Johnny Mac" McDaniels, and Bill Manley. In another corner, he saw Kevin, John Bradshaw, and some of their security police buddies. They were seated with a half-dozen girls, who wore brightly colored New Year's hats, around three tables pushed together underneath the ceiling painting of the two women performing cunnilingus.

"Gary!" Kevin yelled above Steve Miller's "Jet Airliner" blaring from the jukebox. Kevin jumped up from his seat, ran over to his friend and put an arm around his shoulder. "Glad to see you could make it."

Gary smiled. "Just like old times, huh, Kevin?"

"It's good to see you out," Kevin said. "I was worried about you."

"Yeah, it's good to see you too, buddy," Gary said. "The old Gary is back."

Kevin grabbed Gary's right arm and pulled him through the crowd to the table. "Hey look, everybody! Look who decided to join the party!"

"Hey, Gary!" John yelled. "Long time no see."

"Gary, John, and I came down on the plane together from Charleston over a year ago," Kevin explained as he introduced Gary to some of the new guys at the table.

"If you don't mind, Kevin, I'm going to sit with some of my friends from the barracks," Gary said, pointing to the tables where Ben, Jack, and the others were sitting."

"I'll catch up with you later, bro," Kevin said.

Gary moved across the room and joined his friends from the barracks. As soon as he sat down, he had a drink in his hand, courtesy of Jack. Ben, who was working on some female companionship for the night, looked around for any unattached women for Gary.

"How are you doing these days, kid?" Jack asked sliding up a chair alongside Gary and putting his arm around his shoulder.

"I'm much better," Gary said.

"Don't forget if you ever need to talk, you know where you can find me," Jack said with a concerned look on his face. "There are a lot of guys who feel the same way that I do."

"Thanks, Jack. I appreciate that," Gary said.

"*Hola, amiga!*" Ben said, grabbing a woman's thin brown arm as she walked past the table. He twirled her past Jack and the woman he was with and plopped her down on Gary's lap.

The woman, with thick painted lips and shoulder-length hair, giggled and looked up at Gary with large brown eyes. "You and me, fuckee, fuckee suckee, suckee?"

Jack, Ben, and the others at the table laughed.

"That's right, darling, everyone fuckee, fuckee and suckee, suckee," Ben said laughing. "It's the new year!"

Gary looked across the room at Kevin and smiled. He missed hanging out with his friends the way he did a year ago. He was through with Frank, Santiago, Roy—all of them. Ever since J.J. died, he just wanted to get back to doing stuff with his friends like he did when he first arrived and started thinking about life after Panama. In a couple of months, he would find out where his next duty assignment was going to be. Everyone told him that he would most likely get his first choice of assignment because he had not volunteered to come to Panama. He had put in for bases in California, hoping that when he got out in two years he could go to film school.

Kevin raised his Cerveza Panama bottle and tilted it toward Gary as if to salute their friendship. Gary smiled and returned the salute with his drink as the girl he was sitting with planted a kiss on his cheek leaving a cherry red lipstick mark. A few of the guys at the table started singing the Air Force song, which brought a chorus of jeers from a dozen paratroopers from Kobbe, who had commandeered the remaining tables in this part of the bar.

Standing at the bar, with his back toward the table where Gary and his friends were sitting, Luis stared at Gary's reflection in the mirror behind the bar. He ordered another drink and waited.

CHAPTER TWENTY-FOUR

KEVIN HEARD ABOUT Gary's death five days later during the day shift's roll call.

"The body of an airman missing since New Year's Day was discovered in a drainage ditch on the outskirts of Panama City," the duty commander said. "The OSI is working the case along with Panamanian authorities. We've been asked to assist with the ongoing investigation. The name of the airman is Gary Lee Taylor, who was assigned to the 24th Supply Squadron."

Kevin, who hadn't been listening to the commander's brief, bolted upright in the chair as soon as Gary's name was mentioned. He felt his stomach twist in a knot and the Spanish omelet, greasy bacon, and chipped beef on toast doing somersaults in his stomach. He ran for the door and just made it to the latrine just in time.

There were no leads in the case. The last anyone saw of Gary was when he left the Ovalo with a girl. Because of Gary's schedule, it was two days later when he didn't report for work before someone realized that he was missing. Three more days would pass before the Panamanian authorities got around to notifying SOUTHCOM that the badly decomposed body of an American GI had been found face down in a drainage ditch. His throat had been slit.

* * *

Kevin found Frank seated outside a small club in El Chorrillo, underneath a canvas awning. Frank didn't look too well; it looked as though he had been on a three-day drunk. Most of the base had been on a skeleton crew for the holidays and it looked as if Frank had spent his week crawled up inside a bottle. In front of Frank was a half-empty bottle of Ron Cortez; next to it were a metal bucket with a few ice cubes and a bottle of Coke.

"Hello, Rooney," Frank said, looking up at Kevin standing over the table.

"I suppose you heard about Gary, haven't you?"

Frank nodded, pouring himself another drink. He stared at Kevin with tired, bloodshot eyes. He motioned to Kevin to sit down and join him for a drink, but Kevin refused.

"You wouldn't happen to know anything about his death, would you?" Kevin asked.

"Leave me alone, Rooney," Frank muttered as he poured himself another drink. He missed the glass with the rum, spilling most of it on his hand. He licked the rum from the back of his hand and dropped in two half-melted ice cubes into the glass. "If you don't mind I would like to drink in peace."

Because of his friendship with Gary as well as J.J., Frank was a person of interest during the investigation into Gary's death; Kerr had already brought him in for questioning. He reported to work as usual, but everyone who knew Frank and Gary figured it was only a matter of time before the OSI brought him in. Kevin balled his hands into fists. He had a feeling that Frank knew more about Gary's death.

"I ought to fucking turn you in, you son-of-a-bitch," Kevin said, grabbing Frank by the throat.

"A lot of good that would do you," Frank said. "The OSI has already got my number."

Kevin released his grip and pushed Frank down onto the seat. In the process, he banged the table, sending the bottle of rum and glass crashing to the ground.

"I'm not finished with you yet, Costello."

Frank leaned over and tried to pick up what was left of the rum bottle and fell off the chair. He tried to stand up, using the chair to support himself but fell back down, cutting his hand with a broken piece of glass.

"If I were you I would talk to Buck Smith. However, I don't think he's going to be much help to you," Frank mumbled. He looked down at his hand and wiped off the blood. "He would never have let this happen."

"Who?"

"Buck Smith," Frank said, looking up at Kevin. "You can find him under the Central Intelligence Agency in the phone book."

Frank lowered his head and mumbled something about being as good as dead.

* * *

After Kevin had left Frank, he went back to his barracks and calmed himself as best he could with a bottle of Jack Daniels and some Kansas. He stretched out on a bean bag chair, closed his eyes and felt the warm whiskey coursing through his body as he listened to "Carry on my Wayward Son". Of all the songs on the album, this one resonated the most strongly for him The song was recently featured in the movie, *Heroes* that he had seen with Gary at the Quarry Heights base theater. Although the movie wasn't that big of a hit, both he and Gary liked it a lot.

"I'm going to make movies like this one day," Gary had said as they walked down the road from Quarry Heights to Fourth of July Avenue after the movie let out. "Maybe not as cheesy, but movies that will make a person feel good inside."

"I'm sure you will," Kevin said, smiling. "Just don't forget about all us little people once you make it big."

Gary's eyes had twinkled, the way they always did when he was amused about something before he flashed that toothy grin of his. "You got it, bro."

Kevin was startled out of his reverie by a knock on the door. Instead of getting up to see who it was, he took another drink, settled back on the bean bag chair and closed his eyes again.

There was another knock at the door; this time louder.

He slowly pulled himself out of the beanbag chair and stumbled across the room to the door. When he opened it, he was startled to see Inés standing in front of the door. She was dripping wet. Through one of the large windows, Kevin could see that it was raining very hard.

"How dare you accuse Frank of having something to do with Gary's death," she screamed, her eyes blazing and lips trembling. "He thought the world of him."

"Inés, please—"

"Go to hell, Kevin!"

Down the hallway, a door slammed. Gary, fearful that someone would notice and hear the scene she was making, pulled her into his room and shut the door.

"Here, dry yourself off," Kevin said, grabbing a towel hanging on a metal towel rod on the door and handing it to

Inés.

Inés had a wild look in her eyes as she took the towel from Kevin and dried her face and hair. Despite being wet, he could smell a hint of her perfume that he liked so much.

"Is it true?"

"Is what true?"

She tossed the towel onto a chair. "You turned Frank in, didn't you?"

"I did no such thing," Kevin said, "but I should have."

"What are you saying?"

"Frank's responsible for Gary's death, I'm almost sure of that," Kevin said staring at Inés. "Frank's mixed up with some drug smuggler and that's why Gary is dead. Frank or Gary must have double-crossed him."

Inés's eyes widened with fear. Frank didn't tell her much about what he did with Vega but she was close to Guerra and it was no secret what Guerra did when he wasn't at his store. She also knew that Guerra and Vega were close and sometimes did business together. Whatever suspicions she had about either man, she kept them to herself. She clutched the necklace around her neck, the one Vega had given her and trembled at the thought that Frank was somehow in trouble.

"I have no idea what you're talking about," she said, trying to hide her fear. "Frank would never do anything like that. He might be a lot of things that you despise, but he would never let his friends down or put them in harm's way."

"You have no idea who he is, Inés," Kevin said.

"That's enough, Kevin."

"Inés, I was told to spy on him to see what I could find out about his relationship with Vega. I was supposed to find out what I could from Gary, but I couldn't. Maybe if I had, Gary would still be alive."

Inés removed her hand from the necklace. "What do you

mean, 'spy' on Frank?"

"Enough of this, 'I don't know what my husband is up to' act, Inés," Kevin said. "Are you that blind?"

"Kevin, *le dije que era suficiente.*"

"I should have known better than to get involved with you," Kevin said, his face red with anger as he glared at Inés. On top of Gary's death and Frank's possible involvement, the combination of the whiskey and Inés coming here touched off a powder keg. "You were no better than your friend, Rosa, trying to fuck as many men as you could to find the perfect husband. I hope you're happy now."

Inés slapped Kevin on the side of the face. "You bastard! How dare you say that? I cared about you, but you were too immature and jealous if another man even looked at me."

Kevin's face still stung where she slapped him. She looked at him with her big dark eyes. Her lips were trembling. She raised her hand to slap him again, but Kevin caught it this time and held on tightly. She tried to free her hand, but Kevin held onto it as he did with the other one. They gazed into each other's eyes and Kevin slowly released his grip. When his lips met hers, she couldn't stop the trembling that shimmered and quivered through her body. She did not fight him; instead she immediately succumbed to her primal desire to be one with him again. She wrapped her arms around him as the intensity of his kisses increased hoping that he would not stop. She already felt the wetness seeping through her panties and her hips tightening in anticipation. Then she felt his hand inside her panties, his soft fingertips slowly moving lower as he slipped off her panties with his other hand. She softly groaned when he slid a finger into her wetness, then another; she arched her back and whimpered in his mouth as he rubbed her sensitive bud with his two fingers.

Inés felt a tingle course through her body as Kevin's

fingers slid deeper inside of her. She gazed into Kevin's wild eyes as he removed his fingers from inside of her; she tasted her wetness on his fingers. Her eyes widened as she felt his hands behind her knees and felt her body being lifted off the floor and onto a wooden desk. Tears streamed down her face as she felt him enter her. Kevin hugged her against his chest and kissed her neck and ears. Frank had always been rough with her when it came to having sex, which she had come to enjoy, but she had never forgotten how gentle it had been the times she made love with Kevin. But this time it was different and she wanted more. He felt her body tighten as his thrusts went deeper and harder. He had never made love like this to her. It was hard and rough and she didn't want it to stop.

Both wanted to exorcise the guilt from their souls and numb the pain. There was no love; only unabated desire.

"Your roommate," she said, gasping for breath. "Will he—"

Kevin shook his head as he grabbed her from behind and lifted her up from the desk. He pushed her against the cool wall of the room and lifted up her ass. She threw her head back and grabbed her breasts as Kevin's thrusts increased. She pinched her nipples and wildly kissed his neck. She wanted him badly, wanted him deep inside of her. With each painful thrust, she felt her body lift off the wall. She wrapped her legs around him and held onto his back, her long fingernails digging into his shirt and skin.

"Hurry, Kevin," she finally said.

She felt her inner muscles quiver and her body tremble with anticipation as he thrust harder and faster until they both finally climaxed and collapsed on the floor.

After Inés had called her father to check on her child, they made love again, this time in bed. Afterward, they lay next to each other and listened to the rain falling outside.

"We're getting married, Kevin," Inés said after a few minutes.

Kevin didn't say anything as he turned and stared at the ceiling.

"I know you hate Frank for what he did, but he's been a good man. He thinks the world of Esmeralda," she said. "I know all about the drugs and what he's been doing, but he says that he's going to stop all of that and I believe him. He just wants to save up enough for us and then he'll get out of this once and for all."

Kevin turned and looked into her face. "I think it's too late for that, Inés. Frank is mixed up with the wrong crowd. It's only a matter of time before he gets caught."

"You're not going to—"

Kevin shook his head.

Inés pulled her arm free and sat up in bed. She drew in her legs and stared straight ahead. "I'm sorry about your friend, Kevin, and I'm sorry about us," she said, blinking back the tears. "I really did like you. *Simplemente no estaba destinado a ser.*"

Kevin thought about what Inés had said. *It was just not meant to be.* "I'm sorry too, Inés."

* * *

After Frank had recovered from his three-day drunk, he was ready to take on Vega. He burst into Vega's office. Vega was seated behind his desk with a naked woman on his lap.

"Is it true?" Frank asked pointing a finger at Vega.

"Sit down, Frank," Vega said in a calm voice, as he pushed the woman off his lap. He gently slapped her on the ass as she grabbed her clothes and scurried out of the room. "Can I get you something to drink?"

"Fuck you," Frank said.

One of Vega's bodyguards started to move out from behind the desk, but Vega held him back with his arm.

"Get him some water," Vega said.

"The killer was at my goddamn party, Alejandro. He was in my house and followed my friend and then killed him," Frank said. His eyes narrowed and nostrils flared as he continued to stare at Vega. "When we talked at the Paradiso Discotheque that night, you assured me that nothing would happen to Gary."

"A man doesn't get to where I am at without being cautious, Frank. You of all people should be aware of that. There are always certain risks that one takes in a business proposition, and those risks are what make our business a dangerous one. Your friend got caught in the middle, and though his untimely death was a tragic one, there was nothing I could do to stop what had already been put into motion."

Frank continued to glare at Vega, the veins in his neck tightening as he clenched his teeth.

"You haven't accused me yet, Frank. Why is that?" Vega asked looking up at Frank. "Is it because you're not sure, or because you're worried that you could be next?"

Luis Soto was standing near the desk. He leaned over and whispered something to Vega, who frowned when he learned what had happened. Vega looked up at Soto and gave him a dirty look before he turned his attention back to Frank. When Frank took a few steps toward Vega's desk, one of his bodyguards reached for his weapon, but Vega waved him off.

"Did you or didn't you order someone to kill Gary?"

Vega shook his head. "It wasn't me, Frank."

"We're through, Alejandro."

"I wouldn't be so sure about that, Frank," Vega said, taking out a Cuban cigar from a wooden box on top of his desk. "We're through when I say we're through."

Frank eyed the two bodyguards who had their hands on their weapons. He knew better than to tempt his luck any further and slowly backed away from Vega's desk.

"Go home, Frank," Vega said. "I understand you haven't been home for a couple of days. You need to take care of that little woman of yours. When you sober up, we'll talk again."

*   *   *

Something that Costello said about Gary's death bothered Kevin. *Smith wouldn't have let it happen.* Kevin didn't know anyone named Smith, but there was one person who might know.

"Major, I've got a question about Taylor's murder," Kevin told his commander.

Kevin's commander looked up at Kevin standing in front of his desk. "What is it, Rooney?"

"There was this guy that Gary knew or maybe it was the other way around," Kevin said. "His name was Smith. Costello said that if we want to find out what happened to Taylor we should talk to this Smith guy."

Major Fletcher looked uneasy and shuffled some papers on his desk. The base commander was furious—the deaths of two airmen in a span of two months and an ongoing OSI investigation. However, that was just the tip of the iceberg.

"Rooney, would you please shut the door?"

Kevin shut the door and returned to Fletcher's desk. His commander motioned for Kevin to pull up a chair and sit down.

"What the hell were you doing talking to Costello?"

Fletcher was a fair and amiable person; ever since Flagg and Gordon tried to recruit Rooney for some of their dirty work, Fletcher had a soft spot for Rooney. However, right now his commander's tone didn't sound amiable.

"I just wanted to see what he knew."

"You stay away from Costello."

"Sir, I only—"

"You stay away from Costello. You got that, Airman?"

"But, Sir—"

Fletcher cut Kevin off. He felt sorry for Rooney, but his hands were tied. The OSI and DEA had taken over the case, and according to Gordon, Costello was off-limits. "It's best you drop this, Rooney. No good will come from this. As tragic as your friend's death was, you and I both know he was mixed up with the wrong people."

"What about this man, Smith? I bet if we talked to him we—"

"Airman, maybe you didn't hear me. This case is closed."

"Yes, Sir."

Kevin wanted to say something else but knew better. It made him all the more curious about Smith, however. He turned and started for the door when his commander stopped him.

"Rooney?"

"Yes, Sir?"

"Things are not always what they seem. Remember that."

CHAPTER TWENTY-FIVE

AFTER NEARLY SIX months of negotiations—from February 15 to August 10, 1977—Panama and the United States hammered out two new canal treaties that would eventually turn the canal and its operations over to Panama. It would take almost another year—the following April—until the U.S. Senate finally got around to ratifying the second, and most important treaty. The Panama Canal Treaty provided that on December 31, 1999, Panama would assume full control of the canal, as well as its defense.

The night before the Senate voted on The Treaty Concerning the Permanent Neutrality and Operation of the Canal, there was an uneasy peace across the isthmus. Most Zonians were forlorn and apprehensive as their fate was being decided in Washington, beyond their control. They knew their days in paradise were numbered if the treaties were ratified. There was genuine concern Panamanians might take to the streets again like they did in 1964 or random bombings like the ones in 1976 if the Permanent Neutrality Treaty wasn't passed. There were also rumors that Torrijos threatened to sabotage the canal. U.S. Secretary of State Cyrus Vance feared that America's relations with Panama would be shattered, the country's standing in Latin America damaged immeasurably, and the security of the canal itself placed in jeopardy. Buck, who had already made a few phone calls, had a hunch it was going to be close.

On the third floor of Building 714, at Howard Air Force Base, a few guys from CAMS and supply were hanging out in Hector Garcia and Bill Manley's room, going through a case of Heineken and also feeling a little uneasy.

"This time tomorrow, boys, we could be in for some fireworks. And I'm not talking about the kind we shoot off on the Fourth," Bill said, grabbing another beer from the refrigerator and popping it open. Bill had been with the 101st in Vietnam, got out and drove a taxi in D.C. before he decided to go back into the military. Tall and wiry, with a hot temper, he was constantly in trouble and fought with most everyone, but he was a lot of fun to be with, so everyone tolerated him.

"They wouldn't try anything if they knew what was good for them," Vince Flanagan said. Vince had been at Howard less than a month, but just enough time to get on everyone's nerves in supply. Everything to him was a conspiracy.

Jack shook his head. He was one of the last of the old crew, one of the Panama and Howard old hats, who had recently extended for another year. He also didn't care much for the Heineken, opting instead for his usual drink, Jack and Coke. "You boys just have to hope that old Omar doesn't lob a hand grenade or some C-4 into one of the locks. That'll scare the folks in Washington."

Around the room they went, Bill, Hector, Vince, Jack, Ben—everyone voicing their concerns and opinions. They listened to The Who's "We Don't Get Fooled Again" followed by Barry McGuire's "Eve of Destruction" and Creedence

Clearwater Revival's "Have You Ever Seen the Rain?" The Vietnam vets in the room got quiet and reflective. Someone passed around a joint. No one feared a raid on this night.

Later in the night when the Heineken ran out, and all that remained was a six-pack of Pabst Blue Ribbon, most people retired to their rooms. Jack and Ben walked outside the room and stood in front of one of the large sliding glass windows that overlooked the parade field. The base was eerily quiet that night, as though everyone was doing the same thing at the same time.

"What do you reckon?" Ben asked, sticking a Marlboro in his mouth and looking out the window. "What do you think will happen if the treaty is not ratified?"

"I don't think there's anything to worry about," Jack said. "Those boys in Washington will do the right thing."

* * *

President Jimmy Carter came to Panama in June amid student demonstrations in Panama City and resentment from Zonians for having turned the Canal Zone and the canal over to Panama. A C-5 Galaxy transport landed at Howard and was quickly surrounded by secret service as the President's limousines and Marine One helicopters off-loaded. Kevin watched from the flight line as the secret service took care of everything. He joined some of his friends who went to Fort Clayton two days later to hear Carter speak after the ratification ceremony. It was the first time he'd ever seen a president up close though it was behind the roped-in area with everyone else hoping to get a closer glimpse of the President and the chance to shake his hand. His buddy John Bradshaw, whose family knew the President, had the best seat in the house. He was selected to be part of Carter's security detail.

There was a very large turnout with just as many service members as Zonians. A couple of Zonians made some special posters for the speech: "Carter: the Best President Panama Ever Had." Many Zonians were still furious over the treaty Carter had signed, even though there had been other treaty negotiations over the years. As one more progressive and informed Zonian put it, "Carter just completed the negotiations and took the heat for them." Ironically, the negotiations—ongoing since the Ford administration—had laid the groundwork prior to Carter's later and more famous negotiations. They were an important factor in the Ambassador's handling of the October 1976 bombing incidents. The ambassador used those negotiations as a carrot to get cooperation from Torrijos to downplay the events, for the sake of the negotiations.

When both treaties were finally ratified, the first one in March and the second one in April, most Zonians were depressed, dumbfounded, and angry. Many of them were in tears and felt abandoned by the United States. Some gathered with family to console each other as if there had been a devastating death in their family.

After the speech, Carter walked toward the crowd and walked the line shaking hands with those lucky enough to be in the front. Kevin and some of his buddies, who were standing close to the front, pushed their way forward to shake Carter's hand. He was now just a few yards away from them. Kevin was just about to reach out and shake the President's hand when someone tapped Kevin on the shoulder in an authoritative way. At first, he thought it was someone he knew, and as Carter slowly moved down the line where Kevin was standing, he held his ground. When the person tapped him on the shoulder a second time, Kevin turned around and was about to say, "What's your problem?" He came face-to-face with a color-coded pin on the left lapel of a dark suit jacket. He looked up at the stone-faced, six-foot-two secret service agent towering over him, who was scanning the crowd for potential problems and moved out of the way as the agent moved past him. By the time Kevin turned around, Carter had already moved down the line and was headed toward Marine One.

*   *   *

The weekend before Kevin DEROS'd back to the States, his friends decided to throw him a party outside the security police barracks. They got steaks from the commissary, the wives prepared baked beans and potato salad, and they bought up all the Heineken at the package store. Someone set up their stereo outside, and Jackson Browne's "Running on Empty" blasted from a pair of speakers.

Kevin and John Bradshaw were seated at a picnic table watching their buddy, Mark Hamilton, cook the steaks on a grill constructed from a fifty-gallon drum. They passed around a bottle of Jack Daniels and chased it with swigs of Heineken.

"I still can't believe they're sending your sorry ass to Minot, North Dakota," John said, grinning. "Talk about a choice duty assignment. You're going to love it there."

"Lucky me, huh?" Kevin said. "And a SAC base no less."

"You know how many seasons they have there, don't you?" John asked.

"Okay, I give up," Kevin said, grabbing a handful of potato chips from a plastic bowl. "How many?"

"Two. Cold and fucking cold," John laughed. He lucked out. He had orders to Warner-Robins. If he wanted to, he could go home on weekends.

Kevin looked at John and for a moment, felt sad. He thought about when they arrived in Panama with Gary a little over two years ago. Kevin remembered sitting in the terminal at Charleston AFB with him all night, waiting for their MAC flight to Howard the next morning. He had listened to Gary talk about how he was going to study filmmaking and go to Hollywood. Kevin had never known anyone so full of life and dreams. He still couldn't believe that Gary was dead.

"I thought we would all leave together," Kevin said.

"You're talking about Gary, aren't you?"

"Yeah."

"He was a good kid."

"He sure was."

Kevin and John were quiet for a few minutes as they drank their beer.

"Remember that time when we were at the striptease show at the NCO Club, and one of the strippers tossed her bra in the air," Kevin said. "And it landed in Gary's lap and he wouldn't give it back."

"And her old man, a chief master sergeant in CE was sitting across from us!" John said laughing. "Boy was he pissed. I thought for sure he was going to come over and hit Gary."

Kevin smiled. "Or that time when we saw him stumbling out of an apartment building, the one where the girls from The Foxhole took their customers? He was pulling his pants on, and nearly getting hit by a taxi. When we asked him what happened, he flashed that toothy smile of his and said he was trying to catch the last Canal Zone bus back to base."

"Good times, indeed."

"To Gary," Kevin said, raising his bottle and clinking it against John's bottle.

"To Gary," John replied.

Kevin slowly took a drink. He looked around at all the people who gathered for his farewell party. It was hard to believe that his tour had gone by as quickly as it did. Mark took a break from cooking and joined Kevin and John at the picnic table.

"Did you hear about Costello?" Mark asked.

Kevin shook his head. Ever since Gary's death, he had managed to avoid Costello on base. Kevin once saw Inés at the BX shoppette; as soon as she saw him, she hurried out. He knew that Costello and Inés had gotten married a few weeks back in the base chapel and that Costello had extended for another year. He thought that he had been able to forget them both and move on, but he guessed he hadn't. "What happened?"

"He got busted by the OSI."

"You're shittin' me," Kevin said.

"Uh-huh. Got him for smuggling drugs."

"No, shit."

"And they also arrested another airman, Gus Santiago."

Kevin recalled the time he was called into the First Sergeant's office after getting involved in a brawl downtown with Frank. That was when he first heard about Santiago and the drug ring he had on base. He had been asked to find out what he could about Costello. If only he had approached Gary liked he had been asked—

"Santiago squealed like a stuck pig," Mark said. "When the smoke clears from this, half the base will probably be looking at Article Fifteens."

"Damn."

There was poetic justice after all.

* * *

Although Buck had promised Frank that he wouldn't rain on his barbecue, the OSI had other plans. Unlike the past, when the security police raided the barracks, there was always someone in the barracks who knew something was going down and made all the necessary phone calls. Everyone used to joke that it was the Howard's version of the DEW Line—the Distant Early Warning system that was a system of radar stations in Canada and the Arctic Circle that were set up to detect Soviet bombers. As soon as someone learned that a raid was going down, someone would get on the phone and warn the other barracks. This time the OSI made sure that none of the single junior enlisted men knew what was coming down. This raid was conducted by E-6 personnel and above from other squadrons on base and only certain individuals were being targeted.

Santiago went down and when he started singing he brought the heat down on most of the drug ring, including Mike who immediately fingered Frank, who had no idea what happened until he came to work the next day and was immediately detained at the main gate. After spending the rest of the day in a detention cell, someone up the chain of command called in a few favors and Frank was spared jail time for the second time in his life. However, he was given an Other Than Honorable Discharge. It could have been worse for Frank. He was looking at serious prison time.

Flagg was there, but he wasn't looking too happy as Frank walked out with Inés and her daughter. Santiago got twenty years for dealing drugs; Mike got ten years and a Bad Conduct Discharge.

"You are one lucky son-of-a-bitch, Costello," Flagg said as Frank walked past him. "You must know some pretty important people in some high places to let you walk out of here without having to serve any time."

Frank, on the other hand, didn't think he was so lucky.

CHAPTER TWENTY-SIX

ALEJANDRO HAD ONLY killed one person in his career, though he had ordered the deaths of three others, but that didn't make what he had to do any easier. Sitting at his desk in his office, he sipped a *Seco con vaca* and stared at the man slumped in the chair in front of the desk. The man—hands and feet tied to the chair—had been sitting in this same slumped position with his head hanging to the side, for nearly thirty minutes. Unable to speak, (his mouth had been taped shut with a strip of gray duct tape) the man's labored, shallow breathing through his nose sounded like air slowly being released from a tire. His blue shirt was tattered and splattered with blood. From a cut on his lip, blood dripped onto the floor forming a small puddle.

Guerra and one of Vega's bodyguards, Arturo, found the man in a small bar in Colón and brought him to the hotel in Panama City. They took turns beating him for an hour, trying to extract what information they could before they brought him upstairs to Vega's office.

"You, my friend, were very, very stupid," Vega said,

slowly getting up from his chair and moving to the front of his desk. "Did you think I wouldn't find out? Do you realize how embarrassing this is for me and how many people I have to pay off to make this go away? People talk *mi amigo*. People talk and people get hurt."

The man tried to lift his head to no avail. After the beating by Guerra and Arturo, the man had little strength left. He had already given up trying to free his hands from the nylon cord, which had them tied to the chair's wooden armrests. He was already resigned to the fact that he wasn't going to walk out of here alive.

"Diego, what would you do if you were me?" Vega asked, turning to his friend standing next to the desk.

Guerra looked at his boss and grinned. "If I were you, I would make sure that he never does what he did again."

"See, even Diego thinks that I should kill you," Vega said, sitting on the edge of his desk and staring at the man in front of him. "But then I think about your poor wife and family."

Vega sipped more of his drink and leaned forward on the desk. "Did I ever tell you that I was an orphan? My father was a mean drunk and beat my mother. You know the kind of man I'm talking about—the kind that uses his fists to settle an argument or make a point. Almost every day when he came home he beat my mother. Sometimes it was over the smallest, simplest of things. Maybe he didn't like coming home to a messy apartment or he didn't like what my mother had prepared for dinner. Maybe he didn't like the way my mother looked at him when she smelled the alcohol on his breath. One day, my mother had too much. She took a butcher knife from the kitchen and slit his throat while he slept. The police came and arrested her two days later. I was just a child of seven and ended up living on the streets until one day, this man saw me picking through garbage in the back of his hotel. He felt sorry for me and brought me inside. He and his wife raised me and when the time came, and he died, all of this became mine. And I don't intend to lose what I've worked so hard to hold on to. If someone gets in my way, I have no choice but to set an example. You do understand that, don't you? You do understand my position. It would be bad for business—not to mention my reputation."

Vega reached down and ripped off the strip of duct tape from the man's mouth. The man shrieked with pain. "Now I would like to ask you one more time, what did you tell them?"

The man opened his mouth as if he wanted to speak, but the words got lost in a gurgling, gasping sound as he fought hard to breathe. With his larynx crushed and his lungs filling up with blood and fluid, he couldn't speak even if he wanted.

"We dined together. We drank together. I invited you to my home. I went to your daughter's baptism. And this is how you repay me. If you were me, you would be doing the same thing."

The man, sensing what Vega was about to do, used what little strength he had left to free his hands, but the nylon cord was tied too tight and only dug into his wrists. Vega turned around to grab a knife that he had on the desk. He got up from his desk and slowly walked around to the back of the chair.

"This is nothing personal my friend, "Vega said, staring into the man's bloodshot, tired eyes, "but considering the damage you caused to my reputation, you leave me no other choice."

And then Vega slit Luis Soto's throat.

"What should we do about Costello?" Diego asked after he and Arturo had disposed of the body.

Vega sat back in his chair and put his hands behind his head. Soto was collateral damage for killing the airman;

Costello was a different story. Although he was still smarting over having lost nearly twenty-five thousand dollars, it could have been worse. Neither Santiago nor Frank had given him up. There would be ways that Frank could work off the money he had lost when the OSI and police busted him. Frank had a wife and two kids to think about. Men in that kind of situation would do almost anything to extricate themselves from it.

"Let's just sit tight for a while," Vega said leaning forward. He picked up a pair of metal tongs and dropped some ice cubes into a tall glass. He then filled the glass with a third of Seco and topped it off with some fresh milk. "Remember that bar TJ's?"

Diego nodded.

"We might have some use for Frank there now that Santiago is no longer with us."

"Can he be trusted?"

Vega sipped his drink and smacked his lips. "If not, he can always join Luis."

CHAPTER TWENTY-SEVEN

THE DEHAVILLAND TWIN Otter aircraft buffeted some strong headwinds as it started to make its descent. The pilot did his best to keep the plane under control as it suddenly began to buffet wildly as it flew through a thunderstorm squall. The passengers in the back tightened their seatbelts and gripped the armrests. One of the passengers, Omar Torrijos, felt as though he was going to throw up.

The plane shook wildly as it bounced around in the sky. The airfield was not that far away. *Just a few more minutes.* Torrijos closed his eyes and settled back into the seat as the plane bounced up again. *Soon we will be on the ground.* A peal of thunder boomed close to the plane and a flash of white light exploded.

In a fateful twist of irony, the man who had brought the most change to Panama would not live long enough to enjoy the benefits of having secured one of the most important political accomplishments in his country's history. His aircraft slammed into the side of a mountain, and he was killed instantly. Torrijos, who once said that he didn't want to go into history, but wanted to go into the Canal Zone, got to do both.

When Buck learned of Torrijos's death, he was meeting with one of his military counterparts at Quarry Heights. As a precaution, bases were put on alert. There were some who immediately pointed fingers at the CIA for having something to do with Torrijos's death. Truth be known, the circumstances surrounding the airplane crash *were* duplicitous, considering the fact it took two days to report the accident. Some said it might have been Torrijos's sympathy and support for the Sandinistas; others said that he could no longer be trusted as a key ally in Central America.

Then there were those who pointed fingers at Torrijos's number two man.

Buck was one of the few people who realized that Noriega's rise had nothing to do with the Agency's complicity, rather, it simply happened during a period when the CIA was going through some difficult times. Although Noriega had been in bed with the CIA since the sixties, he was more a product of a paradigm shift than any collusion with the Agency. He was a product of the times. Nonetheless, the Agency had come to depend upon Noriega for what he could bring to the table. He was more than a necessary evil. He was a major player in Central America. Only those who had been closely following Noriega since the seventies knew about the drugs and the money laundering and the Agency wanted to make sure that it stayed that way. There was always *that* fear— the damage that could be caused when someone learned what was going on and went public with it. If Noriega continued to support the current administration's policies in Central America he would, for the most part, get away with anything, for better or worse.

There was only one way that the Agency would know for

sure what Noriega really had in mind. Someone was going to have to meet with him. And the Agency had the perfect person for the job.

Buck caught a taxi outside his apartment and took it to the outskirts of the city where he boarded a *chiva* to Santa Rosa. He could have driven, but he needed to keep this as low-key as he could. No one on the bus paid any attention to the gringo sitting by himself at the back of the bus. It took more than two hours to reach Santa Rosa, a sleepy, one-cantina village at the foot of a small mountain. He was early, so he went into the cantina, ordered a Coke, and sat at a table. On one wall, posters of Omar Torrijos and Roberto Duran were prominently displayed. Out back, in a leafless, emaciated tree, Buck watched a group of vultures hold court; below the tree, three piglets busied themselves in a mud hole while a goat stood sentry. At the end of the crudely constructed bar, which looked as though wooden packing crates had been nailed together, a woman around fifty talked to the bartender and then pointed to Buck. It was the sort of a place that a person could come to if they wanted to disappear. In the distance, he heard the familiar thump-thump-thumping of a Huey's rotors beating the humid air. He finished his Coke and went outside. The Huey landed in a field just beyond the cantina stirring up clouds of red dust and other debris. Two Guardia Nacional got off and escorted Buck to the waiting helicopter.

It was only a fifteen-minute flight to another small village on the other side of the mountain. The Huey landed in a clearing about fifty yards from a modest two-story stone house. Buck leaped off the helicopter and covered his face with his hands to protect it from the dust and debris kicked up by the blades. As he approached the house, there was no mistaking the man sitting underneath a canvas awning sipping whiskey.

"Do you think you could have found a more clandestine place for us to meet?" Buck asked, grinning as he approached Noriega. "Not counting the bartender and a female customer back at the cantina and your men, there's not a soul around, though the three pigs and goat I saw outside the cantina seemed a bit curious."

Noriega smiled. "Nice to see you too, Smith."

Though they had met that one time at an embassy function, Noriega had also done his background checks on Buck. "He's just an analyst," Vega told him. "He just pushes a pencil. You have nothing to worry about." Noriega wasn't convinced. He knew all about Buck's intelligence missions in Vietnam; he knew that Buck wasn't a team player when it came to policy.

"What's wrong, you suddenly worried that someone will see you talking to the CIA?" Buck asked grinning.

"Relax, my friend," Noriega said, motioning for Buck to sit down across from him. "You are safe here. Would you like a drink? I know it's probably too early in the day, but there's nothing like alcohol coursing through your veins to get you going."

"No thanks," Buck said, pulling up a chair and sitting down at the table across from Noriega. He looked nothing like the feared officer he had been in the Guardia just four years earlier. "We've got ourselves a little problem."

Noriega laughed and motioned for one of his aides to bring him another drink. "Why is it always business with you spooks? Can't we just talk as friends?"

"We are talking as friends, Manuel."

"What's the problem?"

"You're not pissing in anyone's pool, are you?"

Noriega grinned. It was no mystery to Buck and the

others back at Langley that Noriega was now in bed with some of the Colombian drug cartels, specifically Pablo Escobar, who was suddenly on everyone's radar screens. Noriega's drug deals had always been more of a hobby than some lifelong pursuit, but he upped the ante by teaming up with Escobar. With Torrijos out of the picture, Noriega had his sights set on something bigger. He wanted all of it now.

"Ever since Torrijos died, people have been pointing fingers at us saying that we had something to do with it. Take some time off. Give yourself and the missus a nice holiday cruise. I hear Contadora Island is quite nice this time of the year. When you come back, you'll not only feel refreshed but also things will have quieted down by then."

The grin died on his mouth as Noriega's mood immediately changed as he glared at Buck waving a thick finger at him. "Is this why you came all the way out here, to tell me? You tell Kelly or whoever it is pulling the strings that we had a deal."

"Manuel, I mean no disrespect."

"When I was in Washington, *everyone* treated me with respect!" Noriega yelled. He slammed his fist on the table for emphasis, knocking over his drink, which sent his aide scurrying to clean up the mess and fetch another drink for him. "Well, things are about to change here. And you also might want to tell him, or whoever else is still snooping around down here to back off. Your country doesn't need to be embarrassed, especially now of all times when you are about ready to support the Contras. If someone were to, say, go to your *New York Times* or your *Washington Post* and start rattling off your dirty laundry list, that wouldn't be too good for your President, would it? It would be such a tragedy for you and them if your training bases and staging areas were suddenly closed."

Buck was afraid of that and he warned Washington that if

Noriega got too strong they would have a hard time reeling him in. With the Singing Sergeant's Affair still in the back of Buck's mind and others, there was no telling what Noriega would do with the information he still held onto. They need Noriega, for better or worse. Buck stared at Noriega and knew that whatever he said next, he would have to choose his words carefully.

"We appreciate everything you have done in regard to providing training bases for us, but in light of Torrijos's death, there are a lot of people who think we were behind it," Buck said, in a cool and calculated voice. "You know how some people are, Manuel. There are even people *here* who think we had something to do with it."

Noriega might have thought he could play hardball with Buck and others, but Buck knew that Noriega needed protection if he wanted to continue his drug operations without the DEA breathing down his neck. It was a nasty, dirty little game they played with Noriega and the stakes got higher all the time.

"I thought you gringos had bigger balls than that," Noriega said. "But maybe that's only in the movies."

"We just want you to take it easy for a while, that's all. There are some people who want your head on a platter."

Noriega grunted and sipped his drink.

"How does it feel being a messenger?" Noriega said, staring at Buck with cold, dark eyes. "You're nothing but the CIA's whore."

Buck wiped the sweat from his brow. He expected as much from Noriega. "Then I guess we both know what it is like, don't we?"

Noriega's eyes stayed locked on Buck.

"Manuel, everything is fine," Buck said in a reassuring tone. He knew better than to let down his guard with someone who had made a living out of squeezing intelligence out of his friends and enemies. "We appreciate what you have been doing down here, it's just—"

"You're goddamn right you appreciate what I'm doing here," Noriega said, jumping up from his chair, nearly knocking over the table. Noriega paced back and forth like a wild animal in front of Buck. "You've got a lot of nerve to come to my home and start telling me what I should and shouldn't do. Don't forget that you need *me*."

"Yes, Manuel that is true," Buck said doing his best to calm Noriega and salvage their meeting. "We're all in this together and it is to our mutual advantage that we see eye-to-eye on certain matters for our best interests. We might not always like to hear the things we should, but that doesn't mean we should stop listening."

Noriega stopped pacing and stared at Buck before he sat down. Buck's little speech did the trick for now.

"*Me alegra oír eso*," Noriega said. His aide returned with a fresh drink. Noriega gulped half and immediately felt better. "See, it's good to air out our differences. It's good to clear our heads, *sí*? We wouldn't want anything to jeopardize what we have worked so hard to attain."

"Of course, Manuel."

"Good, then let's have a drink together," Noriega said, motioning for his aide to fetch him a fresh drink and one for Buck.

"Okay, Manuel."

One thing was for certain, when Buck got back on the helicopter and headed to Panama City two hours later, Noriega remained a shrewd player in this ongoing drama. He was right about one thing: the CIA needed him, but he needed the CIA just as much.

231

He's not finished with us. Buck gazed outside the opened door of the helicopter. *It was just getting started.*

PART II

CHAPTER TWENTY-EIGHT

BUCK HADN'T HAD a good night's sleep for over a decade thanks to Noriega, who was a cancer eating away at the soul of the CIA. While agencies like the CIA were responding to various crises around the globe—the Soviet invasion of Afghanistan, the Iran Hostage Crisis, El Salvador, the marine barracks bombing in Beirut, Cubans in Grenada, and Sandinistas in Nicaragua—Noriega had been the one constant. Ever since Torrijos mysteriously died in a plane crash in 1981, Noriega had been an unstoppable juggernaut. Time and time again, Buck and others subscribed to the lesser of two evils logic when it came to Noriega. He was their man in Panama for better or worse, but he had long since worn out his welcome.

As Buck liked to put it, "He's not just an SOB; he's *our* SOB."

Sitting in his cramped office, Buck drank the last of his cold coffee and grimaced. His once sandy red hair was now almost white, the lines on his forehead and the wrinkles underneath his eyes more pronounced. In front of him was a copy of the latest incident report involving Noriega's Dignity Battalions and the cable that he sent to Langley. It was bad. The Dignity Battalions—paramilitary units, which were part of Panama's Defense Forces (PDF) to defend the country from foreign and domestic enemies—had become part of Noriega's strong-arm tactics to terrorize civilians, threaten opposition leaders, and more recently harass U.S. military personnel and dependents in Panama. This time the battalions had gone too far when schoolchildren were targeted.

The veins on Buck's neck tightened as he slowly read the report: nine school buses, containing more than one hundred students, were stopped by the PDF for traffic violations. It could have gotten ugly real quick and the schoolchildren could have been put into harm's way when military police from Fort Clayton occupied the buses preventing the PDF from taking the children off or moving them to another location. The words, "held at gunpoint" jumped off the page. The standoff between the military police and the Panamanians lasted for nearly three hours until one of Noriega's henchmen negotiated with the provost marshal from Fort Clayton and ended the crisis.

It was getting more difficult to look the other way while Noriega continued to flaunt his arrogance and defiance. Kelly, who had been the most sympathetic, was long since gone, transferred to a new post. Brent Mitchell, the new station chief, was catching a lot of heat from the director who was catching a lot of heat from the President. As far as Buck was concerned, the buck did not stop with him; instead, a better analogy would have been that shit flows downhill, and it was piling up outside his office which felt more cramped now than it did ten years earlier.

Buck was so engrossed in the report that he didn't see

Mitchell walk into his office and sit down on a brown leather chair in the corner.

"All's well that ends well, right Buck?" Mitchell said.

Buck looked up and nodded. "It could have been worse."

"Thank God cooler heads prevailed," Mitchell replied. "That provost marshal was one steely-eyed cop. We ought to send him a case of Johnny Walker."

"You know, his kid was on one of those buses."

Mitchell shook his head. "This shit has got to stop."

Buck stared at Mitchell and nodded.

"Thanks for taking the point on this one, Buck."

"Just earning my keep, boss."

Mitchell laughed. "I've got to brief the Ambassador in an hour. Is there anything you would like to add that's not in the report?"

Buck thought for a few seconds and smiled. "Ask him to spring for the case of Johnny Walker."

Buck knew that one day the United States was going to catch heat for its continued involvement with Noriega. Although Buck's headaches with Noriega started back in the 1970s, it wasn't until Noriega assumed command of the Panamanian Defense Forces that his misery began in earnest. After years of letting him have his way with his drug smuggling and money laundering, it became increasingly difficult to rein him in. However, as long as he continued to support American policy in Central America, especially with the ongoing fighting in Nicaragua, Noriega was their go-to man. He assuaged America's worst fears of a Cold War showdown in Central America and for that, Washington had been willing to look the other way. And in the process, Noriega had put both countries on a collision course that was not going to end well.

Ironically, the Singing Sergeants Affair, which had

inextricably conjoined Buck and Noriega from the very beginning, had gotten lost amidst the Iran-Contra Affair and Noriega's grip on Panama. Inasmuch as the affair had everyone scrambling to do some major damage control, Buck and others would soon have bigger fish to fry. By then, the Agency would be taking flak from all sides as Oliver North and company raised the stakes in Central America. As for Rodriquez and his partners in crime, they were doomed to be a footnote to history for the time being.

In the beginning, Buck had no problems with his conscience. He learned that one had to look the other way when it came to dealing with Noriega. He had warned his superiors for years that they didn't know Noriega as much as they thought they did and left it at that. Buck's conscience, however, had started bothering him, and it made him sick when he thought about the monster they had created. Whereas he once said, "We're in bed with this guy and we'd better get used to it," now he had a different attitude: "How can we get rid of this guy?"

The only thing that changed for Buck was that he had been promoted to one of the top intelligence officers in Panama, which invariably meant more late hours and more headaches. Late at night in his modest apartment, it took Buck three or four glasses of bourbon and a couple sleeping pills to fall asleep and even then he tossed and turned all night. Sometimes he got in his car and drove around all night, usually ending up at one of his favorite watering holes or the bar in the Intercontinental Hotel where he often observed the comings and goings of a host of shady individuals who were in some way connected to Noriega which meant more headaches for Buck. Though Estevan's wife had introduced him to some of her friends, Buck still preferred the company of ladies working the hotel bars or the bars on J Street where he drank away his blues and disdain.

The file he started to compile on Noriega in the late seventies took up space in six boxes, and there was more information coming in daily. Buck felt that he knew Noriega better than anyone else and knew the dangerous game that he was playing. There was a method to his madness that was pure, cold, calculated. What most people couldn't understand was that Noriega was still an intelligence officer at heart; he didn't make a move without first weighing all the options, and then making his move. Nothing in his life had been left to chance. He was the master of the subterfuge and knew how to play his enemies off one another. And in the end, Noriega always got what he wanted.

* * *

Noriega got sloppy though. His greed and quest for more power—absolute power—slowly started to erode his power base and for the first time, people were not afraid to speak out against him. In the past, prison time and torture usually did the trick for those who did, but times had changed. The death of Dr. Hugo Spadafora, one of Noriega's more vocal critics changed everything. When Spadafora's mutilated and decapitated body was found stuffed inside a U.S. mailbag across the border from Panama in Costa Rica in 1985, not even the staunchest supporters of Noriega could look the other way. Although he was still on the CIA's payroll, Buck knew that it would become increasingly more difficult to convince the American people that he was an *asset* when he was systematically oppressing his people.

Buck had enough on his plate watching Noriega when Oliver North and company ratcheted up tensions. Buck met North once, at an embassy function, and thought he was too much of a prima donna. He was using the bathroom when North staggered in and started urinating in the urinal next to Buck.

"You're that Noriega expert, aren't you?" North asked, turning to Buck. North stuck out his chest proudly and gave Buck the once over with narrow, suspicious eyes.

"Something like that," Buck replied smiling. He was impressed that North knew who he was.

"I know Noriega, and you're no expert," North said brusquely as he zipped up his trousers and left.

Buck happened to look down at his tan chinos and noticed that some urine had accidentally splashed onto his pants legs.

"He's just going to complicate matters down here for us," Buck later told Mitchell about his feelings about North when he learned that Noriega had met North in Washington several times. "He's giving Noriega too much of a leash. I'm afraid it's going to come back and haunt us."

"It's out of our hands, Buck."

Complicating things turned out to be a bit of an understatement; it ended up being a public relations nightmare for the Agency. It wouldn't be long before North and CIA Director William Casey were gone. Had it not been for the continued Cold War tensions with the Soviet Union, the scandal might have had more far-reaching consequences.

Buck couldn't help but feel guilty for the small role he played in the scandal which had gripped the nation when it blew wide open in November 1986. Buck thought for sure he would be one of the first casualties, but as he soon found out, he was no different than Noriega: Buck was just as much an asset to the company as Noriega was.

Buck sat back in his chair and looked at all the reports and memos cluttering his desk. Most people, including himself, realized that given the fallout from the Iran-Contra Affair and public opinion regarding anything to do with Central America, the best course of action was for the United States to wait for change to occur from within. The Agency wanted to stay away from any military action—overt or covert. And the Republicans, gearing up for an election year didn't want to lose any ground to the Democrats who were already out for blood.

The best hope for a solution to the Panama problem would be something similar to what happened in the Philippines when Marcos was forced from power. Or better yet, next year's elections in Panama could finally force Noriega out.

Since June of 1987, that was what Washington and others hoped would happen. In a twist of irony, or as Buck liked to call it, *in the better late than never* department, the CIA finally got around to removing Noriega from its payroll. Of course, that wasn't going to dissuade Noriega in the least. There was one last-ditch attempt to negotiate with Noriega—to persuade him to step down for the good of the country and hold free elections. Buck knew Noriega wouldn't budge, but other than taking military action, what else could Washington do?

And if all the reports coming into his office were any indication of how ineffective these attempts to deal with Noriega were, they only provoked him more. There was one report after another about an incident involving U.S. personnel in Panama and Noriega's Panama Defense Forces. It was becoming more difficult for Washington to turn the other cheek. Last year alone, there were over three hundred incidents, which ranged from harassment and threats to physical detainment and assaults.

In one of the more violent incidents in April, at a fuel tank farm near Howard Air Force Base, Marine Corps guards exchanged gunfire with approximately thirty intruders.

* * *

After Mitchell had left, Buck picked up the teletype and stared at the message again. *The PDF had gone too far this time.* Buck popped a couple Excedrin into his mouth and washed them down with the last of his coffee. If Noriega continued down this road, it wasn't going to turn out well for either side. And Washington was already looking down this road. Since early 1988, when Noriega was indicted by two federal grand juries in Florida on drug smuggling and money laundering charges, the wheels of justice had started turning against him. After the indictments were handed down, the Joint Chiefs of Staff had come up with an operation plan (OPLAN) which called for the defense of the Canal Zone, evacuation of civilians and the neutralization of the Panama Defense Forces. The question was, when push came to shove, just how far did the President need to be pushed before he responded?

Buck felt sorry for the President. Since taking office, he had been doing as much as he could without raising too many flags, but considering that he and Noriega had a long history, there were no surprises there. The President was both shackled by the previous administration and changes in the Agency—he wasn't about to make any move against Noriega without first weighing all their options. In the back of his mind, the President knew the path they were traveling was a dangerous one that put America and Noriega on a collision course. It was a high-stakes game of chicken to see who was going to flinch first.

In the meantime, it had been business as usual for Buck who kept a close watch on Noriega as best he could.

"We're running out of options, Buck," Mitchell said the other day. Mitchell was idealistic and, more importantly, didn't have the Iran-Contra taint on his résumé. He was a lot more methodical and pragmatic. He had been burned by people like Noriega and believed there was only one way of dealing with men like him. "There are some who say we should wait and see. There are others who want blood now. The problem is, we also have a lot of blood on our hands."

Buck nodded and smiled, the same way he had for the past ten years. The current administration had recently given the Agency three million dollars and was granted greater freedom to use whatever force was necessary to remove Noriega from power, though assassination was not on the table—at least, no one wanted to admit that it was. Although Buck had brought Mitchell up to speed, there was a lot that Mitchell needed to learn. Buck hoped that Mitchell was a fast learner.

"What about this contact you have in the city?" Mitchell asked. "How reliable is he?"

Buck had kept Mitchell in the dark about the true relationship he had with Vega the same way he had done with Kelly. The fewer people knew about Vega, the better it would be, in the long run. Vega might have been Buck's go-to person in Panama but he was also Buck's insurance, and if things didn't go as planned, his escape clause, if someone needed a fall guy. In the meantime, Buck let everyone believe that Vega was still a valuable asset.

"He provides us with enough information for us to keep paying his rent," Buck said.

That was just a half truth. Buck knew that his friend was playing both sides. Vega also needed some insurance in case Noriega was suddenly removed from power. It wasn't easy keeping tabs on his friend when he was too busy to talk when Buck called him, or the other times when phone calls were not returned. Buck had a hunch that his friend had been expanding his operations which could later become an embarrassment to Buck, as well as the Agency. Buck should have cut loose Vega years ago, but even then it would have already been too late.

"Just make sure he doesn't cause us too many headaches," Mitchell warned. "We don't need for anything to come back and bite us in the ass, if you know what I mean."

Buck knew exactly what Mitchell meant. With everyone scrambling to find an alternative way to remove Noriega, Buck found himself on a different journey, a collision course—one which had been long overdue—with his friend. Buck knew that there was only one way this was going to end for the two of them.

*　*　*

Buck was almost certain he was being tailed when he left his office that evening. He had been tailed in the past, but since Spadafora's death, Noriega had been keeping a closer watch on Buck and others just to keep things interesting. He had also been stopped by some of Noriega's minions for traffic violations on three occasions and detained for a few hours until he was let go. Buck liked all the attention he was getting which meant that Noriega was more concerned about his own standing which the Agency.

In no mood for any cloak and dagger nonsense, Buck ducked into the first bar he came across and found a seat in the back. There was just enough of a crowd that no one paid any attention to the gringo sitting by himself. He ordered a beer and pretended not to be too conspicuous as he kept an eye on the door and waited for a woman to finish using a pay phone not far from where he was sitting. If he were going to be here for a while at least he could do some work. It had been a while since they last talked.

As soon as the woman finished, Buck walked over to the pay phone and deposited a few quarters. The phone on the other end rang ten times before someone finally answered. In the background, Buck could hear Bon Jovi's "Wanted Dead or Alive" playing on a jukebox and a chorus of drunken banter around the person holding the phone.

"Hello, Frank," Buck began. "How the hell are you?"

CHAPTER TWENTY-NINE

AFTER FRANK WAS kicked out of the Air Force, Vega took care of him, setting him up in a bar, TJ's, which once had been a popular Zonian hangout in the seventies. The original owner, who had also been a prison guard, had been stabbed to death. It was a way not only to appease Frank, who was still angry over having been busted, but also to make sure that Frank would also be able to pay him back one day. Ironically, the inmate who had stabbed the guard was a former associate of Vega, locked up for murdering one of Vega's rivals. Vega wanted the club, located just a few blocks away from the Mercado and used the bar as a front for selling drugs to service members, now that Santiago was behind bars.

Frank wasn't the only one hurting after Santiago had been busted. It had been costly for Diego—close to one hundred thousand dollars' worth of cocaine confiscated and nearly fifty thousand dollars in cash. Vega never let Frank forget about their little arrangement. Although Vega never came out and said that Frank was working off his debt, Vega used Frank to recoup his losses. With the flow of cocaine into Panama, courtesy of Escobar and Noriega, it was the perfect arrangement. The bar was Vega's insurance and the perfect front for whatever drug smuggling he continued to do under Noriega's nose.

When Frank had been busted, he had no one else to turn to; Smith had left him high and dry. Although Smith called in the beginning to find out what he could about Vega, Smith hadn't lifted a finger to help. Frank had no family to speak of: both his parents were dead and he hadn't talked to his older brother in over a decade. Once out of desperation he went to the U.S. Embassy but there was nothing that he could do. There really was only one person who had been there for him. And as much as Frank despised Vega for what happened to Gary, Vega was the only person there for him. If he was ever going to get out of the jam he was in now, he was going to have to depend on Vega.

Everything he had saved up had been confiscated—as was the kilo of cocaine he was caught with. Shortly after being kicked out of the Air Force, Inés gave birth to another daughter, Adrianna. Inés managed to save up some money, but it wouldn't be long before that well dried up. Her father helped out for a while, but then he had had a heart attack and died. Running the bar was not an option; it was all he had if he was going to pay back Vega. He dealt some drugs on the side, but it was nowhere near the kind of action that Santiago had years ago.

There was something more, however.

Years after Gary's death, Frank still couldn't forgive Vega for not stopping it. One day, he would get back at Vega and Smith for getting him in this predicament into the first place. Until then, he was just biding his time until the right moment came along when he could pay off his debts and get as far away as he could from Panama. Frank hoped that moment came soon. He knew the country was going to hell; Noriega had seen to that. There was no telling when everything could collapse all around him.

Then out of the blue one day, Smith called. Except this time, Frank wasn't buying any of it. He didn't even give Smith a chance to get in a word edgewise. As soon as Frank knew who it was, he hung up on Smith.

"What's wrong, Darling?" Inés asked as she watched Frank drag himself into the kitchen after he had come late from the bar one night.

He opened the refrigerator and peered inside. "Do we have anything to eat?"

It was one of the nights when she stayed up late waiting for Frank to come home from the bar; one of the nights she couldn't sleep because she was worried about him. He had been spending more and more time at the bar and coming home later and later. Sometimes he didn't come until the next morning, reeking of alcohol and cigarette smoke. In the beginning, she worried that he might be sleeping with one of the girls Vega had working at the bar, especially when she and Frank's love life lost the spark it once had. When she confronted Frank about it, he responded by shouting and blaming her not trusting him.

"I can cook some—"

"Never mind," he said, slamming the refrigerator door shut and knocking off one of Adrianna's drawings. It was the one of her and Frank playing in the park. Frank picked up and tried to put it back but it fell down again. He tried again with no luck.

"I'll take care of it," Inés said, taking it from Frank and putting it back on the refrigerator.

Frank glared at Inés before he moved across the room

and plopped down on a rickety wooden chair across from Inés. From a crumpled pack of cigarettes, he pulled out a crooked cigarette, straightened it out as best he could, and stuck it between his lips.

"Is there something you want to talk about?" she asked sitting down across from Frank.

"No." Frank snapped. He took a long drag off the cigarette and exhaled slowly. "It's nothing, Inés. Why don't you go to bed?"

"You don't have to take it out on me," she said.

"I'm sorry."

Inés knew how much it pained Frank that he couldn't provide for her and their daughters as much as he would like. The bar that Vega had set him up paid the bills and put food on the table. In the beginning, she had been grateful to Vega for taking care of them. Frank's buddy, Santiago, hadn't fared as well. However, what worried her most was that she knew Frank was selling drugs on the side again, unbeknownst to Vega and Guerra, even though he promised her that he was through with that. She shuddered at the thought of Vega finding out and what he would do to Frank. Her father had left her a little money which she had managed to put aside for a rainy day but with two daughters in school and the money he owed Vega, it was never enough.

She gazed at Frank and grabbed his hand. The years had worn him down.

"We're going to be okay," she said. "Things will get better for us."

Frank wasn't so sure.

When he finally crawled into bed after he had taken a shower, he heard Inés softly sobbing. He didn't mean to snap at her like he did earlier in the evening. He put his arm around her. She grasped his hand tightly and placed it on her breast. For the first time in a long time, he felt aroused.

"You're right, Darling. We'll get through this," he finally said, gently kissing her ear. "I don't know how yet, but we'll get out of the predicament we're in. One day I'm going to make this all up to you and the girls."

Frank waited for an answer, but Inés had already drifted off to sleep.

CHAPTER THIRTY

THE DREAMS WERE always the same for Kevin. They always started with him in his old barracks at Howard. He recognized some of the people he had been stationed with, his buddies John Bradshaw and Brent McBride. They were not surprised to see him; instead, they seemed to be happy that he was back in Panama and usually asked him what had taken him so long to come back. Depending on what was going on in his life at the time—a new assignment or relationship problems—his buddies offered him advice about what he should or shouldn't do. When Kevin asked how he would be able to leave, his friends told him that he would never be able to leave.

The next part of the dream was also the same: he was on a bus traveling across the Thatcher Ferry Bridge. When he looked toward the canal, he didn't see any ships transiting; instead, he saw a line of coffins floating toward the bridge. The rest of the dream was a little blurry until he saw Frank walking with Inés. He didn't recognize where they were, but Inés was in her wedding dress and Frank was wearing a suit. They both motioned for Kevin to come closer to where they were standing. At first Kevin thought it was their wedding, but as he approached them, they moved to the side and there was a coffin on a white pedestal. Kevin started trembling as he approached the coffin, afraid to see who was inside. Sometimes he woke up before he could see who was in the coffin; other times, he looked inside and saw Gary's lifeless body, his eyes open, staring up at him.

Kevin usually woke up in a cold sweat and needed something strong to settle his nerves. A couple of times he was tempted to call his buddy John, who had gotten out of the Air Force after his father suffered a stroke, to tell him about the dream.

He had been at Minot for a little over a year when he recalled having the first dream, which at the time he figured it had something to do with the anniversary of Gary's death. Then the dreams began to occur more often—first once a month, then two or three times a month. They also became more vivid and frightening.

Kevin did tell his girlfriend, Clare, about the dreams. However, he left out the part about Gary.

"Sounds like you miss being there," Clare said one morning after he had woken up in a cold sweat. She sat up in bed and wrapped a sheet around her body. She watched Kevin in the bathroom splashing cold water on his face. "Did something happen to you that makes you miss it so much?"

Kevin never told her about Gary or Inés. He had locked all that away, or so he thought, when he left Panama. Seeing Gary's lifeless body at the end of the nightmare always shook him up the most—especially in some of the dreams when his friend opened his eyes and reached out of the coffin as if to strangle Kevin. A couple of times when he woke up he was soaked with sweat. Without question, Kevin still felt guilty for not having been able to prevent his friend's death. He had been one of Gary's last friends to have seen him alive that night. And he still felt guilty for sleeping with Inés after he had found out what happened to Gary.

"It's a long story, Clare," Kevin said, walking back into the bedroom. He had been at Norton Air Force Base for only a few months after having spent a year in Korea at Kunsan Air Base. After Kunsan, he had had enough of barracks life and got himself an apartment off base.

Since leaving Panama, Kevin had gone on to have a lackluster, though honorable Air Force career. He received high marks on all his Airman Performance Reports and was awarded a couple medals along the way, though everyone received them for just doing their time and a good job. He had recently reenlisted, and it wouldn't be long before he would be thinking about life after the Air Force.

Clare curled a finger around a strand of blonde hair and looked at Kevin with her big blue eyes. They met at the community college where he was taking some courses in criminal justice.

"Have you ever been back there?" she asked.

"No, I haven't," Kevin said, sitting on the edge of the bed.

"Maybe that's why you have been having these dreams," she said, snuggling up to Kevin. "My psychology professor told us that the reason some people have the same dreams about the same place and people is they are harboring some deep-seated guilt or anxiety about that place and the people they once knew there. He said it's our subconscious taking over. Is there something that you're trying to repress because he said that's another reason we dream about the things that we do?"

Kevin shrugged. He was taking the same class with the

same psychology professor this semester. "I don't know."

"Maybe you ought to go back there one day if you can," Clare said, resting her head on his shoulder. "Maybe if you could go back there you could put these dreams behind you once and for all."

If it only were that easy. He knew why he had these nightmares, but he couldn't tell her. Clare was probably right, about laying to rest the ghosts of his past; though it wasn't like he could hop on a plane and fly back to Panama. When he had re-upped for another four years, he could have put in for Howard and probably could have been stationed there again. The Air Force usually took care of people who had been in for a while and were planning on staying in for longer by giving them their choice of assignment. However, there was something keeping him from doing that. For better or worse, he wanted to keep that part of his life in the past. He was just going to have to deal with the dreams and the ghosts as best as he could.

"Yeah, maybe one day," Kevin said, putting his arm around Clare.

Panama had been in the news a lot recently—not so much Panama, as it was about Manuel Noriega. There were all sorts of allegations about drug and arms smuggling, money laundering, as well as Noriega's connection with the Iran-Contra Affair. Kevin sometimes wondered just how much of this was going on when he was stationed there. At the time, Panama was in the news a lot, but it was only because of the canal treaties. He still cringed when he thought about Gus Santiago and Frank and their little drug smuggling operation and how it might have had something to do with Gary's death. Just as much as he would never be able to forgive himself, he would never be able to forgive Frank. Then there was that time after he had gotten in a fight downtown when the OSI wanted him to spy on Frank and Gary. Maybe if he had done what they asked of him, Gary wouldn't have ended up dead.

The fact was he had been thinking a lot about the two years he was stationed at Howard. At first, he wanted to put it all behind him—Gary's death, Inés, even the Article Fifteen he got for what happened outside Napoli's. He just wanted to forget about everything. There were too many painful memories for him.

It wasn't until he bumped into Wayne Bouchard who was TDY at Kunsan and the two of them started reminiscing about Panama and Howard when Kevin started missing Panama. Although he had only been at three stateside and two overseas bases since Howard, those assignments paled in comparison— those two years he spent in Panama, for better or worse, were a yardstick for which he measured all his other assignments. It was true what some of his older Air Force buddies had told him, ones that were nearing the end of their twenty or thirty-year careers, that no matter where you went and hung your hat, you never forgot your first assignment.

Of course, it was much more than missing the good times he had when he was stationed at Howard. Even if he had gone back to Panama, as Clare suggested, there would always be that dark cloud hanging over him.

After his most recent dream about being back in Panama, one night after Clare had gone to bed, Kevin dug out a photo album from a box in the living room closet and sat on the balcony with a bottle of Corona looking at some of the photos he had taken when he was in Panama. It had been a while since he had last looked at them, but as soon as he opened the album he was overcome with a wave of nostalgia as he journeyed back in time. Perhaps they could help him exorcise the demons which had been causing him the nightmares.

Most of them included the usual assortment of barrack's grab-assing, goofing off, and hamming it up for the camera with his buddies. There were a couple blurry Polaroids of his buddies and bar girls, even one of him with one eye shut and the other half-open, his arm around a buxom girl at the Paris after having downed three Motherfuckers in less than twenty minutes. He grinned as he continued to flip through the pages, stopping to pause at various photos. Each photograph told a story and had its special memory for Kevin. There was one of Thatcher Ferry Bridge taken from the top steps of the administration building in Balboa, and one of him standing in front of Miraflores Locks with his friend Brent (who was holding a copy of his hometown newspaper for his family back home) as a ship transited the locks. There was another one of him sitting with John Bradshaw on a rocky outcrop above Galliard Cut with a container ship in the distance moving toward Miraflores Locks and one of him and a couple of his buddies gathered around a ten-foot boa constrictor that someone had managed to drag up to the third floor of the barracks. Kevin grinned when he remembered how one of his buddies walked out of his room and shrieked when he saw the snake. They caught a lot of flak for that stunt when their first sergeant heard about it the next day.

He flipped through a few more pages of photos which included ones of him on patrol, or standing outside the armory with his M-16 at his side, striking the best John Wayne pose he could muster, and a few pages of photographs of Kevin and his buddies at Goofy Falls, a popular swimming hole out past Tocumen International Airport until he came to the ones he had of Gary. Kevin bought a Polaroid Land Camera at the BX and went through two packs of film that night—starting off at the NCO Club and ending up at the Ovalo. There was a photo of Gary, with his hair slicked back, doing his very best impersonation of The Fonz, sans leather jacket, by giving two thumbs-up and saying, "Aaaayyyy," another one of him gnawing on a stick of monkey meat outside the Ovalo and one of him inside with a girl sitting on his lap. There was another one of them taken standing in the shallow water at the Fort Kobbe beach after the tide had gone out with the shark net behind them. They both had an arm around each other's shoulder and in each of their hands a can of Pabst Blue Ribbon. Kevin liked that photo of them the best.

There were a few empty spaces where photos had once been; ones he had removed quickly in a drunken rage. He hadn't thrown them all away, however. He still had a photo of him with Inés sitting around a campfire on Venado Beach, not too far from the back gate of Howard. John and Brent were there, as were a couple other guys from the squadron with their girlfriends and wives. It was the only photo he still had of Inés.

He closed the photo album and drank the last of his Corona. Someone in the apartment complex had a radio tuned to a local rock station he heard one of his favorite songs, Don Henley's "Boys of Summer" which seemed apropos for how he was feeling this night, especially the part when Henley sang about not being able to go back to one's past. He settled back in the chair, gazed up at the stars in the sky, and for the first time, in a very long time, thought about Inés.

CHAPTER THIRTY-ONE

THE TELEPHONE RINGING in the living room woke Buck up from a sound sleep—one of the first nights in a long time that he slept well, thanks in no part to a couple extra glasses of scotch before he went to bed. When he left the office earlier that evening, there had been another report of Panama Defense Forces harassing military personnel. These reports were becoming too much a part of his daily routine. Although he decided it could wait until morning and came home, it might have ended up being more serious.

He staggered into the living room, stubbing his toe on a table, causing him to nearly lose his balance and fall over, cursing at himself for putting the table there in the first place.

"Hello," Buck mumbled into the phone.

There were a few seconds of silence before the person on the other end began to speak.

"Buck, it's me, Estevan," his friend said on the other end. His weak voice was fraught with pain. "Buck, Estefani—"

Before his friend had a chance to finish his sentence, Buck knew that whatever happened to his goddaughter was going to be bad.

"She's dead, Buck. My little baby's gone."

Buck felt as though someone had punched him in the stomach with a two-by-four. "Oh my God."

On the other end, Buck could hear his friend softly weeping.

"I'm on my way over now."

Thirty minutes later, Buck was sitting in the restaurant with Estevan and his wife. Estevan had made them some coffee. Outside traffic droned along Vía España. A few passersby, noticing a light on inside, tried the door, but when they discovered it was locked, moved on down the sidewalk to another restaurant or café.

Buck sat across from his two friends and listened to Estevan explain how Estefani had died. It was the same table that the two men had sat at over the years talking about their lives, sharing their happiness as well as their sadness. It was here where Buck had sometimes bounced Estefani on his knee or helped her with her homework. It was from this table where he had watched her grow over the years into a beautiful and caring young woman. Buck stared at his two friends and slowly shook his head as Estevan told him as much as he knew.

"She had gone to Miami with some classmates after graduation and while she was at the airport, she collapsed," Estevan said slowly, his voice choked with emotion. "By the time the paramedics arrived and tried to resuscitate her it was too late."

"I'm so sorry, Estevan," Buck said, reaching across the table and grabbing his friend's hand.

"When I talked to her last, she was so happy that she was able to help out with paying off the debt I owed Vega," Estevan said, wiping away a tear. "That's just the kind of person she was; she was always thinking about other people and not herself."

Buck nodded. He knew that Estefani was a good daughter; after her mother was diagnosed with cancer, she took a year off school to help her father at the restaurant. Buck had been so proud of her the day she graduated from one of Panama's top universities where she studied medicine. He looked over at Ascension, who dried her eyes with a lace handkerchief.

"*Un padre nunca debería tener que enterrar a uno de sus hijos*," Estevan said, his voice trembling.

Buck nodded. There was nothing more tragic for a parent than to have to bury one of their children.

"I just don't understand, Buck," Estevan continued, his voice weak. "She had never been sick a day in her life. People her age just don't die of a heart attack."

The last time Buck saw Estefani had been five months earlier. Estevan had closed the restaurant early that evening and the two men caught up on each other's lives the way that friends who hadn't seen each other for a long time did. On this night, however, there was a somber underpinning to their conversation.

Business hadn't been good for Estevan. As more and more new restaurants popped up along Vía España, Estevan found it challenging to compete with them. Thinking that he needed to expand his restaurant, he had borrowed ten thousand dollars from Vega. However, he had difficulty paying back Vega. Buck offered to help out, but Estevan didn't want any more help from his friend.

"You've done too much already, Buck," Estevan said. "Thank you, my friend, but this is something that I have to do on my own."

"Let me talk to Vega," Buck said, worried that his friend would never be able to pay back Vega. "It's the least I can do. I'm sure he'll work something out with you."

"How do you know, Vega?" Estevan asked with a surprised tone.

"I've known him for a while," Buck said matter-of-factly, hoping that Estevan wouldn't inquire about the relationship he had with Vega. "He's a reasonable man."

Estevan nodded, but he wasn't so sure about Vega being a reasonable man. Estefani didn't say anything as she cleared off the table. She had stopped at one point to listen to what her father and Buck had to say about Vega. She could understand why her father would go to Vega—he was well liked by most everyone up and down Vía España and in Chorrillo and was always quick to help out, for a price—but paying back Vega was much harder than he imagined. Estefani wished that there was something she could do to help her father.

"You're just as beautiful as your mother," Buck said, looking up at Estefani. She was tall and thin as her mother and wore her long jet-black hair curled. "You've got her eyes and smile."

Estefani blushed as she finished clearing off the table and brought coffee for the two men.

Estevan watched his daughter sweeping the floor in the kitchen. "She goes back to the university next month. And then—"

Estevan's voice trailed off. He knew what kind of man Vega was and how difficult it was going to be to get another extension. Vega had already given him two extensions already and threatened to take over the restaurant if he didn't come up with the money. And if he lost the restaurant, there was no way that he would be able to pay for the rest of his daughter's college expenses.

"You must be very proud of her," Buck said.

"More than you can imagine."

"Everything's going to be all right, Estevan," Buck said. "This business with Vega, we'll be able to work out something."

After Buck had consoled Estevan and his wife, he went back to the office and made a few phone calls to arrange for Estefani's body to be brought back to Panama. He couldn't believe that his godchild was gone. He poured himself a tumbler of bourbon from the bottle he kept in the bottom drawer of his desk. She had been so full of life when he had seen her last, talking about what she was going to do after she graduated—especially helping out her father and mother for all the sacrifices they made—which made the information surrounding her death all the more painful and tragic.

The person on the other end had put him on hold. He sipped the bourbon and relished in its warmth as it coursed through his body numbing the pain.

"Mr. Smith?" another person asked finally coming back on the line. "This is Detective Tony Rogers of the Miami Police Department."

"Yes, Detective," Buck replied.

"May I ask, what is your relationship to the deceased?"

"Like I told the other person, she is my goddaughter," Buck said, refusing to think of her in the past. "I'm handling all arrangements on behalf of the family."

"I see," Rogers said.

And then what Rogers told him next caused the glass to slip out of his hand.

"The circumstances surrounding her death are part of an ongoing criminal investigation," Rogers continued. "We are still waiting for the toxicology reports, but we have every reason to believe she was transporting cocaine. We have her traveling companion in lockup right now, but she's not saying anything."

Buck couldn't believe what he was hearing. He grabbed another glass and filled it with bourbon.

"What do you mean *transporting* cocaine?" Buck asked.

"She was one of those mules," Rogers said in a cold, calculated, *just the facts* voice. "You know, someone transporting cocaine or heroin. She must have had thirty balloons in her stomach. A couple of them burst when she was standing in line at the immigration counter. She went into cardiac arrest. It's all in the coroner's preliminary report, which I can send to you if you'd like. There was nothing that the paramedics could do. We'll be able to release the body once the Dade County Medical Examiner has completed all the tests."

"Did her friend call anyone?"

"She called someone in Miami," Rogers said.

"Miami?"

"It was some local attorney, Hernando Lopez," Rogers replied. "He's as shady as they come. Do you want his number?"

"Yes, I would."

After thanking Rogers for his time, Buck made a few more phone calls, used his Agency pull, and within twenty-four hours, Estefani's body was flown back to Panama aboard a military flight. He called in a few favors from some friends at Howard and arranged for an ambulance to transport her body to a funeral home not far from Estevan's restaurant. He also had one of his buddies at Langley run a background check on the attorney. Rogers was right. Lopez made a living representing the dregs of society. However, he had also a list of

Colombian and Panamanian clientele who were caught for
various drug offenses, including smuggling as well as their
known associates and contacts in Panama City and Bogotá.
One name jumped off the list: Alejandro Vega.

There was one more thing that Buck had to do; he
cringed when he thought where it would lead him.

At the funeral three days later, a large crowd gathered to
pay their respects and offer sympathy to Estevan and
Ascension. It was one of the saddest funerals Buck ever
attended. Not surprisingly, Vega showed up with two of his
bodyguards. Buck watched Vega work the crowd as though he
were running for public office instead of paying his respects to
Estevan and Ascension. When Vega reached the end of the
row where Estevan and his wife were sitting he looked up and
noticed Buck on the other side of the room. He nodded his
head once to acknowledge his friend.

"What a tragedy," Vega said, clasping Buck's hand. He
had walked across the room to meet his friend. "I can't believe
that she just died in the airport. Tragedy has no boundaries."

Buck glanced toward Estefani's casket at the front of the
room and watched a pair of mourners, two of Estefani's
classmates, kneel down in front of her casket to pray. "She
meant so much to a lot of people."

Vega cast a sideways glance at his friend. "That's right,
you were her *Padrino*. I am sorry for your loss, my friend."

Buck nodded and watched more mourners silently file
past the casket. Some stopped to pray; others made the sign of
the cross before they slowly moved to the back of the room.

"What I don't understand is what she was doing in
Miami in the first place?" Buck asked. "Her father had a hard
enough time putting her through school as it was."

"It was a graduation present," Vega said matter-of-factly,

looking around the room to see if he recognized anyone else. "She always told me that she wanted to visit Miami. It was the least I could do for her."

Buck furrowed his brow and stared at his friend. "That was awful nice of you considering the debt her father owed you."

"I just wanted to do something nice for her," Vega said, detecting the sarcasm in Buck's voice. "As for the debt, you and I both know, now's not the time to bring that up."

Something wasn't right. There was something that Estevan had said that bothered Buck. He said that Estefani was helping out with paying off the debt he owed Vega, but the way that his friend had put it, she had already taken care of the debt. As far as Buck knew she didn't make anything helping out at the restaurant and didn't have a part time job at school. And then there was Estefani's traveling companion and the attorney in Miami. The more he thought about it, the more it bothered him.

On the other side of the room, one of Vega's bodyguards motioned to Vega that they had to leave.

"Don't be a stranger, Buck," Vega said, putting a hand on Buck's shoulder. "We should have dinner one of these nights."

"Yes, we should, Alejandro," Buck said.

"So unfortunate and tragic," Vega said, shaking his head. He looked in the direction of Estevan and Ascension. "Just last month I was telling them that they had done a fine job raising their daughter. Now, she's gone."

Buck couldn't recall a time when Alejandro had showed this kind of emotion, at least not in public. "Yes, she was everything to them."

Vega glanced at his bodyguard and motioned that he was ready to leave. "She was a good daughter, that's for sure. When she came to me and told me that she was worried about her father losing the restaurant, what was I supposed to do? I offered her some cash, but that was not enough. She wanted to do more. You knew how she was. She could be so stubborn just like her old man."

The word *stubborn* hung in the air and made Buck's stomach twist into a knot. That's when Buck realized that his friend might have been responsible for Estefani's death. He knew all about the young women he recruited to move his cocaine; young women he lured with the promise of a better life, even though they risked their lives.

"Take care, my friend," Vega said, clasping Buck's hand before moving toward the door.

Buck stared into his friend's dark eyes. "Yes, you too, Alejandro."

Although there was no way to prove it—he doubted the girl in the Dade County Jail was going to start talking—he had a strong hunch that Vega had recruited Estefani as a mule to transport cocaine to the States. It sickened him when he thought about his friend taking advantage of Estefani and using her as one of his mules. Buck could feel the anger swelling up inside of him. He hadn't felt this kind of anger since Vietnam when his unit came across a village that had been destroyed by the VC. Most of the villagers had been rounded up and executed. A week before, U.S. troops had provided food and medical supplies. It was the kind of anger which made him tremble inside; the kind of anger that over the centuries, men allowed to destroy all that was holy and good as some kind of false justification for the evil that men do to others to perpetuate their good fortune. Noriega, Vega—they all just got more personal for him.

CHAPTER THIRTY-TWO

ONE LAZY, QUIET afternoon, Frank's luck was about to change when a stranger entered TJ's. Most of TJ's patrons were younger airmen, soldiers, or Zonians who came for the drug deals which took place in the back rooms or the ones who loved to shoot pool on the three regulation-sized pool tables which no other bar or club had in town. People who came to TJ's already knew about the place. No one wandered in off the street.

"Nice little bar you got here," the stranger said, wiping off his brow with a handkerchief. He spoke with a gravelly voice and an American accent that Frank guessed was probably Texas. The man ran a hand through his matted, damp white hair and stared at Frank. "Are you TJ?"

"Excuse me?" Frank said, walking down the length of the bar to where the man was sitting.

"The name out front, it says TJ's," the man said, putting his handkerchief away. "I don't know how anyone can stand the heat and the humidity here. Are you TJ?"

"No, that was the previous owner," Frank said, wiping off

the bar in front of the man and tossing down a coaster. "I never got around to changing the name."

"Don't see too many gringos owning bars like this in the city, do you?" the man said.

"No, you don't."

"A person would have to, let's say, have the right connections, right?"

The man was making Frank nervous with all his questions. A stranger didn't walk in here off the street and ask those kinds of questions without knowing something about the bar, not to mention the owner. Maybe it was Smith's way of checking up on him or maybe it was one of Vega's associates. He heard Diego talk about this American, Daniel Patterson, who smuggled drugs and arms for Noriega. He had never seen Patterson; maybe it was him.

"Yes, that would be true," Frank said. "What can I do you for, mister?"

The man looked at all the liquor bottles on the shelves behind the bar in front of a cracked yellowed mirror.

"You know, what I could go for is a Cuba Libre," the man said. "That is what most people drink here, right? It's not just rum and Coke, is it?"

"Cuba Libre it is," Frank said as he started to make the drink for the stranger seated at the bar.

"Do you know the history of the Cuba Libre?" the man asked. "Most people don't, you know."

"Yeah, I've heard some of the stories," Frank said, dropping some ice cubes into a highball glass.

"Supposedly the drink dates back to Havana right after the Spanish-American War," the man said as he watched Frank make the drink. "Some soldiers were sitting in a bar one afternoon and one of them ordered a drink made of rum, Coca-Cola, and a lime wedge. When the soldier got his drink, he turned to his comrades, raised his glass and said, *'¡Por Cuba Libre!'* in celebration of Cuba's independence, hence the name, *Cuba Libre* or Free Cuba."

"Yeah, I've heard that version," Frank said filling the glass with two parts Bacardi.

"I'm sorry, I haven't properly introduced myself," the man said, holding out his hand for Frank to shake. "My name's Chip Ramone."

That was just one of the aliases he used; Skip Gordon was another.

Frank set the man's drink on the bar and shook his hand. "Frank."

Ramone took a sip of the drink and smacked his thin lips. "Yes, that's the way I like them. Just enough fresh lime. Most bars here just serve you Coke and whatever rotgut rum they've got behind the bar."

"I thought you said—"

"Life's been a little rough for you these days, hasn't it?" Ramone said, taking another drink. "Two daughters, in debt to Vega. How much is it now, Frank? Twenty thousand dollars? That's got to be rough."

An expression of fear washed across Frank's face as he stared at Ramone—if that was even his name. "Who are you really?"

Ramone smiled. "Who I am is not important; what I can do for you *is*."

Frank looked at Ramone with a quizzical expression on his face. "Excuse me?"

"Let's just say you and I have a mutual acquaintance."

"Vega?"

Ramone shook his head and sipped his drink.

"Smith?"

Ramone nodded. "Things have gotten complicated down

there as you and I both know. Noriega is out of control. Panama has become a dangerous place for people without the right friends. Buck asked me to check up on you."

"I don't need anyone's help," Frank said. "And as far as Smith is concerned, you can tell that son-of-bitch he can go and fuck himself. He promised he would help out. For ten years, I've been sweating my ass down here no thanks to him."

"Could be worse."

"How so?"

"You could have been sweating your ass in prison the past ten years."

"What's the difference?"

Ramone smiled. "Good one, Frank. Well, my friend, this is your lucky day."

"How so?"

"I can make all your problems go away, just like that, Frank," Ramone said, snapping his fingers.

Frank turned around and grabbed a bottle of bourbon from the shelf behind the bar. He reached under the bar, found a glass, dropped in some ice cubes and filled it halfway with the bourbon.

"I doubt that," Frank said.

"How would you like to make enough money to settle all your debts here and take your family back to the States?"

Frank's brow furrowed as he thought about what Ramone had said. Whoever this Ramone fellow was, he had obviously done his homework. Frank took a large swallow of the bourbon that made him wince. The warmth of the liquor immediately helped to calm his nerves.

"Why do you want to help me?" Frank asked. "And more importantly, how do I know this is not a set-up? How do I know you're not working for Vega?"

"I guess you will just have to trust me, won't you?"

"The last time I trusted someone I got kicked out of the Air Force."

Ramone grinned. "That was most unfortunate, but you do realize it was the only way that we could protect you."

"Protect me? You and your buddy Smith and whoever else you work for at the Agency hung me out to dry."

"You're the one who got mixed up with Guerra and Santiago. We were only taking advantage of an opportunity, and sadly, things didn't go the way we would have liked them to at the time."

Frank didn't say anything. He poured himself another shot of bourbon.

"Buck feels bad about everything. He wants to make it up to you."

"A CIA agent with a heart *and* a conscience," Frank said. "You guys are too much. You tell Smith that if he wants to talk to me, he knows—"

"No can do, pardner," Ramone said.

"What's wrong? Smith scared to show his face around here? You tell that son-of-a-bitch he's got my number if he wants to talk."

Ramone laughed. "Buck warned me that you wouldn't be too receptive. And yes, it wouldn't be too healthy for you—or him—if he were seen here. Do you catch my drift?"

"Vega?"

Ramone nodded. "But right now, let's forget about your past relationship with Smith. Forget about your debt to Vega. Forget about everything that went down before. Let's talk about today, right here and now."

"Go ahead."

"What do you think Vega will do when he finds out that you've been skimming off a few ounces of cocaine here and there and then turning around and selling it?" Ramone said.

"The only reason you're still alive is because you and your wife are close to Guerra. He's Esmeralda's godfather, right?"

"How did you—?"

"That's not important right now," Ramone interrupted. "What is important is what I can do for you."

Frank gulped down bourbon and winced again as it traveled down his throat. There was no denying that he wanted to get back at Vega. He might have owed Vega his life for being there for him when no one else would lift a finger to help—including Smith—but Vega was still responsible for his friend's death. As long as that dark, troubling cloud continued to hang over Frank, he would never feel safe or secure.

"What exactly do you have in mind?"

"Do you know those C-130s that regularly fly in and out of Howard?"

Frank nodded. He knew they were from Air Guard units from the States on regular ninety-day rotations in support of Operation CORONET OAK, which provided airlift for the Southern Command as well as for other contingencies such as humanitarian missions. And until he got busted, some of those C-130s were the ones he used to smuggle his packages of Panama Red back to the States.

"Yeah, what about them?"

"Every Friday one of those C-130s flies back to the States and returns to Howard on Monday. A person could fly, say, to Texas or South Carolina on Friday and be back at Howard first thing Monday morning and no one would be the wiser," Ramone said. He smacked his lips and motioned to Frank that he wanted another drink. "Now, let's say for the sake of an argument that a person wanted to bring with them, say a certain amount of contraband and bring it on board the aircraft without any fear of being detected. That person could easily transport it to the States, hand it over to a third party, and still have time to take in the sights before getting back on the C-130 for the return trip to Howard with a suitcase full of cash."

"You're not suggesting what I think you're suggesting, are you?" Frank asked.

Ramone smiled and took another drink. "There's one thing I didn't mention in that story; supposedly one of those men in the bar that day had been one of Teddy Roosevelt's Rough Riders. Imagine that, the man responsible for making the Panama Canal a reality also indirectly introduced the Cuba Libre to Panama. And here you and I are today. Ironic, wouldn't you say? Of course Coca-Cola wouldn't come out until the early 1900s, and the Rough Riders had already left Cuba by then, but you have to admit, it makes for a good story."

"Mr. Ramone, I'm serious."

"Can we please dispense with the formalities? Chip, please," Ramone said. "I'm serious, too, Frank. This is your ticket out of paradise."

"What kind of contraband?"

"Do I have to spell it out for you, Frank?"

"Cocaine?"

Ramone nodded.

Frank thought hard about what Ramone had proposed, his curiosity already piqued. If someone was going to make a move against Guerra or Vega, they might want to use him, knowing his past as well as his current economic situation. And though it would mean putting his ass on the line, he had nothing to lose. This stranger was right, all it would take was smuggling a couple of kilos of cocaine and all his troubles would be over. He could pay off Vega and get the hell out of Panama. And with the way Noriega was running the country, it was time to get out. Whatever the risk, it was worth hearing what Ramone had to say.

"Cocaine, huh? Go on."

"There's this fellow who lives near Albrook. He's a GS-10, ex-Air Force. He married a Panamanian and decided to stay here. He's your point of contact," Ramone explained. "All you need to do is show up with a duffel bag containing the cocaine."

"It's that simple, huh?"

"You of all people should appreciate that," Ramone said, sliding a piece of folded paper across the bar. "Just deliver the cocaine to this address and our friend will do the rest."

Frank unfolded the piece of paper and looked at what had been written on it. "I don't get it. You want to help *me* sell cocaine? Since when was the CIA in the drug business?"

Ramone grinned. "Who says the CIA is behind this?"

"You guys are crazier than I thought."

Frank looked at the piece of paper in his hand. It all seemed too simple which made him all the more reluctant to go through with it. The downside? If Vega or whoever else was involved found out about this, there would be no way that Smith or Ramone would be able to protect him.

"I know what you're thinking, Frank," Ramone said, sensing that Frank was mulling over the proposition and worrying about it. "You're probably wondering if this is all on the up and up. Maybe you think this could be a setup. Maybe you're wondering if I'm DEA or worse, if I am working for Vega. If I were you, I would probably be wondering about the same things. A stranger comes into your bar and starts talking shit like this, well, that's got to raise a few flags. But here's the clincher, Frank. You've got to ask yourself this: Who stands to gain the most from this if this *is* on the up and up?"

Frank stared at Ramone. "That's easy for you to say."

"You're right about that, Frank. After all, anyone who tries to make a move against Vega is just asking to end up in a ditch with their throat slit."

Frank thought about Gary and felt his insides twisting into a knot. Outside a car or truck backfired, startling Frank, who quickly turned and gazed toward a window near the entrance.

"What's going to happen one day when you finally fall from his graces? Things are changing here fast, Frank. You are about to become a liability. I'm offering you a way out."

Frank turned back around and furrowed his brow. He still wasn't sold on the idea. "Smuggling cocaine back to the States? You call that a way out? No thanks, buddy."

Ramone grinned and sipped his drink.

"Besides, I don't see how this is getting back at Vega," Frank continued. "If anything I'm just helping him make money. Why go to all this trouble—"

"Yes, that is true," Ramone said. "Why go to all this trouble if what one truly wants to do is get back at someone where it would hurt the most?"

"Wait a minute, you're not suggesting what I think you are—"

Ramone smiled. "Buck said you were a fast learner."

"You're going to steal his cocaine, aren't you?"

"How about one more Cuba Libre for the road?" Ramone finished his drink and slid the glass across the bar. "Steal is an awful word. Let's just say we're going to divert some of his cocaine to teach him a very valuable lesson on how *not* to treat your friends."

"If all you want to do is set Vega up for whatever you and Smith are concocting, why don't you and the boys at the CIA, DEA, or whatever agency you work for take care of it yourselves? That's how you earn a living. Why drag me into this?"

"Could you add a little more rum this time, Frank?"

Ramone asked as he watched Frank make him a fresh drink. "The last one was a little weak."

Frank glared at Ramone before he poured some rum into the glass and then stopped. "You're using me to get Vega, aren't you? You're going to have me put my ass on the line, so you don't get your hands dirty."

"When you put it like that it sounds so awful. We're not that bad."

Frank snickered. He squeezed a wedge of fresh lime juice into Ramone's drink and ran the lime wedge around the rim of the glass. "I wouldn't be so sure about that."

"Don't worry, we're going to be with you every step of the way."

"Why don't I like the sound of that?" Frank asked, sliding the fresh Cuba Libre to Ramone.

"You're going to have to trust us on that one, Frank," Ramone said. "You and I both know there's only one way out of this predicament you've gotten yourself into with Vega."

Frank poured himself another drink. He was caught between another rock and a hard place. Frank had trusted Smith before, but it didn't work out too well for him. Although he had managed to save up a close to a thousand dollars, there was no way he would be able to get his family out of Panama without some help. Ramone was right; there was only one way out. "Tell Smith I'm interested but if this doesn't work out, I want to make sure my family is protected."

Ramone nodded. "Buck has already got that covered."

"Tell me, Ramone, why is the CIA so interested in helping me out now?" Frank asked. "You guys probably have plenty of stooges in Panama that would love this kind of action."

"Much better," Ramone said, taking a drink and licking his lips. He set the glass down and stared at Frank. "Let's just say that your interests and our interests are one in the same."

CHAPTER THIRTY-THREE

SEÑORA DOMINGA BONILLA Castillo sat nervously in the home of her best friend Rosalie Lopez, who was in the kitchen making coffee. Dominga knew she had taken a risk coming here, in an upscale neighborhood located next to the Thatcher Ferry Bridge, but there was no other way she would be able to carry out her husband's wishes. Right now, the meeting that she would soon have with two CIA agents was the only thing that stood between her husband and the man who could assist with the plan to remove Manuel Noriega from power.

The risk she would be taking wouldn't be anything like the one her husband would soon be taking if this meeting went the way she hoped.

Outside, a car door slammed, and Dominga jumped, spilling a glass of water on her dress. A few seconds later, when she heard someone pounding on the door, her heart skipped a few beats.

"They're here," Rosalie said, walking into the room carrying a tray with four cups of coffee on it. "Now you tell them everything that you told me and everything's going to be all right."

*   *   *

Major Moisés Castillo was the young and charming commander of the Panamanian Defense Forces Fourth Infantry Company which was in charge of security at the Comandancia—the headquarters of the PDF. He had everything going for him: a trophy wife at home, the respect of his men, and the respect of the man who could punch his ticket for career advancement, Manuel Noriega. However, Castillo had become disillusioned with the man he once looked up to and admired. Blinded by his professional pursuits, Castillo had soon discovered that Noriega did not have the best interests of his countrymen in mind. Although it had been easy in the past for Castillo to turn a blind eye, after the recent elections, it became obvious to him that his boss was not the same man who had courted his expertise. Like many of the young officers who had blindly followed Noriega, they had also looked the other way whenever Noriega's disreputable actions came to light. Noriega, for Castillo, was out of control and the only way to put an end to it was to remove the man from power.

One night, he confided to his wife about how disillusioned he had become while serving under Noriega.

"He's destroying our country, Dominga," he said. "He doesn't care about our people anymore. Just the other day he said, 'either you are with us or against us.' He has no qualms about killing innocent people. Maybe the Americans have been right all along trying to remove him from power."

Dominga had harbored similar feelings about Noriega for months. She knew that the man her husband once admired was destroying their country.

"What can you do about him?" his wife asked. "If he finds out you're making a move against him he'll have you killed."

For weeks, Castillo had been thinking of how he could remove the man who had grown fond of him. He knew that the only way it could work was to convince some of the junior officers that they needed to ask Noriega to step down. Castillo didn't want this coup to turn violent and deadly. There already had been too much violence and bloodshed. He hoped that Noriega, when he heard their demands and concerns, would do the right thing. However, he knew that they wouldn't be able to do it alone. That was where he needed his wife's help.

"That's a risk I am willing to take, Dominga. Somebody has to make a move against him," he said. "If we could enlist the help of the Americans, we might be able to make this work."

Dominga looked up at her husband with her big brown eyes. She had never seen her husband like this, and it turned her on.

"What about that friend of yours, Rosalie? She's a general's secretary at Quarry Heights, right?" he asked. "Is there any way possible you could pass some information along to her about my plan that she in turn could give to her boss?"

"I think so," Dominga said.

The die was cast. That night, when they made love, it was some of the best lovemaking they had had in a very long time. It would also be the last.

*   *   *

Buck hadn't been too crazy about the plan when he sat down with Castillo's wife and another agent. First of all, he didn't like how the woman had used one of her friends who worked in Quarry Heights to arrange this little meeting. Second, and more importantly, could Castillo be trusted? On the other hand, if there was a move to be made against Noriega without raising too many red flags, this might be the way that Noriega would finally be removed from power. Although this was something he and others had hoped for, Buck had guarded optimism. The details of the coup were sketchy: Castillo, who had assembled a group of young officers, was hoping that Noriega would simply give up for the greater good of the country when he saw that a coup was in the works. However, what bothered Buck and others the most was that the success of the coup was dependent upon assistance by the U.S. military. Without it, according to Castillo, the coup would fail.

Buck wasn't too keen on involving the U.S. military, and neither was the new SOUTHCOM CINC, who still wasn't sold on the idea.

"If I could talk to the SOUTHCOM commander—" Castillo began when he finally had the chance to talk to Buck.

Buck shook his head. "That's not going to happen. This has to be done on your own. If anyone connects us or the U.S. military to the coup, it's game over."

"Yes, I understand," Castillo said in a weak voice.

It was a half-baked idea at best—to surprise Noriega in his headquarters, capture him, and turn him over to the Americans—but the group of young officers led by Moisés Castillo felt that if they could get some support from the Americans, they could easily overthrow Noriega.

At least that was what Buck felt. It could solve all their problems in one fell swoop.

Although a coup was the best way for all of this to end, the United States had a few tricks up its sleeve. For months, the United States had stepped up its military exercises in the Canal Zone—as part of the 1988 OPLAN that now had a name, OPLAN Blue Spoon—primarily as a psychological ploy to convince Noriega that the United States was planning a military operation against him. The message was simple: either Noriega stepped down or they were coming to get him.

"They're going to serve Noriega up on a platter for us," Buck said when he met with his military counterpart at Quarry Heights. "This is a golden opportunity for us to remove Noriega from power without looking like we had anything to do with it. We might not get a chance like this again."

Noriega had to go; there was no denying it, and everyone agreed. The problem all along was not a matter of what to do with Noriega, rather, how to make it look like the Americans had no part in it. This was not going to be like an episode of the TV drama *Mission: Impossible*—a show that Buck liked watching back in the 1960s—where the team would infiltrate a dictator's country and remove him from power without anyone being the wiser, right before a commercial break. This operation was going to take a little thought, but not what Castillo and his wife had in mind. Planning a coup over coffee and cookies was more like an episode of *Charlie's Angels*.

On the other hand, Buck, like a few others, was worried that it was all a ploy, cooked up by Noriega to see what the Americans would do. To be sure, he was one of Noriega's confidants and had squashed the last coup attempt. Buck and others had their reservations about Castillo and rightfully so. If this was a ploy to force the American hand, then Noriega could announce to the world that the Americans were deliberately trying to oust him from power by intervening in Panamanian affairs. The commander of SOUTHCOM, who had recently assumed command a few days earlier, thought he had caught a break with having to deal with Noriega once and for all. However, he had his doubts about the coup, especially when he found out that it had been the wife of the coup leader who had first approached U.S. officials, not to mention suspicious of Castillo's ability to actually pull it off. There were other officials who felt that the coup was an attempt to humiliate the new commander of SOUTHCOM as well as the United States. Panama's latest Noriega-handpicked president just so happened to be at the United Nations; if the coup attempt was only meant to embarrass the United States, the Panamanian president would be able to make an announcement and have the whole world watching.

* * *

Buck monitored the unfolding coup all morning with a few officers in the command post inside Quarry Heights, but the information coming in was spotty at best. Despite conflicting reports, the coup was proceeding as planned though it had been delayed for a few hours, which worried everyone inside the command post. The plan was to have everyone in place before Noriega arrived at the Comandancia, the headquarters of the Panama Defense Forces. Any delay could prove disastrous.

As Buck watched officers listening to radio chatter, he was overcome with a strong feeling of déjà vu tinged with irony. His father had been in the same command post during the 1964 riots, monitoring radio chatter and directing troop movements.

"Please repeat, Tango Foxtrot," one of the officers, his voice fraught with tension, said into a radio. "What can you see?"

There were a few seconds of static and white noise and what sounded like small-arms fire emitting from the radio the officer held in his hand. Then, a voice with a metal edge to it, said, "There's some shooting in the compound."

"Jesus, Castillo went ahead and did it," Buck said, no longer able to hide his emotions.

One of the officers, Colonel Charles Greer, walked away from a wall map of Panama City that he had been looking at and joined Buck at the back of the room.

"Your first coup?" Greer asked.

Buck grinned and poured himself a cup of coffee from a coffee urn. "Is it that obvious?"

"Just a little," Greer said smiling. "It's kind of like being an expectant father. You've done your part; now it's up to the powers that be to deliver."

Buck sipped the bitter coffee and nodded. "How about you?"

"My third," Greer said, pouring some coffee into a Styrofoam cup. "Trust me; they get easy after the first one."

"What do you think his chances are?" Buck asked.

"About fifty-fifty," Greer replied. "I hope your boy pulls it off. It will save us all a major headache down the road."

Tell me about it. Buck still had reservations about the success of the coup, not the least of which was what Castillo would do with Noriega when it was all over. There was no way that Noriega was going to go quietly.

"It's still too early to tell, Buck, what exactly is going down," Greer said. "You don't want to go popping any champagne yet."

Although his money hadn't been on Castillo in the beginning, now that the coup was underway, Buck had a change of heart. There wasn't much the United States could do at this point without raising too many flags. Folks were just going to have to sit back and wait and see what happened. He remembered the meeting he had had with Castillo's wife. Here was a woman who was putting everything on the line because she believed in her country and her husband while she served coffee and cookies. When she handed Buck a cup of coffee on a platter, her hand was hardly shaking. Buck hoped her husband had that same steely-eyed resolve to pull off this coup.

*   *   *

Some operations are doomed from the beginning, where nothing goes according to plan, but at least the mission or operation can be aborted without too many repercussions. Then there are the missions that run afoul after they have gotten underway, and there's nothing that can be done to stop them. When Castillo and his men started their coup, it was a combination of the two. Without the full support of the U.S. military in Panama, there was no way they would be able to carry out the coup attempt successfully.

There was no way that U.S. officials could contact Castillo once the coup started, which only added to the confusion. Although the U.S. military would be able to offer some support, such as having a detachment of marines take up positions at the Bridge of the Americas and blocking Fort Amador, they wanted to avoid any confrontation with the PDF. To be sure, the United States had to be discreet about any use of military units lest it would be interpreted that they had a hand in the coup. However, miscommunication thwarted the coup attempt. Castillo had requested that three roads needed to be blocked by U.S. forces if the coup was to be a success; however, only two roads were blocked which allowed Noriega's forces to stop the rebels.

Everything went according to plan in the beginning but then it fell apart. Castillo waited until the last minute to tell his forces about the coup and what he intended to do; he hoped that his relationship and friendship with Noriega would be enough to convince him to step down in the best interests of the country. However deep their friendship ran, Castillo seriously underestimated Noriega. Shortly after Noriega arrived at the Comandancia, Castillo's forces attacked. Timing had been everything, making certain that the coup didn't start until after Noriega arrived, but luck was with the general that morning. As soon as Noriega realized what was going down, he barricaded himself in his office. Men loyal to him managed to hold back the rebel forces and radio for help. Immediately PDF forces were on their way to Amador to come to the rescue of their beleaguered comrades. At that moment, the coup was, for all practical purposes, over.

U.S. authorities remained in the dark for most of the coup. At first, reports said that Castillo had Noriega in custody and was ready to turn him over to U.S. authorities. Then it was learned that Noriega's forces had been able to turn back Castillo and that Noriega had escaped unscathed—a little shaken up, but no worse for the wear.

* * *

Castillo and some his officers were dead. Noriega had rounded up the conspirators and put a bullet into their heads. And when the moment was just right, Noriega emerged and beamed at cameras to let the world know that he had survived and that he was more powerful than ever. He was like a boxer who had survived a grueling ten-round fight; though battered and flustered, he was still standing when it was over. The press had a field day with the photo opportunity he gave them for the world to see: wildly brandishing a machete, Noriega put an exclamation point onto the failed coup attempt and issued a warning to anyone else who tried.

In Washington, it didn't take long for the fallout from the failed coup to resonate strongly from Capitol Hill to the Oval Office. Politicians from both sides were lining up to criticize the man who once wined and dined Noriega for not doing enough. Of course, the President took it personally. Noriega had embarrassed him for the last time.

In his Panama City apartment, Buck had been watching news reports from the United States via the *Armed Forces Radio and Television Network*, but he didn't need any of the Washington pundits who had been consulted by the networks to make sense out of what had just happened. They were going to spin the news the way they saw fit. The press was having a field day with the coup attempt and everyone, it seemed, was looking for someone to blame.

He looked in on his girlfriend Lucinda asleep on the bed. Buck met her at a Fourth of July party at the U.S. Embassy, and the two hit it off immediately. He smiled when he thought back years ago when Estevan's wife told him that he should meet a nice woman and settle down. Ascension would approve. He told her to stay home, just in case things got a little ugly, but when he came home from the office, she was waiting for him in the lobby with a carryout from an Italian restaurant down the street; the food was still on the kitchen table.

He poured himself another tall tumbler of bourbon. He took a drink and winced as the warm liquid coursed through his body. It was just one more failure, one more setback that put a damper on more than the evening. There was going to be a lot of fallout from this and heads were going to roll, and one of those heads was probably his. Ever since he got back home, the phone had been ringing off the hook. He had tried getting hold of Vega, but his friend wasn't answering his phone either.

Buck figured his friend was keeping a low profile in case Noriega started cleaning house after the coup attempt.

He moved out onto the balcony and sat down with his bourbon. It was quiet in his neighborhood. He looked up and down the palm tree lined avenue. By now the Panamanians were talking about how Noriega survived the coup; he was going to be stronger than ever. He wondered how many people cared about what was happening in Panama. In most cases, people only reacted after something had happened ignoring all the warning signs in the process. Washington had ignored all the warnings for years and had paid dearly. If Washington wanted Noriega out of the Panama, it was going to take something on a much larger scale now. On the other hand, there was always another way to take care of this problem once and for all. The military had already been preparing for just such a contingency; perhaps Castillo didn't die in vain, after all.

There was something else that Buck needed to do of a more personal nature before this ill-fated coup attempt had come along and put his plans on hold. He walked back inside and sat down on the sofa in the living room. He poured himself another glass of bourbon and made a phone call. The telephone on the other end rang ten times before someone finally answered in a groggy voice.

"Hello, Frank," Buck said, swirling the bourbon around in his glass. "We need to talk."

CHAPTER THIRTY-FOUR

VEGA WATCHED FRANK get out of a banged-up yellow Pinto and walk toward an apartment in Diablo Heights near the back gate of Albrook Air Force Station. What Frank was doing in this high-end rent district near the Air Force base was no mystery to Vega, who had been keeping an eye on his investment making certain that Frank delivered as promised. Frank walked slowly with his head hunched in case someone was watching him. In his left hand, he carried a faded green duffel bag. When he reached the entrance to the apartment, he stopped and looked over his shoulder before he knocked on the door. About a minute later, the door opened and Frank walked inside.

Vega tapped the steering wheel of his black Mercedes and continued to stare at the apartment waiting for Frank to emerge. Vega was well aware of the risk he was taking in this recent venture with Frank, but what troubled him the most was the distinct possibility that Frank was playing him.

Six weeks earlier, Vega was all ears, just as Ramone

prophesied when Frank told him about a plan he had come up with to smuggle up to forty kilos of cocaine. If Vega wanted to keep his little drug smuggling operation off Noriega and Escobar's radar screens, Frank's little plan was perfect.

The only problem was could Vega trust Frank?

For Frank, it was déjà vu when he walked into Vega's office and told him about the plan; it was in this same office that Frank had first met Vega and started them both down the rocky road they had been traveling for the past twelve years. However, this time he wasn't going in half-cocked. Buck and Ramone had coached him on exactly what to say. All Frank had to do was be convincing.

"Every Friday one of the C-130s deployed to Howard flies back to the States and then returns to base on Monday," Frank began to explain.

"I'm listening."

"We make up some phony travel documents and have one or two people fly back. They don't even have to be military. They can easily carry a couple of kilos in their duffel bags," Frank explained. "Once they arrive in the States, they hand over the duffel bags to one of our contacts and return on Monday morning. No one will know they are gone."

Frank explained everything to Vega the way that Ramone had instructed. He left nothing out; nothing to chance. Frank knew that Vega was desperate, not to mention greedy.

It was a *good* plan. Smith and Ramone had seen to that.

"That's all there is to it," Frank explained. "It's the simplicity of this plan which makes it so beautiful."

Vega liked what he heard. For the past ten years, Vega had been moving his cocaine by whatever means possible—a kilo here and a kilo there—hardly the kind of action he desired. While it had been easy to divert a couple kilos from the secret labs along the Colombian border and the secret airfields where the cocaine was flown to the United States, it wasn't enough to satisfy his appetite. He had a hunch that Noriega's days were numbered, especially after the last coup attempt, and if there ever was a time to make a move, it was now. As he always told Guerra: "When an opportunity presents itself to you don't pass it up, regardless of the risk." That opportunity had come now.

"Do you have anyone in mind?" Vega asked.

"There are some airmen who regularly come into the bar," Frank said, gesturing to his nose. He figured that would be the best way to convince Vega that this plan would work. "They might be interested if there's something in it for them. If you know what I mean."

Vega smiled. He knew exactly what Frank meant. That's how he had been able to keep his stable of mules happy and content. "What about the security police?"

"Not a problem. We do like we did before," Frank said. "There's always someone who's willing to look the other way for a price."

Alejandro twisted the large onyx sterling silver ring on his finger as was his habit every time he liked a plan or a proposition. The wheels were already turning. "You haven't thought of everything though, have you?"

"What do you mean?" Frank shifted his body on the chair. He didn't expect the third degree from Vega.

"Aren't you worried that someone might recognize you?"

Frank shook his head and finished his Cuba Libre. "All I have to do is drop off the drugs. These guys that I know will do the rest."

Vega paused before he spoke. Handing over all that cocaine to Frank was too much of a risk even for him. He didn't get where he was at without taking chances, but he also had to protect his interests and not let his guard down. The DEA was getting too close for comfort. Another lab had been raided. He knew it was collateral damage—all for show. However, it still worried him. Had the DEA gotten to Frank? The more he wrapped his mind around it, the more plausible it seemed. He was going to have to play this one carefully.

"Do you think I'm stupid enough to give you a couple kilos of coke?"

Frank bolted upright in his chair.

"Alejandro, I swear on my daughter's lives, I would never make a move against you," Frank said, putting on his best poker face and his right hand on his chest over his heart. "You've been there for me as well as my family. You've been like a second father to me. I owe you my life."

Vega stared at Frank as he sipped his *Seco con vaca* and licked his lips. He wasn't touched by Frank's sincerity, but it made for good drama. Vega slowly stood up and walked up to where Frank was sitting. He motioned for one of his men to come up behind Frank; the man pulled Frank off the chair and held Frank's arms behind his back.

"What the hell?" Frank said, an expression of fear washing across his face, as he tried to free his arms. "Alejandro, what's going on?"

Vega ripped open Frank's shirt to see if he was wearing a wire.

"Sorry, Frank," Vega said. "You of all people know that a man in my position cannot take any chances."

"You have to trust me on this, Alejandro," Frank said, tucking his shirt into his trousers. He felt smug with the self-satisfaction that came with the plan knowing that whatever reservations Vega might have, there was no way he was going to back down. He only prayed that Smith and Ramone would come through for him; otherwise this wasn't going to bode well for him. "The way I see it, it's a golden opportunity for you, Alejandro."

"I would like to meet these airmen," Vega said after he had mulled over what Frank said.

Frank nodded. He could tell that Vega had already been sold on the idea. He could easily get a few customers to play along with the idea to assuage Vega's anxieties.

"Just remember, Frank," Vega said with a hard edge in his voice, "I own you until you pay off your debt."

"I understand completely."

Vega held out his hand. Frank gazed into Vega's cold, dark eyes and slowly shook his hand before he turned and started for the door.

"One more thing, Frank."

Frank turned and gazed at Vega.

"Why did you wait so long?" Vega asked, walking back to his desk and sitting down. "There have been C-130s flying in and out of Howard regularly for the past ten years. You could have done this at any time."

Frank bit his bottom lip and thought hard about what Vega said. "I hadn't given it much thought, you know, after what happened before. So, when this airman comes in and tells me how he goes home on weekends by hopping on one of these C-130s, that's when I got the idea."

Vega stroked his mustache with his index finger, thumb under his chin. "Hmm, very interesting. Lucky for us, huh?"

"Yeah, yeah," Frank said, doing his best to hide his nervousness. "Very lucky."

* * *

Vega didn't have to wait long for Frank, who appeared thirty minutes later carrying a different duffel bag. He looked around as though he knew he was being watched and just to make it look good, he pulled down the Chicago Cubs baseball cap and hurried back to his car. If Frank was up to something, he sure as hell wasn't worried about being tailed. Not to mention, if he was aware that he was being tailed, he was doing it right under Vega's nose. Vega didn't like being double-crossed, and that was what Frank was doing right in front of him. If the DEA was about to make a move against him, he was going to need an escape plan. In the meantime, he had Guerra keep an eye on Frank's family. His family would be his insurance; his leverage should anything happen.

Frank threw the duffel bag in the car, got in, and drove away with a sputter and a rumble before disappearing in a cloud of blue smoke.

*　*　*

Frank wasn't the only one who was being watched.

From a window of a second-floor apartment building across the street, Buck peered out through partially opened curtains using a high-powered sniper rifle scope.

"You are so predictable, my friend," Buck said.

This was going to be a lot easier than he had anticipated. The dummy drops were Ramone's idea—just to see what Vega would do. Once all the players were in place, Buck would pull the plug on the operation and Vega, Noriega, even Escobar wouldn't be the wiser. Buck's friends in the DEA, including Danny Patterson, who was brilliant at playing both sides, would swoop in and shut everything down before Vega knew what the fuck had hit him. Buck still had a personal score to settle with his friend and there was no better way than to hit him where it would hurt the most. And then Buck would take care of his friend once and for all.

Now the only thing Buck had to do was make sure that it went according to plan.

CHAPTER THIRTY-FIVE

NO MATTER WHAT Vega had in store for Frank, he was also going to have to deal with his friend Buck one day.

Guerra had warned Vega that Smith was getting too close for comfort—something that Vega didn't take too lightly. Ever since the attempted coup, his friend had his hands full with Noriega, which was good for him. On the other hand, he had a hunch his friend might have had something to do with the DEA coming down hard on Noriega's operations which in turn had an impact on Vega's livelihood. Vega had a good thing going and he didn't need Noriega or Buck messing it up.

With so much cocaine and money flowing in and out of Panama, Vega was certain that no one would be the wiser—even Smith.

"You know if this ever gets back to Smith, he's not going to be happy about it," Guerra said, grinning. "And if this gets back to—"

"I can handle him," Vega said, sipping a glass of bourbon. Kneeling in front of him, one of the hostesses who worked in his nightclub downstairs was giving him oral sex. "Smith has got too much on his plate with Noriega."

The one constant in this high stakes game that Vega dangerously played was his friend, Buck. Though he was concerned that Buck was snooping around where he shouldn't—he knew all about the phone calls to the Dade County Police Department and his attorney's office in Miami—his friend was just as easy to handle. As long as Buck thought he could depend on him for whatever intel he could provide, Vega was untouchable. He thought for sure it would all blow up during the Iran-Contra Affair, but as long as Noriega remained in power, this little drama that Vega had with his friend would continue to play out.

Then there was Danny Patterson, who had become a pain in the ass. Vega knew that Patterson had become Noriega's go-to-man, which incensed Vega all the more.

Vega had never cared much for Patterson the first time he was introduced to him at Noriega's beach house in Rio Hato in the late 1970s. Noriega introduced him as his personal pilot; it was Patterson who was helping Noriega smuggle guns to the Contras as well as drugs to America, using secret bases in Costa Rica. He could never figure out if he was on the CIA's payroll; if he was, Buck certainly didn't know anything about it or didn't want to talk about it. He was just as dirty and corrupt as everyone else, but there was just something about the guy that rubbed Vega the wrong way—maybe it was his two thousand dollar Cartier watch or his three thousand dollar Italian tailor-made suits that made Vega nauseous when he saw Patterson; maybe it was the way he schmoozed with Noriega and other high-ranking officers in the PDF which turned his stomach. Then, of course, it could be that he was just simply jealous.

"It's a dangerous game we sometimes play, Diego," Vega said. He set the glass on the desk and stroked the woman's long black hair before he pushed her head down further on him. He shifted his body in the black leather chair. "This business with Smith, Noriega, and Escobar will work itself out in the end. We have to plan for the future, my friend. We have to think about ourselves."

* * *

It was ironic how that fateful day in 1964 had brought them together and sent them down the rocky road they traveled for twenty-five years. Buck often liked to tell the story of how he had saved his friend during the 1964 riots but Buck never knew the whole story, only the part how he came across Alejandro and helped him get back home. Buck assumed that he had marched into the Canal Zone with the other Panamanian students when he came across Alejandro on the street. However, nothing could be further from the truth.

Vega had gone into the Canal Zone to break into a home on a dare from a member of the gang he ran with in Chorrillo. While he was looking for something valuable to steal, the homeowner, who worked in the commissary came home and surprised Vega. There was a scuffle and Vega hit the man on the head with a glass pitcher, which shattered upon impact. Vega cut his hand on a jagged piece of glass. The man who had collapsed on the floor lay in a growing pool of blood from a serious head wound. That's when Vega panicked, thinking that he had killed the man, and he ran out of the house as fast as he could. He got about a block when he collapsed on the road. That's when Buck came along.

Vega never bothered to find out if the man died or not. It wouldn't have made any difference. He was already telling people how he killed his first gringo.

* * *

After the failed coup attempt, Vega knew that his friend was the most vulnerable. He was surprised that Buck hadn't called him, licking his wounds, hoping that he would throw him something to take away the sting of having been defeated by Noriega. Vega had known about the coup—there was more than one secretary inside SOUTHCOM working both sides—but had sat back and waited to see how it would play out. Either way, he would come out a winner. Noriega might have survived the coup, unscathed, and now stronger than ever, but Vega knew that it would be a matter of time before the Americans tried something—and when they did, he would be ready.

"What should we do with Costello?" Guerra asked.

Vega twisted his thin lips into a wry smile as he zipped his pants. "I'm sure we can up with something creative, don't you think?"

* * *

Guerra waited until his boss was gone before he returned to Vega's office to use the phone. Guerra, who had been one of Vega's faithful associates for almost twenty years, knew that Vega's days, just like Noriega's were numbered. Vega was right. After the failed coup, everyone was vulnerable. It was only a matter of time before Noriega, Escobar, or the Americans put an end to it all. And if that happened, Guerra needed some protection. He didn't feel bad for going behind his boss's back. He also had to think about the future.

The phone rang six times before the person on the other end picked up.

"Smith, this is Diego."

CHAPTER THIRTY-SIX

KEVIN WAS GOING back in time. At least that's what it felt like as he bounced up and down in the cargo section of a C-130 bound for Howard Air Force Base. Forty-eight hours earlier, he had been pulled out of morning roll call and told to report to his commander. He thought he was going to be reprimanded for an incident that happened on the flight line two days earlier when he stopped the base commander and ticketed him for making an improper turn; instead, he was told he was being sent to Panama on a special assignment.

"Panama, Sir?" Kevin had asked, looking at the copy of his orders in hand. He knew that in the past year things had gotten dicey down there and there had been some exercises, but nothing that would warrant having him go there.

"Beats me, Rooney," his commander said, who was equally in the dark about any special assignments to Howard. "Someone must want you down there pretty bad to make this happen in less than forty-eight hours."

Kevin had just enough time to go home to get his duffel bag, which he always had packed for whatever mobility exercises the Air Force conducted, contact his political science instructor that there was the chance he wouldn't be able to take his final exam, say goodbye to Clare and catch a flight from Norton to Eglin. Twenty-four hours later he was back in the air, on his way to Howard.

There were ten other men besides Kevin on the C-130 transport. It was the Air Force's way of having Kevin fly under the radar by having him catch a hop with one of the Air National Guard units that flew weekly TDY missions to Howard. His orders instructed him to report to the 24th Security Police Squadron no later than November 30, but Kevin was still in the dark as to why he was being sent to Panama. With Noriega and Panama in the news a lot, he figured that it probably had something to do with one of the exercises the military was conducting. However, when he asked the other guys on the plane with him, they also had no idea. They were part of a normal Guard rotation to Howard.

He felt the plane shimmy and shake as the landing gear deployed. He turned around and looked out one of the small windows on the aircraft. In the distance, he could see the base coming into view. For the first time in a long time, Kevin was overcome with a strong feeling of nostalgia for having been stationed in Panama. Despite having moved around his entire life, he never felt close to or connected with a place the way he did when he was stationed here.

As soon as the ramp was lowered, and Kevin felt the heat and got a whiff of the vegetation, he smiled. He grabbed his gear and slowly walked out of the aircraft. After all these years, both as a military dependent and an airman, Kevin truly felt as though he had come home.

However, when he walked into the 24th Security Police Squadron's commander's office thirty minutes later, whatever euphoria and excitement he might have been feeling quickly changed to anger and contempt when he saw who was waiting for him.

"Rooney, I would like to introduce you to Buck Smith," Colonel Davis said. Both the colonel and Buck were looking at Kevin's personnel records. "He's here to help us coordinate things on base."

Kevin's jaw dropped as soon as the colonel said Smith's name.

"Master sergeant in ten years," Buck said, looking at one of the documents inside the brown folder. After the failed October coup, SOUTHCOM continued its psychological warfare against Noriega and the PDF. Conducting intelligence briefings for one of the latest exercises was Buck's cover story, and so far everyone had bought it.

"That's rather impressive, Rooney. Your old man did it in ten too, right?"

"Colonel, what's going on here?" Kevin asked, looking at Davis.

"Quite the record, Rooney," Buck said closing the folder. "Your father would have been so proud of you."

"You son-of-a—" Kevin glared at Buck and shook his head.

"What's going on here, Rooney?" Davis interrupted.

"This bastard is responsible for my friend's death," Kevin said with a hard edge to his voice. He stood in front of the commander's desk with his hands balled into fists as he stared at Smith. "My friend and I were both stationed here in the 1970s. My friend got mixed up with one of Smith's associates and ended up dead."

"I'm sorry I don't seem to follow you, Rooney," Davis said. "Mr. Smith requested you to be part of his team to gather information. Granted, with all the shit that's been happening here—"

"Before you go accusing anyone of your friend's death, you should at least hear all the facts," Buck said cutting off Davis. He knew it was going to be awkward finally confronting Rooney after all these years, but he could see no other way around it.

Davis looked at both men with a confused expression on his face. "Do you mind telling me what this is all about?"

"Rooney and I have some unfinished business to attend to, Colonel," Buck said. "I assure you it will have no impact on whatever Washington is cooking up for us down here."

Davis grunted. He still didn't know what Rooney and Smith were talking about. And he certainly didn't like the way Smith came into his office throwing his Agency weight around. "What's with this accusation that you are responsible for some airman's death?"

"Colonel, with all due respect, this is of no concern to you," Buck said, getting up from behind the desk and walking to the door. "This is strictly on a need-to-know basis. Now if you don't mind, Rooney and I have some matters to discuss."

Buck opened the door and motioned for two airmen to escort the commander from his office.

"What the hell is this, Smith?" Davis said. "You can't kick me out of my office."

"Grab a cup of coffee," Buck said, his lips twisting into a grin. "We'll be out of your hair soon."

Davis shook his head and grumbled as he got up from his desk and walked out of the office.

"Jesus, that colonel is sure a tight ass," Buck said grinning. "Bet you're relieved you're working for me and not him."

"Fuck you, Smith."

"I know I owe you an explanation—"

"You think?"

"Just hear me out, Rooney," Buck said, walking back to the commander's desk and sitting down. "We don't have much time."

Kevin continued to glare at Buck; the anger swelled in his chest. "Why did you let them kill Gary?"

"Your friend was in the wrong place at the wrong time," Buck said. "We had a mole supplying valuable intel on Noriega, who was a rising star in Panama's Guardia Nacional. Your friend unsuspectingly got himself mixed up in all this, and because of it was murdered."

Kevin had never forgotten the time when he was summoned to his first sergeant's office after he had gotten into a fight downtown with Frank Costello and asked by the OSI to *spy* on his friend. Although he had only been asked to find out what he could about Costello's connection with a Panamanian underworld figure, he never knew just how much his friend was involved.

"So you sat back and did nothing."

"That's not the way it works, Rooney. You of all people should know that when you have a mole or someone working undercover there are certain risks and liabilities. We couldn't afford to expose our man without jeopardizing everything."

"Who?"

Buck bit down on his bottom lip and wondered if Davis kept a bottle in his bottom desk drawer for emergencies. It wasn't going to be easy to tell Rooney what he had to hear. However, if this was going to work, he had to tell Rooney everything—no matter how much the truth hurt.

"Frank Costello."

Kevin stared at Buck wide-eyed and slack-jawed; then the veins in his neck tightened as anger washed over his face after what Buck had said finally registered with him.

"No, Smith, no" Kevin said, shaking his head and glaring

at Buck. "You're not going to sit there and tell me that Costello was in on this from the beginning."

Buck nodded. He knew that he was walking a fine line with Rooney. He had to be very careful what he said; otherwise, it was game over. "It's not what you think, Rooney."

"What do you mean, 'it's not what I think'?" Kevin clenched his teeth.

"It's complicated."

Kevin jumped up from his chair and started to pace like a wild animal in front of the desk. He wanted to leap across the desk and take a couple of swings at Smith. It would be worth some time in a cell and whatever punishment he deserved. "Where is he now, Smith? Is he still in Panama? I knew that son-of-a-bitch was responsible for Gary's death. I just knew it. And look at you, sitting there with that smug expression on your face. You are just as responsible. Who are you really? OSI? CIA? DIA? All you bastards are alike."

Buck had enough of Rooney's tirade. "Sit down, Rooney. Quit being such a hothead. Boy, you sure are like your old man."

"Smith, if you mention my father's name one—"

"Park it, Sergeant!" Buck yelled the way he did another lifetime ago when he was an instructor at Fort Gulick.

Kevin stood in front of the desk with his mouth agape. It had been years since anyone yelled at him like that. He backed into one of the chairs in front of the desk and sat down.

"That's better," Buck said. "It's good to clear the air. As I said, we don't have much time."

Kevin drew a few deep breaths as he continued to stare at Buck.

"As you already know, Costello was suspected of having some drug connections with a Panamanian."

"Yeah, I remember," Kevin replied.

"That Panamanian was Alejandro Vega, a powerful underworld figure, and one of our operatives."

"You've got to be kidding. You had Costello *spying* on one of your spies?" Kevin said shaking his head. "Leave it to the CIA to come up with something so ludicrous."

"I suppose when you put it that way it does sound rather bizarre, but when an opportunity presents itself to you, it's best to take advantage of it. That's what happened when Costello and Vega's paths crossed. Vega was providing us valuable intel we couldn't afford to lose. If anything happened and that intel was compromised, given Costello and Vega's relationship, Costello could alert us."

Kevin couldn't believe what Smith was telling him. Costello, a spy? None of this was making any sense. "What kind of intel?"

"Mostly Noriega's comings and goings—who he was dining with and who he was screwing. Later it was about his drug and arms smuggling and money laundering."

Kevin shook his head again. This was all too much for him to process.

"Of course Vega was just as dirty and corrupt as Noriega, but he was, for all semantic purposes, the lesser of two evils."

"Why doesn't that surprise me?" Kevin asked.

"You're missing the big picture, Rooney. Central America was where we fought the Third Cold War. One day it's the Russians, the next day it's the Cubans. Maybe tomorrow it will be the Chinese. That's how the world runs these days. The canal was just the tip of the iceberg. At the time, everyone was going apeshit over having to lose the canal, but we were already looking farther down the road," Buck explained.

He wasn't sure if Rooney was getting all of this; many didn't. It had been one thing for people to get all worked up because something was going to be taken away from them, but these same people looked at the world through rose-colored glasses. "Our biggest fear was always the continued threat of Communist encroachment in the area. Imagine what would have happened had the treaties not been ratified. We already knew that Torrijos was talking to the Cubans and who knows what would have happened in Nicaragua if we didn't have Torrijos and Noriega in our pockets."

"Spare me the lecture, Smith," Kevin said with a sarcastic tone. "I was stationed here at the time, remember?"

Buck grinned. He liked the way Rooney was standing up to him, just like his old man.

"What does all this have to do with my friend's death?"

"I'm getting there, Rooney," Buck replied. He was relieved that Rooney had calmed down "We've got to think three to five moves ahead of everyone else. We all knew that Noriega was going to give us problems one day, but his usefulness with the intelligence he provided in Panama outweighed any of his illegal activities."

"So you just looked the other way, is that it? Just like you did with my friend?"

Buck shot Kevin a dirty look. "Of course not. We knew that one day we were going to have to deal with Noriega one way or another. In fact, it was my job to profile him and try to find his weaknesses, which we could exploit one day should the need arise to—"

"And when Noriega finally wears out his welcome—after you used him knowing how dirty and corrupt he was all along—you have to find a way to get rid of him."

"It's not that easy, Rooney. Yes, he was a trusted ally when it came to our greater interests, specifically dealing with the Sandinistas. It was an entirely new ballgame when Ronald Reagan rode into town and made it clear from day one his policy for Nicaragua. We were off to the races and Noriega was leading the way. And yes, he would end up being indispensable in the greater scheme of things. That's why you can't always think in terms of right and wrong. There are varying degrees of right and wrong. It's all for the greater good. I didn't make up these rules, Rooney. They've been in play long before you and I came onto the scene and will still be in play long after you and I are gone. The sooner you accept this, the sooner this will all make sense to you."

Kevin looked at Smith with a puzzled look on his face. He still wasn't getting it.

"You're not looking at the big picture, Rooney. You've got to take the blinders off, son. Have you ever seen the painting 'A Sunday Afternoon on the Island of La Grande Jatte' by the French painter Georges Seurat?"

Kevin shook his head.

"You probably have; it's really famous. It's on display at the Art Institute in Chicago," Buck explained. "It's this huge fucker displayed on a wall all by itself. People sit and stare at it for hours. Seurat was a genius because the entire painting is made up of dots. It's called pointillism. It doesn't look like much when standing up close, but when standing back, everything comes into focus because our eyes fill in the spaces between these dots of paint. That's kind of how we have been operating the past decade with Noriega and that's why you are having a hard time accepting all of this now. You've got to stand back and look at things from the greater whole and for the greater good."

"That still doesn't explain why you waited so long to do something about him," Kevin said with an air of indignation. He wasn't buying any of Smith's hard sell on the CIA's handling of Noriega. "It's no wonder people despise you guys. You're no better than the people you go after. And then, when you find yourself up against the wall, like you now are with Noriega, you talk about how righteous you are and that you have to do what you do for the betterment of the world."

Kevin, a big film buff, was reminded of a film that he enjoyed watching with Gary not long after they arrived at Howard, *Three Days of a Condor*. A CIA analyst, played by Robert Redford, stumbles across some of the Agency's operations in the plots of books that he reads. At the end of the movie, one of the CIA directors, played by Cliff Robertson talks about how the Agency has to do what it does for the sake of the people it is supposed to protect. Sometimes the truth was stranger than fiction.

"Let's just say we had no choice."

"Of course you did. If you knew he was dirty and corrupt all along, you could have stopped him at any time. Or maybe you didn't want to."

"It's not that easy, Rooney."

"Sure it is. You guys can make a problem go away with a snap of a finger," Kevin said, snapping his fingers for effect.

Buck snickered. "You watch too many movies."

Kevin could see how Buck and the CIA had their hands full with someone like Noriega and the embarrassment he had become. These days you couldn't turn on the news or open a newspaper without some story about Noriega. What he still couldn't understand was what any of this had to do with him being sent to Panama.

"And Vega?"

"He was our insurance in all this," Buck said matter-of-factly. "We thought we could handle him, but—"

"So instead of one problem you have two. Now you have to take care of Vega, so he doesn't become an embarrassment to you. You spooks are all alike."

Buck grinned and stared across the desk at Rooney. It

wasn't going to be easy convincing Rooney what had to be done, which was all the more complicated given Buck's relationship with Vega. He still had a score to settle with his friend, and he didn't need Rooney complicating things. Nonetheless, Rooney and Vega were connected in the high-stakes drama that was soon to unfold. That was a card that Buck was going to have to play.

"Vega is well-connected within the Guardia and the Colombian drug cartels, but he also has an agenda when it comes to his illicit activities. We knew from the beginning that he was playing both sides the same way that Noriega was. Vega's dirty laundry list included everything from money laundering and extortion to drug smuggling and—"

Buck stopped and thought about Estefani. The anger swelled momentarily in his chest before he took a deep breath and continued. "We wet-nursed him because we knew he was indispensable even in spite of his checkered past just like Noriega's. We knew he was in bed with a who's who of Colombian drug lords, even the king of them all, Pablo Escobar. By then he had climbed high enough and was loyal enough to both our sides that he became a key player."

"Jesus Christ, Escobar?" Kevin said. "The plot thickens."

"It most certainly did. The problem was—which brings us to why you and I are part of this drama—was that Vega had gotten mixed up with an airman on Howard and the two of them concocted this little drug smuggling ring."

"Costello?"

Buck nodded. "When we found out about it, we hoped to use the airman to see what more he could find out about Vega's connections with the Colombians that we would be able to use against Vega should he ever become too much of a risk. Sadly, your buddy got mixed up in all of this. Vega was protecting his interests and we were protecting ours."

Kevin's nostrils flared as he stared at Buck. His eyes were wild with anger. "You could have at least warned him at the time, you bastard. You could have come up with some excuse and gotten him off base and out of the country. That's what you guys do, isn't it? You make people disappear all the time. Instead, you sat back and did nothing. You allowed my friend to die and for what? To protect your asses because you were in bed with Noriega."

Buck shook his head. "There was nothing that we could do. You have to believe me. Our operative already suspected your friend had talked to the OSI. Do you remember a guy named Gustavo Santiago?"

That was another name Kevin hadn't thought about for a long time. He still remembered not long before he left Panama when Santiago, Costello, and a few other airmen were busted.

"Santiago suspected your friend all along and alerted Vega," Buck explained. "If we had moved in, we would have tipped off Vega for sure, not to mention Noriega."

"And Costello?"

"Costello was smuggling drugs back to the States on C-130s. He had a nice little thing going until the OSI found out about it," Buck explained. "We stepped in and made a deal with him given his association with Vega, who was about to become a very big embarrassment for us."

"If you can't trust a spy, who can you trust?"

Buck grinned.

"What kind of deal?"

"He would keep tabs on Vega for us and we would make sure he didn't see the inside of a cell at Leavenworth."

"An offer he couldn't refuse?"

Buck smiled again. He was beginning to warm up to Rooney.

"But that didn't work, did it?" Kevin said.

Buck nodded. "We didn't know that Vega had already made a move against your friend. He had one of his men, Luis Soto, follow him home one evening and kill him."

Kevin bit down on his bottom lip and stared at Smith. After all these years, he had finally found out what had happened to Gary. A great weight had been removed from his heart.

"There was no way we could tell anyone what happened without jeopardizing our operations here. I'm sorry."

"And this is all for the greater good?" Kevin said. "Leave it to you guys at the CIA to come up with shit like this."

Kevin had a difficult time processing everything that Smith was telling him. Who would have thought that Frank and Gary had gotten mixed up in all of this because of their little drug operation and that there was nothing that anyone at the time could have done to protect them? It all started to make sense to him now. He remembered a night when he had gotten into a fight with Frank outside an Italian restaurant in Panama City. There had been a Panamanian man at the table with Frank and Gary. Maybe one of those men had been Vega. If not Vega, someone connected with him. Gary had also been with them that night. Smith was right about one thing: Gary got caught up with the wrong crowd.

"Where is he now?"

Buck didn't think it was a good idea to tell Rooney; there was no telling what Rooney would do, but if Buck's plan was going to work, he needed both Rooney's and Costello's help to create the diversion to take care of Vega so that none of this would ever be traced back to Buck or the Agency. Likewise, Buck couldn't tell Rooney about the plan that he and Ramone had put in play that would hit Vega where it hurt the most; nor could he reveal how Costello was a part of the plan. One thing was for certain, given Frank and Kevin's rocky relationship in the past, it was the perfect cover story if he needed one. As long as everyone played his part no one would get hurt.

"He's still here, isn't he?"

Buck nodded.

"There's something more, isn't there? Something that you need my help with, right?" Kevin asked. "Three days ago I was pulled out of roll call and the next thing I know I am on a C-130 bound for Panama. What the fuck is going on that you need my help?"

Buck was quiet for a few seconds. He knew what he was going to say next was very important to bring Kevin on board—even if it meant lying a little. "He double-crossed Vega and now we have reason to believe that he's got himself caught up in something that if it goes down, he's going to put himself in harm's way."

"That's why you brought me here. My being here has nothing to do with a military exercise. You just want to save your ass in case Vega starts talking. Why don't you call out the hounds and bring him in yourself? Better yet, if Frank got himself in shit with Vega, you guys or the OSI—not to mention the DEA are better equipped to deal with it than me. That's how you make your living, right?"

"Yes and no."

"I don't follow you."

"We're afraid that Vega is about to make a move which could jeopardize our ongoing operations here."

"I still don't understand why you dragged me down here."

"We have very good reason to believe that Frank and his family are in immediate danger—danger that includes your daughter."

CHAPTER THIRTY-SEVEN

AFTER ALL THESE years, Inés was still a sensitive issue for Kevin. Although he had been in a few relationships, he had never forgotten the time he spent with Inés nor what Frank had done. He knew he had been a fool for not trying to win her back after Frank stole her away. He had been so immature about it and let his pride get in the way. And then, after Gary died, and he had sex with her, he felt so guilty about it, he just wanted to forget about her—but he couldn't. There was a part of him that still loved her. Now, thanks to Smith's revelation, their paths would cross again but not the way he had imagined they would.

On the way to Frank and Inés's apartment, Kevin couldn't believe how much Panama City had changed since he last was here eleven years ago; buildings and streets were hardly recognizable anymore; antebellum landmarks and signage had been replaced with shiny new structures promising a better life which were just as much a testament to the country's prosperity as it was to the impact of all the illegal money which had been pouring into the country, thanks to Noriega. Shiny new glass and steel buildings rose along Balboa Avenue in stark contrast to the crumbling, decaying squalor just blocks away. Appearances could be deceiving; Noriega had seen to that.

Kevin remembered the time he had gone to the Intercontinental Hotel—not far from where he was now—with Steve Wilson, Gary, and John. That had been the night Steve had hit a stroke of luck at the craps table, and in an hour had tripled his paycheck.

Steve had been bragging how the previous weekend he won fifty dollars playing craps and wanted to try his luck again. He had started off small, lost a few times, but after he had won back the money he lost, he had gotten serious and had put down his entire paycheck.

"Are you crazy, Steve?" Gary asked him.

"Trust me," Steve said, with a wild look in his eyes. "I know what I'm doing."

Kevin and the others shook their heads and enjoyed the free drinks courtesy of Steve, who shared the ones the waitress had kept bringing to the table. It had been good to get out and do something different after what had happened between him and Inés. Steve did know what he was doing; in about thirty minutes, he had tripled his winnings.

"Come on, Steve, give us some of the money before your luck runs out," Kevin said.

"The only way to win big is to bet big," Steve said, blowing on the dice for good luck.

He bet everything and lost it all.

Steve had been unfazed by what had happened. They ended up back at the Ovalo, where in a few minutes, Steve had a girl on his lap giving him a hand job.

"Can I borrow ten dollars?" Steve asked sheepishly. "I think this girl likes me."

Kevin, John, and Gary fished in their pockets for some crumpled bills and tossed them on the table until they had enough money for Steve. That's what buddies did for one another. No matter how bad things got or if someone's luck ran out, one always looked out for his buddies.

Thirty minutes later, the taxi turned down a quiet tree-lined avenue. The buildings were much older in this part of the city though newer ones were being built. He recognized the neighborhood immediately. It wasn't far from the old Lux Theatre where he saw *Rocky* when it came out in Panama.

The neighborhood also brought memories of another kind for Kevin. A few months after Inés had left him for Frank, he had ended up in the Paris by himself, drowning his sorrows in one Cuba Libre after another. One of the girls, who worked in the bar, was also feeling down that night. It was her six-year-old daughter's birthday back in Colombia. Together, they sat at a table in the back and drank until the girl, Sarah, asked him if he would like to go home with her. She just wanted to be with someone that night away from the bar and the hotel with the semen and bloodstained beds. She just wanted to be held by someone.

After Kevin had paid the bar fine, they slipped down a side street and quickly grabbed a taxi which took them to the same part of town where Kevin was at now. They sat up talking for a while. She showed him a photograph of her daughter and explained that after her husband died she tried to find a good job; however, she couldn't find one even though she had a college degree. He ended up spending the night with Sarah after they made love. In the morning, he offered her some money but she refused.

He never saw her again.

The apartment building was located at the end of the

street. He paid the taxi driver and then slowly walked toward the entrance. Sweet smelling flowers filled the air; a radio somewhere played Roxette's "The Look."

He climbed up the narrow staircase to the third floor. Inside one of the apartments, a child wailed; in another a television blared. His heart was pounding in his chest. He slowly walked down the hallway to the apartment at the very end. He stood in front of the door and took a deep breath. He knocked three times on the door. Inside he heard the metallic click of a lock being unlocked and then the door partially opened. Inés looked out and stared at the man standing at the door. It took her a while before she recognized Kevin.

"Kevin?" Inés said, gasping in shock. "Oh my God! What are you doing here?"

Inés continued to stare out the crack in the door at Kevin, still in shock at seeing him standing outside before she unlatched the chain and opened the door. Although she wore her hair shorter and had put on a little weight, she looked just as stunning as she did the first time he saw her outside the NCO Club on Howard nearly thirteen years earlier. They both stood looking at each other, not quite sure what to say. On the way over, Kevin thought about all the things he would say to Inés once they were together; now he didn't know what to say. He didn't know whether they should hug or not. Finally, Kevin broke the awkward moment and lightly embraced Inés.

"It's nice to see you, Inés," Kevin said, removing his arms from around her body and stepping back.

Inés smiled and ushered Kevin into the tiny apartment. Kevin looked around the room with a worried expression. He tried to see if there was anyone in the adjoining rooms, but the glare from bright sunlight spilling in made it difficult.

"He's not here," Inés said, "if that's what you're worried about."

Smith had assured him that Frank wouldn't be home, but Kevin was still worried about having to confront Frank.

"I can't believe it's you," Inés said. Her eyes twinkled brightly and dimples formed on both cheeks as she gazed at Kevin. "After all these years, here you are standing in my kitchen. Can I get you something to drink? Coffee?"

Kevin shook his head. "No, thanks. I'm fine."

"Are you back at Howard?"

"No, I'm here temporarily," Kevin said curtly. He wished this could have been a more pleasant reunion. It was awkward enough for him seeing Inés after all these years and the feelings that he still had for her.

She moved across the room and sat down at the kitchen table. Kevin followed her and sat down across from her. As Kevin continued to look around the room, an eight-by-ten photograph in a metal frame on a wooden stand not far from where he was sitting caught his attention. In the photograph, taken at some beach, were Frank, Inés, and their two daughters. Kevin shuddered when he looked more closely at one of the daughters. Although she closely resembled her mother, he couldn't believe he was looking at his daughter.

"They're in school," Inés said, noticing that Kevin had been looking at the photograph.

"Excuse me?" Kevin asked in a startled voice.

"My daughters, they're in school now," Inés replied, and then paused, staring down at her hands in her lap. There were only three people who knew who Adrianna's biological father was, but she wouldn't be able to keep it a secret for much longer. When she looked up, Kevin's gaze met hers.

"They're very lovely," Kevin said, his eyes watering slightly, as he turned and looked at the photograph one more time. "They take after their mother."

Inés blushed and looked closely at Kevin.

"Do you know how many times I reached for the phone at night wanting to hear your voice?" she said. "I cared about you so much. I wanted to call you and tell—"

"I thought about you, too."

Kevin told her about the nightmares he had about her, Frank, and Gary. Inés was quiet for a few seconds before she brushed away the tears with her hand. "I should have never left that night."

"We all make choices, Inés," he said. "You and I made ours one night a long time ago."

Inés bit down on her bottom lip. She looked down at the floor and then lifted her face and met Kevin's gaze. "I'm sorry that I hurt you, Kevin. I liked you a lot, but—"

"But it would have never worked," he said. "We both got what we deserved, but right now I need you to listen to me."

"What are you talking about, Kevin?"

"I need to know if you and your daughters have somewhere safe to go."

"What's going on, Kevin?" she asked with a worried expression on her face.

"Frank's got himself mixed up in something bad again," Kevin explained measuring his words carefully. "I don't think you and your daughters are in any immediate danger now, but—"

"You're scaring me, Kevin," Inés said, her voice fraught with fear and tension. "I don't see you for over ten years and then all of a sudden you show up here one day telling me that we're in danger. What's this all about? Why are you doing this again?"

Kevin gazed at Inés. This wasn't going the way he intended. "I know what must be going through your head, but you have to trust me about this."

"Frank sometimes said that he never could trust you

because you might have been working with the OSI and you might have been the one who had him arrested."

"Inés, please," he said calmly. "This has nothing to do with that."

"Who told you this?" Inés's eyes widened and her upper lip trembled.

"I can't say."

"Frank was right. You can't be trusted. Why did you even come back here?"

"Inés, stop it!" Kevin said, raising his voice.

She was startled by the tone of Kevin's voice. She knew what Kevin was talking about; she knew that Frank was involved with Vega again and that they were planning to smuggle drugs to the States. Frank told her that everything was going to be okay; how this was going to be their ticket out of Panama. Her crying became more uncontrollable as her worst fears were confirmed.

"Inés, I would never do anything to hurt you or your daughters," Kevin said.

She looked across the table at Kevin and nodded.

"After Frank got kicked out of the service it was really hard for us. Even though we had some money saved, it wasn't enough," she said, wiping away the tears. "We had no one else to turn to. Vega was good to us at first, but only because Frank had to work off his debt. He still owes Vega close to twenty thousand dollars. Frank said that he's working on something that when it's over he'll be able to take care of his debt to Vega once and for all. And then we'll be able to leave Panama."

Kevin cringed when Inés mentioned Vega's name. He felt sorry for Frank now that he knew more about Vega and his reputation. Kevin looked across the table at Inés. *If only she knew what I know.* He should have never given up on her like he did. All of this could have been prevented.

"Frank is in more trouble than he realizes, Inés," Kevin said. "He's double-crossed Vega."

An expression of fear washed across Inés's face as she looked up at Kevin. "What?"

"There's one more thing, Inés."

"Yes."

"I know about our daughter."

CHAPTER THIRTY-EIGHT

IT TOOK A moment for Kevin's eyes to adjust to the dimness as he stood inside the entrance to TJ's. His eyes darted from one side of the room to the other as he slowly moved toward the far end of the bar through a maze of chairs and tables. It didn't look like anyone was inside even though the lights were on outside.

The bar had seen better days judging from the cracked grimy walls covered with faded and torn sports and beer posters. The long concrete bar, which was covered with brightly colored ceramic tiles, was cluttered with empty Cerveza Atlas and Panama beer bottles, empty highball glasses, and ashtrays filled with cigarette butts. In the center of the bar was an open Napoli's pizza box with the remnants of a half-eaten pizza. The humid, cool air reeked of stale cigarette smoke and the sweet aroma of Panama Red.

Kevin had come here a few times with some of his buddies when they heard about the regulation-sized pool tables and imported beers. It had been mainly a Zonian hangout, but when some of the working girls from the bars down the street heard about the GIs that went there, the atmosphere and the clientele changed.

Somewhere in the room a radio played Warren Zevon's "Lawyers, Guns, and Money"—a popular song the last time Kevin was in Panama—the irony of which was not lost on him.

"Welcome back, Rooney."

Kevin squinted his eyes in the direction of the voice and saw Frank seated at the end of the bar smoking a cigarette with a bottle of bourbon in front of him. Kevin sat down a few stools away from Frank.

"How are you doing, Frank?" Kevin asked.

Frank had put on some weight and his jet black hair was thinning. His face was puffy and pasty looking.

"I'm getting by."

"You look like shit, you know?"

Frank laughed and started coughing. His voice was raspier, too.

"I've had worse days," Frank said, picking up the bottle and filling his glass. "Drink?"

Kevin nodded. "Why not?"

Frank slid off the barstool and nearly lost his balance as he staggered behind the bar. He grabbed a glass, slammed it down in front of Kevin, and filled it with the same bourbon he was drinking.

"To better days," Frank said, raising his glass and tipping it toward Kevin, who tossed his glassful down his throat and winced from the bourbon's potency.

Kevin wiped off his mouth with the back of his hand and motioned for Frank to pour him another.

"So tell me, Rooney," Frank continued, twisting mouth into a wry smile, "what brings the prodigal son back to Panama?"

"Knock it off, Frank. You know why I'm here."

Frank nodded. "That's right, Rooney. You and I have some unfinished business."

"You're right about that, Frank," Kevin had promised himself that he wouldn't start anything with Frank. But Frank was way ahead of him.

"What you did back then was reprehensible—accusing me of killing Gary," Frank said, putting his elbows on the bar and leaning toward Kevin, "but nowhere as low as trying to convince Inés that I was responsible for his death."

"Listen, Frank—"

"No, *you* listen, Rooney," Frank said, gazing at Kevin with hooded eyes. "Inés told me everything."

Kevin finished his drink and stared back at Frank. He didn't like where this conversation was headed. "Frank—"

"Maybe you still hadn't accepted the fact that you lost Inés and that was your twisted way of getting back at her."

Kevin moved back a little from the bar just in case Frank decided to take a swing at him. "That's not true, Frank."

"Then maybe fucking her *was*."

Kevin had a feeling that at some point Frank was going to confront him about what happened that night if Inés had told him everything, but he was still caught off guard by Frank's brusqueness. "Frank, I can explain—"

"Explain what? That you fucked her to get back at me?"

"Frank, it was nothing like that. Yes, I was angry, and I wanted to hurt you, but I was just as angry at myself for not stepping forward and doing something when I had the chance."

"So you fucked her and that was your way of making everything better, is that it?" Frank took his hands off the bar and poured himself another drink.

"Frank, what I did was wrong—very, *very*, wrong," Kevin

said as calmly and sincerely as he could. Although he had backed away from the bar and out of Frank's reach, he was still afraid that Frank would come at him. "I'm terribly sorry."

Frank hadn't said anything about Kevin's daughter, which Kevin didn't know how to interpret. Either Frank was waiting for the right moment or he didn't want to talk about it.

"And that's going to make everything better?" Frank continued to glare at Kevin. "Fuck you, Rooney."

Frank gulped down the drink he had just poured and winced just a little as the whiskey went down his throat. He had said what needed to be said and hoped that it was enough to make Rooney squirm. Rooney had always been a goody two shoes, and that's what Frank counted on most now. He figured Smith had already told him about Adrianna, which was all he needed for the plan to work.

"Yeah, I deserve that, Frank. I was so worked up about Gary that I didn't know what I was doing," Kevin said. "My best friend was killed and his death led back to you."

When Frank found out that Inés had gone to see Rooney and that she had slept with him, he was furious. However, he knew she still had feelings for Rooney. She was just as worked up about Gary as he and Rooney were. "He was my friend, too."

"You could have at least warned him given your association with Vega."

"So you know all about Vega, huh?"

Kevin nodded. "Of course. Maybe you were only trying to save your ass again."

"That's where you are wrong, Rooney," Frank emphasized. "As a matter of fact, I did warn him. I told him that it wasn't worth the risk anymore. I told him not to screw up his plans about getting out and going to film school. Where the hell were you at the time? If you ever got off that high horse of yours, maybe you'd see things differently."

Kevin frowned and shook his head. "He looked up to you. You were like a big brother to him. Why, I don't know."

"Listen, pal, I haven't stopped thinking about that kid's death for one day. I've carried my cross just as much as you have."

Kevin and Frank sat quietly for a few minutes. Kevin debated whether or not he should come clean about how he had been asked to spy on Frank, but decided not. After all these years, thanks to Smith and Costello, Kevin finally found out what happened to Gary that night and that Frank—though Kevin still didn't think too highly of him—had tried to protect their friend. Kevin finally had a peace of mind.

"I take it then that you've already talked to Smith," Frank finally said. He couldn't be sure what Smith had told Rooney. It was best to play this one close to the chest. For now, the less Rooney knew, the better. "What a messed up world we live in, huh?"

"You tell me."

"Who would have thought that you and I would end up this way?"

"Yeah, I guess it was in the stars."

Frank grunted and looked at Kevin. "So what exactly did Smith tell you?"

"He told me about your buddy Vega and the mess you got yourself into down here if that's what you mean."

Frank nodded and poured himself another drink. It was always easier to swallow the truth when he was numb. "Bet you're surprised that Smith and I ended up together, aren't you?"."

"I'm not surprised about anything anymore."

"Well, you know what they say," Frank said. "The road to hell is paved with good intentions."

Kevin snickered. "There is one more thing—"

"I know." Frank gazed across the bar at Kevin with a worried look on his face. "Vega wants me dead."

CHAPTER THIRTY-NINE

MARINE LIEUTENANT RANDY Ortiz had been looking forward all week to dinner with his friends at a new restaurant in Panama City. With Christmas just a little over a week away, Randy wanted to get an early start on celebrating the holiday. His buddy, James Martin, had been to the restaurant with his Panamanian girlfriend the week before and all week he raved about the food. Although it was going to be his first Christmas away from home since enlisting in the Marines, he wasn't feeling any pangs of homesickness. And he certainly wasn't apprehensive about driving into Panama City.

Ortiz was well aware of the problems some service members and Americans had when they left the Canal Zone. For the past year, service members stationed at bases on the Atlantic and Pacific sides of the canal as well as American officials and citizens continued to be harassed by members of Noriega's Panama Defense Forces and the Dignity Battalions, as a way of getting back at the United States for economic sanctions which had been levied against Panama in an attempt to remove Noriega from power. Service members and their dependents had been robbed, beaten, arrested for no apparent reason, and even raped. Despite warnings and advisories from commanders, personnel were not restricted to their bases and movement in the Republic of Panama was not limited.

Lieutenant Mark Campbell, who had been in Panama for a little over a year, was no stranger to the harassment campaign. Two months earlier, he had been pulled over by Panama Defense Forces for apparently having a broken taillight. Detained for more than two hours by the Panamanians, Mark was finally let go after he paid fifty dollars. He was behind the wheel again of his tan-colored Impala this evening—the one he bought from a fellow marine, who rotated back to the States three months ago—worried that he had taken a wrong turn. Campbell, Ortiz, Martin, and another officer, Greg Harmon, had left the Officer's Club on Fort Clayton at 8:30 on their way to the Café Habana.

"Now where is this restaurant located?" Randy asked from the backseat. "I hope it's not too far. I'm famished."

"It's just down this street," Martin said as he pointed to an intersection where Campbell should turn. "You guys are going to be in for a real treat. Randy, don't forget this one's on you, buddy."

Ortiz smiled. He had bet his friend that if the Chicago Bears—who were having a dismal year after starting out four-and-oh—beat the Detroit Lions, Martin, who was a Lions fan, would spring for dinner. The Bears lost.

"Are you sure?" Mark asked, turning down the one-way street where Martin had pointed. Campbell, who had never driven in this part of the city, had been driving down a maze of one-way streets for the past fifteen minutes. "It doesn't look as if there's anything around here that looks like a restaurant."

Martin looked at the decaying, graffiti-covered buildings and shook his head. None of the buildings looked familiar to him. Then again, when he had come to this part of the city with his Panamanian girlfriend, they had been in a taxi and she had done all the talking. "It's got to be around here somewhere."

"Oh, shit," Mark muttered.

Two cars ahead of them on the street was a PDF checkpoint. Mark looked in the rearview mirror to see if he could back up, but there was a truck behind their car. The four men nervously looked out of the windows at the checkpoint and the five PDF soldiers.

"We'd better get out of here, Mark," Greg said, as he watched one of the soldiers point his AK-47 automatic rifle at the car.

"We didn't do anything wrong," Mark said, keeping a firm grip on the steering wheel as he watched in the rearview mirror as two more soldiers approached the car with their weapons readied. Across the street, he could see a small crowd gathering. "There are too many people around for them to try something. They just want to scare us."

Ever since the failed coup attempt two months earlier, Noriega's Dignity Battalions had stepped up their harassment of American troops and their dependents. Routine traffic stops for no other reason than to just harass had increased.

"They're doing a good job," quipped Greg with a nervous smile.

"Nothing like a little excitement on a Friday night," Randy said, in an attempt to assuage their anxiety as he looked at the crowd beginning to gather around the car. "You'd think they had never seen a car filled with Americans."

A crowd of around fifty people had gathered on both sides of the street and watched this drama unfold. Some of them, members of Noriega's paramilitary Dignity Battalions, pointed at the car and yelled for the PDF soldiers to take care of the fucking gringos. One of the PDF soldiers motioned for the four men to get out of the car.

"This doesn't look good," Mark said as another PDF soldier approached the driver's side of the car. "These guys mean business."

"Let me try to talk to them," Randy said. "I don't think my Spanish is too rusty."

Nervous laughter filled the car.

"*Disculpe ¿hay algún problema?*" Randy asked one of the soldiers closest to the car on the passenger side. "*¿Podemos continuar por acá?*"

"What did you say?" Greg asked.

"I asked him if we could get through here," Randy replied.

The soldier didn't say a word. He just stared at the occupants of the car as he tapped the door with the barrel of his automatic weapon, motioning with his head that he wanted everyone inside to get out.

"Jesus, what should we do?" Mark asked.

The next sound they heard—a metallic click—sent a chill down their spines: the PDF soldier had chambered a round.

"Mark, get us out of here, buddy," Greg said staring at the soldier.

"We're boxed in here," Mark said. "There's a truck behind us."

By now, the car in front of them had gone through the checkpoint; without thinking of the consequences, Mark stepped on the gas and sped through the checkpoint nearly hitting a PDF soldier who had tried to stop the car. The five PDF soldiers who had initially surrounded the car, immediately opened fire. Randy was hit in the back and Greg was hit in the arm. As Mark sped past the PDF headquarters, a dozen other soldiers opened fire. The rear window was shot out spraying everyone with glass; other rounds peppered the side of the car.

"Randy's been hit!" Greg screamed, not noticing the blood trickling down his arm. "He's not moving!"

Mark had his foot all the way down on the accelerator as he sped down the narrow, crowded street. Pedestrians jumped out of the way as he frantically honked the horn. A deliveryman carrying three cases of Cerveza Panama barely got across the street in time, but the beer wasn't as lucky: the man lost his grip and the three cases crashed onto the sidewalk. Mark looked in the rearview mirror and was relieved that the PDF weren't following them. He sped through an intersection and was nearly hit by a truck. When he looked in the rearview mirror again, he saw that the truck had crashed into a parked car.

"Greg, how's Randy?" Martin asked in a frantic voice.

"There's blood everywhere and he's not moving," Greg replied, his voice shaky.

"Hang on!" Mark said. "We'll be at Gorgas Army Hospital shortly."

Mark turned up another street until he came to Avenida de los Mártires. Five minutes later, they pulled up in front of the emergency entrance at Gorgas Hospital just inside the Canal Zone. However, they hadn't gotten to the hospital fast enough. Randy succumbed to his wounds twenty minutes later.

Unknown to the four Americans, a U.S. Navy officer, Richard Garza, and his wife were also stopped at the same checkpoint just an hour before, and they witnessed the PDF's actions. They had been on their way back to the Rodman Naval Station after attending a Christmas party. When the PDF soldiers realized that Garza was most likely military, he and his wife were detained. While the soldiers manning the checkpoint debated what to do with Garza and his wife, Mark, and his friends were stopped at the checkpoint.

From where they were parked, Garza and his wife saw the drama and the tragedy unfold. Hoping to discourage these witnesses, the PDF held the Garzas for four hours, during which time they were beaten. He was repeatedly kicked in the head and the stomach and had loaded automatic weapons pointed at his head. Mrs. Garza, after she was slammed against a wall and sexually assaulted by three of the PDF soldiers, was forced to stand with her arms above her head for over an hour.

By the time they were finally released and news of Ortiz's death had spread like wildfire throughout the U.S. military installations across the isthmus, advisories were issued for service members living off base and other personnel were recalled.

*   *   *

In Washington, the President had had enough. There would be no tomorrow for Noriega. His time had finally come. And perhaps, given the wave of the euphoria that the President and the nation was riding following the fall of the Berlin Wall, there was no better time, from a public relations point of view, to remove Noriega from power without too much fallout. After consulting with his advisors and the Joint Chiefs of Staff, the green light for the invasion of Panama—Operation Just Cause—was given.

After he had given the order, the President put on his best holiday face and joined his family and friends around the Christmas tree in the Blue Room where they sang carols and drank hot apple cider. He knew that at the same time, elements of the 82nd Airborne were already on their way to Panama.

Later that night, after he had been briefed by his advisors in the Situation Room, he stepped outside.

"God help us all," the President said as he looked to the cold Washington sky.

*   *   *

Buck had just gotten out of the shower when someone from Quarry Heights called him and told him that H-hour would be at one o'clock in the morning on the twentieth.

He sat on the edge of the bed with a towel wrapped around his body and poured himself a tumbler of whiskey. Underneath a thin blanket, Lucinda murmured that Buck should come to bed. He picked up the phone and dialed a local number. It rang five times before the person on the other end answered.

"It's on, Kevin. You know what to do."

CHAPTER FORTY

IF MANUEL NORIEGA thought he was living on borrowed time, it certainly wasn't the night that the United States commenced Operation Just Cause. And why should he have worried? For the past two years, he had been able to outsmart the United States and stay in power. Time and time again he believed that the United States would never resort to military action to have him removed. Even the stepped-up military exercises the past few months—which some of his staff interpreted as a precursor to an invasion—did not faze Noriega.

"If they're going to come and get me, let them," Noriega had said on more than one occasion as he flaunted his bravado in front of friends and aides. "And if they do, they will be making a very big mistake. Nobody fucks with Manuel Noriega."

Noriega was about to be taught a very valuable lesson and fucked with in a very big way.

After a night of drinking and partying, early in the morning of December twentieth, a groggy and angry Noriega was woken up by his aides and told of a possible military invasion by the Americans. Although reports of an invasion were sketchy at best, there were indications of fighting taking place across the country, including Omar Torrijos International Airport, not far from where Noriega had shacked up with a prostitute. Right now, his aides had to get him to one of the two cars they already had waiting for him.

"One more thing, Sir, you're no longer president," one of the aides, who most assuredly risked being shot on the spot whether he told the truth or not, said. "We have reason to believe that Guillermo Endara is going to be installed as president."

Noriega didn't go for his pistol. Instead, he rubbed his deeply pocked face and worked up some saliva in his mouth to remedy a bad case of cottonmouth. In the process, he liberated a pubic hair with his tongue, which had been stuck between two of his teeth. He picked it off his puffy bottom lip and examined it before flicking it onto the floor.

"I'll get that son-of-a-bitch first," Noriega said, looking for something to drink on the nightstand. "Get on the phone and—"

"Sir, we're under attack!" another aide shouted, bursting into the room. "We need to get you out of here and to a secure location."

Noriega refused to believe that the Americans would resort to military action, grumbled and got out of bed. In the distance, gunfire and explosions could be heard. He was not going to like how the rest of the day and the week were going to go for him. The man, who just days earlier had proclaimed himself Maximum Leader of Panama, barely had enough time to escape his bungalow.

They came from a half-dozen posts across the United

States. Not since the Vietnam War had America flexed its military might, and when it was over, it would be one of the shortest military operations in American military history. At one o'clock in the morning, designated H-Hour by SOUTHCOM, approximately 26,000 soldiers and marines, half of them already deployed to Panama, launched synchronized assaults at over a dozen military targets while securing American assets and personnel at another twelve locations across the isthmus. A military operation of this size involving the coordination of key troop deployments with forces already on the ground and multiple targets had never been attempted. The military exercises which had been conducted—in some instances right in front of the PDF—paid dividends. If the United States was going to go into Panama and pluck Noriega out of there and bring him to the States to stand trial, they needed an operation that left nothing to chance.

And if ever the United States needed a shot of red, white, and blue and a chance to flex its military might to right a shitload of wrongs, it was Operation Just Cause.

One of the first targets of the invasion was to seize Omar Torrijos International Airport and neutralize a PDF company as well as the Panamanian Air Force, but more importantly, to prevent Noriega from escaping. Timing was everything. The last plane scheduled to land at the airport was before midnight, which would be more than enough time for the passengers to clear immigration and customs and get out of the airport. However, the plane was delayed an hour which meant that when the attack began, those passengers would still be in the airport.

Noriega barely managed to escape one of the roadblocks set up by the Rangers who had neutralized the airport. He nearly pissed himself in the backseat of the car when he realized how close he had come to being captured. His PDF units were not so lucky. Across Panama, there were additional coordinated attacks on various targets—either to neutralize PDF units or to prevent them from reinforcing beleaguered units already fighting for their survival. At the Paitilla Airfield, not far from the U.S. Embassy, a Navy SEAL task force cleared the airfield, destroying Noriega's private jet, denying him other means of escape. The United States slowly began to tighten its grip and create a dragnet around the city.

Besides the seizure of the two airfields, another one of the main targets and objectives of the invasion force was the Panama Defense Forces La Comandancia Headquarters located in the heart of Panama City, just a few blocks away from Vega and the Mercado Hotel. Attack helicopters and a mechanized infantry unit led the assault. The chatter of automatic weapons reverberated through the narrow streets leading to and from the PDF headquarters. M113 armored personnel carriers crushed through the neighborhood with little resistance though the forces had to be vigilant against small-arms fire from apartment buildings that hemmed in the Comandancia. Tragedy was averted early when an AH-6 "Little Bird" observation helicopter was shot down. Although the helicopter crashed into the courtyard of the Comandancia, the two-man crew were not injured and managed to escape over the wall of the compound and link up with one of the armored personnel carriers that had arrived on the scene.

The noose around the PDF tightened. With each target taken out and neutralized, the chances for individual units to link up diminished. Throughout the night and through the morning on the Pacific and Atlantic sides of the canal, as well as the interior, the targets that the various U.S. task forces hit continually weakened the PDF and prevented them from striking back or helping out other units. At the same time, the noose was getting tighter around Noriega as more targets—

possible escape routes—were taken out.

Fifty miles from Panama City at Rio Hato, near Noriega's beach house, two Ranger battalions of almost 900 men were sent to secure another airfield as well as neutralize two PDF companies of about five hundred soldiers, including the 7th Company, the company that came to Noriega's rescue during the October coup. The Air Force also got to try out one of their newest aircraft, the F-117A Stealth Fighter. Two F-117A Stealth Fighters, which had flown nonstop from an airbase in Nevada each dropped a 2,000-pound bomb, nicknamed *The Hammer* in the vicinity of the PDF barracks. Although one of the bombs missed its target, an AC-130 gunship and helicopters joined in by taking out selected targets before the air assault by the Rangers, which immediately neutralized the threat.

Noriega, who thought the United States would never resort to military action (even when one of his PDF soldiers shot and killed an American four days earlier), had created a shit storm that was not going to stop until he was caught. It was, as one soldier from the 193rd Infantry Brigade from Ft. Clayton eloquently put it, after having secured Fort Amador on the Pacific side of the canal, "We came, we saw, we kicked fucking ass."

* * *

Frank heard the fighting from his apartment. He walked out on the balcony to watch parts of the city light up like fireworks. He already knew what had to be done; he had been planning this for weeks, and now thanks to the U.S. military, he was going to have the perfect cover. He had weighed all his options and knew what the consequences would be for him, as well as his family. There was no other way.

It was ironic in a twisted sort of way how everything had come full circle for him. When he signed on with Smith, he never imagined that it would all come down to this. And then for Rooney to show up, that was, for lack of a better expression, poetic justice. When this was all over, perhaps the world would once again spin the way it had been meant. Everyone would be able to get on with their lives.

Everything *had* come full circle.

In the distance, he watched a fireball rise from some dark neighborhood. There were more flashes of light. He would be driving right into the middle of the storm, but he had no choice. What had been set into motion years ago would all come to an end this evening. He finished a cigarette and poured himself a glass of whiskey. He thought he would be nervous, but after having thought through everything, he surprisingly had a peace of mind for the first time in many years.

He went back inside the apartment and on the top shelf of the closet in the living room, he felt around for the pistol and the three clips of ammunition that he had bought from an acquaintance three weeks earlier. He took off his wedding ring, attached it to a gold chain Inés had bought for him on their last anniversary, and slipped it inside an envelope with the note he had written to Inés explaining what had to be done and apologizing for all the grief he had caused her. He thanked her for giving him the best years of his life and for their two daughters. He knew that Adrianna wasn't his, but he didn't want Inés to know that he knew. That was okay; he made sure Smith took care of that for him.

He then kissed his wife and daughters on the forehead for the last time.

CHAPTER FORTY-ONE

EVER SINCE THE day he saved Alejandro's life, Buck had been on a collision course with his friend. Although it had been Noriega who had kept the two men friends, none of that mattered now. Buck had a debt to settle and Alejandro had no idea that his best friend was coming to collect.

Noriega would have to wait.

Buck removed a photograph from his wallet and looked at it. The photo was taken of him and Estefani at her father's restaurant the last time he saw her. After he had found out that her death was the result of a drug overdose, he did more digging, and that's when he discovered that it had been Vega's cocaine that she had been transporting. And it wasn't just one trip. Over a five-month period, she had made four trips to Miami—all paid for by Vega. That's how she was helping her father pay off his debt, but that was more than enough to pay off whatever Estevan owed. Vega had been using her all along to move his cocaine. Buck shuddered when he thought about seeing her in the casket and how devastated her parents had been. He shuddered when he thought about how smug Vega had been at the funeral. Tonight he would take care of everything. Ever since he found out that Vega had a hand in the death of his godchild, there was only one way this was going to end.

He slipped the photo back into his wallet and gazed through the windshield of his car. He had parked a block down the street from Vega's hotel—out of the line of sight of anyone standing watch in front. From here, Buck could see anyone who walked in or out of the front entrance. But there was something else which concerned him more. In the distance, he heard gunfire and a series of explosions. Overhead, an AC-130 gunship circled. Green tracers lit up the sky. He took a risk being here knowing very well that the U.S. military was already assaulting the PDF headquarters, but it would also be the perfect cover for Vega to escape.

"Well, my friend, I have other plans for you this evening," Buck said, touching the Glock 17 on the seat next to him.

Buck never forgot the first person he killed. It was not long after he had arrived in Vietnam. His platoon had come across a village and taken into custody two South Vietnamese suspected of collaborating with the VC and providing them with intel. The operation went exactly as they had planned. They had taken custody of the two VC and were waiting for the helicopter to extract them. It had been extremely hot that day, hotter than most days in the Delta. In the shade of one of the hooches, the men tried to keep cool. Buck sipped the tepid water in his canteen and wished for something ice cold. Then, as if someone had read his mind, a young woman showed up carrying a basket. She set the basket down, reached inside, and pulled out two bottles of Coke dripping with water.

There was a kid in his platoon, Harris, from Alabama or Mississippi, Buck never got to know him well enough to find out, who leaped up when he saw the Cokes and ran toward the basket. Buck opened his mouth to yell at the kid that the basket was probably booby-trapped, but it was too late. Harris reached into the basket and grabbed one of the bottles that were wired to a claymore mine. When the smoke cleared, Harris and two other soldiers were dead; three more were seriously wounded. The woman who had brought the basket had been wounded in the explosion. When she tried to crawl away, Buck walked up to her slowly, took out his pistol, and calmly shot her in the back of the head.

There would be others that he would kill in Vietnam, but that woman and the bullet he put in the back of her head had haunted him ever since. She had been the only person he'd ever shot in cold blood, but that was about to change. From where he was sitting, he could see one of Vega's bodyguards standing outside the entrance. He picked up the Glock 17 and held it in front of him. With seventeen rounds in the magazine and two more magazines in his back pocket, he hoped that was enough for the evening. Mitchell was more than happy to provide Buck with all the firepower he needed. He didn't ask Buck why, but he had a hunch. "Just make sure it doesn't come back to us," was all he said.

The problem was getting past Vega's bodyguards. There was no way Vega's men standing guard outside were going to let Buck walk right in without first notifying their boss. And there was no way that Buck was going to get past them without having to neutralize them. Once inside, there would be more bodyguards. His fears were compounded by the fact that Vega's men were probably already jumpy by the attack on the Comandancia and would shoot at anything that moved.

While Buck was running through his options, a car pulled up in front of the hotel. The driver got out and before the two bodyguards could do anything, the driver shot them both at point-blank range.

"What the fuck—"

Buck couldn't believe what he had just seen. Whoever it was must have known the bodyguards to have gotten that close to them. The driver walked up to the two bodyguards writhing on the ground and put a bullet into each of their heads. Before entering the building, the person glanced to the right and then to the left and then turned around as though he knew he was being watched.

"Costello."

This was not how Buck envisioned the night unfolding. He had told Costello to stay put and wait for further instructions. He jumped out of the car and dashed across the street. In the distance, he heard sporadic automatic weapon fire. There was no mistaking two of the most distinct automatic weapon sounds in modern warfare: the AK-47 and the M-16.

He stopped at the entrance and looked down at the two bodyguards, admiring Costello's handiwork before he moved inside. There was a flash of light at the top of the stairs and then the sound of someone or something falling to the ground. This was so unlike his friend to let someone get this close. There were a few lights on in the lobby, but it appeared that the hotel had not been opened for some time. That wasn't the only thing that got Buck's attention.

In the middle of the lobby, a couple of crates and modular containers stood, ready to ship. Vega was also using the invasion to his advantage. There was no mistaking the blocks of C-4 on the sides of some of the containers. Buck figured the amount of plastic explosives could take out the hotel and most of the block.

He slowly walked up the winding staircase to the second floor where he had seen the flash. Lights in the corridor flickered. Shadows from fires burning outside danced on the walls. When he passed a window, in the distance he could see a ball of fire rising into the sky. The headquarters of the PDF were just a few blocks away, and Buck knew, from having sat in on some of the security briefings, the headquarters were one of the first targets to be taken out. There wasn't much time; the last thing Buck wanted was to be picked up by U.S. forces patrolling the area.

Buck proceeded down the hallway to Vega's office. There was another bodyguard on the floor with a bullet in his forehead. Frank wasn't that bad of a shot. Buck leaned up against the door and listened. He could hear two men talking—the voices were definitely Vega's and Costello's. Buck held up the Glock, took a deep breath, and kicked the door open.

"What took you so long, Buck?" Vega asked, backing away from his desk. He had a pistol pointed at Frank, who was standing in the middle of the room. "I thought you'd never get here."

"It's a little crazy out there tonight," Buck said.

"So I've heard," Vega said grinning. "And as you can see, we have ourselves a little situation right here. He tried to shoot my ear off."

Buck could see blood trickling down the side of Vega's face. He also noticed more suitcases next to his friend's desk. "Going somewhere this evening, Alejandro?"

"Smith, this is of no concern to you," Frank said, keeping his pistol aimed at Vega's head. "You just back away and let me take care of this."

"That's where you're wrong, Frank," Buck said. "Alejandro and I have some unfinished business to attend to. Don't we, Alejandro?"

Outside, an explosion rocked the neighborhood. The sporadic gunfire, which had been faint earlier, now seemed much closer. Shadows from a fire burning somewhere in the neighborhood danced across one of the walls.

"What are you talking me about?" Vega asked. "This *pendejo* came in here shooting up the place and threatened to put a bullet in my head before you finally decided to show up."

"You threatened my family, Vega," Frank said, the veins on his neck tightening. "For that you are going to pay dearly."

"Do you see what I had to put up with, Buck?" Vega said. "Let's take care of this *hijo de puta* and get out of here while we can."

"That's not going to happen, Alejandro," Buck said, slowly moving toward the middle of the room where Frank was standing.

Vega furled his eyebrows. "You and I had a deal. You get Noriega and I walk out of here."

"*Did*, Alejandro."

"Buck—" Vega began.

"What's it going to be, Frank?" Buck asked, glancing at Frank out the corner of his eye. "Are you going to shoot Vega or are you going to let him walk out of here?"

Vega couldn't believe what he just heard. His friend was betraying him, and he was going to let Costello do his dirty work. Buck slowly moved toward Frank. He wasn't about to let Frank shoot his friend; things had gotten too messy already, but that's what he wanted Vega to think. Very carefully, Buck came back around Frank and knocked over an ashtray that crashed to the floor. Frank, nervous and on edge, jumped when he heard the crash and turned to see what it was. That was all the distraction Buck needed to come up behind Frank and with one quick martial arts move, disarm him.

"*Bueno, bueno,* my friend. I see you haven't lost any of your skills." Vega walked out from behind his desk and started to move to the center of the room. He still had his pistol aimed at

Frank. "You had me worried there for a second. Now, what do you say we end this drama and get the hell out of here?"

"I'm sorry, Alejandro," Buck said, turning toward Vega and pointing the Glock at his head. Out of the corner of his eye, Buck saw one of Vega's men moving into the room. "Tell your man that's close enough. Frank, sorry about this, but this is between Vega and me."

"Buck, I love a good drama, but do you mind telling me what the fuck is going on?" Vega said, motioning for the man behind them to put his weapon down and to move back. "We don't have much time."

"You got that right, Alejandro, but not *we*, you," Buck said.

"My friend, you've been with the Agency too long," Alejandro replied. "You really ought to hear yourself sometime."

"What bothered me the most when I found out about how she died, was how you could look me in the eye at her funeral knowing very well that you were responsible for her death," Buck said in a cold, calculated voice.

"Who are you talking about?" Vega asked.

"You know exactly *who* I am talking about," Buck said staring at his friend. He could feel the anger swelling up inside. "Estevan's daughter, Estefani."

"Is that what this is about?" Vega asked. "Buck, I thought I knew you better than to take a personal interest in these matters."

"What's going on, Smith?" Frank asked.

"Jesus, she was just a kid, Alejandro," Buck said. "How could you let her be one of your mules?"

Vega grinned. "My friend, she wasn't as innocent as you thought. She came here begging me to do something to help her old man. You know me, when an opportunity presents itself, I never back away."

"You bastard!" Buck yelled. "You're talking about the daughter of one of my friends. She was my godchild."

"That's got to hurt, but business is business, Buck," Vega said. "You of all people should appreciate that."

"That's why I've got to do this," Buck said coolly. "Now, Frank!"

Before Buck could fire his weapon, an explosion outside shook the building, which paused the standoff between Buck and Vega. Chunks of plaster rained upon the men who ducked as best they could to avoid getting hit by the falling debris and choking dust. Buck, only slightly fazed, immediately fired one round at Vega. It hit him in the shoulder but not before he managed to get two rounds off at Frank, hitting Frank in the arm and shoulder. At the sound of gunfire, Vega's bodyguard had come to the assistance of his boss, firing two rounds at Buck. One grazed the side of this head, but the other slammed into his shoulder knocking him over a chair and onto the floor. Frank lay writhing on the floor; his pistol was a few feet away. He heard Buck moaning not far from where he was. He could feel his blood-soaked t-shirt clinging to his body. Out of the corner of his eye, he could see Vega moving toward him. Frank tried in vain to reach for his weapon with his good arm, but it was beyond his grasp. He grunted and groaned as he tried to roll his body over to the weapon, but was unable to move fast enough.

"Not so fast, Frank," Vega said, stepping on Frank's wounded arm and pointing his weapon at Frank's head.

The pain was excruciating as Frank tried to free his arm while still trying to reach for his pistol.

"I'm sorry about this, Frank," Vega said. "If it's any consolation, I wanted to do this in front of your wife and daughters, but a man can't have everything."

Frank tried one more time to free his arm, but Vega was enjoying the moment, watching Frank writhe in pain as he applied more pressure to Frank's arm. Frank closed his eyes and waited for the shot that would end his life, but when he heard it, he felt no bullet ripping into his body. Instead, as he looked up, he saw a large red stain growing across Vega's chest. Vega's mouth was agape as he stared at Buck, who had put the round in his chest. Buck then spun and caught Vega's surprised bodyguard with a round between the eyes. Vega slowly looked down at his bloodied chest and then looked at Buck before he fell back against his desk. Buck walked up to his friend and calmly stuck the barrel of the Glock into Vega's mouth. Vega had the same wild, frightened eyes that he had twenty-five years earlier when the scared, skinny kid looked up at Buck for help.

"*Esto es para Estefani,*" Buck said as he pulled the hammer back on the Glock. "*Nos vemos en el infierno, mi amigo.*"

Blood and bits of gray matter splattered the desk. Buck looked down at his friend one last time before his attention turned to Frank writhing in pain on the floor. Outside, another explosion ripped through a building adjacent to the hotel. Inside Vega's office, the concussion from the explosion knocked out most of the windows. Glass and dust flew through the air, filling the room. After the dust had cleared, Buck checked on Frank whose wounds needed immediate attention.

"We don't have much time," Buck said, spitting out a gob of blood. He looked down at his bloody arm. It wasn't as bad as it looked. He wondered where Guerra was, but right now that was the least of his worries. "Vega's got enough C-4 downstairs to take out an entire city block. He wasn't taking any chances."

"Thanks for having my back," Frank said.

Buck nodded, helping Frank to his feet. "Don't mention it. Thanks for having mine."

The two men slowly staggered out of Vega's office and moved toward the staircase. Through one of the broken windows, they could see and hear the fighting taking place outside. There was another explosion that caused more plaster and glass to rain on the two men. The distinct, throbbing pum-pum-pum sound of a .50 caliber machine gun, which sounded like a kettledrum as it echoed down the narrow streets, meant that the U.S. forces had already breached the Comandancia compound.

Another explosion rattled the hotel. Buck lost his balance and fell down the steps.

"Smith!" Frank yelled.

CHAPTER FORTY-TWO

KEVIN RACED ACROSS the city in the dark blue van he signed out of the security police motor pool two days earlier and pondered his situation. He knew he was taking a big risk going anywhere in the city with parts of it already occupied by U.S. forces and many of the major thoroughfares were already closed. He had no other choice if he wanted to get Inés and her daughters to safety. Thanks to Smith's phone call he had a heads-up on the timing of the invasion, but by the time he got downtown, the invasion was already underway.

He passed a burning car in the middle of the street. A group of young Panamanians, oblivious to the vehicle, danced around the burning wreckage, their shadows cast upon the side of a building. Another group of Panamanians emerged from an electronics store carrying television sets and boom boxes. Either they were getting a jump on the looting or things were happening a lot faster than he had anticipated. Either way he didn't want to be out here any longer than he had to; just get Inés and the girls and get back to Howard as fast as he could. He was angry at himself for not getting them sooner. Two youths crossed the street right in front of the van and he slammed on the brakes to avoid hitting them. One of the kids, no older than sixteen, stared at Kevin for a few seconds and then started laughing uncontrollably.

Other than the looters, there were no other people or traffic on the street Kevin was driving down. He knew to stay off the main thoroughfares until he got to the apartment. What he feared most was coming across U.S. or Panamanian forces and getting caught in the line of fire. As he turned down the street where Frank and Inés's apartment was located, he heard gunshots and what sounded like machine gun fire. There was the sound of a helicopter somewhere, rotors beating the cool air. An AC-130 gunship circled overhead providing fire support wherever needed. Someone on a bullhorn was shouting in Spanish for people to stay indoors.

Adrenaline coursed through Kevin's body. In all his thirteen years of service, he had never been in a situation like this; however, when he was at Minot, security forces were constantly on alert. He wondered if he would have to use his weapon tonight. Smith had given him a Berretta M9 just in case things got a little dicey. The other day, Kevin had returned to his room in the transient barracks and found a box on his desk with the weapon and ammunition inside along with a note which read: *You will need this.*

A car pulled out from a side street startling Kevin as he swerved to avoid hitting it. *We're in for one hell of a shit storm.* He heard an explosion somewhere followed by small arms fire. He gazed up through the windshield and saw the flashing anti-collision lights of a low-flying aircraft overhead. He suddenly had a terrible thought. What if Frank and his family were not there when he got to the apartment? What if Vega had already gotten to them?

Halfway down the street, he glanced in the rearview

mirror and noticed a car driving erratically, as though it were trying to catch up to Kevin. Thinking fast, Kevin stepped on the accelerator and drove up onto the sidewalk in front of the apartment building. He got out of the van and was just about to reach for the Berretta-M9, but at the last moment, the car swerved and drove up on the sidewalk. It continued along the sidewalk for a few yards before it crashed into a palm tree a few yards from where Kevin was standing. He held his weapon at his side as he slowly approached the vehicle. Wisps of smoke escaped from underneath the hood. When the driver's door was thrown open, Kevin pointed his weapon at the driver, but dropped it back to his side when he saw that the driver was Frank, who slowly got out of the car and staggered toward his friend. Frank had a gunshot wound in his shoulder and a deep gash across his forehead. Blood was trickling down the side of his face. Halfway toward Kevin, he fell to the sidewalk. Kevin ran to him and helped his friend to his feet.

"Inés," Frank said, gasping for breath. "We've got to get her and the girls out."

In the light from the streetlight overhead, Kevin could see that Frank's injuries were bad.

"What happened, Frank?"

"Vega."

"Did he get away?"

Frank shook his head. "Everything happened so fast. He's dead."

"Smith?"

There was another explosion not far away and more small-arms fire.

"I don't know," Frank said, wincing from the pain. "There was an explosion and he fell down the stairs. He got buried under some rubble. I barely got out in time."

Frank's knees buckled, but Kevin caught him in time and

helped him to the van.

"We have to hurry," Frank said, wincing from the pain. "Vega had some of his men following me. They were not too far behind."

Kevin looked out the back of the van and noticed that a car had turned down the street and stopped. If it were Vega's men, there was not much they could do to stop them. His best bet was to get Inés and the girls, put them in the van and get everyone the hell out of there.

"You hang on there, Frank," Kevin said. "I'll be right back."

Kevin grabbed the Berretta and ran into the building, bounding up the stairs as fast as he could. This time, there were no televisions or music blaring from inside apartments up and down the floor where Frank and Inés lived. The city was on fire and people were locked behind doors cowering in darkness hoping that the nightmare would end soon.

"Inés, it's me, Kevin! Please open the door!" Kevin shouted.

He heard movement inside the apartment that sounded like a chair or some other piece of furniture being pushed away from the door followed by the metallic click of a lock.

The electricity was off in the apartment, and Inés had a candle burning.

"We have to go now, Inés," Kevin said, moving over to a window and peering outside. If Vega's men had followed Frank back to his apartment, they were waiting to see what he would do next.

Inés gasped when she noticed the weapon in Kevin's hand. "What's happening, Kevin?"

"There's no time," Kevin said in a tone that startled Inés and frightened her daughters. The youngest one started crying. Kevin glanced at Inés whose eyes were wide with fear. "I'm sorry, Inés. I've got a van outside. Frank's in the back. Vega's men most likely followed him here. When we get downstairs, I want you and your girls to run to it as fast as you can when I give you the signal."

"Frank!?" Inés screamed. "He's here? I don't understand. He left me a note saying that he was going to take care of—"

"Inés, we have to go, now!" Kevin lifted up Adrianna.

"*¿A dónde vamos mami?*" Adrianna asked, turning her head and looking at her mother.

"*Vamos a ir a dar un paseo con este hombre amable,*" Inés replied gazing across the room at Kevin and smiling.

Kevin's Spanish might have been rusty after all these years, but he did understand this nice man is going to help us.

"*¿Dónde está papá?*" Esmeralda asked.

"*Está afuera,*" Inés answered.

Kevin walked over to a window that looked out on the street below, which was empty of any cars. In the distance, he could see the sky lit up by green tracers from the AC-130 gunship circling that part of the city. If he wasn't worried about Vega's men coming after them and if Frank wasn't hurt they could hunker down here and wait until things quieted down; however, it was too late to change the game plan. Kevin knew that Vega's men would be coming after them; the question was, would he have enough time to get them safely back to Howard?

"Okay, let's go," Kevin said, moving to the door and ushering Inés and her daughters out.

When they reached the ground floor, they stopped at the entrance. Kevin peered out the door. He couldn't see the car that he had seen earlier. The street was still empty. He breathed a sigh of relief.

Then a voice froze him in place.

"That's far enough," Guerra said, walking out from

behind a concrete column in the lobby. He had a pistol in his hand. "Please drop your weapon and kick it over here."

Kevin did as he was told. He turned and faced Guerra. In the fluorescent pallor which filled the lobby, Kevin thought he might have recognized the man, but just couldn't quite place him.

"*Diego, ¿qué estás haciendo?*" Inés screamed when she saw that it was Guerra. She couldn't understand why Diego had a gun pointed at Kevin. "*Fuera de Frank. Tenemos que llevarlo a un hospital.*"

"*Lo siento, Inés,*" Guerra said, backing up a few steps.

"*¿De qué estás hablando?*" Inés asked. A look of fear washed across her face as she held her daughters. Adrianna started crying. "*¿Pasando a Diego?*"

Guerra still hadn't gone for the Berretta on the floor. Kevin noticed this and hoped that Inés would find a way to distract him. He moved a few steps to the left. Now he recognized the man. It was the night at Napoli's when he got into a fight with Frank. They had been sitting at an outside table when Kevin and his friends walked past the restaurant. Guerra had tried to intervene, and Kevin had taken a swing at him.

"That's far enough, *hermano.*" Guerra, who was also having a hard time placing Kevin, studied the man standing in front of him and finally remembered. "I remember you now. You used to be stationed at Howard. You're the one who—"

Upstairs, a door slammed shut, which startled Guerra just enough for Kevin to go for his weapon. He dove onto the floor, grabbed his Berretta, rolled over three times and got off three shots before Guerra realized what had happened. Kevin, who had competed in the Air Force's Tactical Urban Warfare Competition at Lackland Air Force Base, used the same moves that won him top honors two years in a row. Though he had won those awards with his weapon of choice, a Smith & Wesson .38, the Berretta was his second choice. The first shot was too low and off target, hitting Guerra in the shoulder and knocking him back, but not off balance. Guerra tried to get a shot off and shot high over Kevin's head. It was the only shot he would take and the last one of his life. Kevin took careful aim and put the second shot in Guerra's chest and the next one in the middle of his forehead.

The person who had slammed the door upstairs walked into the lobby just as Kevin put the last bullet into Guerra. When she saw Guerra's body on the ground, she started screaming and ran back up the stairs.

"Inés, we have to go," Kevin said, starting for the door.

Inés just stood there, horrified, still holding her daughters close and staring down at the spreading pool of blood around Diego's lifeless body. She used to call him Uncle Diego—he was Esmeralda's *padrino*.

"Inés! Come on, let's go!" Kevin yelled, hurrying Inés and her daughters out of the building toward the van. He glanced down the street and noticed a pair of headlights come on and then another pair as they hurried to the van. Kevin heard both cars revving their engines.

"Shit," Kevin muttered as soon as he saw the headlights and heard the engines.

Inés also saw them.

"Kevin?"

"Everything's going to be fine," Kevin said calmly, sliding open the van's side door. "Just get in the van."

Inés and her daughters got into the van as Kevin kept an eye on the two cars down the street. Kevin figured the occupants of both vehicles were waiting to see what he would do next. As soon as Inés saw Frank and all the blood, she started screaming while her daughters cried.

"Frank, oh my God," Inés cried as she cradled her husband's head in her arms. "Why, darling, why?"

"Inés, I'm sorry," Frank said, his voice weak from the loss of blood. "I never meant to hurt you or the girls."

"I know, darling," Inés said pushing Frank's matted hair off his forehead.

Kevin climbed into the van and moved to the driver's seat. He quickly shoved a fresh clip into the butt of the Berretta. He had two more on the seat next to him. Although it might be enough for whoever was in the two cars waiting for them, Kevin wasn't about to find out.

"Everyone, hold on back there," Kevin said, turning around in the seat. He started the van, slammed the gear selector into drive, and gunned the engine.

The van's rear tires spun on some dead palm fronds before it took off down the street heading straight for the two cars. Kevin knew that gunning for the two cars with the lights off was playing a dangerous game of chicken, but he hoped the element of surprise would work to his advantage. When he got within fifty yards of the two cars, he switched on the lights and hit the high beams momentarily blinding the drivers of both vehicles. If the occupants of both cars had any designs on firing their weapons at the van, they had little time to react as the van sped by. The two drivers immediately turned their vehicles around on the street and began to pursue the van.

Kevin didn't bother to see how close the two cars were behind him as he turned the corner and headed down Balboa Avenue. He hoped that his little maneuver back there was enough to give him a head start, but the cars soon caught up with the van. In the distance, the sky was lit by flares and fires as U.S. forces continued to take out targets in the city. The van raced down the avenue at speeds topping seventy miles an hour, but the two cars stayed close. Kevin's best bet was to get back on Avenida de Los Mártires, and from there, cross the Thatcher Ferry Bridge to get back to Howard. At least that was the plan he was improvising; if he couldn't get through there was always Fort Clayton or Albrook, which were on the other side of Balboa. If he could just put enough distance between himself and the two cars in pursuit, they would have a good chance to make it. Kevin turned off Balboa Avenue and sped down a side street. His maneuver worked. When he looked in the side mirror, he couldn't see either of the cars.

After traveling down the side street for a couple of blocks, they ended up on Vía España. *This is where things could get dicey.* Kevin gazed at the side and rearview mirrors for any sign of the two cars. There was no mistaking the gunfire and explosions in the distance and what appeared to be a couple of buildings on fire. The street they were on now was festooned with brightly colored Christmas decorations—Santa Clauses, reindeer, even a couple of snowmen which made everything about this night seem all the more surreal, but not as surreal as one larger-than-life plastic Santa Claus that had "Noriega is a Pig" spray-painted across the front.

Kevin mulled over the evening's events. What a fucked-up night. Smith was dead, as was Vega. Guerra lay in a pool of blood back at the apartment. Frank was barely hanging on to his life. Somewhere in Panama City this evening, U.S. forces were closing the net around Noriega—if he hadn't already managed to escape. Too bad Smith wasn't going to be around to see it. He would have appreciated how this night was unfolding.

Tonight, everything had come full circle—Noriega, Vega, Frank, and Inés.

In the back, Frank started coughing up blood.

"Hurry, Kevin!" Inés shouted.

"You hang on there, Frank," Kevin said, as the van

356

rounded a corner and nearly sideswiped an abandoned taxi. "We'll be out of this in no time."

Kevin stepped on the accelerator as the van careened around another corner. He swerved to avoid hitting another abandoned car, which was on fire, and he lost control of the van as it rode up onto a sidewalk. An octave above the revving engine, more gunfire echoed in the distance. He turned the wheel abruptly, avoided taking out a concrete bench, and turned back on the road, but in the process losing valuable time. However, they had made it. They were on Avenida de Los Mártires. From where they were at now, it was at least another twenty minutes, maybe less before they would be at Howard. He just hoped that the bridge was still open. He knew that one of the objectives was to seize the bridge to prevent PDF forces from launching a counterattack, or perhaps even sabotaging the canal, but if there was a roadblock—

"You heard Kevin, darling," Inés said, clasping Frank's right hand which felt cold and clammy. "Everything's going to be okay."

Frank looked up Inés and smiled. His body already started to feel cold from the loss of blood. "It looks like we'll finally be able to go home."

"Son-of-a-bitch!" Kevin yelled, looking in the rearview mirror.

The two cars had suddenly reappeared and were gaining on the van.

CHAPTER FORTY-THREE

LENNY JACKSON, WHO was with the 536th Engineering Battalion and a detachment of marines on the western side of the bridge, couldn't believe what he was seeing; there was a van speeding right at them. The hastily erected roadblock wasn't much, but it would be effective; they had an Army M920 truck with a lowboy trailer with a bulldozer on it, which completely blocked the road. There was also a triple row of concertina wire before the barricade. In case that wasn't enough to stop someone from getting through, there was more than enough firepower with M16s, M249 Squad Automatic Weapons—SAWs, which were light machine guns—and shoulder-fired grenade launchers.

"What do you reckon, Sarge?" Lenny asked his squad leader as he watched the van speeding across the bridge. "Suicide bomber?"

The men had been briefed on the possibility of suicide bombers taking out their roadblock. His sergeant had also seen

the vehicle speeding over the bridge and started to bark orders. The marines had already taken up positions behind and on either side of the truck. The men of Task Force Semper Fi were ready for whatever was coming their way.

* * *

Once they got across the bridge, Kevin knew they would be safe. When he looked in the rearview mirror and didn't see either one of the two cars, he breathed a sigh of relief. Traveling down Avenida de los Mártires, the two cars had been the least of his worries. He could see the flashes of light and hear the explosions just blocks away from where he was driving. Gunning the van down the avenue was more than running a gauntlet and avoiding detection by U.S. or PDF forces, it was threading a needle. Overhead, one of the AC-130 gunships circled and began to open fire on some targets with its 20mm, 40mm, and 105mm weapons. A fireball rose from the middle of El Chorrillo as more explosions rocked the neighborhood. Fortunately for Kevin, the gunship overhead had created so much damage, the smoke from burning buildings and wreckage on the streets was the perfect cover for the van to run that gauntlet without being detected. It was also the perfect cover for the two cars that were still pursuing the van.

This smoky cover was further exacerbated by PDF and Dignity Battalion soldiers deliberately setting fire to buildings in El Chorrillo to conceal their withdraw. As a result, thousands of refugees began to flee the area, which compounded attempts by U.S. forces to cordon off the area and provided another diversion for Kevin. The fires set by these withdrawing forces cast an orange glow over the neighborhood juxtaposed against the silhouettes of darkened apartment buildings.

Kevin glanced over his right shoulder to check on Inés and the others in the back. Inés tried to comfort her two crying daughters while she tried to make Frank as comfortable as she could. He turned his attention back to the street just in time as he swerved to avoid hitting a group of young Panamanians brandishing automatic weapons and machetes as they ran from one of the burning buildings onto the street.

Although Kevin had managed to put enough distance between the van and the two cars chasing it, what he hadn't counted on was a roadblock across the eastern approach to the Bridge of the Americas. It was too late to turn around and try to go through Balboa to get to either Albrook or Fort Clayton. Even if he stopped before the roadblock, there was no way that Vega's men following him would let the van get through.

There was only one course of action to take.

"Hang on!" Kevin yelled as he pushed the accelerator all the way to the floor. "Everyone get down!"

Halfway across the Bridge of the Americas, Frank stopped breathing.

"Frank!" Inés yelled.

*   *   *

Lenny Jackson had been in Panama for almost a year, and he was getting tired of one exercise after another. First it was Sand Flea then it was Nimrod Dancer. *Who the fuck came up with these names?* Lenny grabbed his gear and headed out of the barracks to the waiting deuce-and-a-half earlier in the evening. Panama was nothing like his buddy Evan Murphy described, but that was ten years ago. Murphy talked about how laidback it had been serving here. "Spend a little time in the Panamanian bush," Murphy told Jackson, "and then head on downtown to spend time in some Colombian bush."

This time it wasn't any exercise. It was for real.

Lenny could care less about the geopolitical backdrop to Operation Just Cause—that's what the brass was calling it to avoid any international fallout from invading Panama. (How could someone fault an operation that was a "just cause"?) On a personal level, he despised Panama's Defense Forces and even more, the Dignity Battalions. He knew a couple of guys who were harassed by the Dignity Battalions, which everyone started calling the Dingbat Battalions. A couple times when Lenny was hanging out at one of his favorite off-limits watering holes, there was always one or two off-duty dingbats checking out the GIs and if the need be, call for one of their on-duty buddies to serve up some harassment. Lenny once watched one of these dingbats rough up an airman from Howard just for looking at him the wrong way. If he had the chance, he relished the thought of roughing up a couple of those dingbats just out of spite.

The van speeding across the bridge was no more than three hundred yards from the roadblock. Lenny wished they had some more firepower like one of the Marine's LAV-25s or one of the Army's M-113 armored personnel carriers. If the car was a suicide bomber, they needed to take it out before it got any closer.

* * *

As soon as the marines and the soldiers saw that the van was not going to stop, they immediately opened fire. Kevin tried flashing the headlights on and off, hoping that would signal that they were friendly, to no avail. He ducked down as the windshield was shot out, spraying him with shards of glass. Unable to see, he did his best to steer the van toward the side of the road, but in doing so—given the high rate of speed that the van had been traveling—it clipped the edge of the trailer and slammed into a tree. Kevin banged his head on the steering wheel when the airbags failed to deploy and he felt like he had broken a couple ribs, but that was the least of his worries. Within seconds, six marines surrounded the van.

"Get out of the van now!" one of the marines yelled as he aimed his weapon at Kevin.

The engine sputtered and knocked as Kevin, dazed from the impact, followed orders, slowly taking his hands off the steering wheel. He raised them high enough for the marine lance corporal to see. The acrid smell of rubber and oil filled the interior. "It's okay, Inés. We'll be out of here soon."

"Now, keep your right hand up so we can see it and slowly get out of the vehicle," one of the marines closest to the van yelled above the din of screaming from the back of the van. "Move out of the van now!"

Kevin nodded and slowly opened the door. He was immediately slammed to the ground. Pain shot through his body. He thought he was going to pass out. His chin and cheek scraped the surface of the road as one of the marines held his body down. Two other marines had their weapons still aimed at Kevin as two more approached the rear of the van.

"Don't you fucking move, or I'll blow your fucking head off," a tall marine said as he aimed his weapon at Kevin's head.

"I'm an American. There's a woman and her two daughters and an American civilian inside. He's been shot up badly!" Kevin screamed, pointing to the van. Kevin tried to reach inside his shirt and pull out his dog tags and security pass to show the marines standing over him, but couldn't reach them. He was still having a difficult time seeing due to the glass that had cut his face. "I'm Master Sergeant Kevin Rooney here on special assignment."

"I don't care if you're John fucking Rambo," the marine yelled again. "Keep your head down, or I swear I'll blow it right fucking off!"

Kevin's explanation didn't help his situation as he felt the flash suppressor of the M-16 pressed against the back of his head and one of the marine's size ten combat boots squarely planted on the small of his back. Kevin's mouth tasted the cool, oily asphalt that his face was pressed against.

"Jesus Christ!" one of the marines still watching the bridge yelled when he saw two more vehicles racing across the bridge.

Kevin turned his head slightly to see what all the commotion was about. The marines didn't have the chance to check Kevin's identification or help Inés and her daughters. Right now, they were more concerned about the two cars traveling at high speeds toward the roadblock. Thinking that the two cars were with the van, the marines and soldiers immediately opened fire on the two approaching vehicles. After having been surprised by the van, the marines and soldiers used all of their firepower. The driver of the first vehicle was shot in the head and after the car spun out of control, it crashed head-on into the lowboy trailer, not far from the van. It exploded into a ball of fire, spraying hot shrapnel around the roadblock and wounding the two marines closest to it. Two of the car's occupants were still alive, screaming as they tried to escape the burning vehicle.

In the meantime, the group of marines surrounding the van worked to quickly rescue the occupants in the back before the burning car threatened their safety. The second car, unable to stop in time, clipped the back of the van. It was immediately hit by a salvo of automatic weapons, but it continued down the road for fifty yards before it veered off the road and crashed into a palm tree. One of the occupants, dazed from the impact, got out of the car with an AK-47, and was immediately gunned down.

From where Keith was lying, with the side of his face still pressed against the pavement, he could see the three vehicles burning and heard the screams of the men who hadn't been able to get out in time. He heard the girls crying and Inés screaming to save her husband. He heard one of the marines yell for a corpsman. Suddenly, the gas tank in the van exploded, followed by another explosion which showered hot metal and other debris on Kevin and the marines gathered around him. Kevin lowered his head and breathed slowly. He was going to have a lot of explaining to do, but at least Inés and her girls were safe.

EPILOGUE

IN THE AFTERMATH of Operation Just Cause, parts of the city were still on fire, especially El Chorrillo, which was one of the areas hit hardest during the operation. By the time the fires were brought under control, thousands of families had been displaced and thousands more sought refuge. Looting continued in parts of Panama City, which further complicated matters for U.S. authorities who were forced to divert personnel to secure the city. There was still sporadic fighting in Colón and other towns where PDF soldiers were holed up and would continue for a few days.

Noriega, who believed, up until the very end before his empire crumbled, that the United States would never intervene militarily because of his past relations with the various agencies who he had been in bed with, ended up on the run for days while the U.S. forces conducted nearly fifty operations to flush him out. Finally, on Christmas Eve, after hiding out in a car in the parking lot of a Dairy Queen, Noriega slipped into the Vatican Embassy—a man desperate for salvation and redemption.

With Noriega hunkered down in the embassy hoping that some country would grant him asylum, an Army PSYOP unit started blasting music from large speakers outside the embassy in an attempt to drive out Noriega. First, it was a day of Christmas music, followed by a barrage of rock and roll hits from "I Fought the Law" to "Welcome to the Jungle." The press had a field day writing about how demoralizing as well as cruel it was, but the majority of the people who had been following the Noriega drama loved it. Finally, the man who, weeks earlier proclaimed himself the Maximum Leader of Panama had had enough. On January 3, after days of negotiations between the U.S. State Department and the Vatican, Noriega quietly walked out of the embassy and was immediately taken into custody by U.S. authorities, put on a plane, and extradited to the United States.

On national television, the President assured Americans that everything was okay. They had their man. Peace was restored. Panama had a new president. The country could get back to preparing for the eventual turnover of the canal in ten years.

Kevin spent over a week in a ward at a military hospital recovering from his injuries. Separated from the other patients, Kevin had no contact with anyone other than the nurses and doctors who came into his room. He had no idea what happened to Frank, Inés, or their daughters. None of the nurses or the two doctors who checked on him said anything to him. When he asked them about what happened, they pretended as though they didn't hear. Other than the medical staff, no one came into his room until two officers came in and told him that he was being transferred to the bachelor officer quarters on Albrook. It wasn't until the day before he was transferred when someone finally told him about Frank, Inés, and their daughters.

"Your buddy didn't make it," an airman, who brought Kevin his lunch, said. "His wife and daughters are fine, though."

Kevin stared at the tiny Christmas tree that someone had brought into the room for the holidays. He had completely missed the holiday because of all the medication he took for the pain. There was something about the way the airman had said that his buddy had died that weighed heavily on Kevin's soul. Though he had despised Frank ever since Gary's death, trying to get to safety with Inés screaming for him to drive faster and Frank fighting for his life in the back of the van that put the screws into him. As much as he hated Frank, Inés was a widow, and their daughters were without a father.

"What about the operation?" Kevin asked, rolling over in bed and glancing at the airman. "Is it over?"

The airman nodded as he started for the door. "Yeah, they finally caught the son-of-a-bitch."

Kevin grinned and rolled over in bed. He thought about Vega lying dead in the Mercado Hotel and Guerra with a bullet in his head back at Frank and Inés's apartment. Everything *had* come full circle. Kevin stared at the Christmas tree and the blinking lights, and for the first time in a very long time, wept.

*   *   *

"I think we're good here, Rooney," Johnson said, closing the legal pad and putting it back into his briefcase. "We'd like to thank you for coming here today and helping us with our investigation."

"That's it?" Kevin asked. "Four hours ago you were about to hang my ass out to dry."

"We just wanted to corroborate your story with that of another witness," Johnson said smiling. "We're sorry for all the formalities and any inconvenience we might have put you through. We just had to make sure that there are no loose ends in case there is a real investigation down the road one day."

Real investigation? The only other witness Kevin could think of was Inés; they surely wouldn't have called her to testify unless this was all a diversion. Kevin glanced toward the two-way mirror again. *Who was on the other side?*

"You've got to be kidding me," Kevin said looking at Johnson and Collins. "The next thing you're going to tell me is that there was no tape in the video camera."

Collins stood up and slid his chair under the table. "You catch on fast, Kevin."

"You're not Air Force, are you?" Kevin said, staring across the table at Johnson. It was all making sense to Kevin now. Smith wasn't here, but his colleagues were tying up all the loose ends. Someone up the chain of command had to cover his ass. "You guys work for Smith, don't you?"

Johnson looked at his partner and then looked toward the two-way mirror. The airman first class smiled and put away her legal pad. She hadn't written anything.

"Rooney, a lot of things are not always what they seem at first. Sometimes we have to create appearances to ensure that the truth is not compromised. The story that you just told might seem quite incredible, almost unbelievable to someone not familiar with what we do, but we're all in this together and though our motives are not always clear, we all want the same thing. If it hadn't been you, Rooney, it would have been someone else. Wasn't that what Buck told you? That's the way the world turns," Johnson said. "We're all on the same team, Rooney. Don't you ever think otherwise. Noriega, Vega, your friends Gary and Costello—they were all minor players in this drama, but each one had a role to play. It was all about people just like you. In ten, twenty, thirty, even fifty years from now, what do you think people are going to remember most about these events? We all have our parts to play in this, Rooney, and you just played yours."

Johnson looked toward the two-way mirror and nodded. Their boy had done just fine.

In the other room, Buck looked through the glass at Rooney on the other side and smiled. "See? I told you he didn't have anything to hide. I told you that he would come through for us."

In the back of the room, Frank slowly stood up, favoring his injured shoulder. "Rooney never was good at lying. Has everything been taken care of?"

Buck nodded. "As you requested. The money has been transferred to an account set up in her name with a trust fund for each of the girls."

"What about the cocaine?" Frank asked.

Buck looked at Ramone and the other men in the room. "What cocaine?"

"Oh, I see," Frank said, raising his eyebrows. "We're playing that card now, are we?"

"Let's just say for the sake of an argument that it's been disposed of," Buck said, casting a sideways glance at the gray-haired man, Daniel Patterson. "Ain't that right, Daniel?"

Patterson nodded.

"Do you think Escobar is going to miss it?" Frank asked.

"We'll worry about him later," Patterson replied.

Buck and Ramone laughed.

"I've got a question for you, Smith," Frank said as he walked over to Buck. "When we were back at the hotel, what did Vega mean when he said that you two had a deal?"

"Vega thought that I had come for him to help him get out of the country if something ever happened to Noriega," Buck said. "He didn't count on me finding out what happened

369

to Estefani."

"She must have been some woman," Frank said. "I'm sorry about her."

Buck was quiet for a few seconds. "I loved that girl as if she was my daughter. When I found out what he did to get back the money he loaned her father, there was no way I was going to let that bastard live."

"I thought he was your friend?"

"Friends don't kill their friend's children," Buck said.

The two men looked through the two-way mirror and watched Rooney push his chair back and stand up. Rooney walked around the table and shook hands with Johnson and Collins.

"By the way, I forgot to ask you, how does it feel to be dead?" Buck asked grinning.

"Other than this bullet hole in my shoulder, it feels no different than when I was alive," Frank said smiling. He looked at Ramone and then at Patterson and Buck. The smile disappeared from his face. "It had to be done this way, right? I mean there was no other way?"

"It's the only way we can guarantee their safety," Buck said. "As long as certain people think you're dead, they're going to be okay."

"What's the cover story?"

"'The body was burnt beyond recognition' is the story we released to the media. There were enough burnt bodies in the car to make it stick," Buck explained. "Fortunately for you and us, there were plenty of witnesses who saw the van explode after the second car hit it. In all the confusion of getting your wife and daughters out, and the possibility of more vehicles trying to get through the same roadblock, no one is sure they ever saw you before you were transported out of there. All the marines and soldiers we interviewed have the same story: there were four survivors in the van."

"It worked out nice for us, didn't it?" Frank said.

"Couldn't have planned it any better," Buck said. "Next time though, when someone tells you to stay put, you should listen."

Buck and Frank watched Johnson and Collins leave the room followed by the airman first class and technical sergeant. Before Rooney left the room, he turned and twisted his lips into a wry smile as he gazed at the mirror.

"Does Rooney know?"

Buck shook his head.

"So that's it. I'm dead."

Buck grinned. "Get used to it."

* * *

After he said goodbye to Inés and the girls, and watched them get on the Freedom Bird, Kevin walked outside the terminal. There was a lot of talking that the two of them were going to need to do when Kevin eventually joined them, which also included Kevin getting to know his daughter.

Inés. He was already missing her. They hardly said much to each other on their way to Howard; though as they neared the MAC terminal he felt her take his hand and squeeze it. She had on a simple black dress and a black hat and large dark sunglasses, which reminded Kevin of the Italian actress, Sophia Loren. When they walked through the terminal, most people stopped whatever they were doing and stared at her. Since the night Kevin rescued Inés and her daughters, they hadn't seen each other until yesterday. Kevin had taken care of all the arrangements for them to fly back to the States on the Freedom Bird; surprisingly, he had little difficulty getting them assigned a seat.

She didn't say much about Frank. Kevin got the impression that she had been preparing for this day for some time, as though Frank's death had always been in the cards for her. In fact, Kevin thought that she looked rather peaceful and subdued considering everything she had been through. He could still see her leaning over Frank's bloodied body, holding onto his hand. He could still hear her screaming in the back of the van to drive faster so they could get Frank to the hospital. Kevin would never be able to get that out of his mind.

As Kevin walked out of the terminal, he saw a recently arrived airman with a duffel bag at his side standing at the edge of the parking lot. Kevin experienced a feeling of déjà vu seeing himself standing there in the same parking lot waiting for his ride thirteen years ago when he arrived with Gary and Frank. It seemed so long ago now, almost as though the memory wasn't even his. Time sometimes played tricks like that.

"Just arrived, huh?" Kevin asked.

The airman turned around to see who was talking and nodded. "Guess I just missed all the excitement."

"Just a little," Kevin said smiling.

The airman took off his cap and wiped the perspiration from his forehead. He noticed that Kevin's arm was in a cast and that he still had some cuts on his face that hadn't fully healed. "Were you part of it?"

Kevin looked at the airman and nodded.

"I watched it on the news with my family," the airman said, squinting in the bright sunlight. "They were worried about me coming here."

"Things have quieted down here since then. You're not going to have anything to worry about."

A van pulled up and stopped in front of the airman.

"My ride," the airman said, opening the door and tossing

in his duffel bag.

"Have a good tour," Kevin said.

"I hope so."

Kevin waved to the airman and watched the van drive away. He walked to the edge of the terminal parking lot and stood behind a chain-link fence. From where he was standing he would be able to watch the plane take off. He thought about Clare back home. Although he was finally able to talk to her when he was released from the hospital, he didn't say much other than that he had been injured in an accident and that he would be coming home soon. Ironic, it was Clare who said that he should go back to Panama to lay the rest the ghosts from his past. He dreaded the conversation they were going to have when he finally went home.

"Where will they go?" a voice behind Kevin asked.

Kevin smiled when he recognized the voice. "I've arranged for them to stay with my sister in Tampa for a while."

"Until you can get them, right?" Buck said, walking up alongside Kevin.

Kevin nodded. "That's the plan. They're going to need some time to process all of this. After that, we'll just have to wait and see. By the way, I want to thank you for expediting their passports and visas."

"I owed you a favor. Besides, it was the least I could do," Buck said. "I'm sorry about Frank. He saved my ass, you know. If it hadn't been for Frank, I probably wouldn't be standing here."

Kevin nodded. He was also lucky to be alive. At any point during that night, one of Vega's men could have gotten to him before he managed to rescue Inés and her daughters.

"Why did you go to the hotel?" Kevin asked.

"Vega and I had some unfinished business."

"What kind of unfinished business would that be?" Kevin

asked, shading his eyes from the sun as he looked at Buck.

"The kind that gets a person killed," Buck said.

They watched as the boarding ramp and the AGE equipment were pushed away by the ground crew. The engines whined loudly as the plane slowly taxied down the flight line, past rows of C-130s, toward the end of the runway.

"When you told me that Vega had put out a contract on Frank, you knew that I would make sure that Inés and the girls got out, didn't you?" Kevin asked.

"It wasn't my idea. It was Frank's," Buck said, measuring his words carefully. "Frank told me how much you had a thing for Inés. I found out about your daughter by accident. Of course, Frank knew all along which is probably why he made sure you were here. He wanted some insurance in case things turned bad, which they did. Believe it or not, you were the only person he trusted."

Kevin thought about what Smith had said. After everything they had been through eleven years earlier, Frank counted on the one person who had despised him the most. "And you made sure to pull the right strings?"

"Thinking like a true analyst, Rooney," Buck said. "If things went south, I figured that you needed to be here to take care of your daughter. Besides, after your friend's death, it was the least I could do."

"Guess you have a heart and conscience, after all," Kevin said smiling.

"Let's say I have a soft spot for happy endings."

The plane reached the end of the flight line and turned onto the runway. Of all the places that Kevin had been stationed at or gone to on TDY, Howard was the most beautiful and would always be near and dear to him. What other bases could boast a runway that extended out to the Pacific Ocean? Even the rows of white stucco barracks and enlisted residential quarters with the reddish-orange tile roofs and manicured lawns looked more like a resort than a military installation. They say a person never forgets their first duty assignment, and that was especially true for Kevin and how he had always felt about Howard. Without question, the time he spent in Panama and Howard was the best time of his life. No matter where life's journey had taken him and where it would take him next, there would always be a part of him here. He wasn't the only one, either. There were countless people who felt the same way.

"That's not really why you brought me down here, is it?" Kevin said after a while. "You could have easily gotten Inés and the girls out of here with, or without me."

Buck looked at Kevin with an inscrutable look on his face. "Yes, that's true, but I had some unfinished business."

"Unfinished business?"

"Vega."

Kevin was silent for a few seconds thinking about what Smith had told him about Vega and then it all made sense to him.

"You killed him?"

Buck nodded.

"Because of Noriega?"

"Let's say it was for both professional and personal reasons."

Kevin turned and looked at the crowd gathered along the fence waiting for the plane to take off. At the very end of the fence, Ramone looked toward Kevin and Buck, gave a nod of his head and smiled.

"There's been something I've been meaning to ask you—"

"Let me guess, you want to know how I knew your father?"

"Yeah, I would."

"It was back during the war. He helped me out once at Cam Ranh Air Base. I was this cocky second lieutenant who didn't know any better. You know the type. Someone who thinks they're above the law. Well, your father saved my ass one night at the Officer's Club," Buck said grinning.

"What happened?"

"I punched a guy's lights out."

Kevin furrowed his brow. "You did *what?*"

"I got into a fight with this civilian contractor who was giving one of the Vietnamese go-go dancers at the club a hard time," Buck explained. "He was sitting at a table next to mine yelling a string of obscenities at her. Really mean, vile stuff. I told him to cool it. When he didn't, I took matters into my own hands. We tore the place up really good. There were tables and chairs flying this way and that way. The poor girls on stage were screaming as they tried to get out of the way. It was a like a scene out of an old western movie. Everyone joined in. Fighter jocks fighting grunts; marines fighting everyone"

"What happened next?

"Your father and three other SPs arrived and sorted out the mess. Boy, was he pissed when he found out that a grunt had started the ruckus and laid waste to the club. Of course he hauled us both in and a couple fighter jocks and marines," Buck said grinning. "His commander was furious and was going to throw the book at the lot of us. However, when your old man found out what really happened, he stood up for me and told his CO how it wasn't my fault. The CO let me off with a stern warning to stay clear of the club while I was at Cam Ranh. However, the marines and the contractor didn't fare too well."

"That's it?"

"Afterward your old man came up to me in the chow hall thanked me. Turns out this same contractor had pulled this same shit before but no one had stood up to him until that night," Buck said. "Your father didn't take shit from anyone, but he was a fair man."

Kevin smiled.

"Your father was a good man, Rooney," Buck said. "Everyone that I knew at the base spoke highly of him. He would be very proud of you."

"Thanks."

They both shaded their eyes with their hands as they watched the plane position itself on the runway for takeoff. The low rumbling "moo" sound of the aircraft's Rolls-Royce engines revving up in preparation for take-off echoed across the runway and the flight line.

"I'm going to hate to leave you here," Kevin said. "As much as I despised you for the past, you're not a bad SOB, after all."

Buck grinned. "I wouldn't be so sure about that."

"What do you mean?"

The captain of the plane pushed the throttle forward as the plane started down the runway. The plane needed a little more than three-quarters of the runway before it finally lifted off the runway as it flew out over the Pacific Ocean. Kevin and Buck continued to watch the plane climb higher in the sky until it banked to the left and finally disappeared into the clouds.

"Well, it looks like you're going to be stuck with me for a while longer," Buck said. "You've been reassigned to a task force that I've been asked to lead. There's going to be a lot of work cleaning up the mess we made down here."

Kevin looked at Buck and smiled.

"You know, this could be the beginning of a very

interesting relationship."

"Don't go getting all Claude Rains and Humphrey Bogart on me," Kevin laughed, referring to the final scene in one of his favorite Bogey movies, *Casablanca*. "After all, you're *still* CIA."

Buck grinned. "Not if I can help it."

.

AUTHOR'S NOTE

Several books were extremely helpful to my understanding of Panama's history, the Panama Canal Zone, Manuel Noriega, and Operation Just Cause. In particular, I point to David McCullough's *The Path Between the Seas*, Walter LaFeber's *The Panama Canal The Crisis in Historical Perspective*, Frederick Kempe's *Divorcing the Dictator, America's Bungled Affair with Noriega*, John Dinges's *Our Man in Panama*, Matthew Parker's *Panama Fever – The Epic Story of the Building of the Panama Canal*, and Herbert and Mary Knapp's *Red, White, and Blue Paradise*. Specifically, Dinges and Kempe's books were insightful and informative regarding the "Singing Sergeant's Affair" the 1976 Canal Zone bombings, and the October 1989 coup attempt. I highly recommend each one of these books to learn more about the history of the Panama Canal Zone, Manuel Noriega, and the eventual invasion of Panama, Operation Just Cause, which brought about his downfall.

ABOUT THE AUTHOR

Jeffrey Miller has spent over two decades in Asia as a university lecturer, language instructor, and writer, including a six-year stint as a feature writer for *The Korea Times*, South Korea's oldest English-language newspaper. Originally from LaSalle, Illinois, he relocated to South Korea in 1990 where he nurtured a love for spicy Korean food, Buddhist temples, and East Asian history.

He is the author of eight books including *War Remains, A Korean War Novel*; *Ice Cream Headache*; and *When A Hard Rain Falls*.

He currently resides in Daejeon with his wife Aon, and four children, Bia, Jeremy Aaron, Joseph, and Angelina. If he's not working, writing, or reading, he's usually chasing little kids around his home.